Ms. Peggy Bartlett
1385 NE 13th Pl.
Canby, OR 97013

D1774112

WHISPERS

THE SECRET WATCHERS
Book Two

Enjoy your reading adventure

LAUREN KLEVER

www.thesecretwatchers.com

Copyright © 2013 Lauren Klever. All rights reserved, including the right to reproduce this book or portions thereof in any form whatsoever without permission.

This is a work of fiction. Names, characters, places, brands, media and incidents are either the product of the author's imagination or are used fictitiously. The author acknowledges the trademarked status and trademark owners of various products referenced in this work of fiction, which have been used without permission. The publication/use of these trademarks is not authorized, associated with or sponsored by the trademark owners.

Acknowledgements

To my wonderful friends and family who have spent countless hours reading, discussing, brainstorming, encouraging and administering many hugs... THANK YOU! This book is for you!

I would like to give special thanks to: Mom for being my first cut editor, my dad and boys for the use of their words and thoughts and my husband who puts up with me.

To my special friends who have gone the extra mile for me and The Secret Watchers, 'thank you' is not nearly enough. I hope seeing your name in print will help a little! Cipriana and Sharon Mabaet, Marty Herdener, Lora Porterfield, Julie Postlewait, Sheila Senger, Andra Odegaard, the Hamann family, the Anderson family, Janet Barrera, Amanda Wall, Cindi Etten, Bryce Duncan and Sally Paulson - you are... the best!

ONE

The sun beat down on us, hot and merciless. The whistle blew and we ran yet another set of wind sprints, as sweat dripped into our eyes and our gear rattled. Adrian and I could take the running, push-ups, sit-ups and drills in the damp Oregon heat of August. Many on the team had puked when daily doubles started. Our mentor, trainer and personal coach, Earl White Eagle, had kept us in shape all summer and believe me, we were thankful. The final whistle blew and I for one wanted to cheer. I was ready for this to be over and our season to begin.

I snatched up my water from the sidelines and took a long drink of the now warm water, some of it dribbling down my chin and neck. Adrian clapped me on the back on his way to his gear.

"Now that's what I'm talking about," my dad enthused as he reached my side. "You are looking decent out there. We just need to work on your hands a bit. We don't want you dropping the ball during a game, right? Maybe we'll throw the ball when we get home."

He had to be kidding! I had just been through my second practice in one day. I caught way more passes than I missed and I was fast. I could also get by almost anybody because I could anticipate their moves. All the fighting I had done under White Eagle's tutoring had left me in great shape for football. He wanted me to have as many skills as possible so that I could defend myself in any way necessary. He was still convinced that something big, bad and ugly was coming for me. We'd see. For now it was all football - all the time.

School was starting in a week and our first game was a week from Thursday. It was just preseason but still a real game would be much better than practice. Adrian joined us and we all loaded up in our SUV. It was... interesting having my dad back in my life. He still didn't believe that I had any special abilities. He let me train with White Eagle but he ignored the rest. In fact he didn't even want to hear it. He tried to pretend that he never had a nervous breakdown and left us for several months at the end of last school year.

My brothers have welcomed him back like nothing was wrong but it's taking a lot more for me to repair our relationship. Having someone not believe in you can put a real damper on reconciliation, I've found. I think that my father would like to keep us compartmentalized: work in one space, his father's family in another and us in a third. I don't work like that. I know my parents loved each other passionately once. They did, after all, run away together against the wishes of my grandfather. He thought my mom wasn't worthy. He cut off my dad and swore he didn't want to see him again. He's loosened up over the years but lately he's been acting strangely again. Mom and I tend to be cautious and reserved when it comes to my grandfather. We both believe that trust is earned. We will freely give it once but after that, if you blow it, you are on your own to earn it back.

We dropped off Adrian at his house and then headed for our own. I paused when I got out of the SUV and watched the setting sun. I draw my peace from nature sometimes. When I have to deal with my dad I find that I have to refill my well of peace more often.

"Come on. Let's throw the old pigskin at bit," Dad tried to convince me again.

"No Dad. Thanks, but no. I just finished my second football practice today. I'm tired, I have laundry to do and you know what they say about too much of a good thing. Besides, I have three more days of daily doubles. Give it a rest, okay?"

"Fine, don't say I didn't offer," he said abruptly. He gave me a frustrated look and headed inside.

I try, but everything comes out wrong when I talk to him. My gift seems to be the gorilla in the room. I don't know what to do about it either. White Eagle and my mom both tell me to have patience. I took a deep breath of evening air and looked again to the sky.

The redness had seeped away, like melted chocolate dripping off a strawberry. The streetlight popped on and night began to wrap itself around me. Stars flicked on and the moon rose in the purple-black sky. Still, I breathed in the cooling air.

I have always been partial to the in-between times. I am fascinated by the time before day leaves and night comes and vice versa. Some people find a kind of sadness in the space between night and day, going and coming. I find that new beginnings can be refreshing.

I took another breath to calm myself before I had to face my dad again. My feelings regarding him were so confused. I loved him but I didn't like him very much right now. I also worried about my... friend, Lucie. She had not spoken to me since our Washington D.C. trip last June. I had emailed, texted and tried to call her. She was ignoring me. She had told me that she needed time to think. I guess she had decided that I was just too dangerous or too much trouble to be around, yet I had seen her in the stands just yesterday watching us practice. To be completely fair, she may have been watching someone else. Her brother played varsity so she was not there to watch him.

I desperately wanted to let go of my feelings for her. She had let me go. I needed to let her go. Now if only my dreams weren't haunted by her face. I walked up and sat on the front porch with my back against the pillar and my head tilted up so I could see the stars better. I tried to let my thoughts go and just make pictures out of the stars.

The front door banged open. "You still out there? What's with you? I thought you had laundry to do. You're wasting time. We could have been throwing the ball," Dad grumbled at me.

I didn't even turn around. "I do have to do laundry, Dad. I was just taking a moment to relax." I could hear the bitter tone in my voice. I tired to clamp down on it. I began to wonder if that tone would be locked into my voice forever when I spoke to him. I felt myself drifting into a cold place where meanness could so easily take over.

The front door slammed. I could hear my mother once again coming to my rescue. That too made me angry. It wasn't her job or her problem to solve.

"Brad, what is with you? Why are you so hard on him? He doesn't drink, smoke, do drugs, have piercings or tattoos. Give him a break. He is playing football like you wanted and his grades last year were the best they have ever been. Please don't start his freshman year like this," she said, both hurt and angry.

"Why do you defend him like that? He is getting weird hanging out at that pawnshop all the time. He still thinks he sees things. He and his buddies act like they're part of a secret club and that White Eagle guy is the ring leader. I don't like it. Why can't he just be normal? He better not do anything weird when we go see my father this Christmas!" Dad replied in a grouchy voice.

"What? My mother is expecting us in Arizona. We haven't been to visit them since they moved. We made plans last week. You were right there when I was talking to her..."

"We'll go later. Maybe for spring break. We'll send a nice gift. She was here in July and you and the boys have not been to Florida in four years."

"We have not been invited back since Lucas had a two-year-old temper tantrum because he was overtired. It's a long flight for a little guy. How was I to know he'd throw up on your dad when he tried to pick him up? Please remember that it was Owen who finally calmed him down. But that's beside the point. Why are you doing the dictator thing again? We used to discuss things. What is going on?"

Mom's voice had gotten fainter and fainter. They must have walked upstairs. I sighed. They didn't used to fight and if they did it wasn't in front of us. I didn't know what was going on with my dad but he wasn't the man he used to be. These days he was always grouchy when he came home from Atlanta or Miami. After he was here for awhile he would mellow out and almost be like he used to be.

Now every time he came home I tried to sneak a peek at his stuff but I just couldn't *see* anything. All of his belongings were gray to me. I had mentioned the phenomena to White Eagle. We could not make heads or tails of it. It was almost as if things belonging to my dad were muffled, gagged or disguised. I was getting better at reading people although my dad was a whole other matter. When he would first come home from business trips he was even harder to read than usual. As his time went by with us it became easier and then the cycle would start again the next time he came home.

I finally wandered inside to take a shower and start some laundry so that I could have clean gear for tomorrow. As I walked past my parent's room I could hear the rumble of the heated discussion continuing. I took my shower and gathered all my dirty clothes. On the way to the laundry room I noticed that my brothers were doing a great job of ignoring the arguing. Lucas was watching cartoons, Alex was playing a game on the computer and our lovable Lhasa Apso, Beggar, was lying on her doggy bed wagging her tail.

"Hey guys," I said on the way past, "want to play a board game after I get this started?"

"Nope," Alex said.

"No thanks," Lucas added. "I gotta go to bed soon anyway. I just hate listening to... ya know," he said pointing at the ceiling.

"When does he leave again?" Alex sighed.

"Come on guys. Give him a week and he'll mellow out. He always does."

"It sounds like we're going to Florida for Christmas which is cool 'cause Grandpa Ryer has a pool but I like my Arizona grandma better," Alex added.

"We'll have to wait and see, won't we? Be patient guys. It'll all work out."

I sincerely hoped that it really would all work out. I checked my watch. It was time for Lucas to go to bed. It was getting late for an almost first grader and he needed to be ready to leave for school at a quarter after seven in just a week.

"Come on, Lucas. Let me throw in a load and then let's get you ready for bed. I think Mom is still busy. I'll read to you tonight. Alex, you get forty-five more minutes and then come on up and brush your teeth."

"Yes, Mother," he flipped back at me causing Lucas to giggle.

I started my load, then herded Lucas upstairs to watch him brush his teeth and then supervised the rest of getting ready for bed, making sure that his dirty clothes made it into the hamper instead of all around it. I opened up his sheets for him and he slid into his twin bed. Then I flipped the covers back and lay on top resting my head against his headboard. Lucas snuggled into my side and each of us held half of his favorite book. We were on the last page when Mom came in. She mouthed a 'thank you' from the door and then came over to kiss Lucas good night. She kissed me too, sighed and then just looked deep into my eyes. I had gotten to where I could almost read her mind. Tonight I keenly felt her regret.

"Love you, Mom."

"Me too!" Lucas added.

"And I love both of you! Where is Alex?"

"Right here, Mom. Owen said I had forty-five minutes."

"You are the smartest fifth grader I know," Mom told him proudly.

"Yeah, I know. I'm your favorite too and don't tell the others!" Alex laughed back at her.

It was a family joke with us. Mom always told each of us that we were her favorite. She often did it when the rest of us could hear and added, don't tell the others. It always made us laugh and always lightened the mood. I hugged my brothers and Mom goodnight and headed for bed myself.

Drifting off to sleep, I thought about Lucie for about the millionth time. I wished I knew what she was thinking. I guessed the puzzle of her heart would have to remain a mystery. I wished that she at least would have remained my friend. It hurt so bad to have her completely shut me out. I wasn't perfect and neither was she. Nobody's perfect. I just wished she would give me another chance. I could keep her safe if she'd let me. I felt confident about that now.

The rest of daily doubles passed mostly painlessly. Dad and I ignored each other which worked pretty well for me. Adrian sprung plans on me for another blind date on Saturday.

"Oh why not," I sighed, as Adrian's mom took a turn picking us up Friday.

"I can hardly wait until you have your license. Think of the fun we'll have!" Adrian said in a dreamy voice.

"You find ways of having plenty of fun already," his mom sharply retorted. "You're lucky I'm letting you out on Saturday. You're way behind on your chores. You better be caught up by date night or you aren't going. You're just lucky that Amy's mom picks you up as often as she does. You are just like your father! You're lucky you're cute!" she griped at him.

I sat in back and tried to keep a straight face. Adrian and his women! His mom was usually a really sweet and easygoing person. They dropped me off and I waved them home. Adrian would text or call later with Saturday's plans.

Dad had been called back to Atlanta early. From my perspective it was a pleasant surprise. Mom and my brothers had taken him to the airport while I was at practice. The three of them were watching a movie when I dragged my tired body in the door.

"Hey Bud, how was it?" Mom asked in that special way she had that made us all feel loved.

"Fine, I'm tired. I think I'll have a shower and then sit with you for a bit, okay?"

"Sure! I'll make some popcorn," she replied happily.

I wandered into the laundry room and dropped most of my gear. I sprayed my shoulder pads, helmet and the insides of my cleats. I dropped my jersey, tee and socks into the washer and headed upstairs. I took a clean tee and pjs from my room and dragged myself to the shower. I let the hot water beat on me to relieve some of my muscle ache. Adrian and I had survived daily doubles and there was talk of being moved to the junior varsity team!

I had washed so much of my own stuff lately that my hamper was nearly empty when I checked it. I had even washed my sheets yesterday just to make a load. I took the hamper from my brothers' room and headed downstairs. I had to have something to make a full load with my practice gear.

"I'm stealing dirty clothes so that I'll have enough stuff to make a load," I said to the room at large.

"Thanks Owen," Mom said as she held up the popcorn bowl. "We're ready for you."

I groaned a bit as I fell into our loveseat. Mom smiled at me. She knew I was beat. My brothers were too absorbed to notice me.

"Mom, I don't have details but Adrian wants to set me up on another blind date. He wants to go out tomorrow. Would that be okay?"

"Sure, honey, if you want. I'll find a way to get you there."

I watched the movie for awhile. When my eyes began to burn, I shut them for a moment and the next thing I knew there was a comforter over me and the room was completely dark. I could hear the dryer rumbling in the next room. Thanks Mom! I headed upstairs, brushed my teeth, crawled into bed and fell back into a deep and dreamless sleep.

I awoke when the sun touched my face the next morning. I could feel the built-up lactic acid in my body. Yuck, morning. I stretched and gingerly rolled out of bed. I made my bed and tossed my pjs onto the end. I pulled on some cargo shorts and found a tee. I ran a hand over my jaw. I needed a shave but who cared? I rolled downstairs. Alex was out back poop scooping and Lucas was throwing the ball for Beggar. Oh yeah, the lawn. I pulled out my cell phone and texted White Eagle, "2 lawns to hit. Be in later." As I was closing out my cell, Mom came in from the laundry room with a basket of my laundry.

"Hey, sleep okay?"

"Yeah, I guess. I'm just wiped. Football is a different kind of practice than what we do with White Eagle."

"That's why he encouraged you all to try a sport this year, right?"

"Yeah, I think I'm glad that football season is short. I've missed the pawnshop this last week. I bet White Eagle has a ton of stuff for me to *look* at. He's had Marlo watching the news for anything weird that might mean a job for us. We had so little to do this summer. About all we did was return some of Clive's stolen merchandise to its rightful owners." What a mess the whole Clive thing had been. He had terrorized Max and forced him to sell stolen goods at the pawnshop or Max could count on losing a niece or nephew at school. Then when Clive thought I got too interested in the situation he had one of his coconspirators try to scare me off. He and his two buddies finally gave me an ugly beating at the mall, one died in the process, and then Clive and Darren tried to kill me too by tossing my nearly unconscious body down a ravine. Darren, the only one still alive, was behind bars for murdering Clive. Crime really doesn't pay.

We had also returned a little kid who had wandered away from her parents while they were moving. Her parents had been distracted and she was lost and confused. Adrian will gloat about that one forever since he was the one who saw her hiding. It took me almost twenty minutes to talk her out of the bushes so that we could return her to her anxious parents.

"I'm proud of you – you know that, right? Did I tell you that I decided to substitute at the school this year? I think I will mostly just teach at Lucas and Alex's school for now."

"I'm proud of you too, Mom. I also think that it was really nice of Sarah, our part-time nanny, friend and guardian angel, to help watch Lucas and Alex while you went back to school. I figured you had something up your sleeve. No subbing at the high school huh?"

"Not this year. It's too far from my kindergarten roots," she laughed. "Hey, I'm curious. I know that they moved you and Adrian to J.V. I heard they moved Calvin too. How is that going?"

"He's over Lucie so we are pretty successful at ignoring each other. He also plays defense so I don't see him lots. I haven't seen him do anything obviously bad lately either. Maybe he learned his lesson. I can hope anyway. I tangled with him enough last year."

As I poured milk on my cereal, Mom asked, "How about Marlo? How is soccer going for him?"

"He doesn't hate it. He's decent at it too. He's not the best one on the team but he is far from the worst."

My brothers came pounding into the house feeling like they had earned some cartoon time for their 'hard' work. Mom smiled at them and released them from drudgery. I headed out to cut the grass. I popped in my ear buds and turned up my tunes. Sadly it brought back memories of the day Lucie had watched me cut the grass. "Get over it stupid," I growled at myself, "she doesn't want you."

I finished our lawn, Sarah's lawn and used my skateboard to get to the shop. I hardly ever used it anymore. The hum of the wheels and the feeling of flying still spoke to me. I took a moment in a clear spot to spread my arms wide and feel the wind. Glorious.

I arrived at the shop after Marlo and Adrian. Max had given Adrian a ride, but Marlo had jogged over. He was much more focused these days than Adrian was. Marlo was still full into his healthy living regime too. He had helped his mom create a whole healthy line for her catering business and it was doing really well and kept her super busy. His dad had gotten a promotion and was gone a lot so Marlo was free to do all kinds of Marlo-esque activities including helping me out. His folks loved that he was at the shop, at soccer or hanging out with us. They thought he was safely supervised. Good thing they didn't really know. He had spent all summer collecting a variety of equipment that would aid us on any missions that came up. Marlo knew gadgets.

Adrian also had a lot of freedom. He spent most of his time with his Uncle Max, the owner of our pawnshop and now, training facility. Max had purchased the shop years ago with an inheritance. Adrian's dad was a silent partner with his share of the same inheritance. Adrian's mom worked days at a spa and his dad worked nights as the night manager of our local Denny's. Adrian's sister spent a lot of time with their mother's sister. As long as Adrian was home for dinner, the magic hour at his house, life was golden.

My boys, as I liked to refer to them, were the best. Adrian's uncle didn't know everything about us but he did know a little. Fortunately, we had him convinced that the less he knew the better. He continued to stay out of our business as long as we didn't make trouble for him and with Darren still in jail and the other two dead – he'd deluded himself with a false sense of security. I know you can't trust the villains in this world.

Adrian was dusting and straightening merchandise when I arrived. Marlo was doing his usual gig as bookkeeper. He had also earned Max's everlasting gratitude by organizing and filing his quarterly taxes for the business. It was the other reason that Max stayed out of our business. All of our hard work also netted us all the great gear that we wanted that came into the shop. Marlo had done the paperwork and we had gotten the appropriate signatures so that we could work for Max at minimum wage. Marlo set it up so that he paid us in product, at fair market value of course.

With Marlo doing the books, we had also found out that White Eagle really was not just an employee but had used his savings to be a third partner in the business. It explained a lot really, though I wasn't sure why he had kept it a secret. I guess we had just assumed wrong and he had never corrected us. He just smiled in that secret way of his.

I said "hey" to everyone up front and strolled into the back to see what White Eagle was up to. He was busy working on a chainsaw but to my dismay I saw that every other open spot on the work benches and counters was filled with new items for the shop. The item that first drew my attention though was a black Kawasaki KLR series bike.

"Wow? Is that yours?" I asked excitedly.

"At the moment. I bought it at the auction that Max and I went to. She needs a little work. It's been garaged for several years," White Eagle replied with a twinkle in his eye. "Maybe you could help me fix her up."

"I'd like that," I said with a smile. I approached the bike. It wasn't really calling to me but there was something *off* about it. I reached out a hand and gently touched the grip. Images swam before my eyes. I felt bombarded by all the images it was showing me. I lost sight of the shop and was sucked into what I was seeing. It was coming at me faster than I had ever witnessed before. I was almost afraid my brain would short-circuit. I couldn't seem to let go. Then just as suddenly as the images had started, they stopped and the bike was silent.

"Where did you get this bike again?" I asked, feeling dazed and confused.

"At the auction last Sunday. I can tell you its history from the auction sheet though. Why?"

"First of all, I didn't sense the darkness about it. It was almost like it was hidden or disguised. Once I touched it... it was like it had been dying to talk to me and it wouldn't or couldn't shut up. I do know this though, its owner is missing - he was taken. The person who took him did something to the bike, then left it behind. I don't know what else is here that I need to *look* at but this one is big. We'll need Sarah and Marlo. We may even need Evelyn, your police contact. I need Marlo to catalog what I saw and to start some initial research on this guy."

"Marlo told me that he would be back as soon as he could after you came in. Do you want to look at the other stuff?"

"I don't know - I hate to clutter the images I have here. Maybe I will see if the bike can give it to me again." I closed my eyes and reached out. I ran through the images again. I focused on as many little details as I could. Where were the images coming from? What year were the images from? I was so absorbed that I didn't hear Marlo come in.

He cleared his throat to get my attention. "So it begins, yeah?"

I nodded. Marlo pulled up a fresh spreadsheet to catalog information. Over the summer Marlo had gotten some new software. He could now record my voice and have the computer transcribe it for us. He could then go back and pick out the important bits. I closed my eyes and replayed the images, telling him what I saw.

I opened my eyes and paused for a moment in indecision. Marlo waited patiently. White Eagle had returned to his chainsaw. "Let's do the rest of the items and see what we find." I used my *other sight* to look at each item. Marlo separated them into two piles. One pile for clean items that he would later catalog for general inventory and another, smaller pile of items that I needed to *look* at more closely because they had something to *say* to me. Items that had been touched by darkness were thick and oily feeling to me. They seemed to almost suck the light from around them, like a black hole. Items that were touched by goodness glowed with a soft light and had a happy, almost sleepy hum about them. Most items looked completely normal if they had nothing to *say* to me or they appeared grayish in color which I had come to learn meant neutrality.

Marlo and I quickly went through the rest of the items. They all had small stories to tell. A toolbox held some interest for me though. I started with the toolbox; sure enough, it had belonged to the man who was taken. As I watched the images unfold it became clear that he had some kind of gift. It appeared that he was either a very new *watcher* or was soon to be discovered. The wrench inside the box showed me the same two men that I recognized from what the motorcycle had shown me. The young man who was taken was... Trevor, his name was Trevor Vance... The *watcher stalker*, I bet my life on it, was the other man and he had been in Trevor's garage.

Marlo and I cataloged every piece. White Eagle listened and thought, saying nothing. More and more this summer he was pushing me to make the decisions. He would offer his opinion if I asked.

"Marlo, let's pull in our contacts. I think we are looking at about 2003. The motorcycle was manufactured in 2001. Trevor bought it new. Missing person cases sometimes go to the FBI so maybe Sarah could do some digging around with her old contacts." He nodded and got to work.

"White Eagle, would you please call Evelyn and see if she could scare up the old files for us so we can read the reports? I would like to meet with the person who put this bike up for auction and see what other leads develop. The toolbox and the tools in it also belonged to our missing person. We are looking for a *watcher stalker* and I would bet money that his talent is covering his tracks. I think he did something to hide the bike. The images were there but the darkness I usually see and feel was gone.

It didn't matter that it was Saturday. In our line of work, justice never sleeps and neither do the bad guys. I wondered how I would make it until we had the information we needed. I am a man of action and I hate waiting. Tuesday was the first day of school and it would be really awesome if we could get going on this one before school started. The guys and I didn't have much time between school and football, or soccer in Marlo's case, but we would make do. We had before.

I had completely forgotten my promise to Adrian. "Owen, dude, its time to go get ready! Marlo, are you sure you don't want to come? I can still get a girl for you."

"I told you, I have sworn off women for awhile. I'm too busy to date anyway. As it turns out though, I have a date with Sarah tonight to share some information on a potential case."

"Have fun with the ninety-year-old."

"She's not ninety!" White Eagle, Marlo and I all said in unison.

"Whatev... she's old, but if it gets us a job – I'm game. Hey, Owen, can your mom or someone get you to my house? Amy's mom will pick us up there at six."

"Okay. I'll be there." What had I done? Oh well. It would be a distraction for awhile.

White Eagle and Marlo shooed me out of the shop so they could continue their work in peace. I took my board and rode it home. I hadn't left myself much time to get ready. I showered, shaved, brushed my teeth and put on my usual date clothes. Having learned my lesson from an overeager Katie last year, I made a point to tuck in my shirt and wear a belt. I was not in the mood to have a chick I didn't know well, putting her hands on my bare skin. Adrian thinks I'm crazy but I want to know a girl before we become... involved.

Mom smiled at me when I came downstairs. "I know why the women chase you. You do look very good in black with your dark coloring and beautiful brown eyes. I should see about getting you something in a dark red tone. That would bring out those eyes! Your birthday is coming soon. What do you think?"

"I don't know. Clothes are fine I guess. I do seem to destroy them at an alarming rate."

"If you could find a way to stay out of fights it would save your clothes and your hide, you know."

"Sure, Mom, I'll work on that," I said with a laugh. "How do you suppose I let Adrian talk me into this again?"

"You're a nice guy and you are trying to get Lucie out of your head. Just try to have fun. Knowing Adrian, the girl will, at the very least, be cute!" Mom added with a smile for me.

Mom loaded up my brothers in our SUV and we all headed for Adrian's. They would drop me off and then hit the grocery store. I was glad I was missing that one. Grocery shopping is not my favorite. Give me yard work any day. Adrian was waiting out front as we pulled up and right behind us was Amy's mom. My mom asked my brothers to wait and she stepped out to say 'hi' to Amy's mom. I'm sure Mom just wanted to know who I would be with for the next four hours.

Amy's mom looked familiar. When Amy stepped out of the car with her friend I made the connection. It was the little redhead from our Washington D.C. trip that Adrian had found so fascinating. She was the first girl that had ever tongue-tied him so maybe there was hope. Amy's friend was... interesting. She was tall, almost as tall as me. She had a quiet confidence about her which was explained when I discovered she was an athlete. She played sports year round. Her passion was volleyball. She also had older brothers. She was the least girly girl I had ever met.

She reached out a hand to shake mine at our introduction and I knew looking into her bright green eyes that she would fall into the friend category. Her name was Melody and she went to high school on the other side of the river. She and Amy had been childhood neighbors but had kept in touch.

As dates went, it was a good one. Melody was easy to talk to and never once tried to hang on me. The best part was that she ordered a burger, fries and a soda – a real one, not diet. Now this was a chick I could relate to. Adrian rolled his eyes at us but we had a great conversation about our favorite sports teams and what we liked to do to work out. Amy giggled indulgently. She said that she was more the cheerleader type. Both girls were smart and loved to read. They also had the same taste in movies. Tonight we were seeing a romantic comedy. I was hoping it was heavy on the comedy.

The movie was actually okay. Melody shared popcorn with me and we both watched the movie. Adrian spent most of the movie either looking at or kissing Amy. Amy wanted to watch the movie so she did a good job of keeping Adrian in line.

Amy's mom picked us up at the theater after the show. She dropped off Adrian and me. I told Melody that I had enjoyed our time together and that I would see her around. I didn't ask for her number and she didn't offer. I had texted Mom but I had not heard back yet. I was trying to decide my next move but Adrian insisted I come inside.

I don't spend much time at Adrian's with both his parents working oppositional shifts. Amber, Adrian's bossy sister, wanted to know all about our date. Here was another woman that Adrian could not charm. Amber is okay in small doses. I'm just glad I don't have to live with her. She would start in at the middle school this year. I couldn't believe she was in sixth grade. She seemed so young and tried to act so old.

Mom finally got back to me. She had put my brothers to bed so she was trying to decide what to do with me. Should she see if White Eagle or Sarah could get me or stay with my brothers or what? I solved it for her by offering to run home. It didn't make her happy but it would only take a few minutes if I cut through the grade school. Mom and I both hated to bother our generous friends.

TWO

I was restless on Sunday as I often am when I'm waiting to get going on a case. The waiting is murder. I knew Marlo would call as soon as he had something for me. I helped Mom do a frenzy of chores. I went for a run. I lifted some free weights we had in the garage. I paced. I ran through my Tai Chi exercises. I gave up and called Marlo at two.

"If I had something for you I would've called. Evelyn told White Eagle that she couldn't, or was it shouldn't, get into the cold case files until Tuesday. Sarah took the basic info and said she would do some digging. She had some old friends that she was hoping to reconnect with. Why don't you read a book or watch a movie or something? Or come over here. We haven't gamed in a long time. You're good in a real fight. Let's see if you remember how to do it in the virtual world," Marlo exclaimed.

"Deal!" I practically shouted at him.

Mom happily released me into Marlo's care. I think she was tired of the nervous energy. Both Alex and Lucas had friends over so I think she was about full up on boys and craziness.

Marlo's parents welcomed me like family. I love to go to his house. He's an only child. His dad is some kind of computer engineer who is just as geeky and friendly as Marlo. Marlo's mom is a sweet lady who I've always liked. She used to have a real hard time getting me to talk much around her but this last year I've found it's getting lots easier. I guess I'd always found her a little oppressive; now I realize that she genuinely cares about me and what I think. She's just a little more gregarious and outgoing than I'm used to.

I headed up to Marlo's man cave with a tray of healthy goodies and diet sodas from Marlo's mom. He'd added a second flat screen. His computer hummed and whirred and many images flashed by. His laptop was plugged in and running also.

"What's up?" I asked indicating all the electronic activity as I set down the drinks and tray.

"I have carefully saved up and planned all my purchases. I also watch the pawnshop carefully and tag any items that come in that will help us and then we buy them with our 'pay'. I'm keeping aside money to pay our taxes just in case but I'm trying to watch our earnings so that we come in just under the wire and with the trip last year... well Max, White Eagle and Adrian's dad wrote that off as a donation. So... oh never mind, I see your eyes glazing over," Marlo said with affection.

"I'm sorry Marlo. Maybe I need to see it on paper. I appreciate everything you do. I just don't understand all of it."

"Well then, let's do something you do understand! But first, to answer the question you must have really been asking... What am I doing on the computers? I am looking into the public records on our new case... Trevor Vance. I have pulled all the newspaper articles I can find, I know how much is in his bank account and his interest rate is terrible. He should have invested. I've also found out where he was last seen and who his parents were. Well, his mom is still around. She is now living with his sister in Astoria. That's why they sold Trevor's stuff - his dad passed away and his mom couldn't afford to keep the house."

"What are we waiting for then? Road trip!"

"Don't you want to wait for Sarah and Evelyn? Don't you think we should get the complete picture? The guy has been missing for over seven years – what's a couple of days? For once, let's not rush in," Marlo advised.

"I guess - it just seems like our plans don't always work out like we think they should. Our gut instinct seems to work pretty well."

"Is that what you would call what happened to you at the mall last winter when Clive, Darren and that other guy got their hands on you and tried to kill you?"

"That was an unfortunate situation, but I healed up fine and they killed each other except for Darren and he's behind bars. So, I'd say we did pretty well!" I defended.

"Now you sound like Miles. I know that you have a little Miles in you. He was a reckless guy. You were never reckless, just a little on the adventurous side. Try to channel the best of Miles and not the ugly bits. I don't want to see you hurt."

I looked at my wristwatch and thought about what Marlo was saying. Almost a year ago the watch had called to me in the pawnshop and awoken my gift. With White Eagle's help and some training I had enhanced my natural ability to see the images that objects showed me. I knew now that I was seeing snippets before my powers awoke fully, but I had dismissed them as an overactive imagination or my own memories floating to my consciousness. As my abilities grew and I bonded more fully with the watch, I came to know its owner, Miles, and eventually absorbed all that he was during the time he owned the watch. I now had his abilities and mine. White Eagle had never seen anything like it in all his years of training *watchers*, including Miles. My mom and Miles had similar gifts. My mom is an exceptional reader of body language. Miles could read the temperature of the room, so to speak. He knew if people in a room had good or bad intentions and he knew when something bad was going to happen. Marlo was right. I was forgetting what it was like to be *normal* and not get extra information all the time.

I now knew when danger was coming. I could find the danger in a room. I knew who was going to cause a problem and I knew if any objects in a room had been part of something bad happening. I was the most powerful *watcher* White Eagle had ever seen and he said he still didn't know everything about me. He was waiting for the next shoe to drop. I figured that combining my gifts with Miles' gifts just made me look like I had more ability.

Miles was a great guy and had taught me a whole lot with the memories that were contained in his watch. Miles had been a good person who loved his wife and his job. He had been a police officer and a private investigator. His memories showed me his talents in full detail. I had learned many fighting skills from him and combined with White Eagle's teaching it did make me a bit formidable. I also had Miles' investigative abilities; too bad so much had changed since the 1980s when he had been killed. He had a good heart, had integrity and was loyal. All the things I wanted to be. Being *watchers* meant that people like me and Miles were driven to right wrongs. It was our job to bring back balance. The only bad thing about it was that now I had the memories of a man of thirty-four dancing around in the head of an almost fifteen year old boy. It did make for a strange mix. The older I got the less weird it was, but still.

"You're right, Marlo. I do tend to dive in where angels fear to tread. Part of it is Miles' personality but part of it is our need to bring balance. If something dark happens and we know about it we *have* to fix it. It becomes almost a physical thing, like the need to drink or eat or even breathe. I will try to remain more circumspect, okay?"

"Just remember, Miles didn't have the technology that we do. We're way ahead of where he would've been. Now let's take your mind off of work and goof around a bit. We'll hear from Sarah soon."

Marlo had me so absorbed in a shooter game that I hardly noticed when his computer dinged at us. Marlo put on a headset, kept playing and moved to his computer all at once. He neglected his character, which was quickly killed, so I paused my character while he respawned. I became aware that he was talking to Sarah. Yipee. We were moving forward.

Marlo signed off with Sarah and quickly typed a bunch of stuff into his computer. He popped out a small flash drive that I hadn't noticed and shut down his laptop. "She wants to see us," he said as he loaded his laptop into its case. He then password-secured his computer and looked back at me, clearly wondering why I'd not moved yet.

"Marlo you truly are a technology wizard," I said in amazement.

"I am getting better all the time. Now come on!" he replied exasperated.

We hustled downstairs. "Hey Ma, Mrs. Lando needs a hand with her yard. Okay if we go help? I have my cell phone," Marlo said with all the aplomb of a seasoned bureaucrat.

"Sure honey, let me know what the deal is with dinner. I can reheat for you or let me know if you are eating with her, okay?"

We headed out at a jog. Sarah was clearly watching for us because she had the door open before we even hit her driveway. She ushered us right inside and into her study. She had rearranged it significantly from when she was robbed last fall. I also noticed more about the room. I had been fooled into thinking it was the basic office of a normal older lady. Today I saw the truth. Sarah had slanted her blinds so that no one could see in. She had added some recessed lighting. What had appeared to be a simple floor to ceiling cabinet actually held a high-tech computer system. She had a file folder on her desk which she flipped open as she sat down, indicated that we should take the two chairs on the other side and slipped on her reading glasses all at the same time.

"Wow Sarah, your FBI roots are showing," I said in amazement.

"I'm so glad to be back part-time; retirement was boring!" she said with a big grin. Then she cleared her throat and got down to business. "I've been able to reconnect with an old friend and colleague. I've been transferred back to my old division under him. It was getting pretty quiet when I retired and they needed to transfer some folks. It seems that things are picking back up and he could use my expertise as a consultant. I'll keep your involvement a secret just like I used to with many of my old contacts. Some of them came out and worked for the bureau. It's a tricky balance and you are too young yet, in their eyes anyway."

"This is really good news for us then, right?" I queried excitedly.

"Absolutely. It gives me better access to information. It also gives me a little more latitude to explore things we are interested in. Now for the best part... Trevor Vance was turned over to the FBI. This is a copy of his case file," she said as she tapped a finger against the file on her desk. One thing I had always loved about Sarah Lando was the fact that she was real. She loved to garden so she kept her fingernails short, neat and clean. None of that long glamorous stuff for her. The same was true of her hair and makeup - simple and minimal. She was too young to be my grandma and a bit too old to be my aunt but she certainly felt like family to me.

I remembered when her handyman had tried to rob her last year and he had pushed her down her basement stairs. I'd tried to save her but in the end she had come to my rescue by clobbering the guy with a baseball bat. Back then I still believed it was from her softball days. When Clive and his band of not so merry men had threatened my family she had reactivated her FBI status so that she could be part of our security detail.

I was rudely drawn back into the present by Marlo's elbow digging into my ribs. "You're doing it again. Pay attention. You need to know this stuff!"

"Trevor has been missing since March of 2004. He was last seen at..." Sarah began.

"A bar on McLoughlin Boulevard," I interrupted.

"Yes - same bar - still there - same name," she continued, giving me a frown. "Marlo, I will have you research the bar to see if it has the same employees and ownership. The house where Trevor lived has been sold but I want to at least drive by and see if you sense anything. Then we need to see if we can see his mother and sister. I want to know if they know anything and I hope they still have some of his stuff so that we can see if you get any more images. Marlo gave me a list of what you seen so far. White Eagle is worried. If you are right about this *watcher stalker's* abilities he will be very dangerous. I have someone new for you to meet also. Her name is Joy and she is a forensic artist. We need the *stalker's* picture so that Marlo can research him. Joy should be here in about..."

The front doorbell sounded and Sarah smiled. "Here she is." She got up to let in her new friend. I could hear their soft voices in the entryway. I felt for a vibe. Joy was a good person. I could not feel any darkness about her. As she came around the doorway, Marlo and I stood. I think Marlo's tongue about fell out of his mouth.

Joy turned out to be a young Asian woman with long elaborately twisted hair all caught up on her head. She wore a gold silk shirt with a mandarin collar and dark brown slacks. On her feet were fancy gold sandals that made *my* feet hurt just to look at them. Even her toenails were painted a golden color. She had a big smile and friendly light brown eyes.

"How do you do Owen, I am Joy Soeng," her musical voice sounded as she reached for my hand, "and you must be Marlo," she added reaching for him next.

"Nice to meet you Joy," I said looking at Marlo who still had ahold of her hand and had said nothing. It wasn't very nice of me but I started to snicker.

"Well then," Joy said, extracting her hand, "let's get to work."

She pulled a tablet out of the case she had strapped over her body like a messenger bag. Sarah showed Joy to the working side of the desk and then sat in a chair in the corner. Joy pulled several pencils out of her bag and went to work. Faster than I would have imagined the image took form. She asked me careful questions and showed me her work periodically to check my mental image versus what was coming out on the page. I nearly gasped when she turned the finished work around. She had captured our *watcher stalker* perfectly. Her drawing was so realistic it nearly looked like a black and white photograph. I thought we were done but Joy pulled a laptop out of her bag and set to work again. She used a hand scanner, that had Marlo drooling all over again, and scanned her drawing and then asked me questions about color and shading.

Marlo watched her computer work intently. He couldn't help himself and quickly began to ask her questions about her hardware and software. I was soon lost. I snuck a peek at Sarah who was smiling from her chair. She stood and motioned to me. We headed for her kitchen. She had me call my mom and Marlo's and let them know that we would not be home for dinner. Then Sarah had me start to make a salad as she pulled out several containers with Marla Saggio's Catering stamped on the side. Marlo's mom was at it again. Sarah is an awesome cook but Marla is amazing when it comes to Italian food. Soon spaghetti sauce was bubbling and meatballs were warming in a pan. The smell of garlic bread was filling the air and the noodles were draining in the sink.

"Come and eat," Sarah called into the next room.

Marlo and Joy appeared. "Thank you so much for your kind offer, but I must get going. I gave Marlo a copy of my work. You were right, he is brilliant. I look forward to working with him again." Marlo flushed a magnificent shade of red and ducked his head.

"Thanks," he mumbled.

"Thank you, Joy dear, I look forward to seeing you again. Please thank Bob for the loan of your services," Sarah replied.

Joy smiled at her and at Marlo. "It was nice to meet you, Owen. I'm sure I'll see you again as well." She then turned and gracefully left. Her light fragrance was the only hint that she had ever been here.

"Wow", Marlo breathed, "isn't she wonderful?"

"Yes, but a bit old for you dear. Maybe she will still be available in four years when you are old enough. She isn't too much older than you though, I guess. She graduated from college at nineteen and was snatched up by the bureau. She has been with Bob's division for about six months. She frequently works with psychics, of which she assumes you're one, Owen. I did not tell her any differently. She knows how to keep her mouth shut, regardless."

"She's so beautiful and she was only as tall as me with her heels on. I think I'm in love," Marlo added like he had barely heard Sarah.

"Well good," Sarah answered, "Your mother's spaghetti goes well with that. Earl is on his way. Let's strategize."

Oh boy, a strategy session. My favorite – not. Marlo drifted into a chair and rested his head on his hands as he gazed at nothing. I knew he was seeing images in his own mind. I set the table and helped Sarah dish up dinner. White Eagle walked in as the last dish was set down - as if he knew when that would happen. We filled him in on everything we had and planned to drive by Trevor's old house after dinner. Marlo even pulled up the evil one's picture on his laptop. He already had Sarah's computer searching the FBI's database through her secure linkup.

We cleaned Sarah's kitchen while Marlo checked the computer's progress. Then we loaded up in her sedan and headed for Trevor's. His house was just off of McLoughlin between the bar he had disappeared from and the pawnshop. Marlo pulled up the new owners' information on his laptop. They were a retired couple. We had decided on an angle but we thought we would start with a drive-by just to check it out.

The street was quiet as most folks were likely eating their dinner or were out. A neighbor two doors down was cutting the grass. No one else seemed to be about. I decided to hop out and have a closer look. The only idea we had come up with was to pose as lawn boys. We didn't have a better idea so I decided to go for it.

I picked up the small stack of flyers that Marlo had created. We already cut our lawns, plus Sarah's - so what was one more? - and 'Lawn Boys' was born. We could fake it until the weather turned bad and then tell them that we quit.

I walked up past the garage giving it a touch on the way – I caught a few images. I was building a big picture out of all the little bits. It was like putting together a three dimensional puzzle.

I bravely went up to the front door, knowing the others had my back – well, were watching from Sarah's sedan anyway. An older lady answered the door. I sensed that she was a good and trusting person – I hated to lie to her. I handed her a flyer and asked if I might trouble her for a glass of water.

I used all the skills and strategies that White Eagle had taught me about posture, body language and tone of voice. I tried to look as young and small as I could, yet capable enough to cut her grass. I sold her on the lawn job and I was in. I could feel Marlo cringing in the car. I had just promised him I would be more careful.

I *felt* the house – it had been sad for a long time but now it was happier. It had nothing else to show me. I even *looked* at Trevor's old room without going down the hall. It had nothing to say. I needed a closer look at the garage though.

I thanked her for her time, reminded her to call my 'mom', Sarah Lando, to book the lawn job and drank the water. I handed her the glass and then walked to the front door. She let me out and I headed back to the sedan. "Let's roll. The house has nothing to say. The garage showed me a couple of images and there is a strong pull coming from inside. The owner of the house should be cal..."

Sarah's cell chirped. "Hello?... Why yes it is... You would? Wonderful... Let me check the schedule... Why yes, we do have an opening tomorrow. Lucky you, it was a cancellation. We're open at ten in the morning. Would that work for you?... Wonderful. May I suggest a mow and edge?... Good, good, I'll send both boys. Yes, twenty dollars would be perfect. It is an average sized yard, isn't it?... May I call back and check their work? Lovely... Yes, he is a fine young man... Oh yes, a very hard worker and so is his brother... I would say about an hour and a half... You have a wonderful day too. Bye now," Sarah said with a grin that lit her face. "Isn't this fun? You're in! Earl can bring you over or shall I?" she asked, looking at White Eagle.

"I'll bring them, as well as the mower and edger, in the truck. You may come if you wish, my dear," White Eagle replied.

"My dear?" Marlo and I mouthed to each other from the back seat. We straightened up quickly as Sarah turned her attention back to us in the rearview mirror as she drove. "Marlo, are you up for this or should we put in a call to Adrian? I think sending the three of you is overkill."

"I've got this one. I can handle retired people."

White Eagle and Sarah turned to smile at each other but they didn't break down and laugh. I turned my lips in and pressed them together to keep from smiling myself. My cheeks hurt from the strain. Then I remembered the way Marlo had handled his mom earlier. He was getting good.

White Eagle had us back at Trevor's old house at two minutes to ten the next morning. We had our gear unloaded and were ringing her doorbell at ten on the nose. The lady of the house told us to go ahead and get to work. I started edging and Marlo started mowing. When he passed me he stopped to scoop up the clippings that got in the flower beds. I was thankful that we had brought the mulching mower so that we would not have to rake and bag today. We were trying to make her lawn look like we really did this for a living. My brain was busy working on a way into the garage. I knew I had to get in there before we finished the backyard and we were almost done with the front. As my brain concocted and rejected about five different scenarios, Marlo got lucky. He went to ask if they had a yard debris bin. They kept it in the garage. She would open it for us.

Marlo dumped his handful of grass and offered to switch me jobs so that I could get a chance at the garage. I walked around and picked up two handfuls of stray bits of grass and headed for the bin. She was poking around out there trying to keep an eye on us. Grrrr. I asked her politely how she wanted us to get into the backyard and then followed her around to the side gate. I thanked her and restarted the mower. I finished the front and started on the side yard, headed for the gate. I was getting ahead of Marlo so I tried to pick up the extra bits of grass again. She was still in the garage. My third trip back there the phone finally rang and she went to answer it. I knew I didn't have much time. I'd already scoped out where I would start my search.

On the house side of the garage were shelves. Behind the shelves was the wall. No wait – in the wall, behind a piece of missing drywall and near the bottom. I listened for her voice. It sounded like she was talking to Sarah. Ah yes, checking on our work. Hurry,

hurry my brain screamed. I knelt down and reached past the bottom shelf and into the crevice. At first I felt nothing. I strained a little further scraping my arm but I touched a book. I knew in an instant it was Trevor's and it was what I was after. I quickly pulled it out and stuffed it in the pocket of my cargo shorts. Thank goodness it was small. I took a brief moment to reassess the garage. Nope, nothing else. I stepped to the edge of the garage and gave a quick wave to White Eagle before hustling out back to restart the mower. Marlo was nearly done edging. I cut grass like a crazy man until I sensed her approach. I slowed back down to normal speed. In my haste I had missed a bit so I went back to fix that spot and leave some nice even lines. Marlo took the edger back to the truck and began collecting stray clippings again. As soon as I was done I took the mower to the truck. White Eagle helped me load the mower. I told him to look busy while I got out the book. I bent to tie my shoe and left it on the rear tire. In one smooth move White Eagle had collected it and was back in the truck. The lady was just paying Marlo. We both thanked her. She went back in through the garage closing the door behind her.

Marlo and I climbed back in the truck and sighed heavily as White Eagle pulled out. Sarah sat up from her slouched position in the front seat. "Good job, guys. It's Trevor's journal. I'm glad I called though; I didn't think she was ever going to leave that blasted garage!"

"I hope it was worth it," I said in a disheartened voice.

"Oh it was. From what I have skimmed so far and shared with Earl - he was a potential *watcher*. He thought he was going crazy or that he was seeing ghosts. Instead of finding a mentor he found a *stalker*. It happens sometimes, I understand."

"Yes, it happens," White Eagle replied. "It is sad, but it happens. I'm so thankful that I found you," he said looking at me. "You'd have been a great loss."

"Owen is strong. I was suspicious of him myself. If I hadn't seen the dramatic changes in him this last year I would have put him in touch with someone from my old team. A dangerous move maybe, but Owen would have been worth it," Sarah added.

"I didn't get many images from the journal but I would agree with what you said. I get the strong feeling that Trevor was afraid of the *stalker*. He knew that there was something *off* or *wrong* about him. I feel that he was torn between protecting his parents and running away. I wish I could hear what was said. With each meeting the terror grew. I don't think the *stalker* was sure about Trevor until just before the end. I think most of the information we get will be in his writings," I said, feeling a little let down. I wish I could've pulled more images out of it.

"Well, now we can freak out about high school starting tomorrow and hope we hear from Evelyn. Then we can make our beach jaunt," Marlo added, his mixed feelings plain in his tone.

"Don't worry Buddy, school will be fine," I said with more enthusiasm than I felt.

Sarah promised to read the journal and give us a report after our collective practices. There would be no pawnshop time for us except for the weekends until fall sports ended. We practiced everyday after school until five thirty and we needed time to do, oh joy, homework.

We dropped off Marlo and headed for my house. It was time for one of my favorite meals. It's not the food or time of day, but the company. Last year as part of our protection detail, while my dad was out of town, we would eat with Sarah and White Eagle. Today's conversation focused on school. Lucas was the most animated, but then first grade was a big change for him. With football practice happening, I felt like school had started already. Alex had mixed feelings. He really liked the lady who would be his teacher but he liked his free time too. He wasn't thrilled about getting back on a schedule. Mom was pretty excited to go back for her first year of subbing. She hadn't taught since Alex was born and she was ready for a change. Once we had my brothers fed and off doing their own thing, we filled Mom in on our latest adventure and told her that we had tentative plans to go to the beach.

Beggar barked once and the front door banged open. All of us turned in surprise to the doorway to the entry hall and there stood my dad, scowling in at the table. I saw White Eagle's eyes lose focus as he looked at my dad. Mom and Sarah both popped up.

"How about some lunch?" Sarah offered.

"I didn't realize you were coming in today. I would have picked you up," Mom said in a surprised voice.

I took my cue from White Eagle and *looked* at my dad also. There it was again, that strange something I'd been noticing. There was a fogginess about him. He was still neutral gray but this was different. I realized that it had been increasing since I'd first looked at him last spring. Then it hit me and I shot White Eagle a look. He looked a little puzzled but I knew what I was seeing. It was like with the motorcycle. It was hidden and so was Dad but who would do that and more importantly – why?

"Can I help you bring your stuff in, Dad?"

"Yes, I think I will have some lunch. Thank you, Mrs. Lando. I didn't realize we were hosting a neighborhood meeting," he replied stiffly. "You may take my bag upstairs, Owen."

White Eagle stood up and started clearing the table. I took off with Dad's bag. It too seemed to be gray and foggy or muzzled. Interesting. There were some images but it was like trying to watch a corrupted video; the pictures were incomplete and scratchy. If this was the same person who touched the motorcycle, they had grown in ability or it was a different but similar gift. Why had I not seen this before? Or was it so subtle that I'd missed it. I didn't dare open his bag for fear he would notice. I would have to sneak a peek later.

I walked back downstairs but Sarah and White Eagle had already left. I was disappointed but I knew the feeling. When Dad first comes home none of us want to be around him. I could feel an argument brewing. I had been avoiding my father but today I thought I would try something new. I sat down at the table and watched him, waiting for my opening.

"What?" he nearly barked at me. I saw Mom's hackles go up but I kept my eyes on Dad.

"I was wondering how your trip was." I said calmly.

"Fine."

"You were in Atlanta this time, right?"

"Yes," he said, giving me a hard stare.

"I was just wondering if you could tell me what you did while you were there." I used that same calm tone.

"I worked," he said a little gruffly and then he loosened up a bit. My mom was pretending to clean the counters but watched out of the corner of her eye.

"I'm working on a new project," Dad finally continued. "I'm helping to develop a new type of adhesive. We are..." His eye seemed to almost glaze over. It was odd. It wasn't the kind of look someone has when they are trying to remember – it was the kind of look you might have when you are trying to forget. He stayed like that for so long that Mom and I looked at each other. His lunch was forgotten, his fork teetering in his slack hand.

"Brad?" she ventured.

That was all it took to snap him back. "Ready for school tomorrow?" he asked in a normal voice like nothing had happened.

"Yes, I'm good, thanks. I think I'll go put everything together though." I sent my mom a look to let her know I would talk to her later. I figured I had about five minutes for Dad to finish his lunch. I was definitely going to look in his bag. I walked out of the kitchen and then lightly ran up the stairs. I headed for my parent's room and quickly unlatched Dad's bag. As fast as I could I laid everything out in careful order. I ran my hand over everything without touching it to really focus. Most items were layered in fog but I kept coming back to the bag. Something was drawing me in. The bottom of the bag had a double layer. Between the layers was a business card with a handwritten number on the back. His spit kit also was different. It was especially foggy which of course made me suspicious. Deodorant, razor, toothbrush, floss, shaving gel, aftershave, pills. Wait - pills? What did Dad take? It was from a pharmacy in Atlanta. It looked like an antidepressant. But something didn't feel right. I slipped one pill out of the bottle and quickly pocketed it. Crud. I heard footsteps on the stairs. I jammed everything back in his spit kit and then repacked and latched the case. I looked around frantically for a place to hide. I zipped into the master bathroom and on into the closet. I silently slid the door shut. I looked around inside the walk-in closet for a place to hide. At a loss, I slid the window up and silently removed the screen. I laid it out on the edge of the roof and listened. Dad had gotten on his cell.

"Hello? Dr. Rozenelle? I think I just had one of those episodes in front of my wife and son… Yes… But I wanted to be here for their first day of school. Maybe I could just see someone here… Yes, I understand… Yes. I have arranged to be at my parents for Christmas break. You can see Owen then. He has delusions; he thinks he can see things. I'm sure you can help him… Yes, Doctor. Goodbye."

There was a brief pause and I heard the beep of the ended call. Then I heard Dad open and rummage in his bag. I watched through the crack in the closet door. He brought the spit kit in to the bathroom. He opened it and unloaded it onto the counter. Then he picked up the pill bottle, shook one out and took it. He returned to the bedroom and started unpacking. I was afraid the closet was next so I crawled out the window and shut it as far as I could. I would have to deal with the screen later. With my toes on the skirt-roof I held onto the upper gutter and prayed it would hold. I worked my way to the end of our wraparound porch then eased myself down onto the skirt-roof. I slid over the edge and then dropped into the back yard.

I cut across the back of the house and headed in the back door. Mom dropped what she was holding in surprise - fortunately it was a loaf of bread so it made virtually no sound. I held a finger to my lips in the universal sign of silence. Her eyes were open so wide that I could see the white all the way around.

"I swear I will tell you later. If Dad asks, tell him I went to do some yard work for Sarah, okay?" I whispered frantically, hearing Dad's feet upstairs.

Mom nodded and I headed back out the backdoor so as not to be seen. I started off at a jog. I hit the four foot cyclone fence with both hands, vaulted over in a parkour-type move and then ran for Sarah's as fast as I could. White Eagle's truck was still in her driveway. Yes! It took a bit for my knock to be answered. I waited impatiently bouncing from foot to foot. White Eagle answered the door looking very surprised to see me.

"I have to talk to you both. Something is up. I need your help," I burst out.

White Eagle flung the door wide and I rushed right into Sarah's office. With the cabinets closed you would never know they hid all that technology. I stood staring at the cabinet, my hands loose at my sides trying to collect my thoughts. I turned abruptly when I heard the tread on the floor behind me. White Eagle and Sarah stood shoulder to shoulder looking appropriately serious.

"There is definitely something going on with my dad. I have some information and we need to start researching it right away. Most importantly, he is taking a new medication. We need to know what it is. We also need to track down this card," I said whipping them out to show Sarah and White Eagle. "Dad has been coming home acting strangely, as you know. You may not know that he and his stuff have been coming home looking *foggy* to me. I thought it was just Dad's neutrality. Now that I saw the motorcycle as *hidden*, *smudged* or *foggy*, I see that the same thing is going on with Dad. Whatever *spell* he is under may or may not have been enacted or created by the same person, but they are very similar, which is what gave me the idea in the first place. It's just that what is being done to Dad and his stuff is much more sophisticated and subtle. I'm sorry if I'm not using the right words, I just don't know how to describe it. I feel strongly that I am sensing someone's ability, just like I can tell when you are using your ability, White Eagle."

"Well I'll be darned," White Eagle managed. "What made you question the card and the pills?"

"I checked out Dad's bag after you left. I found the card buried under the layers of Dad's bag itself so it may be old or nothing but it is dark. It's like it got missed when his stuff's images were ruined. I forgot that part. I only get bits of images like you would from corrupted media. Someone has found a way to block what I *see* from objects. As far as the pills go – I didn't know that Dad was taking anything. Though it is true that he may not have told me – his spit kit was especially blank or foggy, which of course drew my attention. I also overheard him on the phone. He asked for a Dr. Rozenelle - the same as the name on the pill bottle. He said he thought he had an 'episode' in front of my mom and me. Then he almost whined that he wanted to be here for our first day of school. Dad does not whine. Then he asked if he could see someone here. He also said that he had arranged for me to come during Christmas break and the doctor could see me then. He added that he thought I have delusions and that I think I can see things. He ended the conversation by saying he was sure the doctor could help me," I said. I tried to sound calm but I think some of my nausea and fear showed through.

Sarah's phone rang. It was her landline. We all looked at each other. Sarah put a finger to her lips to tell us to be quiet. She hit a button and then answered the phone.

"Hello?"

"Mrs. Lando?"

"Yes."

"This is Brad Ryer. Is my boy there?"

"Why yes Brad, he is. Thank you so much for the loan. I do just love your boys so. They are always so helpful and generous."

"I'm here doing yard work," I frantically mouthed to her.

"He's helping me with a little yard work. Do you want me to get him for you?"

"Ah, no. I just need to know... I mean, I like to know what he is up to. Thank you for your time. Please send him home the minute he is done." Click.

Sarah disconnected her phone but continued to stare at it as if it would provide her with some clues. I could fool my dad about the yard work, no problem - I would be sweating by the time I got home from nerves alone. He had me that riled up. What was going on with him? He had never checked up on me before like this. He'd always trusted Mom.

"Did I mention that I need your help?" I asked in a forlorn tone.

"Owen, this is bad. What in the world? Let me see that pill." Sarah was so distressed that she was all business now. Lucky for us, stress brought out the best in her. "I will scan it for a visual and I will have a chemical analysis done. What did you notice about the bottle?"

"I recognized the medicine name as an antidepressant from an ad on TV. The pharmacy looked like the mom and pop variety. It was not a big name that I recognized," I answered.

"Earl would you..." Sarah started.

"I'm calling Marlo right now to get on the business card. He has access to the best software to research that kind of stuff," White Eagle interrupted.

"Owen honey, it's Monday. Please go drag my garbage, yard debris and recycling bins to the curb. Then run in circles or something in the backyard until you are sweaty, then roll on the grass to get dirty and go home. I promise I will give you the information I have in the morning. Leave for the bus but come here instead. I will drive you and Marlo to school. I know that your mom is taking the little boys so that she can volunteer in the morning. I will report to her as soon as I can pry her away from your dad.

I hugged her. I wanted to cry. At least I knew I'd done all I could and that I had the best help that money could buy and it cost me nothing but a few chores. I hugged White Eagle too. It was a show of affection that we didn't often share but I knew that he loved me just as much as she did. I may not have any of their blood in my veins but they meant more to me than some of the people in my family who did.

I did everything Sarah had suggested and then I dragged my feet on the way home. I wasn't sure what I would face there and I was not looking forward to it. It wasn't even dinner time yet.

When I walked in the house I was surprised to find my family playing a board game at the kitchen table. Mom took one look at me and suggested a shower before I joined them at the table. Besides cleaning up it gave me a chance to collect my thoughts and put on my poker face for Dad.

I couldn't wait for the day to end so that I could escape to school. I did find irony in that thought because it was only last year that I was counting the days to graduation. I had to do something about my dad but I could do nothing until I knew more. It was killing me. I wasn't too worried about my first day of high school. I was kind of worried about seeing Lucie. It had been like seventy-two days since I had seen her. What would I say? What would she say? Would we hear from Evelyn on Trevor? What would Sarah have to report? Knowing my luck I would have nightmares. I just hoped I could sleep.

I was mentally exhausted by the time I went to bed. My thoughts had chased around in my head like a dog after a squirrel. I worried about stuff I could do nothing about and I knew better.

I was right about the nightmare. Dad, like his old self, was in mortal combat with my strange new dad. It was horrible to watch my father attack himself like that. We stood in a deserted city intersection in the dead of night. Everything looked brittle, cold and forsaken. There was no sound except for the sickening thuds of fists hitting flesh. The buildings stared down at us with black sightless eyes. Only the streetlights provided the slightest illumination and that was wispy and weak.

I wanted to help my *old dad* but I couldn't reach him - invisible hands held me back. I felt like I was trapped in thick gelatin. He looked like he was losing and I was powerless – I couldn't even cry out or beg for help. My *old dad* fell to his knees and my *new dad* moved in for a killing blow. I finally broke free, rushing forward only to have my *old dad* disappear like smoke. My *new dad* smiled at me in a horrible and twisted way. My grandfather appeared behind him and I realized that he was holding strings attached to my new dad like he was a marionette. The city intersection was smudging into fogginess. I realized that the only light was now coming from me. I glowed like I imagined White Eagle saw my power. I then realized that my grandfather too was attached to strings and the faceless figure holding his strings was making everything disappear as well as manipulating my grandfather. I was shining brighter and brighter as everything else was fading away. Out in the distance I heard a broken cry, "Owen, help me." My *old dad*.

I woke up hopelessly twisted in my bedding, my face wet with tears and my body damp with sweat. The last time I felt this hopeless, I was lying broken at the bottom of a bank after Clive had beaten me and Darren had run me down with a car at the mall. I extracted myself from my bedding and stood to stretch. My phone beeped. I looked at it in utter amazement. I had a text from Lucie. I about dropped the phone, I was so surprised.

"couldn't sleep. thinking of u. Hope u r ok. Have a good day 2morrow."

I read it over and over. I couldn't decide if I should respond or not. I didn't want to sound overeager or anything. I didn't have a clue what to say that wouldn't scare her off again. In the end I fell back into bed and prayed for morning to come.

THREE

I had a different start time this year so I saw no reason not to get up with my brothers. They had to be at school by seven-thirty and I now needed to catch the bus just before eight. I showered quickly and dressed in jeans, and a button up shirt. I packed the football gear I would need for today's practice and headed downstairs. The kitchen was the usual early morning, school day, crazy. Beggar had mellowed after our other dog had been poisoned by one of Clive's guys and had died. Of course she was five now, so maybe her age was showing. She was hiding under the table hoping for dropped food. Ron, the cat was weaving in and out of Mom's busy feet as she tried to simultaneously get breakfast ready, feed the cat and find Lucas' missing sock in the laundry basket. I took over cat duty and then started in on my own breakfast. Missing socks were not my department; I had enough trouble keeping track of my own. Dad was hidden behind the morning paper ignoring the pandemonium. I got everyone going on pancakes and eggs, then served myself. I took a couple of protein bars for snacks and put them in my backpack. I was trying to decide if I should pack my lunch or buy one at school. Dad was still buried in his paper so I started cleaning the kitchen as Mom and my brothers headed out the door.

"Have a great first day," I said trying to sound enthusiastic.

Dad grunted from behind his paper. Why whine about being home and then not participate? I finished the kitchen, folded the rest of the clothes in the basket for Mom and then went ahead and packed a lunch. Dad had said nothing to me nor had looked up from the paper so I picked up my gear and backpack and headed for the door.

"Where do you think you're going?" he questioned in a grumpy voice.

"To the bus stop," I answered patiently.

"You're an hour early. Where are you really going?" Now he was scowling over the top of the paper at me. What the heck?

"No, really, I catch the bus at just before eight," I tried in a calm voice. Then I remembered the schedule on the fridge. I have never been happier that Mom is so... compulsive. "Here, look," I said handing him the schedule.

"Mmm," he grunted and went back to the paper.

"So, I'll see you tonight I guess," I ventured, trying to figure out what was going on. As the silence dragged on I wondered if I was dismissed or if he was okay. "Dad?" I peeked over the paper and his eyes were glazed again. He seemed to snap out of it and looked at me startled.

"What did you say?" he asked, seeming almost like his old self.

"I have football practice after school. I'll see you tonight, okay?"

"Okay, have a good day," he said sounding nearly normal.

My worry was intense as I left the house and headed for Sarah's. Marlo was already there. I prayed that my dad would not slip back into weirdness and come check on me at the bus stop. Marlo said I looked like a train wreck. I told them what had happened this morning and about my strange dream. Sarah suggested I put it out of my mind for now and focus on school since there was nothing I could do at the moment and she would keep an eye on Dad as best she could.

She shared with us that she had sent the image of the medicine I had stolen from my dad and the med itself to her lab for quiet processing. Whatever it was, it was not what was listed on the label. She figured whatever they were giving him, it was too much for his system. On the Trevor front she did not have a lot more from the journal. At first the guy who called himself Willie, seemed interested in Trevor's bike. The bike was the 'in' and got Trevor to open up a bit. At first he was happy to have a friend who didn't think he was losing it but things went downhill fast. Although she looked forward to hearing what was in the cold case file she felt that we needed to go see Trevor's mom and sister. I was the best detecting tool we had.

"Look, my dad seems to be really suspicious of me right now. I won't be able to go anywhere until he goes back out of town and right now I don't know when that will be." I wondered if I sounded as frustrated as I felt. How could so many things be happening at once? How was I supposed to deal with it all and school?

"It *is* going to be alright Owen, we have each other. You are not alone," Sarah said with a soft look in her eyes. "Let's get you to school. Right now just think about school and football... or soccer," she said with a smile for Marlo. "I will take care of things here. I will also go catch your mom while she is still at school, Owen."

We loaded up and headed for our first day of high school. At the moment I could not think of anything else I could do. It wasn't so long ago that I had wished for more excitement. This is not what I had in mind.

Marlo and I consulted our schedules and double checked the map of the school layout. There would only be freshman here today but still, there was no need to look any more weak than we had to. We thanked Sarah for the ride, took a deep breath, nodded at each other and headed for our first class. Geometry seemed to last forever. We were used to having class last around fifty minutes instead of almost an hour and a half. Now we would have four classes each day, on alternating days instead of seven classes every day. Lots of changes. The next period I had Biology. I wondered if I would see Lucie. Surely if I had been bumped up in science, she had been too. Marlo had Biology as well but of course it was with the other section. I wished we had more classes together.

It was weird to be in a class that was nearly empty. Many of the other students would be sophomores. There were only five freshmen in this class. I knew all of them from middle school but we were more acquaintances than friends. I had the feeling that every one of my organizational skills was going to be put to the test this year. Fortunately I had Marlo, the organizational wizard, on my team. Marlo and I had all the same classes again this year and again only a few were at the same time. It was a relief when the bell rang.

I ate one of my protein bars since lunch wasn't until after one and then I wandered into World History. There were several kids I knew in this class. Instead of choosing a seat based on the people present, I chose by location. I have learned that I prefer the right side of the room and I prefer not to have my back to any doors or windows. If I can watch a door, that is optimal. I like to know what is coming at me. I still don't like to draw attention to myself, so I choose a seat near the middle of a row when I can. Some days it's easier than others to get the seating I like. I was doodling in my spiral, waiting for class to start, when the gentle scent of citrus and springtime washed over me. I'd know that combination anywhere. I looked up to see Lucie hesitating by my desk.

"Hey, Lucie," I said softly.

"Owen," she replied. She wore navy slacks and a pale blue button up shirt. She bit her lip and then took a seat directly behind me. Great. Now I would never be able to concentrate. While the teacher took roll, I turned slightly just to look at her. She had looked like she wanted to say something but she wouldn't meet my gaze. I brought together all the good times we had shared, in my mind and then rested my hand on hers for a moment. I imagined sending my goodwill her way. I wanted to tell her that everything would be okay and that I was still her friend, if nothing else. I wanted her to know that she could still count on me. She looked at our hands and her eyes widened a bit. She met my gaze for a moment and then moved her hand away. I turned back around determined to concentrate. I wasn't sure what her look or the movement was meant to communicate to me.

As much as I tried to focus, I found that I was super aware of her. If I concentrated, I could pick up her scent. When she spoke, I listened. Every movement she made I was aware of too. She must have been just as aware of me. At the end of class, I turned right to see if she wanted to go to lunch and she zipped left, past my desk and out the door, faster than I would have thought possible, yet, I reminded myself, she had chosen to sit by me during class. Maybe there was hope.

I got my lunch from my locker and made my way to the commons. I looked around for Lucie. She was nowhere to be seen. Marlo and Adrian didn't even have this lunch. I started out at a table alone. When Lucie came down the stairs she looked at me and moved to another table. Sigh. Jesus wandered over and plopped down next to me.

"Whazup?" he asked.

"Not much, you? Do you feel uncomfortable being here?"

"Nah, I feel a little nervous though. After the trouble I almost got into last year, I'm not looking forward to tomorrow when some of my sister's ex-boyfriend's crowd will be around," he admitted.

"I know they gave you some trouble last year so stick with us. I didn't see you this morning but what do you have the rest of today and tomorrow?"

We checked our schedules – we would have Choir and Spanish together tomorrow. He also had Global Science with Adrian. Jesus got sucked into the drama with his sister Selena's old boyfriend. Selena had dumped the ex when she was a senior because he had gotten involved in drugs and some gang stuff. We thought the ex was trying to get even with Selena when he tried to recruit Jesus into his group of wanna be gang members. Administration tried to keep all gang and drug activity away from campus but if a kid wants to find something bad enough they often can. We had adopted Jesus into our group and he had turned it around.

"Hey man, where are Adrian and Marlo? I thought you guys did everything together," Jesus said, lightening the mood a little.

"Not this semester – we have some classes together but not like last year," I answered.

We settled in to eat our lunches and people watch. Every time I looked at Lucie, she was looking at me and then her eyes would dart away. This was like starting over - all over again. I wished I could figure out what the draw was. Adrian was right, there were lots of chicks out there. Many were just as nice as Lucie and with a whole lot less baggage. There were many that were as pretty but she had been one of my best friends for awhile. This just sucked. Jesus and I parted ways. I told him I'd see him for lunch on Thursday when we had it at the same time again.

I headed for PE and football practice and then finally I would hopefully have some news from Sarah and White Eagle on my Trevor and Dad problems. I was sure that most guys on my team were worried about the upcoming first game of the season. It was the least of my problems.

I was astounded to find White Eagle's truck waiting in the lot for me after football practice. I was immediately overcome by dread. Something must be terribly wrong at home if Mom or Dad didn't come get me. I started running for the truck. White Eagle either saw or sensed my concern. He jumped out of the truck and gave me the hand signal to slow down. I flipped my head right and left to check lot traffic and then hustled a little more sedately in his direction.

"What's going on?" I asked the minute he was within hearing distance.

"Everything's fine. I promise. We'll talk in the truck," he said in his most soothing voice.

I put my gear in the back seat and hopped into the passenger side. I buckled up and looked expectantly at White Eagle.

"Sarah caught up with your mom at the grade school. They were able to find a place to chat. Sarah filled her in. Then your mom went home and discovered that your dad was... gone. He had left her a note. He said that his dad was ill and that he was returning to Florida. Your mom and Sarah did some checking – he is being flown on the company plane. This problem is bigger than we thought or at least it goes higher. You were under the impression that your grandfather had gotten your dad the new job, right?"

"That's basically what I heard. I wonder who is pulling my grandfather's strings though. It's more than the dream I had last night. I have this feeling... Did Sarah tell you about the dream?"

"Yeah, with dreams it is hard to tell what's real and what isn't. It's our brain's way of working things out but the images many not directly relate to anything. I also get the feeling that you are thinking what I am. What is a guy like your dad doing being flown around on the company plane? He is a talented engineer but he is not extraordinary. Why the special treatment? The job in and of itself was a surprise. We have done some research. Your father has had very little to do with his father in years and now that your talent has shown up that has changed. This amazing job came his way and now he is flown on a private plane. I don't mean to be paranoid but I think someone is after you and willing to pay anything or do anything to get to you."

"If they are so well funded why not just come here and get me?"

"I don't know. Why play the games? Why wait and why be subtle? Are they trying to turn you? Are they still watching or not ready for you yet? I just don't know and frankly it scares me but I won't let it rule my life and I sure don't want you to let it rule yours. Be aware but don't stop your life and hide either. For now I think we need to watch and see. I need to find a way to go to Florida when you go. I can't leave you there alone with just your mom."

"Did Sarah learn anything about the drug that my dad is taking?"

"Nothing beyond what you already guessed. We don't have a chemical analysis yet, but it is not what it says it is on the label."

"Did you hear from Evelyn?"

"She pulled the file and was able to get us an electronic version. We have not read all of it yet. There was no evidence from the scene other than the motorcycle so there is nothing there for you to *look* at. We need to go to the coast to see Trevor's mom."

"Have we had any hits on the picture that Joy drew up for us?"

"Not yet. Facial recognition can take time I understand."

"This is why Miles became a PI isn't it – he kept getting pulled into cold cases and it would have looked suspicious if he solved too many of them but as a PI he could feed the information to different people so that it didn't all come back to him."

"That was part of it, yes. He also found that sometimes the need to take care of something he discovered because of his power was stronger than the need to do his paid work. He couldn't keep calling in sick. What you do is not easy. It is a tricky balancing act. You will be able to figure it out and we are here to help you."

"Just this morning, Sarah was reminding me that I am not alone. Do you just know me so well that you know I am worried or am I looking weak and helpless?"

"I would never accuse you of being either weak or helpless! I just know that you are being driven in more than one direction right now. I don't know why things come to you this way sometimes. You have a whole bunch of things going on or it's too quiet. I don't claim to understand it."

"Right now things are getting a little out of hand."

"True."

"Is it just me or does it seem weird to you, that my dad came home yesterday and left already today? Could he just be checking up on me?"

"I really don't know, but it is odd."

We pulled into the driveway at my house and I took in my gear. My house held the festive air that it often did when my dad left or maybe it was my imagination. I tossed my dirty, stinky practice gear in the laundry room and sat down to one of Mom and Sarah's great combined 'cooking genius' dinners. My brothers interrupted each other frequently to tell about their first day of school. They were happy and enthusiastic. No one seemed to notice that I didn't say much.

As soon as dinner was done I was excused to go do my homework. My turn to clean the kitchen would be on weekend nights. I looked at my class syllabuses and pulled out my planner. I dutifully wrote down as much as I could and got to work. Lucas wanted to play checkers so I paused to play one game. He wanted me to put him to bed but my mom talked him out of it. I tried to focus on my assignments and work a bit ahead but I was too distracted.

Mom peeked in a little after nine to tell me that the coast was clear. We found White Eagle and Sarah curled up side by side on the couch watching TV. Mom and I walked on in and sat down.

"I think that I need to let Trevor go for awhile. I think that Dad has become our priority. I'm concerned about the drug someone is giving him and what they are doing to him. I hate that I'm not in a position to miss school. I guess I could have a weird illness but how many times can I pull that one and keep getting away with it? I feel like I'm being pulled in so many directions," I groaned.

"Owen, your dad can hang on for a bit. Let's get some more information. Let's find out what the drug really is. We should know in a day or two. Go ahead and go to the beach this weekend to meet Trevor's mom. It will be okay. Your dad will be all right. I'm sure they'll try to get him back under control and then send him back to spy some more. I feel like they're really after you and that we shouldn't rush this," Mom said softly.

"We agree with your mom. Sarah and I have been discussing this and going over the information we have. We all know that you hate it when there isn't anything you can do. Well right now you can *do* something about Trevor. So let's work on that one. We'll keep looking into your dad and your grandfather. In thirteen and a half weeks you will be going to see your grandfather – let's get you both as prepared as we possibly can. If we must move sooner, then we will," White Eagle said in that calming, assured way of his.

"My plan of attack for the weekend is to leave on Saturday. Lila, I think you should stay with the little boys and let them think that Owen is at the pawnshop like usual. I really don't think we need Marlo or Adrian and I feel greater numbers would be a hindrance for this. I also believe it should just be the two of us and White Eagle can wait in the car. I want him there for safety but I would like to use my bureau ID and tell Trevor's mom that I'm part of a cold case squad. Don't shave anymore this week and we'll put you in a suit. Use your body language to look as old as you can and channel Miles. I'll do most of the talking, then we'll play the rest by ear. What do you think?" Sarah asked.

We all looked at each other, nodding. It was a place to start. I told them I was beat and headed for bed. I hoped that I wouldn't be revisited by nightmares. I was doing all I could at the moment. I made sure my stuff was ready for the morning and got ready for bed. I lay down and tried to run through my relaxation techniques. I don't know when I drifted off but the next thing I knew my alarm was blasting.

I really didn't feel any more rested than when I went to bed. I looked at my haggard face in the mirror. Oh well. No help for it. Stress is bad for the dark circles under your eyes. I squirted some shaving gel in my hand and started to rub it in when I remembered I wasn't supposed to shave. I rinsed off my hand and adjusted the shower temp. The minute it was warm enough I stepped in, hoping to wake up. I reverted to my casual rock band t-shirt, jeans and my last pair of skate shoes.

I headed downstairs and straight for the coffee pot. The kitchen was much more composed this morning. Mom had first day of school paperwork clipped and put into two neat piles to go back to school today.

"Hey, rough night?" she asked sympathetically as she looked at me from the eggs she was cooking.

"I slept like a rock but I still feel tired. I think I have too many worries. I'll be okay."

"Sarah will be here tomorrow. My friend who teaches Kindergarten needs a morning sub so Sarah will be here to get you all to school. Okay, boys?"

Her words were met with a chorus of 'sure' and 'fine'. Mom smiled at us. "I am excited but a little nervous."

"I know you will do a great job," I said with a smile. She was always there for me - the least I could do was support her. I tried to be a little more enthusiastic around my brothers. As soon as they were out the door, I relaxed back into sadness and worry.

I met Marlo at the bus stop and since no one else was around yet, I filled him in on the latest. He was disappointed about the beach trip but he understood. There was a girl he thought he might ask out and he'd see if they could double with Adrian and Amy. Better Marlo than me was all I could think.

"Hey Buddy, call me a coward but since you have to talk to Adrian anyway, do you want to try to break it to him? Maybe he'll be cooled off by our football game this afternoon or maybe he'll still be mad and he'll take it out on the field instead of me."

I knew Adrian wouldn't really be mad but he *would* be disappointed. He hated missing any action but this time I felt that Sarah was right, smaller numbers would be a plus. Now I just had to get through three more days of school and a game.

Marlo, already in his PE gear, and I parted ways in the locker room where I put my stuff for this afternoon. Then I headed for Choir. I hoped I would at least see Lucie again. It was a relief to see her in Choir but she was working hard at ignoring me. Fine, I thought, frustrated. I had Adrian in both Choir and Spanish but I conveniently forgot to tell him about the beach trip in hopes that Marlo could break it to him. I felt a little cowardly but I just wasn't in the mood to deal with his sometimes sharp tongue.

I met up with Marlo in Health. Amy, Adrian's girlfriend, came in just as the bell was ringing and sat by us. Marlo chatted with her about Saturday plans and she thought it was great. Apparently the girl Marlo liked was in his orchestra class and she had said yes. No surprise to me. Marlo was a great guy. Amy joined us for lunch and a couple of her friends came over to sit with us too. It was nice after yesterday though it had been good to see Jesus. One of Amy's friends acted like she was interested but when that opportunity knocked I didn't answer the door. I didn't feel a spark.

Marlo and I headed for English but my mind was already on the game. I jumped when a book was slapped on my desk. I guess the teacher noticed that I wasn't paying attention either. *Romeo and Juliet*, what a deal. I cut my eyes to Marlo. He was looking right at me with his eyes twinkling and his shoulders shaking a bit as he struggled not to laugh. At least I could count on him to fill me in on what I had missed when I zoned out. He would also understand the language of the book.

I was glad to head to the locker room. I saw Lucie heading for the bus. I figured she must have had PE and was just leaving. I guessed she wouldn't be staying for the game. I headed on in and suited up. I stretched a bit and waited for Adrian and the others to get ready. I tried to put everything else out of my mind and focus on our plays and our coach. We ran through all the pregame stuff that had to be done. I kept working on focus.

It wasn't raining and it wasn't too hot. The sky was a clear deep blue with a few puffy clouds hanging around. The stands were mostly empty with a smattering of parents scattered about. I saw my mom, brothers, White Eagle and Sarah in the stands. Adrian's dad was also here and so were Amy and some of her friends.

Fate was smiling upon us. Everything went right. Everyone was where they were supposed to be when they were supposed to be there. I imagined that we actually looked pretty good. Some of these guys had been playing together for quite awhile and that helped.

Lucie's old boyfriend Calvin was even minding his manners. Now that we were at high school and he was away from Lucie, he didn't seem as antagonistic toward me but I avoided him whenever possible. He thought of himself as a super star. I just did as I was told. He had been moved to a quarterback position and I was one of the receivers so sometimes I got the 'privilege' of working with him. I stayed out of his way and tried to catch whatever he threw. I let him take all the credit no matter how awful his throw. He was hinting at being moved up to junior varsity. I was here to learn some new skills.

I was surprised when the coach pulled me aside after our debriefing. I had seen the JV coach on the sidelines but thought nothing of it. Apparently he was there taking notes. He liked the way Calvin and I worked together which I thought was the world's greatest irony. We would practice with our team and then attend the JV game tomorrow. Then we would start practicing with the JV. If we played as well as we did today the move would be for the rest of the season. Calvin was not hip to my presence but he was so anxious to move up that he was willing to go with me if that was the way to get there. Next I saw them speak to Adrian and I held high hopes that he would move with me.

After we were left alone by the coaching staff I asked Adrian what they had said. Yep, he was moving up. Yay, team. He was fine with not going to the beach. He had JV to look forward to and a date with Amy. His life was perfect. I wished I could say the same.

Our families greeted us as we left the locker room. I was happy to be heading home. I waited to spring the JV news until we were a bit away from the rest of the kids and parents. Everyone seemed really enthusiastic. I guess I should have been but I was so worried about everything else that I couldn't really get excited about it right now.

Mom decided that dinner would keep so we went to pizza instead. My brothers even partook in some arcade games. The atmosphere was fun and noisy. There were a few other team members' families there. White Eagle and Sarah joined us as part of our extended family. It was nice to sit and relax. I found that all the racket acted as white noise and made me sleepy. I had a few aches and pains from being tackled but none of it was too bad. I rested my chin on my hand and scanned the room - nothing out of the norm was going on. I shut my eyes and felt the room. Nothing felt out of place so I left my eyes shut and let my mind drift. Mom, Sarah and White Eagle were talking quietly. Mom and Sarah were working out a modified training and babysitting schedule. White Eagle was working on karate with my mom and brothers twice a week after school for an hour. I drifted. The hum and background sound began to evolve and change. I could hear Lucie... crying softly. I opened my eyes with a start.

"Tired? Ready to go? I'll round up your brothers. You must have dozed off," Mom rattled at me.

"I thought I heard... never mind. Yeah, let's go."

We parted company and I closed my eyes and tried to focus on Lucie. I could hear nothing but my brothers chattering in the back seat. At bedtime I tried to capture the feeling of the pizza parlor again but I still got nothing on Lucie. I even tried staring at the picture of her from our Washington D.C. trip. I got nothing.

School was a repeat of day one except for Biology. We had all the sophomores with us today. We weren't assigned seats so I took one of the spots I like to the right of the room closer to the back than the front. I was doodling in my spiral when I felt the air move and a soft scent tickled my nose. I looked up to see a beautiful girl I'd never seen before. She had medium brown hair that curved under her jaw in front and sloped down to brush her shoulder blades by the time it reached her back. She had magnificent eyes. They were amber brown near her pupil but were ringed darker at the outer edge. I was captivated.

She continued to stare at me. Finally she spoke. Her voice was a surprise, it was deep and throaty like a lounge singer and completely unexpected out of someone so young. "This seat taken?"

"No, go ahead." At least I didn't stammer or stutter and I had kept my eyes on her face the whole time. That had to get me points, right? She slid gracefully into the seat and then unloaded her backpack of the supplies she would need for class. She then turned and looked at me.

"I'm Tess."

"Nice to meet you Tess, I'm Owen," I responded, still glad that I wasn't acting like the idiot I felt like sometimes.

"You any good at science?" she asked, her whole attention on me.

"I did well, you?"

"I'm okay. I need a good lab partner. Maybe that could be you."

"If you like. I don't really know anyone in here so why not," I asked in a friendly voice. She smiled at me. It was a beautiful sight and lit up her whole face. The first thing we got to do together was share a textbook and fill out a worksheet. We read and had to fill in the answers. I quickly noticed that all the vocabulary we needed were the ones in bold. So we finished the worksheet and then went back and read so that we were ready to move on when the teacher was. Tess had me a little worried by her words but she seemed to be plenty smart.

"Save me a seat next week, okay?" she asked with another of her dazzling smiles.

I nodded and smiled back. I started repacking my backpack but looked up to watch her leave. She looked back at me from the door before she turned the corner. She liked me. Good. I could use a distraction. I had barely noticed during class but as she had left the room I realized that she was wearing a glitter decorated, close fitting t-shirt and low cut jeans. When she moved I caught a flash of tanned skin just above her belt. Wow.

I thought of both Lucie and Tess as I sat in World History. Lucie sat on the other side of the room today. She gave me an odd look. It was almost as if she wished that she could sit by me. So why not do it? She was nowhere to be found at lunch and neither was Tess. Jesus ate with me again and then it was off to PE, football practice, grab some grub and be back and suited up to sit on the sidelines of the JV game.

FOUR

Sarah surprised me after my unbelievably long day on Thursday. After school, practice and the JV game all I wanted to do was eat, sleep and squeeze in a bit of homework. Instead I was pounced on when White Eagle dropped me off at the door. While Mom told me about her first day back teaching, she had me dress in one of Dad's old suits. They started with the pants and a white dress shirt. As soon as I was decent, Sarah and a friend of hers stepped into Mom's room.

My surprise turned out to be a tailor. Mom and Sarah had been thinking and planning again. I was beginning to think this thinking and planning stuff was a really bad idea. After much twitching around of the clothing on my body, the tailor said that it could be done and proceeded to pin me into the clothing. Last she had me put on the suit coat and the whole twitching thing began again as I was assaulted by images of my dad in a meeting with my grandfather and a man I didn't know. Dad's body language showed me that he was both angry and scared. My grandfather looked determined, yet angry, too. He felt... manipulated. The third man was clearly in control. Whatever he wanted them to do they were not happy about but for different reasons. The third man was doing something to both of them. Perhaps he was using his power on them. Was he a manipulator? I looked at my grandfather's desk. A newspaper was on it. I forced my attention there. It was two days before eighth grade graduation!

While the tailor was at work on me, Mom and Sarah went through Dad's ties. They brought out three for her to approve. She chose the subtle gray and black stripe to go with the serious black suit. The shoulders almost fit and would not need to be altered. She needed to hem the pants, take in the waist and bring in the back some. On the jacket she needed to shorten the sleeves a bit. The dress shirt was fine except for bringing it in at the waist. She would deliver the whole outfit to Sarah tomorrow.

"Dad won't be happy," I commented to Mom when the others left.

"Don't worry, in the state he is in right now, he won't even miss it. In the end he will understand. It's an older suit anyway and he hasn't worn it in a long time. Have you noticed that every time he comes home he has a new suit? I've looked at some of the labels. The new suits are high-end and they're being tailored. I'll be relieved when this is resolved."

"Mom, the suit gave me an image. I saw Dad in a meeting with grandpa and another man last June. That other man is the one pulling the strings. I wonder if Joy could sketch him too. How come you and I didn't find this suit before?"

"Maybe it wasn't here Owen, or that fogginess you have talked about wore off? Maybe you should *look* at the closet again. You need to pick out some dress shoes anyway and your feet aren't that different from your dad's. I think your feet could last through your Saturday meeting in his shoes."

I looked at the closet and found nothing. I touched each of Dad's items just in case. Nothing. Mom and I picked out a pair of somber dress shoes and put them in a bag for our beach adventure.

I inhaled my dinner which I knew wasn't good for me. I plowed through my homework wishing I had time for a more careful job. Maybe I'd have time to recheck it before I had to turn it in on Monday. I would take it to the beach and see how things went. I'd have to get good at using any spare moments for study. I fell face-down diagonally across my bed. I'd brushed and flossed but still wore my clothes.

When I woke up Friday morning I had a blanket from the hall closet over me and I was stiff and sore. I hadn't moved all night. Good grief, why was I so tired? I staggered into the bathroom. I was glad that my brothers took their showers at night so that I didn't have to share. I stood under the hot water and rolled my neck and listened to it crackle. I rolled my shoulders and arched my back. I felt... old today. I dried off and slung the towel around my hips and trudged back to my room. I had almost shaved again today. The stubble was showing a bit. I hoped I'd look appropriately old by Saturday because I sure felt like it.

While trying to figure out what to wear, I had a panic attack when I realized that I had not done my laundry. I had clothes for school but did I have clothes for practice? I scrounged up an old tee with the sleeves cut off and figured I could re-wear the shorts from yesterday. I gathered my books for my day two classes and headed downstairs in khaki cargo pants, plain black tee and my new standard footwear, lace-up boots.

My brothers were at the table spooning up oatmeal. "You fell asleep in your clothes!" Lucas giggled. "I came in to tell you good night and you were out."

"I'm sorry, Buddy. I've been really tired." I walked over to him and ruffled his hair. "How's school going? You like being there all day?"

"I'm a big kid now. It's pretty awesome," Lucas replied with enthusiasm.

"How about for you, big guy? School still good?" I asked Alex.

"Yeah, it's good. There's a new girl in our class and she is *hot*. She moved here from California so everyone wants to be her friend but she sits by me," Alex announced proudly.

Fifth grade and into women already – maybe he was taking after Adrian. Did I like girls in fifth grade? I couldn't remember. I took down a mug and poured myself a cup of coffee again and then I fixed some oatmeal. I was trying to decide if I wanted a hardboiled egg when Mom came around the corner.

"Have the egg and be sure to take a protein bar with you today. You must be growing again."

"Stop that," I said a little louder than I had meant to. She looked at me startled and then it dawned on her.

"Oh, my goodness - I'm sorry," Mom said chagrined.

"What?" Alex asked.

He was getting curious about us. I needed to be more careful. I took note of the laundry basket in Mom's hands and quickly changed the subject.

"Mom did my laundry and I feel bad when she does that. I want to be responsible and take care of myself."

I shook the egg at Mom, then peeled and ate it. While my brothers were getting their backpacks I whispered to her, "I'm sorry. It startles me when you read my mind. There may be stuff in there at some point that I don't want you to know."

"I think I'm lucky and not really reading anything but who knows. I only seem to do it to you and I only seem to do it when I don't try. Okay, that sounded really weird. I'll talk to Earl and see what he says. You know it's only because of you that he even tries to help me. My gift is minimal."

"Remember what he said though. Together we are more. Maybe one day you will be powerful. I sure will need you in Florida, especially since I think you will be a big surprise. Dad doesn't know about you. No wait, I think he might. I think I said something about getting my power from you. Damn it. Maybe he won't remember and it will surprise them. We can hope right?"

"Don't borrow trouble. We have lots to learn between now and then. I have to go. I did wash your gym clothes. I felt sorry for you. You were so tired. I love you. Have a good day. I'll see you tonight."

"Love you too, Mom. Thanks."

I took some clean shorts from the basket instead of the dirty ones I had planned to take and rechecked my gym bag and backpack. My mind was already trying to move to Saturday. I had a few minutes before I needed to meet Marlo at the bus stop so I ran back upstairs and checked on the homework I would need to take to the beach. I pulled it together and stacked it so that I could finish getting ready for that tonight. I wanted to get it all prepared so that I could have a good night's sleep – fat chance of that happening I bet. Biology sat on top of the pile. I think my Science papers laughed at me. It reminded me of Lucie and our plant lab. Why couldn't I put her out of my mind? Think of Tess.

I met Marlo at the bus stop. I must have looked like I felt because Marlo, being Marlo, immediately noticed my mood.

"Rough night?" he asked sympathetically just like my mom had.

"Yes, Mother, stress will do that do you."

"This takes me back to eighth grade. I though we had improved your mood and personality over the last year. Why the backslide?"

"Sorry, Mars. I'm really worried about Dad. We're moving forward with Trevor, but I hate waiting until Christmas to handle Dad. I'm also worried about how my grandfather is involved. This one is big, I hope I can handle it. I just don't know enough and it's freaking me out."

"Have patience my friend. I've got your back on this one. I know Sarah is working on it but I have my ways too. I also have Joy's number. The drawing she did still hasn't shown a match. The guy is a ghost. Don't look so disheartened – even people who hide can be found eventually. And if he is hiding, there is a reason, right? You're on the right track; just wait for the train to pull into the station, will ya."

I spent the whole school day waiting for it to end. Not even practicing with the JV squad kept my interest. I worked hard and was focused but I was still mentally tracking the minutes. The best part of practice was *not* working with Calvin. I got to work with the other quarterbacks. The coaches also spent some time checking my speed and agility. Lucky for me my teammates only got in one good sack. I would have some beautiful bruises to show for it later tonight though, I was certain.

White Eagle picked me up as he often did when my dad was gone. It gave us time to connect.

"You know, I really like football but I'm going to be glad when it's over. Right now it feels like it's in the way and it's a long time until the first week of November. I'll be glad to get back to the pawnshop on a regular basis like the old days," I groused.

"You're in an interesting mood, aren't you? You have too many worries and not enough action. You need to solve some of the problems on your plate and you'll feel better. Miles used to get like this. Shake it off. You're doing all you can - quit beating yourself up. I need you fresh tomorrow. Tonight I need to work on aging you. After dinner we will practice being old. We'll be doing some work on your posture, mannerisms and speech. I want you to channel Miles at about age twenty-five. We already have a pretty good start because you know Miles from the time he picked up that watch you wear until he died. I also think just being a *watcher* changes and ages you. It's what it does to your mind, not your body – I would guess your brain is about eighteen or nineteen right now. At some point it will also keep your mind young."

"I've said it before, but it's still odd to be growing up and creating my own memories AND have memories of stuff like I experienced it myself from age twenty-two to thirty-four. So now you're saying I have a double whammy. My brain and thoughts would have aged anyway and I know how to be a twenty-five year old man because I have been one. Wow that sounds nuts even to me. Now I just need to look twenty-five. Think you can do that?"

"Watch us!" White Eagle smiled with confidence.

He drove straight to Sarah's instead of going to my house. I raised my eyebrows at him as he pulled in the driveway.

"Your suit fitting, sir," he answered my unasked question.

Sarah had me take the suit pants and shirt into her bedroom. Her house is simple, clean, neat and organized. I think it fits her personality. She has a love of antiques that shows in her choice of furnishings. I'd never before been in her bedroom but it showed the same personality as the rest of her house. Her bedroom contained mahogany furniture – the kind with fancy brass knobs and pulls with scrolly legs. Her queen sized bed had a chenille spread on it – not something you see much anymore. Most notable was the lack of a TV. She did have side lamps on either side of the bed and a fantastic floor to ceiling built in bookcase that would make my mom drool. It was loaded with books from every genre imaginable. No wonder she was so smart – she must be the best-read person in the state.

I slipped out of my clothes and into the slacks and button-up shirt. Wow! The sleeves were now the perfect length and the tailor had taken in the sides of the shirt so that it was still comfortable yet fitted. The slacks were much better than they had been. They now fit at the waist and weren't so baggy in the backside. I was just tucking in the shirt when Sarah knocked. "Ready?" she asked before poking her head in.

"I guess," I answered, not sure what to expect. I thought I looked pretty good as I admired the fit in her full length mirror.

"Hey, Handsome! She did good, huh?" Sarah beamed at me. "Here are your shoes and I got you a belt."

"Sarah, you have got to quit buying me stuff," I said gruffly.

"I don't have any kids – you're it – so stop complaining. I love you and I can afford it," she replied, scowling at me.

"But Sarah, I can't reciprocate – I can't repay you," I said trying another angle.

"Every time you do the heavy lifting around here or cut my lawn and just by being you – you do!" she insisted.

I gave up and put on the shoes and belt.

"Thank you, Sarah. How do I look?"

She carefully checked me out from top to bottom and from all sides. She smiled a soft, sad smile and patted me on the shoulder.

"You look good, Champ. Now, clip this on your belt, right at your hipbone and we'll go show Earl."

I looked at her extended hand where she held a badge. Super, now I would be arrested for impersonating an officer. I would be with one so I guessed it was her neck. I took it from her and looked at it closely.

"Hey, this is real. What the heck?"

"It was my first. People won't look close. Their focus will be on me. You'll be fine. You look more grown up already." She shook her head and led me out to the living room.

White Eagle looked suitably, no pun intended, impressed. Sarah slid the jacket up my arms and settled it on my shoulders. I pulled my best Miles out of the old memory banks and walked around the room.

"Amazing," White Eagle said, awed. After a visit to the barber in the morning we will have this nailed.

White Eagle worked with me on a perfect Winsor knot that just touched the top of my belt buckle. Thanks to some of Miles' memories it didn't take me long to make my fingers do the job.

I felt half-starved by the time I'd changed back into me, Sarah had hung up the suit and the three of us had walked to my house. Mom had already fed my brothers who were busy with the Playstation. The four of us sat down and put the final touches on our plans for tomorrow. Mom and Marlo still had me on a careful diet so that I wouldn't get too thin during football season. I still felt a little like a science experiment with the weekly weigh-ins and constant monitoring of what I ate. Whenever my weight dipped they had me back on protein bars and shakes. If I gained too much they were watching my exercise. They had to love me. It had been good for Mom and Marlo too though. I used to think of Marlo as my fluffy friend. He was certainly not that anymore. He still wasn't as tall as Adrian and was about four inches shorter than me but he was much closer to my size now. Marlo had carved off most of his extra body fat. The same was true for my mom. She looked much fitter and even younger and less tired than she had a year ago.

After I ate, I joined my brothers on the Playstation to play a Mario game. It was Lucas' new favorite. Personally I was thankful. If I never played checkers again it would be okay with me. I just kept reminding myself that you were only six once and I should enjoy him at this age. Someday soon he wouldn't want to be around me, I was sure. Alex still put up with me though, so maybe we would all stay close.

I went through all my stuff from school and checked my planner to make sure it was up to date. I prioritized my homework and then worked on it for a bit before heading for bed. Tomorrow would be a big day.

My alarm went off much too early but I knew I could sleep in the car on the way to Astoria. I just wished we were going for fun. I loved the beach. I love to run barefoot in the sand and listen to the crash of the waves. I even like the salty, misty damp smell of the air. I have good memories of the beach. If ever I need to really refill my well of peace, the beach would be my first choice. White Eagle had taught me about refilling my well of peace in the desert. It had its own beauty but for me the beach was primo!

I cooked some oatmeal and fried a couple of eggs. I checked the clock. I needed to be at Sarah's house in fifteen minutes. I quickly ate, ran water on my dishes in the sink, washed my frying pan and flipped it upside down on our gas stovetop to finish drying. The dishes in the dishwasher were clean so I unloaded as fast as I could. I was out of time so I left the rest of the dirty dishes in the sink, slung my backpack onto my shoulder and raced out the door. My phone pinged in my pocket.

"sorry I missed you. good luck today. thanx for unloading the dw. love you. Mom"

I quickly texted back and shoved my phone in my pocket. White Eagle and Sarah were just getting in her car. I loaded into the back and we headed for the barber.

"What barber is open at seven in the morning on a Saturday?" I asked curiously.

"He's a friend of mine. His shop is closed. This is a favor. Trust me," White Eagle said from the driver's seat of Sarah's sedan.

Well duh, of course I trusted him. In fact I trusted him with my life – what was a haircut? The barbershop was a small hole in the wall type of place. The guy who owned it was a complete surprise. I was expecting an older gentleman and not a young flamboyant guy who looked like he would be more at home serving the Hollywood set. Turned out he had inherited the shop from his grandfather who was a friend of White Eagle's - of course. I began to wonder if there was anyone White Eagle didn't know or who didn't owe him something.

Dwayne washed my hair and used a razor blade to cut it. He used clippers around the edges and then trimmed my beard and mustache – well what there was of it anyway. This was the first professional haircut I had had in... ever? It seemed strange that he trimmed something that was barely growing but I suppose he had his reasons. He then rubbed something into my beard and mustache area and rinsed me off. Next he put gel in my hair and combed it just so - finishing with his fingers. He whipped the cape off with a flourish and spun the chair so that I faced the mirror. I did a double take. Was that really me? My face looked slimmer and even more adult. I looked like I had a five o'clock shadow – not spotty stubble. My hair looked really good. He had parted it on the side and angled it back from the part and then he had hidden the obvious part. With the suit on I would look... twenty-something. Now, I just needed to act it.

White Eagle and the barber, Dwayne, talked for a bit and then White Eagle said it was time to go.

"Thank you," I said as Dwayne began to sweep the floor.

He just nodded and smiled. We headed for the sedan. White Eagle again got in the driver's seat. Two and half hours to nap and study. White Eagle laughed a wicked laugh as he threw another book at me. I picked it up off the seat. The Oregon Driver's Manual. Oh boy?

"Are you trying to tell me something?"

"Yeah, your birthday is coming. Get studying."

"Gee thanks. Glad I don't have anything else to do."

"I know you were considering a nap." I sighed and hunched in my seat. How did he know this stuff? I pulled out the homework that I had put on the top and began to wade my way through to the bottom. I'm just lucky I can read in a moving car.

The drive went well. Fortunately it's not horribly curvy out to Astoria on Highway 26. Even Highway 101 from Seaside to Astoria is pretty good. We drove into town and headed east toward the hospital. Oddly it seemed like a good place to hide and blend in. We walked in like we were going to visit someone. I ducked into the men's room as a teenager and came out looking like a twenty-five year old man in a suit. Sarah came out of the women's restroom looking pretty darn sharp herself in a gray suit with a steel blue colored blouse underneath. We kept moving to draw as little attention as possible to ourselves. When we got to the parking lot Sarah checked my suit and smoothed me out and twitched it some, ending with the tie. She checked the placement of my badge and gave me a big grin.

White Eagle got in the back seat and Sarah drove. "If we have to do this again it would look better if you drove. I think we would look more believable," she said to me. We stopped three blocks north of our GPS coordinates. Sarah popped open her briefcase and handed me an electronic tablet. She made sure that I could navigate and use the tablet to take notes. She then handed me two pens and a small spiral notebook as backup. She told me to put the pens and spiral into my inside suit coat pocket. She then handed me a very professional looking ID folder with my new FBI ID.

"Don't show it unless she asks. If she looks too close she may catch on to your cover. Look at your picture," Sarah said, all business.

It looked like me but it didn't. There was something familiar about the shot yet not. It was disconcerting. I looked at her for more information.

"Joy did a great job, huh. She took your school picture and ran it through some CGI type software she has, to age you. Then she put in a collared shirt and tie." Sarah sounded proud as she spoke of her friend and sketch artist. I took a closer look and then I could see it. Amazing.

"Well, I'm all set for Halloween."

"Don't even joke about it. The minute we are done I'm locking that back up. We could get in so much trouble! I need you in that house - without breaking and entering. It is the best idea we had but it's dangerous."

"Relax, Sarah, I was kidding."

"Fine, now think old. You are my second. You'll take notes and of course feel the room, the house and whatever else you can get a read on. I will try to ask for what we need but we may end up doing a little B and E too. It isn't my first choice. I'm hoping that she'll just cooperate. Bob, my boss, will back up that I'm authorized to ask questions about this cold case but not even he knows about you. Ready?"

"As I'll ever be, I guess."

White Eagle handed me a tiny ear piece. "I'll be able to hear you with this and you can hear me. It works sort of like a blue tooth device for a cell phone."

I looked at him skeptically but put it in my ear as he handed one to Sarah. She put hers in as White Eagle opened a laptop and connected it to another device that looked like a large cell phone.

"Now step out of the car and say 'test, test, test,' please," he instructed. "Sarah first and then you, Owen. Look for my thumbs up and then let me know if you can hear me."

I did as I was told. I waited for Sarah to speak. When she did I could hear her real voice and a soft tinny version in my ear. I nodded at her. She looked from White Eagle to me.

"Test, test, test, please," I said, looking at White Eagle and smiling at my attempt at humor.

He gave me a thumbs up along with a shake of his head.

"Now, get back in," he said softly and I could only hear him in my ear piece.

"Marlo is going to love this stuff," I said enthusiastically, when I got back in the car.

"It's on loan so be careful with it," Sarah admonished.

"Yes ma'am," I answered smartly, looking out the windshield – showing her I could be serious. We pulled out and drove to Mrs. Vance's home. We stepped out of the car and I automatically checked my pockets for the notebook, pens and ID. I had the electronic tablet under my arm. I checked the badge at my hip and nodded at Sarah to let her know I was ready.

She led the way up to the house with her head held high. I followed behind her trying to mimic her body language. I stood tall with my shoulders back and pressed down. I held the electronic tablet in one hand and held the other loosely at my side. The door opened before Sarah even knocked.

"Can I help you?" asked a small woman of indeterminate age. She looked like she hadn't had an easy life. Her graying hair was curled tightly to her scalp like it was afraid to let go. Her gray eyes hid behind thick lenses in a well lined face. Her clothing was simple - blue jeans, a flannel shirt and Keds.

"Mrs. Vance, I'm Special Agent Sarah Lando," she said showing her identification, "and this is Special Agent Ryer. We are part of a cold case unit out of Portland and I wondered if we might ask you a few questions about your son, Trevor."

"Have you reopened the case?" she asked, sounding both hopeful yet resigned.

"We have some new information and I hoped that..."

"Well come on in then." I could see the hope flare in her eyes. So far I had *read* nothing from either her or the house. She was not happy but she felt better here. She led us into a clean and simple room with minimal clutter. She sat in a well worn chair and indicated the couch.

"I could get you coffee, if you like," she said quietly.

"That would be lovely, if it isn't too much trouble," Sarah said, surprising me. Then I realized that she was hoping to buy me a little time.

"Ma'am, I apologize for the inconvenience, but would it be possible for me to use your bathroom, please?" I asked, using my deepest voice and speaking softly yet confidently.

"Of course. Down the hall and on the right."

The house had looked small from the outside and looked the same way on the inside. It seemed to be a two bedroom bungalow. At this point it was unclear whether or not it had a basement. Mrs. Vance headed for the kitchen and set to work. I headed to the short hall where the two bedrooms were separated by the bathroom. I closed my eyes for a moment in the hall. There was something here. Mrs. Vance had brought something with her. She would not know it for the clue it was, but I would and obviously it wouldn't be hidden like the journal. This was something she remembered Trevor by, something of his. I went in the bathroom and flushed the toilet. As I stood there I realized that an object was reaching for me.

"Sarah, ask her if she brought anything of Trevor's with her that we could look at. I sense a keychain - I need to see it. She keeps it in her bedroom." I hoped Sarah could hear me. I washed my hands. This was frustrating - I knew I needed to touch the key chain to get the images - all I was getting right now was that it had something to tell me.

I went back into the living room and sat next to Sarah. She nodded at me - message received. Mrs. Vance came back with coffee, cream, sugar and a plate of cookies. I accepted a mug of coffee but refrained from putting anything in it, in keeping with my adult persona.

I powered up the electronic tablet and prepared to take notes. They were completely unnecessary as White Eagle would record the whole thing, but it kept with my cover. Sarah began by telling her that we had come across a person of interest.

"Just before your son disappeared did he start hanging around anyone new?" Sarah asked.

"Like I told the police, just that Willie guy. Trevor liked him at first. They had a common interest in motorcycles. Later Trevor said the guy was kind of… creeping him out."

"Could you describe him?"

"He must have been around six feet tall because he was a bit taller than my boy. He had dark hair that he kept cut short. His hair was not as dark as Agent um, what was your name again?"

"Ryer, ma'am."

"Yes, not as dark as Agent Ryer's. I want to say that his eyes were brown but he nearly always wore dark glasses. He always dressed in black leather. He had this weird tattoo. It was on his forearm. Just here," she said pointing at the inside of her left arm. "It was a sword with vines twisting around it. I thought it was a cross at first but one day I got a closer look. I interrupted them in the garage when I heard raised voices. He tried to cover it up. I thought it was strange. Why get a tattoo and then cover it up. Anyway, his skin was dark like he had some African American or whatever black people are calling themselves today, no offense. He was too pale to be just that, you understand. His nose was long and blade like.

His eyes were close set. He gave me the creeps but in the beginning Trevor seemed to like him and he didn't have a lot of friends."

Sarah gave me a look. It was our guy. I felt sure too.

"Just Willie, or did you catch a last name?" Sarah probed.

"Um, let me see. Trev usually called him Willie. The last name was something common. No wait, I know. It was Brown. I thought it was funny at the time because he was always dressed in shades of black and brown and he was... well, brown. You know – brown skin, brown hair and brown eyes."

"The police were unable to find Willie for questioning at the time. He has been linked to a van at the bar the night your son disappeared. We are hoping to find Willie now. The bar is under the same ownership and the bartender is still around so we're looking again."

"I appreciate that you're still trying. I know you won't find him alive. I feel that much but I would like the closure. I want to finally be able to bury my boy and I would really like to have his killer pay for what he has done. I don't want anyone else hurt."

"Do you have anything left of Trevor's that we could look at?" Sarah asked gently as she laid a hand on Mrs. Vance's knee.

"If I had something, would you need to take it?"

"No, we would just like to look if that is okay with you."

"Okay," Mrs. Vance said as she rose and walked to her bedroom. She returned with a small wooden box. She placed it on the coffee table and opened it. The only thing that spoke to me was the keychain. Sarah carefully looked at each item and listened to the grieving mother talk while I held the keychain and absorbed the images. When I had all I could get I handed the keychain to Sarah so she would know I was done.

I choked down a few more sips of my bitter coffee so that I would not hurt our hostess' feelings. Sarah passed the keychain back to Mrs. Vance.

"Is there anything that your daughter could help us with? She was already living down here at the time your son disappeared, correct?"

"I doubt she could help. She was already here so she never knew Willie. My children were ten years apart in age. Trevor was a complete surprise. I didn't think I could have anymore after my daughter. With my husband gone – I wanted to be with the family I had left. You'll let me know what you find, won't you?"

"Yes, we will. Thank you for your time." Sarah smoothly handed her a business card and shook her hand.

Mrs. Vance turned to me with her hand out. I took it in mine and felt a small zing. Her eyes glazed for a moment and she spoke. "You'll find my boy's remains." She blinked at me and stammered a thank you as she released my hand.

"Thank *you*, ma'am," I said as I tried to regain my composure.

I followed Sarah out the door and to the car. We loaded up and Sarah drove to a restaurant where we could change, talk and grab a bite to eat. As soon as we were out of sight of the house White Eagle sat up from his reclined position in the backseat. We handed over our earpieces and I gave back the electronic tablet. White Eagle started laughing.

"You took really good notes. There is hope for you yet. You knew I was recording it – why such a good job?"

"I wanted to keep with my cover. Now, wanna know what I got from the keychain?"

"We do, but I would also like to know why she said that you would find her son's remains." White Eagle was staring at me.

"I felt a little zing when she shook my hand. I think she has a bit of an ability herself. I'm sure she didn't know what she did. Her recall of Willie Brown was amazing, which I also think is her ability at work. She described him perfectly – right down to his tattoo. Now we have a name and, because of the keychain, we have the make, model and license of the van he was driving the night he took Trevor. I also know that his ability *is* to cover his tracks. Trevor dropped the keychain in the bar parking lot when Willie grabbed him. The police gave it back to his mom when they released the bike. The keychain *saw* everything. Willie followed him to the bar, made sure he had had plenty to drink – which he helped along by putting something in it. When Trevor came out to go home, Willie grabbed him and forcibly loaded him into the van. He touched Trevor right over his heart with his bare hand - I think what he did was drain his ability. It was weird to watch. I could of course hear nothing but Trevor looked like he was in great pain. His mouth was open as if he were screaming and both his hands gripped Willie's arm, yet he seemed weakened and dazed. Trevor crumpled to the floor of the van, Willie hopped out; then he touched the motorcycle. He put back on his black leather glove and then jumped back in the van and drove away. He didn't realize that Trevor had dropped his keys."

"These are not abilities that I am familiar with. I need to do some research and think," White Eagle said, concern plain in his voice.

We headed into the restaurant. We asked for a corner table away from everyone. Sarah and I took in our regular clothes to change. When we were all back at our table and lunch was ordered, Sarah uploaded all the new information we had. It was time to play the waiting game again. For the moment I was okay with that. We had made some good progress today.

Now it was all about waiting... We waited to hear about the drug they had my dad on. We waited for information on both my father and grandfather. We were waiting for information on Willie Brown and his van. I hate waiting!

I asked if we could look at the ocean before we left. White Eagle gave me a knowing look but drove south on 101 until we had an acceptable view. I stood watching the surf for several minutes, taking deep breaths of the salt air. I held my arms straight out to the sides and threw my head back. The strong breeze tore at my hair and clothing. It was brisk and refreshing. I closed my eyes and visualized fixing the KLR650 and riding it along 101 with Lucie on the back – stopping to look at all the best views. I dropped my arms, returned to the car and we hit the road for home.

"Feel better?" White Eagle asked.

"Yeah, I was trying to let go of what I can't fix right now."

"You focus on school this week and we will dig up all we can," Sarah said trying to make me feel better.

I returned to my homework and even read a few pages in the driver's manual. I was surprised when we hit Beaverton and traffic slowed down. The trip home had been fast but I had finished my homework until I got more on Monday. I asked White Eagle about working on the KLR. I was happy he had time for me. I had never worked on a bike before.

The rest of the weekend passed with family time, work on the bike and chores. I at least was prepared for another week. I sat on my bed and *looked* at all my school books. They were the gray of normal student life – neither good nor bad – just life. I needed to get back to Jesus and make sure that everything was still good with him.

My mom poked her head in as she was heading for bed. "I know the beach visit was successful, yet you seem..." She cocked her head, looking at me like she was trying to figure it out.

"I have the weird feeling that I'm not doing something that I should be doing. I feel pulled in a bunch of directions and I feel like I lack focus. I tried to look at the ocean today. I felt better for awhile but now... I don't know how to describe it. I feel odd again."

She came and sat next to me, putting her arm around me. She closed her eyes and took some deep calming breaths. I closed my eyes too and thought about the ocean. I could almost hear it and the calm washed over me again.

"Be your best self. It is all anyone can ask of you - including you. I love you. Sleep well."

"Thanks, Mom." I don't know how she does what she does but when it comes to me, she is scary intuitive. I was glad all over again that she was on the team.

School moved by. I felt like someone else was living my life. I kept waiting for news that did not come. I remembered to save a seat for Tess who seemed happy to sit by me and noticed my new haircut. Lucie avoided me. Being with Tess was comfortable and fun. Lucie kept looking at me like she wanted to be by me but every time I tried to approach her she practically ran away. She still talked to Marlo but she refused to talk about me.

Football practice was going well and it looked like I would see some playing time at the game on Thursday. I struggled to keep up with my homework and wished I had time to work on the bike. By Wednesday I found myself in the garage with the music cranked up, banging away at the heavy bag my dad had hung up for me. Mom came and watched for awhile but finally walked away shaking her head.

Thursday was a blur. All I could think about was the game. Adrian seemed to suffer the same affliction. His mind was more on the game and whether or not he would play than on his girlfriend who seemed a little ticked with him.

The game came and went. Adrian and I both got to play for almost five minutes each. I got yanked out after a spectacular blind side tackle. How I was supposed to see that coming, I have no idea. I gained fifteen yards before I was crushed by a guy who felt like he weighed three hundred pounds. Five whole minutes - big whoop. Maybe we should have stayed on the freshman team. I was amazed to see Lucie in the stands. She was nowhere to be found after the game, but I found White Eagle, Mom and my brothers waiting for me.

"We are off to the airport to collect your dad, Owen. He called and asked me to pick him up. I'm sending you home with White Eagle. Good game and I love you lots." She looked like she wanted to say more but instead turned and herded my brothers to our SUV where Beggar waited eagerly to continue her big doggy evening out.

As soon as we were in his truck I pounced on White Eagle. "So, what is she not telling me?"

"Well, the drug your dad is on is no antidepressant. It is a little hard to determine exactly. It's almost like a mild date rape drug. They are trying to control him and confuse him. It's quite the cocktail of chemicals. No one that Sarah works with seems to know just what it is or what it will do. Your mom knows all this information by the way. We don't know if we can switch the drug, mute it or counter it or even if we should. Every time he leaves here they could just adjust it back. The doctor he is seeing is no doctor and the pharmacy does exist but we don't know how they are getting him the drugs. There is no record of it in the pharmacy's files that we can find."

"You see, there we go. We have to go and do some PI work."

"That could take days. I don't want to confide in Max, I can't afford to go, and neither can you – monetarily or by missing school. Hang tough and keep watching your dad. I think he is here to watch you. Keep a low profile and try to act normal."

"Hang in there. Yeah, sure. I'll do that," I said with heavy sarcasm. Did I have a choice though? Not really. "I hate leaving my dad hanging out there in danger."

"This will sound harsh, but he made his own choices. If we jump in now we risk losing the big fish – the man who really holds the strings. We have to move slowly and carefully. I also think that we need to start behaving like we are watched all the time. We need to try to look as normal as possible."

I sighed hugely. "Okay," I finally spit out, not liking the situation at all.

White Eagle drove me home. I started my laundry and grabbed a snack. I texted Marlo and brought my homework to the kitchen table to wait for Dad. I heard the car pull up and went to the door. Beggar charged past me. Alex brought in Dad's laundry and headed straight for the laundry room. I walked down the front steps and out to the car to see if I could help. Mom was taking a dozing Lucas out of the car. Dad was strangely quiet.

"Welcome home, Dad. How was your week?"

"Fine, and yours?" He sounded almost robotic.

"They moved me to the JV football team. I got sacked pretty good tonight though. Maybe you can come to the next game. Can I help unload?"

"This is it," he said indicating his briefcase and small suitcase. Alex got the rest."

I followed Mom into the house with Dad bringing up the rear. Mom headed on upstairs with Lucas. Dad hovered in the entryway like he was almost unsure where to go.

"I'll take your bags upstairs and you can relax for a bit," I suggested.

"Okay," he said almost meekly.

I took his bags on up as I heard the TV come on downstairs. I walked past my mom and held up Dad's bags with raised eyebrows. She shrugged and pointed to her bedroom. I opened the suitcase and *looked* at it. There was nothing here this time and it was that same darn foggy gray. I took out Dad's pills and counted them, once again stealing one to see if they had changed his formula. I quickly took a pad of paper from Mom's nightstand and wrote down all the information off the bottle. Then just for security I wiped it down, put it away and wiped my fingerprints off the rest of the suitcase. If they could *see* like me I couldn't prevent that but I would do everything else I could to avoid detection.

Someone was not careful with Dad's briefcase this time. I would hate to think that they were planting images. Most of the case was gray and foggy but a file in it was interesting. I could see Dad in his new office and in a lab. He appeared to be lost and confused at work. He didn't seem to get much done. His lunch was brought to him each day. I couldn't see every moment but he frequently carried this file folder around with him. I couldn't really understand what the data was showing but it seemed like his adhesive formula wasn't working. I quickly took the contents to our scanner in the upstairs office and ran the papers through the feeder. I rushed to my room and snatched the flash drive out of my computer. Mom was putting my brothers to bed and I could still hear the TV downstairs. I snuck a peek and Dad looked absorbed in whatever he was watching. I rushed back to the office, saved the file to the flash drive and erased my scan. I knew it wasn't totally removed but maybe Marlo could help with that later. I wiped everything down and returned it to Dad's briefcase.

I slipped out of Mom's room and looked into my brother's room. Lucas was already asleep and Alex and Mom were talking quietly. I headed on in. Just in time too. Dad appeared before I completely settled in.

"Well, goodnight. I'm tired. I'm going to bed. See you in the morning," Dad said groggily from the doorway.

"Night, Dad," Alex and I said together.

"Night, Brad," Mom added.

The three of us watched him walk out of the room.

"Is Dad okay?" Alex asked worriedly.

"He will be, honey. I think he's just really tired," Mom said with more confidence than I could have come up with.

I hugged Alex and Mom goodnight and headed for bed myself. I would give the flash drive to Sarah tomorrow. I didn't want to raise any suspicions tonight. I would lay low like White Eagle had suggested.

FIVE

The next morning I woke before my alarm. I picked up the stuff I would need for today's classes, practice and the flash drive. I headed downstairs - apparently Dad was still sleeping so I would not have to make an excuse to him. I whispered my plans to Mom and reminded her of the dance tonight. I wished my brothers a good day, rubbed Beggar's belly and ran down to Sarah's as I quickly texted her and Marlo that I was on my way. Sarah answered her door, in her robe, with her laptop under her arm. Marlo pinged back that he would be at Sarah's as soon as he could. She led me into her kitchen.

"What's up, Sherlock?" she asked playfully.

"I don't know for sure but I think something weird is going on at Dad's work. I mean I found some documents that don't make any sense so I scanned them for you to look at."

"Let's see what you've got." She loaded the flash drive onto her laptop and studied what I'd found. Her wrinkled forehead indicated that she too was baffled.

"These were in a file folder that Dad has been walking around with a lot. Someone was not careful with Dad's briefcase this time. I would hate to think that someone was planting images but I don't know what's possible. Maybe White Eagle would know. While he is looking into special abilities maybe he could see if that is one. Dad's briefcase was gray and foggy like usual but the file was dark. I could see Dad in his new office and in a lab. He seemed to be even more lost and confused and he wasn't getting much done. His lunch has been brought to him every day. It seems like his adhesive formula isn't working out and something about that is really bugging him. When I look at these notes – they look like something that was missed when they went over his briefcase or they weren't in it when they blanked it out. I think Dad is starting to realize that something is wrong and it isn't us that's the problem."

Marlo knocked and we brought him up to speed. He looked at the documents. He said he would check our home computer when Dad was out of the house and wipe any trails I had left.

"Owen, I'm no chemist, but I think your dad is beginning to realize that what they have him working on is not an really adhesive. We know they have him drugged and confused but he is a smart man. What he's working on has sticky properties but I think it is also an explosive or at least flammable," Marlo said, sounding confused.

"That's what I thought too. I'm also wondering why they sent him home if he's realizing that something's wrong. Your mom will have her work cut out for her while he's home," Sarah added.

"Oh, yeah, here's another pill from his bottle," I said reaching into my pocket. "I thought maybe it was different because the shape is the same but the color is off. Can we test again and see what they are doing to him now?"

"I'll get it to the lab today and put a rush on it. Did you eat?"

"No," I answered sheepishly.

"Well boys, you know where everything is. Fix some for me too and I'll go get dressed. I'll take you to school on the way to the lab."

Marlo got cooking straight away and waved off my offers of help. He just wanted a firsthand recounting of the beach and our cases. He finds my texts lacking in detailed info so I brought him up to speed and filled in the gaps.

As he dished up my omelet and whole wheat toast he asked about Lucie. Sarah wandered in as Marlo was plating her omelet and joined our conversation. I commented that I had barely seen Lucie so far this year. I told them that I thought her behavior was strange. I could understand that she was afraid of me so she had avoided me all summer. I told them that she'd tried to connect with me a couple of times but mostly she sat away from me looking as miserable as I felt. I missed her terribly. I told them it was my friend and companion that I missed the most. I reminded them that it was just three months ago that she had asked what she would do without me and now apparently, she could do just fine. In my mind, I added that I had a big gaping hole where she once lived in my heart.

Their advice was to keep doing what I was doing. Be there for her and wait for her to make the next move. I didn't know if I could do that. I still felt this incredible pull where she was concerned. I just couldn't walk completely away even though I wanted to.

Before we got out of Sarah's car, Marlo put a hand on my arm to stop me. "You know what? I do have a thought about Lucie. Remember, regrets don't help anything, you know that - so quit beating yourself up. What happened with Lucie happened. You saved her - that guy in DC was watching her and could have hurt her. In the end it was worth it. Sometimes people can start out one way, and then their experiences change them and they end up completely different. Maybe Lucie is... different."

"I'll try to talk to her at the dance tonight after our home game. It will be a great opportunity and hard for her to make an excuse. If she pushes me away – really pushes me away and tells me to leave her alone, because she hasn't up until now, then I guess I'll have to move on. I hope the gossip is true that she doesn't have a boyfriend. That will make it easier. I know lots of guys are interested in her."

Sarah wished us a good day and Marlo and I went off to our first class. I was feeling a little dark and gloomy as I trudged into the building. When I felt a hand on my arm, I spun around, ready for anything.

"Whoa, hey, it's me. Relax. I called your name a couple of times and you didn't respond."

"Hey Tess, I'm sorry. I was deep in thought. What's up?"

"I just wondered if you were going to the dance tonight."

"Yeah, I'll be there."

"Good - me too. Save a dance for me," she said as she reached up to pat my cheek. "You know, I told you before but your new haircut is really awesome. You look *hot*. Now keep that in your mind today instead of whatever you were thinking about and see if that doesn't improve your mood." She giggled and hustled away leaving me to shout after her.

"Okay, Tess."

Other than lunch with Jesus, the rest of my day was not as bright as the beginning. Practice was grueling. Any guys who played varsity too, got the day off to be rested for the game. The rest of us were about run into the ground. I had the displeasure of working with Calvin again. He was back to being a big showoff. He had gotten to play almost a whole quarter our last game and was feeling pretty superior. I knew he was more bark than bite, but I was letting him push my buttons. I waited for an opportunity to throw the football right at his big mouth. When I finally got it, I smacked him in the helmet so hard it snapped his head back and knocked him flat on his… ass. Inside I was saying 'YES'; outside I tried and failed to look regretful. For my act of defiance I got to run four laps around the track in full gear. The coach made me apologize and do fifty sit-ups and fifty pushups. It was SO worth it. The best part was that Calvin kept his big mouth shut the rest of practice.

I was very surprised to see my dad in the lot to pick me up.

"Hey, Dad. I thought you would've been in to work at the local office today."

"I took the day off. I wasn't feeling well."

Wow. My dad never took a day off. I felt sure they had drugged him differently and it wasn't working like they'd hoped.

"I saw part of practice. Why did you have to run the track and stuff?"

"I lost my temper with a kid with a big mouth."

"Huh, well that happens. Maybe you should've done that breathing thing you do."

"You're right," I said aloud, but in my mind I knew I would do it all over again.

"I thought we could pick up some pizza. What do you say?"

"Sure Dad that would be great." Weird, this was like my old dad was back. I figured I better enjoy it. He continued like a quieter version of the old dad all through dinner. I quickly helped to clean up the kitchen and then excused myself to get ready for the varsity game and dance.

I showered and admired the bruises I had from yesterday's game. I was a little stiff and sore from the blindside tackle I had suffered. I was ready to put the game out of my head; the bruises just brought it up again. I'd heard plenty about it at today's practice and we got to relive it through the video recordings. I put on the deep maroon button up shirt Mom had found for me at the mall and paired it with dark blue jeans. I laced into my brown boots and added a brown belt. I fixed my hair and gave myself a once over in the mirror.

The doorbell rang. I was betting it was Marlo or Adrian. It was my mom's turn to chauffeur. I headed downstairs as Alex opened the front door.

"Who are you spiffed up for?" Adrian asked curiously.

"I'm hoping to talk to Lucie," I said, prepared for the argument I knew was coming. Marlo understood my need to keep trying. Adrian did not. He figured that there were plenty of women out there. If one wasn't available I should just take the next one in the queue.

He rolled his eyes. "Would you get over it already? First you grieved for a month when we got back from DC. Then you were just plain sad and all you did was work out like a crazy man. Finally you focused on football and came back to us a bit, but then school started and you decided to go after her again. Let the wounds scab up and scar already, would ya?"

"Aid, I would like to think that if something happened to you or to Marlo that I would fight this hard to save you too."

"She doesn't need saving you big dope. She wants to move on to someone safer. Geez, you spent all last year pushing her away. Now she's away and you want her back. Do you even realize how crazy that is?"

"I can keep her safe now. I proved that on the D.C. trip last summer and I'm getting better all the time. Even White Eagle says so."

"Yeah, whatev, Bro. I just hate to see you beat yourself up and waste your time."

Marlo was right behind Adrian – thank goodness. Adrian looked like an Abercrombie model as usual. Marlo was wearing Converse and the wildest tie I had yet to see with a dark lavender button-up shirt. It was classic Marlo. I thought it was pretty great that he had his own style. Adrian rolled his eyes at Marlo like he had at me. I threw my leather jacket on as Sarah came in to hang with my brothers and Mom. They had plans to bake later - always a good thing. We headed out with my Dad who had decided to drive. He let us off at the street near the field entrance and told us to have fun. I reminded him that Marlo's mom was picking us up.

Our varsity team did not win the game. We hadn't had a winning team in quite a few years. Lucie's brother did pretty much steal the show though. He seemed to be the main talent. Sadly, the other team figured that out too. Amy showed up shortly after the game started and sat with us. She was pleasant company. I found that I liked her a lot as a person and a friend. I had her in both Health and Spanish. She was bright and we worked well together when we got to team up. If things didn't last with Adrian I felt pretty confident that we could still be friends.

We headed to the Commons for the dance. Adrian and Amy left us at the door to hit the dance floor. I saw Calvin across the way. He nodded his head at me. We had an awkward truce. He was good at sports so at least in that department we had formed a grudging respect. He had a new girlfriend that he was at least decent to so we had nothing to fight about other than his big mouth but that too was under control for now.

I scanned the room looking for Lucie. She was talking to some of her girlfriends across the way. She was leaning on the railing at the elevated portion of the commons. I stood just watching her. She looked good – much, much too good. A slow country song came on. I listened for a moment recognizing the words. How appropriate... *"When the rain's blowin' in your face and the whole world is on your case, I would offer you a warm embrace to make you feel my love. The evening shadows and the stars appear, and there is no one to dry your tears. I could hold you for a million years, to make you feel my love. I know you haven't made your mind up yet but I would never do you wrong. I've known it from the moment that we met so no doubt in my mind where you belong..."*

I leaned against the railing near the attendance office, feet crossed at the ankles and arms crossed over my chest. As often happened, she sensed my gaze and looked in my direction. I could feel the electricity when our eyes met. Neither of us looked away until one of her friends bumped her to get her attention. I watched a heated conversation with much hand gesturing going on, punctuated by several pointed fingers in my direction.

Lucie finally threw both hands in the air and turned to walk away. No wait, she was walking toward me. I held very still, never taking my eyes off her as she made her way in my direction. She looked lovely tonight. She had on low-heeled strappy shoes of a shiny material and the same neat swirly skirt she wore to the dance last year where I finally kissed her. She must have gotten the grass stains out from when Calvin had pushed her down. Tonight she had paired it with a body skimming pale v-necked shirt with a spray of sparkles that ran from her shoulder to her opposite hip. She moved like the graceful gymnast she was as she wove through the crowd. She stopped in front of me.

"Hello, Owen," she said softly.

"Hey, Luce. You look beautiful."

"Good game yesterday. You did a good job. Hardly anyone could touch you and you only got tackled once and you only missed one pass." So we had been reduced to this... polite conversation, like strangers.

"Luce, I miss you. Why don't you talk to me? I mean you are now, but it's not the same. I miss my friend."

"Let's not talk about that. Please?" she begged.

"I think we do need to talk about it," I insisted gently.

"Look, I didn't even want to come over here but they..."

"Let's dance," I interrupted.

"I don't think that's a good idea."

"Sure it is," I answered as I took her hand and lead her onto the dance floor. The music was fast, a popular hit from the radio. I spun Lucie and then released her hand. She smiled a little. She was graceful on the dance floor too, but then I knew that. I had watched her many times over the years. The music slowed. Lucie froze for a moment in indecision. I did not hesitate. I stepped up close to her, putting one hand on her waist and taking her hand in mine. Bryan Adams crooned his song 'Everything I Do, I Do It For You.' Lucie tried to step away again but I kept ahold of her hand. "Lucie, don't go. Look into my eyes. What do you see? I won't hurt you. You don't need to be afraid of me. Listen to the song, hear the words." She closed her eyes and blew out a soft breath. Then she stepped close, released my hand, put both her arms around my waist and put her head against my shoulder. We swayed gently to the music. I tried to keep the erratic beat of my heart down to a slow, soft and peaceful rhythm. I felt sure I was only partially successful. Her scent floated around us as I took in the soft feel of her. I must have grown again because I was sure she wasn't shrinking. The football team listed me at six feet. Lucie must be close to five feet seven inches. Yet she seemed tiny. I wondered if she weighed a hundred and ten pounds. I felt an overwhelming need to protect her, stronger than ever before. *"I would fight for you. I'd lie for you. Walk the world for you. Yeah, I'd die for you. You know it's true, everything I do, oh, I do it for you,"* I softly sang with the end of the song. She looked up into my eyes. Biting her lip, she swiped at a tear. I could tell she was at war with herself.

"You know, Owen, I was once so curious about you. I wondered how you got involved in so many interesting adventures. I thought it was chance. I didn't know that you invited it. I wanted to know so badly, and then once I did, I wanted to erase it. I really didn't want to know. What you do is scary. I don't want to get close to that. And..."

"Lucie, I won't let anything happen to you. I promise," I begged.

"I believe that you believe that, but I have so much... my life is so... complicated. I don't need that extra worry. I really don't want anything to happen to you... I've got to go," she said softly as she turned away. I let her walk away again. I hoped she would come back to me on her own terms.

As I left the floor Marlo caught sight of me. "Hey man, why do you do that to yourself? Better yet, why do you do that to each other? How can you like each other that much and keep denying it? I take that back. I can tell by the look on your face you just told her how you feel. You've pushed her away for so long that she said *no*, didn't she?"

"No, I believe she said, 'let me think about it'. I wish she'd never seen that fight in Washington D.C. It really scared her. She sees that stuff is still happening to me. It's not gonna go away and she's afraid to be a part of that. There is something else going on with her too. She doesn't want to let me in. Would you do me the huge favor of looking into it? I swear Marlo, you've got a great future as a spy for the government."

"Of course I'll look into it. I can't stand to see you like this - or her. It sucks. You are more distracted than ever. You were smart to take all that aggression out on the field though. I can't believe they moved you to J.V. and the coach is talking about varsity."

"I'd rather have more playing time on J.V. than sit on the varsity bench and I told him that. I also don't want anybody to know about that," I told him with a note of crankiness in my voice.

"Dude, a varsity letter as a freshman? You could get all the girls you want. You do anyway. I swear they follow you around like puppies. You have this whole bad boy thing going. It works out okay for me though," he said with a laugh. "They get close to me to get close to you. It's okay for now. It gives me good exposure." He laughed, punching me in the arm.

I couldn't help but laugh too. "Marlo, the girls would love you anyway and I don't believe for one minute they are following me around."

"Geez man, you really are blind."

"Z'up?" Adrian asked as he joined us.

"We were discussing Owen's chick problems."

"Which chicks? The hordes that follow him drooling or Lucie?" Adrian asked, sounded disgusted.

"See? What did I say?" Marlo said sounding superior.

"You two!" I groaned.

"Hi Marlo," said a soft voice. A cute brunette stood near us.

"Hey Michalia, you know Adrian and Owen?" Marlo said by way of introduction.

"Hi guys. Marlo, would you like to..." she flipped her curly head toward the dance floor.

"Sure, why not," Marlo answered, clearly delighted.

"Hey, Aid, is that the girl from orchestra that you guys went out with last weekend?"

"Yep, that's the one. Marlo has been working his magic."

I smiled. Marlo was having fun. Sometimes I wished my life was that easy. Those were not the cards I had been dealt though. Amy came up, said 'hi' to me and took Adrian off for more dancing. I looked around. Lucie was back talking to her friends. Someone was asking her to dance and she was shaking her head 'no'.

It wasn't enough, though most days I made do, just happy to see her – waiting for those times she sat near me or looked at me or I could smell her soft scent of citrus and spring. It was making me feel raw, like a rug burn that never had a chance to heal. I was afraid if she looked too close she would see the hopeless love in my eyes. I had to let her go but some unknown force kept pulling me back. I had come, I had talked to her and now I should go instead of standing here watching her and wishing...

"Hey Owen."

"Hey Tess. You look good," I said and meant it. She had braided a bit of her hair to keep it out of her face and had run it over the top of her head like a headband. She was wearing a colorful sleeveless top that hugged her curves and barely touched her belted low cut white pants. She wore high healed boots to complete her impressive outfit.

"Thanks – you too. You owe me a dance. Let's go." She confidently took my hand and led me onto the dance floor. The song was fast but she kept ahold of my hand. When she twisted and moved I caught flashes of her tanned skin again. Okay, so I'm a guy. I found her flashes of smooth toned belly fascinating. I heard her laugh and I looked up.

"I know my assets and I know how to use them. I work hard to stay in shape. I know you do too." She had moved in close to be heard over the music. She put her free hand at my waist and gently pinched my skin. "I like it. I really like you for your mind though. Don't be fooled." She laughed again and stepped back still holding my hand. Another song began and she did not release me. I liked the way her eyes sparkled and danced. I could tell she was having fun.

"Hey Tessy, I see you're slumming it with a frosh."

"He's cute and fun which is more than I can say for you, Kirk. Now go bother someone who cares," Tess said, turning so that her back was to him once again.

Kirk looked like a thundercloud was forming right over him. Great, another Calvin, and this one was on the varsity football team. I had seen his stats. Kirk was an impressive six foot four inches and two hundred and fifty pounds in his gear. I blew out a sigh fearing the end of another really nice shirt.

Kirk reached for Tess' arm but found my hand on his arm instead. I said nothing but looked steadily into his eyes. I could see the head of steam building.

"We're friends. We have a class together. What do you want?" I used a calm, steady tone. I wasn't afraid to fight but I wasn't going to start it. Finish it - definitely.

"Hey Kirk, what's up?" Oh this was getting better by the minute – Lucie's brother now had ahold of Kirk's other arm.

Kirk looked at Sam and shrugged. "I don't like the frosh rising above their place."

"Ah, Kirk, he's okay. He's a friend of my sister's. He's a good receiver too. If coach has his way you'll be protecting his ass on the field - so play nice," Sam said with a hint on menace in his voice.

"Fine," Kirk barked, jerking out of our grasp and marching away.

Sam shrugged, smiled and walked away himself. We had become the new center of attention. Great.

"How about a drink?" I asked Tess.

"Sure why not." I had a bad feeling that she kind of liked the attention. We got our drinks and things calmed down. Marlo and Adrian came over with their girlfriends and we all chatted.

The rest of the evening passed uneventfully. I watched Lucie some and danced with Tess. Tess also found other partners. I danced once with Amy and with a girl from my English class. Tess made her way back to me as the evening was winding up.

"Care for one or two more dances?" She asked eagerly.

"Sure, why not."

The music was fast and fun. Once again she danced while holding my hand. She moved in close and spoke. "I got in the last request of the night. It should be up next."

"Oh?"

"You'll see or hear, I should say." Well, okay then. She did like to be mysterious. In fact she took great joy in it. The music slowed and changed. Tess moved in close and put her arms around me. She was back far enough that I could see her smiling face. Lady Antebellum's *Just a Kiss*. Oh Boy. She moved in closer and raised up to slowly meet my lips. I guessed that she had watched the movie *Hitch* too because she only came ninety percent. She left the final decision up to me with her lips just centimeters from mine. I waited a beat and thought – why not. Maybe I was channeling Adrian. Maybe I was tired of Lucie pushing me away. Maybe I liked Tess. It's just a kiss, right?

But it wasn't. She had *zing* down, that was for sure. I came my ten percent and she came another five. Her whole body hit mine with a mind-bending kiss. I staggered back a step then held firm.

"That was fun," she said pulling back. "I'll see you in Biology," she winked as the last chord rang out. I watched her walk away feeling a little perplexed. Whoever thought high school was easy, was nuts. I saw movement out of the corner of my eye and turned to see Lucie. She looked... devastated. I was so mixed up myself that I didn't even try to follow her. Marlo fetched me off the dance floor.

"Come on, Romeo. Mom's out front." I followed Marlo out. I saw Lucie getting into Sam's car. She briefly met my eyes and looked away. Great. Just great.

All was quiet when I got home. I locked up and headed upstairs. I didn't want to talk to anybody. Mom looked up from her chair in the corner.

"How was it?"

"Fine, I guess. Mixed up. Girl stuff."

"If you want to talk, I'm here."

"I know. Thanks. Right now I just want to... not think."

"I understand. White Eagle needs you at the shop tomorrow as soon as you can get there. He says they have a lead on the van," she ended in a whisper.

I gave her a hug and whispered an okay into her ear. Then I headed upstairs and went to bed. As I lay in bed thinking, the rain began to fall. I could hear it lightly tapping on the roof. I tried to use the noise to lull me to sleep. I could see Lucie and Tess. I felt mixed up. I liked Tess but I had a feeling that Lucie needed me and was afraid to ask for help. I drifted off to sleep with images of the dance in my head.

At some point I must have been dreaming. My vision switched from the dance to Lucie in her room. Had I ever seen her room? I could visualize it now perfectly. She lay on her canopied bed curled up in ball – all alone. She felt alone physically and mentally. She was hurting and confused. Tears ran down her face. She turned toward the window. Rain shimmered on the glass.

SIX

I awoke early. I remembered when I was not a morning person. I'm still not my best self in the morning. I like to sneak up on the day. It was still raining. Yuck. Well the run over to the pawnshop would help get the women out of my head, right? If not that, then the news on the van that took Trevor Vance away from his family or some karate should do the trick.

I skipped the shower, knowing I was about to get sweaty anyway. I dressed in my rattiest sweats and threw some dry workout clothes in an old backpack. I tied on my running shoes and put an extra pair in the backpack. I only like to get wet when I swim so I threw in lots of extra socks. I texted White Eagle to see what time I should be at the shop. At least there would be no lawn mowing today.

I fixed some warm fuel for my body. I put some eggs on to boil and cooked a big pot of oatmeal figuring I could eat it later if no one else wanted any. I was just running cold water over the eggs when Mom came in the kitchen. She looked longingly at the empty coffeepot. I took pity on her and flipped it on.

"You had it ready to go. Aren't you sweet?" I dished her up a bowl of oatmeal and passed her the brown sugar she likes to put on it.

She sat down at the table looking a little rumpled but otherwise okay. As soon as the coffee stopped sputtering I poured her a mug and started fixing a sack lunch for myself. My phone pinged at me. White Eagle was letting me know that he was on his way so anytime within the next hour was fine for my arrival.

"So what's the deal?" I asked, indicating the upstairs with my head.

"I don't know. He's almost his old self but different. He's even quieter and more subdued. He seems lost in his own house. He asks all kinds of questions about you and your activities but he lacks focus when we answer. Fortunately your brothers don't know much. Alex is a good observer but he protects you. There are things he knows but he doesn't say. We try to make you look as normal as possible."

"Did he notice that I got into his stuff?"

"I don't think so. Did they change his meds?"

"I'm pretty sure they did. I better go while I can. I'll be home for dinner unless I call otherwise, okay?"

"Sure, good luck and I'll do what I can here."

The rain beat down steadily and I was soaked by the time I hit the bottom of the hill. I ran to the middle school and cut through the back. It was the fastest way to the pawnshop and I was already drenched. My shoes squished with each step. I saw again the vision of Lucie watching rain stream down her window and realized I now saw her looking at a daytime vision. She was doing homework but looking longingly out the window. I shook my head and kept running.

I went to the back door so that I would not drip all over the shop up front. I knocked our prearranged knock and White Eagle let me in.

"Aren't you glad I had you help me wire in that dryer last summer?"

"Yeah, the washer too," I replied, panting. I'd run as fast as I could pushing myself to get out of the rain more quickly.

"Go take a hot shower and then I'll fill you in on what we've got. How do you feel about some reconnaissance with me?" He was kidding, right? I *loved* this part of my job.

I quickly did as White Eagle suggested, dressed in dry clothes and came out toweling off my hair. I threw my wet clothes and towel in the washer along with the other dirty towels we had been collecting. I started the load and ran my fingers through my hair to give it some style.

"So, what did you find out?"

"Evelyn got back to me yesterday after work. I slipped her a copy of the drawing of who we now know is Willie Brown. I also gave her the van information. It never hurts to use more than one source or to use the chicken analogy of 'don't put all your eggs in one basket'. This time Evelyn beat Sarah – different sources sometimes have different info. Our 'friend' Willie has a bunch of minor arrests. The *stalker* type often does. I guess when you are bad on the inside anyway, following the rules just isn't in the repertoire. He's wanted for possession and intent to sell. He's also been arrested for B and E and a little smuggling. Up 'till now he hasn't hurt anybody so he's considered a minor player. Here are some current head shots courtesy of our local cop shop. According to Evelyn he dropped off the grid about a year ago. It makes me feel a little wiggly to think that he disappeared around the same time I found you. Here's the rest of the file. I'll give you a few minutes to absorb what we've got so far."

White Eagle went over to the workbench where he constantly had a selection of projects. Things didn't always come into the pawnshop in perfect working order. White Eagle could fix anything and he was teaching us to do the same. He felt that no skill was ever wasted. Just like a good Boy Scout he believed in always being prepared.

I flipped through the arrest photos - our buddy Willie hadn't changed much from the image I saw of him courtesy of the bike and the journal. In the more recent photos his hair was longer and cornrowed. He looked more worn. In one picture he snarled, showing his teeth, which looked awful. I guessed it was drug use that made them look so bad. I had seen photos like this in health and after our experience with a *stalker* in DC, White Eagle had taught us that frequently *stalkers* resorted to drug use when they couldn't get a new *watcher* to suck dry. They had to get a high somehow; if not the real thing, than a chemical high was a good second choice. He had also taught us that *stalkers* generally did two things: either they turned good *watchers* dark or they used the untrained talent by absorbing it by force. White Eagle's theory was that they got a high from draining away someone's talent. Temporarily they would feel more energized and powerful. He was sure there was a downside. As if drug use wasn't bad enough.

Ah Willie, you'll be mean as a snake, I'd bet my last dollar, but the drugs will have dulled your wits. You'll be a powerful but stupid adversary. I was looking forward to this.

I looked at the rest of his file. In addition to what White Eagle had already told me, I saw that the van in question now belonged to a Vivian Davis. Evelyn, bless her, had dug deeper and had found the connection. Vivian's maiden name was... Brown. We would be going to scope out her residence and see if I could get my hands on that van, literally. There wasn't much else in the file.

Vivian lived out toward Boring in what used to be a rural area but was now pretty thickly coated with houses. We loaded up into White Eagle's truck. He had finally succumbed to technology and had upgraded to a smart phone - thank you, Marlo. White Eagle handed the phone to me and had me access the GPS – let's just say he doesn't have it all figured out yet, but he is working on it. At about one app a month it feels like.

I plugged in our destination and we were off – it took us a mere fifteen minutes to get there. We did a quick drive by looking for a place to park and watch Vivian Brown Davis' residence or a place to ditch the truck. Nothing good popped up. So we did a slow drive by and started discussing alternatives.

There was no sign of activity. Houses were far apart but vegetation was relatively sparse. This was not looking good for our side. We drove to the nearest parking lot and paused to discuss our plans.

"I saw the house and two outbuildings. The neighbor to the right has a clear view of the property. There are no vehicles in sight. I do have an idea though – what if I pretended to be an injured jogger and go to her house for help. We want to avoid breaking and entering right?"

"I've got nothing. Let's try it. You're right, I don't want to do any breaking and entering if we can help it. Don't forget to check for dogs."

Super. Now I would have two pairs of wet shoes. Oh well, I just hoped she wouldn't think I was nuts for running in jeans. I looked myself over and took off my lightweight jacket. My t-shirt was one of my oldest rock band shirts that barely fit. It was good for doing dirty work at the shop and chores. My jeans were also old and well worn. The knees were turning white with age and looking a little thread bare. I had a hole starting in the right knee.

"Let me use your knife, would you?" I asked White Eagle.

He gave me a look but passed it over. I worked at the right knee of my jeans to make it look ripped. Then I went to work on my knee itself making one larger cut and a couple of smaller ones. Next I jumped out of the truck and bounced up and down to get the blood flowing. I wiped White Eagle's blade off on the knee of my jeans to make it look messier and clean his blade at the same time.

"Well, I figure you ought to give me about twenty minutes. I will run to her house from here and trip in her driveway. Then I will limp up to the door, looking appropriately damaged, and ask to use her phone. Seeing as how nothing ever goes as planned we'll play it by ear from there." I flipped my cell phone into the cab.

There was a puddle near the truck. I knelt in it to wet my jeans and to make my knee look worse. I splashed some of the now muddy water onto my shirt and hands. I gave White Eagle a thumbs up and jogged off toward Vivian's. I was guessing that this was going to be a really long twenty minutes for White Eagle. He had my cell so I was completely on my own. He hated it when I did that. Last time I went off on my own I ended up nearly dead in a ditch. I was smarter and better trained now.

Just before I reached her house I checked my knee to be sure it was sufficiently bloody. I knelt again faking a shoe tie for a passing car and dragging my knee a bit through the gravel and muck. I gave myself a quick once over – yep – I looked awful. I started running again. I was moving fast past her right hand neighbor. Right at the edge of Vivian's driveway I purposely tripped and did a spectacular belly flop, laying myself out across her driveway in full view. I lay there for a moment and then slowly pulled myself to a sitting position. I played it for all it was worth. I examined my knee, then I pulled myself to my feet and slowly limped up her driveway.

As I went I made careful note of all my surroundings. I didn't hear a dog here but the neighbor to the left had one. There was no other sound except for an occasional car and the wind in the few trees around the property. I had yet to sense anything. It all seemed quiet and neutral.

I limped up to the front door and gave a gentle knock. Even from here the van was nowhere in sight. The outbuildings either stored it or it was gone. One of the outbuildings pulled at me a bit. I turned my attention back to the house as I heard soft footsteps within.

A young dark haired, dark skinned and dark eyed woman answered the door.

"Yes?" she asked tentatively.

"I apologize for bothering you but I wonder if I might use your phone? I fell," I said indicating my battered looking knee, "and I don't think I can run back home on it."

"I'll call for you – just a minute," she said reclosing the door. I could hear the lock click back into place. She returned a moment later with a portable phone in her hand. She kept the security screen closed between us. She asked who she should call, my name and the number. I gave her the information, frustrated that she was choosing now to be security conscious. White Eagle must have answered on the first ring. I checked my watch it had only been seventeen minutes.

"Hello? My name is Vivian. I'm calling for Owen. He was running by my house and fell near my driveway. He is hoping you can come pick him up... Let me give you my address..."

I turned and sat on her front porch and focused my full attention to a scan of her property while she was busy. I didn't feel any danger here. Only the one outbuilding looked interesting. I was hoping that she would think I just didn't feel well after the fall. I started a bit when I realized that she was talking to me again.

"I don't think I've seen you run here before."

"We recently moved out here. I'm trying to find a route I like – I guess this won't be it – it doesn't like me." I leaned back a bit on the porch to rest my back on her house and give her a better view of my knee.

Vivian was loosening up a bit. She unlocked the security screen and sat down next to me on her porch.

"Would you like a drink of water or a bandage or something?" she asked with concern.

I was glad that I had drawn her out onto the porch. "I don't know about a bandage – what do you think?" I asked, pulling up my pant leg and trying to sound a little needy. My knee looked way worse than it really was, thanks to my rolling it in dirty water.

"Oh my goodness! What did you cut yourself on?" she gasped.

"A rock maybe?"

"Let me get you some paper towels at least."

"Thank you."

She hurried into the house and was back in moments. She sat back down, handing me the towels.

I started at the bottom near my shoe to clean up my lower leg. She hissed in a breath as I started dabbing at the knee.

"Its okay," I said as I reached out to touch her sleeve. Nothing. She was not like her brother. I wasn't getting anything useful from her and I wasn't sure how to approach the situation to get her to open up.

I went for generic, hoping to build to the information I needed. "Have you lived here long?"

"I've lived in the area all my life but I am new to the house. It was my aunt's..." Ah, that would explain why I didn't feel her brother here. She continued, "she wanted to keep it in the family. She had no children and my brother... Well let's just say he wasn't a good candidate."

"Is he okay?" I asked hitting her with all the trustworthy and earnest feelings I could dredge up.

"Oh sure, he ah... he lives in Atlanta now." *Wow! Coincidence?* I wondered.

"Really? My dad goes there on business all the time," I said, trying to sound enthusiastic. "Who does he work for?"

"He's not a good communicator, but it's something like, Fredrick, Cooper and Niles," she said, screwing up her face in thought.

"Sounds like a law firm." I had to keep her talking so that she would leak as much information as possible.

"It does, doesn't it? Actually, they're a chemical engineering firm."

"Wow, your brother must be smart."

"He's um... He's different, but what he is doing for them is security. Maybe he's contracted to them and works for someone else? I don't know. I'm just glad he has a real job. It's ironic though, because over the years he... well he seems to find trouble. For the last nine months he's been... good."

"Does he come home to see you?"

"If he came home it wouldn't be to see me. I don't really approve of his... lifestyle."

"I'm sorry to hear that. You seem like a nice person."

"Thanks, he just... well, he even sold me his old van before he left. Sold it to me, the bum, after all I have done for him. He said he needed the money to get to Atlanta and get settled. It ran okay for about two weeks after he left and now... Never mind, I don't even know why I'm telling you this," she said, looking embarrassed and a little confused. "I'm ranting – sorry."

"Don't worry about it. Sometimes you feel better when you get burdens off your chest."

White Eagle pulled in the driveway, turned off the ignition and walked toward us.

"Owen, are you okay?" he asked sounding genuinely concerned.

"Yeah, Uncle Earl, I just didn't think I should run home on this. Thanks for coming. Thank you, Vivian, for your hospitality," I said, pulling myself to my feet. I turned back toward her as she was rising. "Maybe we can repay the favor? My uncle is a really good mechanic. Maybe he could look at your van."

"Oh that's not necessary," she exclaimed looking embarrassed again.

"Oh no, I insist. We're new around here. Let me have a look - at least to tell you what's wrong with it – you did help my nephew. That was really nice of you by the way," White Eagle said using all of his charm.

"Well, okay. I guess. Let me get the keys."

White Eagle and I smiled at each other in silent celebration. Yes! Vivian was right back and all business. I had to remember to limp. We followed her to the building that was pulling at me. She used a key in the padlock and White Eagle helped her to push open the cranky, rusty doors. Vivian moved just inside the door and flipped on a light that barely provided any help to the dimness within. Shelves ran all the way to the ceiling and were stuffed full of old crates and boxes, some trailing their contents out the edges. White Eagle kept her busy describing what the van was doing while I took in the shed. It was about fifteen feet wide and twenty-five feet long. There was at least one crate I needed to get my hands on but I would have to wait for her to be fully distracted. I leaned on the van feigning interest as I absorbed all it had to tell me.

White Eagle kept her talking and continued to show her things in the engine compartment. Then he started asking her for tools. When her back was turned I indicated to White Eagle which boxes I needed to get into. White Eagle asked aloud if I would get Vivian a stool that was visible on the far side of the shed. I brought it over as she returned with a crescent wrench. White Eagle twitched it into position so that her view was blocked to the first box. Vivian sat down and continued to listen to White Eagle as he fiddled with the engine and gave her a running commentary.

I edged to the box and silently lifted it down. It contained some of Willie's belongings. They all spoke to me but none louder than a screwdriver that I knew was Trevor's and had been used to kill him. I took a bandana from the box and slipped the screwdriver out. I wrapped it in the bandana and concealed it in my sock. It would be supported by my shoe and hidden by my jeans. It would also help me remember to limp. The other items in the box just attested to the crimes we already knew about. I was just sliding the box back into place when Vivian realized I was gone.

"You okay, Owen?"

"Yes, thank you. I was just looking for a place to sit. Do you mind if I open the back of the van and sit on the bumper?"

"Sure, you go right ahead. Let me just unlock it for you." As she came around back she added, "I feel guilty keeping you from fixing up your knee. Do you think you need stitches?"

"Nah, it's just stiff and sore. Perhaps though, if you have some handy, a Band-Aid and some antiseptic?"

"Of course. I'll be right back." To White Eagle she said. "I'm going to get Owen some first aid supplies so he can fix his knee. I'll be right back. Can I get you coffee or anything?"

"No, I'm fine. I don't think this will take long. Oh, but you don't mind if Owen hands me tools out of your toolbox do you?"

"No, you go right ahead."

The minute she was out of sight I rushed to the next box. White Eagle quickly dug out all the tools he would need on his own and then began to work on the van again. The next box had a few more items of interest. Lucky for me Willie liked to collect souvenirs. I hoped that he would not miss the screwdriver. I left everything else behind. I put it all back in the box and moved on to the third and final one. I dumped it out on its side to make it look like I had knocked it off the shelf. I knew I was about out of time. I read all the objects that wanted to talk to me and placed them back in the box. Vivian returned when I had a few objects left on the floor that were of no interest to me anyway.

"I'm so sorry," I said right away. "I knocked it off the shelf. I don't think I broke anything. Would you like to check? I'll replace anything I damaged."

"It's not mine anyway. Don't even worry about it. I keep hoping William will send for it." She helped me put the last few items in the box. She returned to White Eagle and I went about tending my knee. Before I was done, White Eagle was encouraging her to hop up front and try to start the van.

The van tried to turn over but the battery sounded weary. White Eagle pulled his truck up and hooked up the jumper cables he kept in the back. In two turns of the key they got the engine to catch. White Eagle told her to let it idle for awhile. He asked her if she had a battery charger. He told her she probably didn't need a new battery; that they just run down sometimes when they sit. She didn't have a charger but she would go for a drive soon to charge it up.

I handed her back her first aid supplies and thanked her as did White Eagle. She thanked us in return for getting the van going. White Eagle told her what she needed to do next to keep it running and we left.

As we pulled out of the driveway he said, "I can tell that you have a lot of information crammed in your head. Why don't you see if Marlo can come to the shop to catalog it? I think he was coming in today to do some bookkeeping. See if we can pick him up on the way back."

I picked my cell up off the seat and called him. Lucky for me he had not left yet. He would even get me another set of clothes from his house. I put my jacket back on over my wet shirt. Marlo is smaller than me but not by too much. I hoped he would bring some shorts because I was not looking forward to wearing high-water pants.

Marlo was ready to go on his front porch when we pulled up. He was wearing his computer backpack and had a small sports bag slung diagonally across his body as well. He had opted for his new contact lenses today, I noted. He was wearing his glasses less and less often. Without the glasses we looked even more alike. He sprung to his feet as we pulled in and was opening the rear door of the truck before it had even come to a complete stop.

"Where's the fire?" White Eagle asked smiling.

"I'm excited to be working on our next case! Life has been getting pretty dull. I love the research. I also have some information for you about your dad's company. I even got into your grandfather's taxes."

"Holy Moly, Marlo! What if you get caught?" I yelped.

"Don't worry. I didn't break into the IRS. I'm not stupid. Your grandfather uses an accountant. I broke into his database."

"Oh, well, that's a relief," I said sarcastically.

"Stop it, you worrywart! I've been learning from Sarah. My tracks are well covered."

White Eagle burst out with a loud guffaw. "I love this! Usually it's Marlo admonishing *you* to be careful, Mr. Dive in Where Angels Fear to Tread! This is great!"

"Okay, okay - tell me what you've got and then when you get the computer fired up, I will tell you what we've discovered."

"Where to start? Okay this may be a little out of order. My brain is churning. I looked at your dad's new job. He no longer works for the same company but they are under the same... umbrella. Your dad is now acting like a consultant or a liaison or something. It is pretty muddy. Your grandfather has a stake in the umbrella company. He's worth almost a quarter of a billion dollars, by the way. Be still my heart." I felt my own jaw drop at the news. "Anyway... Does the name 'Fredrick, Cooper and Niles' mean anything to you?" Marlo checked my reaction - which was epic. I fought to keep my mouth shut to let him finish. "I see that you do. That is where your dad is working on that funky adhesive that is giving him grief. I think that they're making him work on something he doesn't want to work on. Your dad is not a bad guy, Owen. Now back to your grandfather. He has been putting money into Fredrick, Cooper and Niles... regularly. He did pull strings to get your dad that job. I found the paper trial. It's weird though... something isn't right. Someone else has their hand in this - I feel it. Your grandparents have become recluses. A new security firm is watching his house and... coincidence or no? – also taking care of Fredrick, Cooper and Niles. When your dad is in Atlanta he has a personal security detail or is it a prison guard? The same is true for your grandfather in Miami. By the way, the umbrella company is based out of Miami. They took on the Oregon firm the year your dad went to work there. I don't think that your dad knew he was working for your grandfather until recently. Your dad was removed from your grandfather's will the year your parents announced their engagement and then when you were born... Shazam... you were the heir until... wait for it... five months ago. That's when you told your dad about your ability. Now your dad is once again the heir, working for another of your grandfather's corporations, working on a weird exploding adhesive and being drugged. I smell a conspiracy."

Marlo looked at me like I should say something. I think my brain turned off. I could almost feel it processing the information he'd just dumped on me. Maybe I needed a reboot like my computer did sometimes. It was a lot to take in... A whole lot.

We pulled up to the back of the pawnshop and I still sat there. Marlo patted my shoulder and jumped out of the truck.

"I can hardly wait to hear what he has to tell me. I think I just blew him out of the water and that doesn't happen with him." Marlo seemed very pleased with himself.

White Eagle came around and opened my door for me. I turned my head slowly and met his concerned gaze. "Wow," I breathed. I slid out of the truck and landed wrong on my ankle having completely forgotten the screwdriver. I muttered a curse and pulled it out of my sock and shoe, then handed it to White Eagle. I slowly hobbled through the shop's back door behind Marlo's retreating back.

I plopped down on the stool next to Marlo. White Eagle set the bandana wrapped screwdriver next to me on the workbench and went up front to check on Max. "Well, you do win in the jaw-dropping department today. I thought I had you, but you win. Does Sarah know all that you told me? It seems like this is her jurisdiction. I take it there is nothing illegal that you can find, so we are still waiting."

"Yep, nothing illegal *yet*, but we're still looking. We might have something with the drugs your dad is on."

"Hey guys," Adrian said, coming in from the front of the shop. "We don't have any big plans later, do we? Amy is coming by the shop this afternoon and then we're going to a movie. You guys wanna come?"

That's Adrian for you – more interested in girls than anything else. "You go ahead. I don't have a date anyway."

"Oh, ye of little faith. I have Tess' phone number. I didn't figure you would ask for it. I watched you all night last night. She'll go or the next movie tickets are on me!"

Great. "Fine, give me her number," I sighed, resigned. "Do I dare ask what we are seeing?"

"Whatever the women want to see. Duh! Do you think I'm dumb?" Adrian asked, looking at me like I was nuts.

"Let me call Mom and make sure it is okay and then Marlo and I have some work to do."

"Hey, whatev... So long as you will spar with me while Amy's here. I want her to see how tough I am."

Fantastic. Well, I could make Adrian look good for awhile I guessed. Marlo looked like he was trying really hard not to laugh.

"Hey, Owen, why are you all wet?" Adrian asked, just noticing the obvious, "and what happened to your knee?"

"I went on a little reconnaissance with White Eagle and now Marlo needs to record our findings. It's regarding Trevor Vance."

"I woulda gone."

"We thought we would be nice and let you sleep in – besides, sometimes numbers matter and I like to save you for the important stuff. Like... would you check up on Jesus using your social network? He doesn't want to tell me, but I know he's worried and a little stressed - so something is up." Keeping Adrian busy was a key part of making him feel needed, important and happy.

"Yeah, sure. No problem," he said, happy again. "I've got some work to do up front. I'll be back for the Trevor scoop when you're done with the boring stuff."

"Go get cleaned up," Marlo said tossing me the sports bag. "I'll check in with Max and finish loading the software we need. Then I'll do some accounting while you 'fight' with Adrian. I need to work out too, but you guys can last longer than I can anyway. I also don't want to show off for Amy."

Marlo had packed me clothes from the skin out, including electric blue boxer briefs. Well, well, well, who knew? I would be shoeless until mine dried but that was life. I took another hot shower, recleaned my knee, dressed, and took my lunch from the fridge. I removed my wet stuff from the washer and threw the load into the dryer. I tossed the wet clothes I had just stripped out of into the washer with both pairs of shoes and put on the flip flops I kept for emergencies. I called my mom and got approval for a movie date. Then I took a deep breath and called Tess.

"Hello?" her sultry voice asked.

"Hey Tess, its Owen."

"Well, hello there, Handsome, I wondered when you'd get around to calling me. Let me guess... your buddy Adrian has been at work, right?"

"Yep, that's Adrian. He got your number last night, huh?"

"Yep. So what's up?" she asked in a light friendly manner.

"I wondered if you would be interested in going to a movie at the mall with us tonight."

"May...be. Who's us?"

"Adrian and his girlfriend, Amy, and our friend Marlo and his girlfriend, Michalia."

"What time?" she asked, all business.

"Adrian is setting it up. Hang on just a moment and I'll ask him." I headed for the front of the shop.

"Hey, Owen – are you at your house?" she interrupted.

"Nah, Adrian, Marlo and I work at Adrian's uncle's pawnshop on Saturdays."

"Oh – that makes sense. I thought maybe you were hanging out with Adrian to find your courage to call."

"I admit that Adrian asked me about the movie and told me that he'd gotten your number but he was working up front and I was in the back. Adrian doesn't have to hold my hand if that's what you're hinting at. Hang on a sec, Tess," I said, shifting my attention to Adrian. "Hey Aid, do you know what movie and what time yet?'

"The seven o'clock show and we'll have two choices when we get there. We can meet for food first if you want."

"Did you get all that?" I asked Tess.

"I did. I had some other plans but for you I'll change them. I'll pick you up at six. Give me your address."

"Usually Marlo's mom..."

"Owen, I'm a junior. I drive. I will pick you up and play nice with your parents. Don't worry. They'll love me."

"How did you end up in Biology?" I asked, perplexed.

"I couldn't fit it in my schedule last year. I'll see you at six. Be ready." All I heard after that was dead air. She didn't even say goodbye. I looked up to see Adrian watching me.

"She's driving, huh? Dating an older woman. You 'da man, Owen! She's a junior isn't she... and you just found out! I guess you need to spend more time with your buddy, Adrian, and less time working and worrying, don't ya?" Adrian laughed. I didn't even wait for Adrian to regain control of himself. I headed into the back to go to work and to plot my revenge.

I sat down with Marlo and my lunch and focused seriously on all the images I had seen and where I had gotten them from. Where Adrian was concerned, maybe I just wouldn't let him look quite as good when I sparred with him later. Yeah, that would be good revenge. I took a couple of bites, made sure Marlo was ready and then got down to business.

"Let's start with the van... After Willie threw Trevor in the back he drove him to a remote location. I can see a cabin in the woods. They were there for a few days. I think four days judging by the number of sunrises and sunsets. On the fourth day, Willie hauled out Trevor's body. It feels like up on Mt. Hood somewhere. I can see a lake, it's mountainous and there are tons of trees – mostly Douglas fir. If we can ever find the spot I know right where he's buried." Marlo looked at me over the top of the laptop and gulped.

"Mar, the next part is bad. Do you want me to use the audio program?"

"No, I only have to hear it. You had to see it. It's okay. I'll be okay."

"The next item is the screwdriver." I opened the bandana so Marlo could snap a picture for the file. "Trevor had this on him when he was taken. It corroborates the story of the van. Trevor was dragged into the cabin by Willie. He was still under the influence of whatever drug Willie gave him. He handcuffed him to the leg of the wood stove. As soon as Trevor started coming around Willie was on him again. He put a hand on Trevor's chest. I saw the same back arch and what looked like a scream from Trevor. This time it didn't last as long as in the back of the van and Willie seemed mad. He took out a pocket knife and cut the front of Trevor's shirt open. I could see red marks on his chest. This went on for days. White Eagle is right; it looked like it gave Willie a high. I never once saw Willie give Trevor food or water. Trevor came around on day two and seemed to remember the screwdriver in his pocket. He tried to break the handcuffs. Willie woke up and they fought. Trevor took quite the beating and then Willie drained him again. I saw Willie snort some cocaine a couple of times - more so at the end than at the beginning. I think he was getting enough of a high from Trevor at first. On the third night Trevor was begging for water. Willie had finally had it with him because he tried to drain him one last time. I think that nothing was left because in a rage he pulled out the screwdriver and slammed it into Trevor's heart." Marlo looked a little pale and sweaty over the top of the laptop but he was keeping up.

"Next item – a headband. I see a girl of maybe sixteen. I think she's the first victim. He took her from a family picnic. I have the feeling he'd been watching her for awhile. He only drained her once. She was making too much noise so he snapped her neck. It was a sloppy job. He left her behind and he almost got caught. He decided he needed to plan better and be more careful in the future because he got greedy and anxious with this first one. I see him looking at the headband. He feels so good it makes me sick. He wants more – it's a hunger in him now. Nothing compares to this feeling..." I looked at my lunch - no longer hungry; just plain nauseous. Marlo just looked at me.

White Eagle came through the curtain and looked at us. "It's not good, is it?" He came over and looked at the screen over Marlo's shoulder. "Ah, I was right. I have seen it before and I never want to see it again." He put a hand on my shoulder. "It's best that he broke her neck. He was new and couldn't control himself. He would've done much more horrible things to her if she'd lived." White Eagle gave me a little shake to break the vision's hold on me. This is not the part of the job that I love. Catching these bastards makes my day though.

"I've got to get him. I can't let him do that to anyone else. It freaks me out to think he might be connected to my dad," I gasped and scrubbed at my eyes where I felt tears beginning to well.

"What?" Marlo yelped. That's where you know the company name from... Willie? I thought your dad had mentioned the company name."

"No, Mar, when we saw Willie's sister today she told me he is security for Fredrick, Cooper and Niles. Willie's talent is to blur what he is doing. He covered the motorcycle so that a *watcher* like me couldn't read it. His talent is to block *watchers* except that back then he wasn't good at it or it wears off. Now that same fuzzy, foggy, blurry effect is being used on my dad and his stuff. I don't know what you're thinking, White Eagle, but I would be surprised to find two people with exactly the same talent. It feels the same whether I touch this stuff, the bike or my dad's belongings." I closed my eyes. "It's like the same signature or the way families look alike, do you know what I mean?" I asked, looking at White Eagle.

"I think you're telling me that you think that Willie might just be your father's bodyguard when he is in Atlanta and I see your logic. Let's see how long we can keep him home. If it's any consolation, I really don't think he's after your dad. I think your dad is 'safe' from Willie. I also feel strongly that Willie has a master. We need to catch the big fish. For now, let's see if we can wrap Willie up here. If we find Trevor's remains or can link him to the dead girl, he will be brought back here and charged."

I nodded and tried to pull myself together. *He deserves to be dead.* I thought. *Putting him in jail is too kind. He deserves to feel what his victims felt. If it is in my power to deliver that to him, I will.*

"Owen!" White Eagle snapped. I jerked my head up to look at him. "I see that look in your eye and your color just flared. Revenge is bad, evil – it will ruin you like it ruined Miles. It's our job to catch him, not punish him. You are better than he is. You can do this."

Marlo reached out and put a hand on my arm. "It bugs me just hearing it. It must be awful to see. You carry a big burden. Please don't let it drag you down. You're one of the best people I know and there are lots of Willies out there. Don't get hung up on one. Let's get them all. Okay?"

I leaned over and put an arm around Marlo's shoulder. White Eagle hugged us both.

"I'm sorry guys, it's not fair, but we can do this if we hang together."

"You're right, White Eagle. You too, Marlo. I just... for a moment... I'm sorry, I lost it. I was angry and worried. I'll be okay. We have two more items to catalog. There are more victims – Willie keeps souvenirs. We need to talk to Evelyn and Sarah. I don't want to get his sister Vivian in trouble though. She's a nice person and I think her brother has caused her plenty of pain over the years. I know about four victims. I bet there are more. We need to see if there are anymore unexplained disappearances in our area between 2004 and the present. Maybe I need another look at that shed."

"Slow down. Give Marlo what you have. You read this stuff but didn't really process it or think about it right then, correct?"

"Yes, why?"

"I think more will come to you if you let it float up – don't force it. If you still think there is more we can learn at Vivian's, then we'll take care of it next weekend. These people have been dead for awhile. A few more days won't matter. Relax – be a kid for a few hours, okay?"

I could see that he had my best interests at heart. So I took a deep breath and went back to work.

"Next item – a coin – this belonged to another... female of about twenty. He picked her up in a bar. He danced with her and lured her out. She went with him willingly at first. She was a much later victim. The coin was dated 2009. She may be his most recent. He was smoother and more savvy. You don't want to know what he was doing to her when he drained her. He can drain them more quickly now. They don't suffer as much yet it seems like he gets off on the suffering."

"Please tell me that the picture in my mind is not what you are saying... They were right in the middle of... they were having... What girl picks up a guy in a bar and has sex on a first date? Gross," Marlo interrupted.

"Sorry man, it's what I saw. They were at the same cabin as Trevor. We'll find her body near his." Marlo shuddered and White Eagle cringed.

"Now you see my rage?" I asked defiantly.

"I hope he got a raging case of painful herpes or some other STD," Marlo snarled.

"Who has an STD?" Adrian asked coming through the curtain.

"No one. We're working here. Listen if you must but don't interrupt, please," I said in a cranky voice.

"Geez, *chil-lax* would you. I just came back to say that Amy is on her way."

"Thank you, Adrian," White Eagle said solicitously.

Adrian wandered over and looked at Marlo's screen. He read a bit, blanched and backed away. "Never mind. I'll knock before we come back."

"Good idea," I said gruffly. Then I turned to Marlo before Adrian even had a chance to move. "Last item - a comb. It belonged to a young man. I think he happened somewhere in the middle. He was one who Willie tried to befriend like Trevor. He spent his time getting to know this victim. He had his urges better under control.

By now he was looking forward to savoring his victims. It feels a little different when he drains men. He still feels really good, just not quite as creepy. This one may have gotten away. I can see him running through the woods and that is the last I see of him," I sighed, feeling drained myself.

White Eagle rested a hand on my shoulder. "You go ahead with your other obligations. I'm going to talk to Sarah and maybe to Evelyn. We'll make a plan and run it by you tomorrow. For now Owen, work out with the boys and go on your date. I'll be back when I can. Don't beat up Adrian too much. He's a little jealous of you and it sneaks out sometimes. He really does care about you and he is a good friend. Don't push him too far away. We need him. I feel it."

"Okay, I hear you," I said.

"And finish your lunch. You'll need the energy," he grumbled as he left, wagging a finger in my direction.

"Yes, Mother." I called to his back.

Marlo heaved a huge sigh. "I think I'm glad to go do a bunch of bookkeeping. Not even I want to be in this dark world right now. Yuck. I'm delicate – didn't you read my warranty?" He punched me in the arm, collected his laptop and retreated to the front of the shop.

I looked at my lunch. It didn't look too appealing anymore. I choked down a couple of more bites but my stomach couldn't take it. I'd make up the calories tonight at the mall. I'd have to dip into savings tonight too, darn it. I hadn't been earning much since football practice had started. I was behind on my lawn mowing, as well. What should I wear tonight? I ran through my options in my head. I had a dark green collared shirt. If I wore my brown boots I would look even taller. What pants? I had a pair of skate pants I had gotten this summer. They were cut sort of like jeans but looked a little dressier. I also had picked up a new pair of distressed jeans complete with a knee patch. What can I say? I'd been shopping with Adrian who was set on improving my image. I hadn't shaved since Thursday. Maybe I wouldn't so that I could replicate my beach look from last weekend that Tess seemed to like. Why did I care so much?

Adrian knocked, surprising me out of my thoughts. "Hey, you decent back here?" he asked, laughing.

"I never have been," I flipped back.

"Hey Owen," Amy smiled at me. "Adrian said he'd show me how you guys stay in shape. He thinks he's going to kick your butt."

"He does, does he? We'll see. Are you going to fight or watch?" I asked her.

"You'd let me do that? Fight, I mean? I didn't bring any workout gear. Maybe another time you guys can teach me some stuff."

"Quit flirting with my girl. Let's get to it." Adrian barked at me.

Ho, ho – I had found a button to push. This was fantastic! I gave Amy a huge smile.

"Owen, what happened to your knee?"

"He fell," Adrian quickly put in.

"Yeah, I fell. It's fine. Thanks." I gave Adrian a rumpled eyebrow. "You about ready or are you gonna talk smack all day?"

I walked over and got out the gloves and helmets and left my flip flops off to the side.

"No helmets," Adrian said. "How about no head shots."

"Fine," I groused.

We gloved up and fell into our fighter's stances. I realized that Adrian was wearing his nicest, newest workout gear. I, on the other hand, was wearing some of Marlo's old raggedy work shorts and a disreputable t-shirt that had seen much better days. I had bare feet and Adrian was wearing shoes. I hoped he wouldn't step on my naked toes. Beggars can't be choosers, right? It would be great to really break in Adrian's new duds and get a little blood on them. I was not listening to White Eagle's advice – what was with me? Take the high road, I reminded myself, wondering why Adrian was goading me.

"Are we street fighting, boxing, karate... what?" I asked Adrian.

"I don't know. What do you want to see, Amy?"

"I don't know. How about a little bit of everything. Is Marlo coming?"

"He'll be back in a bit," I answered – then turned to Adrian. "How about street fighting and mixed martial arts. Weapons?"

"Weapons later. Maybe we can take her to the shooting range sometime, too."

"You trying to impress her or scare her?" I asked, getting a scowl from Adrian. Maybe I had pushed too far but he was pushing my buttons also.

"Let's go," Adrian barked.

"You first, Sunshine."

Adrian growled and came at me. Maybe he just needed to be in the mood to spar. Nope, I take it back - he was in a weird mood, period. White Eagle was looking more right all the time. Adrian was jealous. Geez, Dope, he didn't want my life, but then the grass is always greener. So far no hits had landed. He was giving it heck but I blocked all he had. I hadn't even tried to hit him yet. Adrian was getting mad and losing focus so I snaked out a leg, hooking his, pulling it out from under him and dumping him on the ground but he sprang right back up.

"She'll like the way you looked doing that move," I said so that only he could hear. Adrian paused for a moment and shook his head.

"Ya, think? Then she'll love this," he said with a grin as he went for a chin shot, snapping my head back. I glared at him and followed up with three quick blows to his chest to back him up, then I spun and kicked him in the same spot landing him flat on his back on the mat again. This time he did not spring right up.

"You okay?" I asked bending over him. Adrian reached up an arm so I reached to help him up. Instead he helped me down – followed by an elbow to my sternum. The air left my lungs in a whoosh. Adrian laughed and got to his feet. He took a bottle of water from the fridge and had a quick drink.

"Street fighting – remember Bro?" He laughed again.

No head shots and street fighting, my butt. Damn showoff. Fine. I could dish it out too. I said nothing out loud. I relaxed back into my fighter's stance. I watched Adrian. I decided to use a little Steven Segal on him and use all his moves against him. The best part was Miles knew about the martial artist and actor turned law enforcement officer. I bet that Adrian didn't. Okay, so I was cheating by pulling up memories from a past I had never lived firsthand but Adrian was pushing it. He circled me and then decided on a kick, but his feet had given him away. I was ready and pulled his leg in the direction he was already moving, sending him off balance with the unexpected move. He recovered and came at me again. He punched this time. I turned sideways letting it brush past my torso and again pushed him past me. Adrian looked frustrated.

I backed up a step and waited. He circled some more hoping I would go on the attack. Finally Adrian gave up and rushed me. At the last moment I moved toward him in an unanticipated move bringing up my arm in a clothesline and knocking him to the mat for the third time. Adrian jumped up and growled at me. He rushed me with a rapid succession of jabs. I never tried to hit him back; I just blocked everything he threw at me. *Smack, smack, smack, smack, snap.*

"Ouch, Dude, what the hell?" Adrian snarled at me. I guessed I had bent his wrist back a little too far.

"Adrian, I apologize. I didn't mean to hurt you," I said sincerely.

Adrian stepped in close. I wasn't sure what he was intending – I was half ready to get walloped.

"I know that. Frankly, it has made you an even better person, but it's hard for Adrian to take. Of the three of us, he was always the most popular – now he feels like he is standing in your shadow. I know you don't want any attention and quite honestly, I like living in someone else's shadow but if Adrian had it in his power to choose, he'd want to be famous."

"He just needs to be the best Adrian he can be. No one needs to be more than that."

"True."

White Eagle still hadn't returned so I checked up front to see what needed to be done. Max had me clean the outside windows and sweep the shop, and then he sent me to the back to finish a repair on a dresser that had come in. It needed a new drawer glide and one handle had been pulled off. Adrian left Amy in my care while he took a shower in preparation for our date. Marlo was back to bookkeeping, having already showered. From what I overheard, Marlo was working on the quarterly taxes. He may be a computer genius but I'm glad that I'm not him.

Amy watched me work and asked questions about what I was doing. I told her that not everything came into the shop in perfect working order and that we fixed what we could. One of the first things White Eagle had taught me was woodworking. He had to when I got angry and damaged a kitchen cabinet last year. Anyway it was a useful skill. I measured and cut a new glide. I drilled pilot holes and screwed it into place. Then I glued a peg into the oversized hole left by the ripped out drawer pull. Later I would sand and redrill it to replace the handle. I looked at my watch. With no White Eagle to give me a ride I would need to run home now so that I would have time to get ready for my date.

"Owen, you're amazing. How come you don't take shop?" Amy asked.

"I really enjoy choir so I take music as my elective."

"Is there anything you can't do?"

"You were supposed to make me look good," he half whined, half snarled in a low voice.

"Aid, you do look good. The back handspring was fantastic. Now quit trying to show off and you'll look even better." I whispered as I looked him hard in the eye trying to communicate with him. He thought a moment and nodded - then held his gloved hands up for me to smack and we started again.

This time it was clean. Adrian fell into our normal routine. He was good but he didn't put in the hours I did and I'd practiced with him so often that I knew what he was going to do. He very rarely surprised me. Marlo came into the back and pulled up a stool next to Amy. I could tell that they were whispering but I couldn't tell what they were saying. Marlo finally came to the edge of the mat and waited. Adrian and I stepped apart. Marlo stepped in and Adrian went to talk to Amy. Marlo was not gloved so I threw my own gloves to the side. Marlo preferred karate. As I sparred with him, I watched Adrian glove Amy and take her to the heavy bag. She didn't seem to mind Adrian being all sweaty. He worked on her stance and form. He showed her how to throw a punch. I didn't know how much she was actually learning but she seemed to be having a good time.

After a half hour when Marlo was slowing down and looking sufficiently sweaty, we stopped. Marlo helped me unload the dryer and fold the towels.

"What's up with Adrian?" I whispered. Though I probably didn't need to bother because he was deep in conversation with Amy.

"He's bugged because we are in Biology and he didn't make the cut. As much as he likes Amy, you are taking out a junior tonight and well... it started last year, but everything you touch seems to turn to gold in his eyes. Whatever you try anymore, you seem to be instantly good at and it feels unfair to him."

"It has to do with my gift, I can't help it. I also absorbed twelve years of Miles' memories. It changed me."

I saw movement out of the corner of my eye. Dang, Adrian. I saw his body go rigid – he was gonna flip a biscuit. Time for me to beat feet.

"There is plenty, believe me. I gotta go. I'll see you guys later." I knew Amy didn't mean anything by what she said, but it would be salt in Adrian's wounds. I went up front to tell Max and Marlo goodbye, then hustled to the back to find Adrian and Amy just ending an argument. He grabbed her somewhat roughly and dragged her in for quite the clinch. I tried to ignore them as I ditched the flip flops, collected my gear and put back on my still damp shoes. Adrian and Amy were paying no attention to me and I resisted the urge to tell them to get a room. I snuck out the back and ran for home. The rain had stopped but it was still overcast and gloomy. My thoughts turned to Tess as I ran. I wondered what this date would hold for me. I didn't think my track record was too good with women. I thought of Katie from last year who had surprised me with her aggressiveness. I'd only seen her a couple of times this year. She had a new boyfriend and seemed happy. Many girls fell into the friend category. Lucie was a conundrum. I didn't know what to make of her. She and I were rarely on the same page anymore. The strange pull I felt for her was still there, just muted some. I would at least like to be her friend. Then there was Tess. Could a junior actually like me? She was bold, funny, smart and confident. What on earth did she see in me?

I walked the last two blocks to my house to cool down and noted White Eagle's truck was in Sarah's driveway. I checked my watch – it was just after five. I needed to hurry. I saw that our lawn had been cut. It probably shouldn't have been cut when it was wet. I couldn't decide whether I felt more relieved or guilty.

Dad and Lucas were watching TV. I headed to the kitchen, calling a greeting on the way past.

"How was work?" Dad asked.

"Okay. I was working on refurbishing a dresser."

"Oh, so that's why you look like that. That doesn't look like good work attire."

"I was in the back almost all day. I did wash the window up front but that was about it. I didn't help any customers today, don't worry."

He still seemed nearly normal and Lucas looked just fine. Huh. Mom and Alex were assembling a meatloaf when I hit the kitchen.

"Tess will be here at six to pick me up so I need to hurry," I said by way of greeting.

"You have a girl who *drives* picking you up? *Hot!*" Alex said with relish.

"Alex, honestly," my mom said, trying and failing to avoid laughter.

"How old is this girl?" she asked when she got herself back under control.

"She's a junior. She's in my Biology class."

Mom gave me a look. I threw up my hands and headed for the shower. I tried to restyle my hair like it had been for my début as a special agent. Part of me wished I had the suit. I buttoned up the dark green shirt I had planned on wearing and debated the pants. I went for the jeans that Adrian claimed were 'da bomb'. I put on my brown leather belt and laced up my boots. I stood staring into the mirror. Shirt in or out?

I heard the doorbell and Beggar bark. I left the shirt untucked. I was out of time. I hit about one out of every four steps on the way down, leaping the last half of the lower staircase as Alex opened the front door. Tess had seen me through the glass by the front door and laughed.

"Hey Spiderman, ready to go?" she asked, still giggling.

"Hello, I'm Alex."

"Well, hello there, Alex. I'm Tess. How are you doing today?" She turned her full wattage smile on him.

"Fine," he blushed. "You have real interesting eyes."

"Alex," Mom said, exasperated, as she came into the entryway – then she smiled at Tess and held out her hand. "Hello, Tess, I'm Lila, Owen's mom."

"Nice to meet you," Tess replied with a smile, extending her hand.

"Over there is Owen's dad and his youngest brother, Lucas." Mom said by way of introduction. Dad smiled and Lucas waved.

"Let's go," I suggested taking Tess' arm. "See you around ten, Mom."

"It may be closer to eleven. I think it's a later showing," Tess replied, giving me a look.

"Ah..." I said stupidly.

"If you're going to be later than eleven thirty call - at midnight you are grounded," Dad said from the couch without looking up.

"Don't worry Mr. Ryer, I'll have him home safe and sound by no later than eleven thirty," Tess answered smoothly. She put a hand over the one I had on her arm and hauled me out the door.

As soon as the door closed behind us, Tess leaned over and whispered. "You are adorable when you are taken by surprise. You look... delicious by the way and you smell... mmm... fantastic." I froze on the front walk with a vision of octopus Katie at the movies last year swimming before my eyes.

"Oh come on, seriously, I don't bite," she said, looking frustrated.

I swear I heard the word 'much' under her breath. Tess drove a snappy lime green Beatle. Of course. I got in the passenger side and buckled up with as much dignity as I could salvage.

Before starting the car Tess turned to me. "I was trying to pay you a compliment. You look good and you smell better than you look. Is that tamer for you?"

"I'm sorry, Tess. You, um, surprised me. You look very nice, by the way." She had kept her makeup simple, just mascara as far as I could tell. Her ears were double pierced with a small diamond higher and little silver hoops in the lower hole. She wore black form fitting pants tucked into gray boots. She had a gray suit-cut jacket over an emerald green blouse that had some ruffle to it. Tess unbuttoned her jacket with a laugh, buckled her seatbelt and started the car. I was trying to figure out why she was laughing.

As she turned her body to back out, I gulped, realizing why she was laughing. With the jacket buttoned she was very conservative – now, not so much. I couldn't help myself, my eyes were drawn right to that place where males are not supposed to look. Women dress like that and then they want you to look at their faces – seriously, we're *only* human. Her shirt was deeply, and I mean deeply, cut in front. I think the first button started at just below her bra line.

"Owen?"

"Yeah?" I asked, snapping my eyes back up where they belonged.

"You like?"

"Um, that sounds like a dangerous question that I'm better off not answering."

Tess burst out laughing. "It's not as bad as you think. I'll show you when we get to the mall. What are we seeing by the way?"

My mind malfunctioned. "Uh..." What did she ask? I swear I heard an audible click in my head as my brain restarted. "I have no idea. This is Adrian's show."

"You know, it's okay if it is about *you* sometimes. You're an interesting mix. I find you fascinating. You're humble, yet it seems like you would have every reason to be a stuck-up snob. People want to be around you but you don't encourage it. You're friendly but you don't reach out. You like to hang where you're comfortable. You can handle yourself but you don't seek out trouble. I look forward to completely figuring you out."

"Ah, thanks? You're right, I don't like the spotlight. I like to just be, but I won't take garbage off people. I don't like it when other people get picked on either."

"I figured that about you. You seem like the loyal type. That girl from the beginning of the dance - she broke up with you, didn't she?"

"Sort of. We were the best of friends last year and now she won't talk to me. I kind of forced her to tell me why yesterday."

"I think she still likes you but... I don't know. Why do people have to make things so complicated? People need to learn to relax, take things as they come and have a little fun."

"Tell me about you. You seem to have me figured out and you met my family."

"I'm no great mystery. It's just me, my mom and my sister. My sister goes to Portland State. She wants to be a teacher which I think is really dumb in this economy but it's her life. My mom's a nurse. I play basketball in winter and do track and field in the spring but my real passion is photography. There I am in a nutshell."

"Tess, I don't think anyone could ever fit you into a nutshell. You are bigger than life."

"Nah, I just seem that way. I'm insecure, like everybody else, on the inside."

"What would a beautiful, outgoing girl like you have to be insecure about?"

"I guess you'll have to wait and see. I can't tell you all my secrets on the first date, right?"

"Yah, okay, Tess," I said with a laugh.

"There, now see? You're loosened up. That's the Owen I like."

We pulled into the mall and found a place to park. As we got out, Tess called me over to her side of the car. I came around and got a full view of her. She was stunning. Her blouse was not quite as low cut as I first thought. The fabric was sheer, I could see right through it to the black halter top she had on underneath. She held her arms straight out from her sides and her jacket flipped over one arm. She turned a slow pirouette.

"What do you think?"

"Stunning and fantastic come to mind."

"There you go! Let's go have some fun. Where do we meet your buddies?"

"At the food court."

"You're such an interesting mix of grown up and shy. Very cute," she said as she reached up to gently pinch my cheek.

I had to laugh – she was so bold and so in control. "Are you afraid of anything?"

"Plenty. I'm just not afraid of you. Should I be?"

"I hope not," I said appalled by the thought.

"May I hold your hand?" she asked smiling with a twinkle in her eye.

"I'm surprised you asked."

"Look Owen," she said pulling me to a stop just outside the food court entrance, "I like you. I won't deny it. There is something about you that pulls me right in. I would happily crawl right up you and... well, never mind. I don't want to freak you out or scare you away. I'll let you take the lead for awhile. It was a good kiss yesterday. Don't wait too long to do it again."

I was at a total loss. She was bold and unafraid. She knew what she wanted and she wasn't afraid to ask for it. She took a step toward the entrance but I stood frozen.

"Tess." She stopped and turned. I flipped my hands out to my sides, palms facing her. "I..." She stepped back to me, right up to my toes. "I don't know what to say. I like you too." I looked down into her beautiful eyes. They almost had hints of green in them today. I leaned toward her just a bit without touching her. She put a hand on either side of my waist and rose up to kiss my... cheek. Hey wait a minute. She laughed and grabbed my hand.

"Come on, let's go find your friends. I'm starving. Let's see if we can get them to go to the Mexican place outside the mall. They're fast. We'll have time and the food is good."

We were the first ones there but we didn't have to wait long. Tess kept up a happy conversation that flowed easily. Everyone liked her and thought she was funny. She made them all feel comfortable. Adrian was reluctant to have Mexican food but he was out-voted. Tess finally won him over with the promise of some peppermint gum she had in her purse.

Tess and I argued over who would pay for her dinner. I reminded her that she drove so it was only fair. She said she worked as a waitress so she had money. I reminded her that I also had a job. I finally won by reminding her that I had asked her out. She relented, laughing. Everyone else laughed at me too. Notice I did not say with me.

Marlo was a perfect gentleman but Adrian had to be slugged by Amy before he remembered where his eyes were supposed to be when he talked to Tess. Tess got quite a few looks I noticed. I bristled a bit when some schmuck whistled at her. Tess took a firmer hold on my hand, looked right at the guy and planted a big kiss right on me. Then she whispered in my ear.

"Remember, I dressed for *you* and not anybody else. Don't let them get to you. I would hate to have to beat someone up defending your honor," she said with confidence.

Now *that* made me laugh.

"Woo hoo," Adrian said, as the kiss ended, laughing also, "way to show that guy who the boss is."

Tess turned and gave Adrian her hundred watt smile. "It really bothers me when guys whistle at other guys like that – it can be so intimidating."

Now we were all laughing and Tess' admirer scowled at us and wandered away to bother someone who was more willing, no doubt. Tess kept holding my hand as we made our way back to the theater. We were there by quarter to seven. We had two movies to choose between. The group decided on the action adventure flick. Yes! It was one I really wanted to see. Tess even let me buy her ticket without an argument. She was still holding my hand and swinging it back and forth between us. Nice. She insisted on popcorn and a soda for us to share. I caved and let her pay for that one. Besides my funds were running dangerously low.

We sat in the seats where the arms raise. Of course Adrian gravitates to those. Tess plopped the armrest down between us and put the soda in the cup holder. "Don't worry," she whispered, leaning in close as I was sitting down, "I still like you." And she closed the distance and kissed me on the tip of my nose, smiled at my reaction, then sat in her seat. "Popcorn?" she offered as she landed.

All I could do was smile and shake my head. She was having fun teasing me, there was no doubt. She was such an unexpected mix – she acted like she had known me for years instead of weeks. I even got to watch most of the movie. She let me watch it. She did not try to touch me or hold my hand. She kept the armrest down. I cut my eyes to her now and then – when I did she smiled at me, then turned back to the movie.

I had ended up on the end. Tess sat between me and Michalia, leaving Marlo to deal with Adrian. Amy seemed to be doing a great job of keeping his attention on the movie, though he did spend a fair amount of time nuzzling her neck.

After the show we walked them out to where Amy's mom was running her taxi service. It felt strange to not be going with the gang. We waved them off and I expected to be heading home too.

"Let's walk a lap around the mall. We've got time and then we can talk and burn off some calories," Tess suggested. She faced me to put on her jacket and my eyes were drawn again to where they weren't supposed to be. I shook my head and reminded myself to be good. Then I took her hand and we started walking. Tess said nothing about my lapse.

"Are you going to follow your sister to PSU?"

"Maybe. I might go to community college for a year first. I don't know what I want to do. I just know I want to do something I love so that it doesn't feel like work. I don't ever want to be so busy chasing a dollar that I forget to live."

"Nicely said," I told her as I smiled down at her.

"How about you?"

"Until a year ago, my great aspiration was to work at the skate shop and get my gear at a discount."

Tess stopped walking and looked at me, startled.

"Kidding! I used to love to skateboard, but I knew it wasn't a career, at least for me. I wanted to work with animals but now I think that I'm meant for some kind of law enforcement. My neighbor works for the FBI and that seems interesting."

"With that big vocabulary of yours I knew you were more than a skater dude. I had you pegged as an astrophysicist," she joked.

"Nah, my mom's a teacher and my dad's a chemical engineer."

"I'm so sorry about the teacher crack earlier."

"No worries, Tess. What you said is true. It's tough to be a new teacher now."

We had made almost a complete loop around the outside of the mall. I was sad that our time together was coming to an end.

"Owen, I like you. I had a good time. I'd like to see you again outside of school."

"I'd like that too, Tess," I said turning to face her. "May I kiss you?"

"I hoped you would," she said stepping into my arms. Lady Antebellum's *Just a Kiss* replayed in my head. This time we really were standing in the moonlight.

"Did I tell you that you smell good too?" I whispered against her lips. I could feel her smile before she kissed me again.

It was nice to kiss someone who wanted to be kissed - someone who wasn't crying, trying to run away or mug me. I could feel hormones running through me, making my chest feel light and electric. She really did have zing.

"Time to go," she said putting a hand flat on my chest between us.

I put my hand over hers. "Okay, Tess."

We walked back to her car hand in hand. "I'm actually looking forward to school tomorrow," she said with a wicked smile.

"Oh yeah?"

"Sure, we have Biology." She did know how to make me smile.

SEVEN

The rest of September and into October became a routine. Tess was my new favorite hobby. I spent time with her whenever I could. She came to every game when she could get off work. We both had an 'A' in Biology. Waiting for information on Willie, my dad and my grandfather was horrible but Tess kept my mind occupied. Lucie was staying far away from me. Not even Marlo could figure out what was going on with her. Jesus still wasn't talking about what was bugging him. When I tried sneaking a peek at his life by touching his stuff I wasn't getting much. Just a few snatches of guys giving him lip and talking smack to him. I caught one ugly glimpse of his sister's old boyfriend. It looked like he might be trying to sell drugs near campus. Him, I would watch for. Adrian's social network was hot on it too, but mostly we were getting rumors and innuendo. All I could do so far was remind Jesus that I was here for him.

White Eagle and Evelyn were able to get the screwdriver admitted as evidence somehow. White Eagle claimed that he found it concealed in the seat of the motorcycle he had purchased at auction. The fingerprints were Willie's - the blood was Trevor's. With his body still missing there was little anyone could do yet. They were working on a warrant to go through Willie's stuff without hurting his sister. Marlo and Sarah were busy trying to track down the cabin on Mt. Hood. There are many, in case you're wondering. Marlo had posted a big topographical map in the back room of the shop and we were hoping to start exploring.

The highlight of September was my birthday on the 26th. All my buddies gave me grief at school. It was not a Biology day but Tess found me anyway as she often did. Lucie was even pleasant to me. She gave me a hug and wished me well. She looked like she wanted to say more but turned and fled as she often did in my presence. My family went out to dinner at my favorite steak house and Mom invited Tess. Dad was still gone. He had spent a whole week with us during which we had gotten him, more or less, back to normal. Mom even got him to cut down on his pills which I think helped. I was right about the pills too. They were a new chemical cocktail variation of the first ones he had. Each time he came home I would try to snatch one to have it analyzed.

Mom authorized me to miss school to take my learner's permit test. We decided to do it during choir so that I would miss as little of the meat of my education as possible. We took all the paperwork we needed and ponied up our five dollars to take the test. I passed. What a relief. I did feel a little silly being chauffeured around by my girlfriend. I was an idol to my guy friends for dating a junior though.

Since Tess could drive I got to experience a whole new kind of dating. Almost every weekend we would try a new restaurant. For someone so fit, I was happily surprised to find that she was quite the foodie. Photography was not her only passion. She liked to cook and she loved to eat! I had no idea so many different kinds of foods even existed. She was courageous and bold as always – even in her choice of cuisine. Her goal was to try food from every nationality. To balance the food, Tess ran. We started running together on Sundays. That girl could kick my ass and I'd been in cross country. Nobody could run like Tess. She was bringing me to a new level. We were at five miles and she was working toward seven.

Halloween was fast approaching. One of the varsity receivers was injured and required knee surgery after a nasty tackle. I was moving up and I wasn't thrilled. It made Adrian even crankier with me than usual. He was back to cheap shots at our Saturday practices and his tongue had gotten pretty sharp too. I tried to be supportive but didn't take any crap either. I did find that he was better behaved when Amy was at the shop so I encouraged that even though it made it difficult to work. Dad was due back in town this week and I wondered how that was going to pan out. His excuse was that he wanted to be home for conferences. My grades were fine so I wasn't worried.

On the next to the last Saturday in October, White Eagle and I were working on the bike and I dumped cleaning solvent all over my shirt. It had rained on the way over again so those clothes were already in the washer. I felt disgusted with myself but White Eagle just laughed. I pulled off my shirt and threw it in the laundry sink with a swish of car soap and lots of water. I was agitating the water when I was startled by a voice behind me that I had not heard in the shop before… Tess.

Oh geez, not now, I thought. "Oh my goodness Owen, what did you do to yourself?" she asked alarmed. I looked down at the pink blooming on my skin from the chemicals.

I quickly grabbed a towel from the shelf, ran water on it and began dabbing at my chest and abs. "What is it?" Tess asked White Eagle who was completely unconcerned.

"Solvent. He'll live and then he'll remember to be more careful next time," White Eagle said with a smile to soften his words.

"Here, let me!" Tess said slapping my hands out of the way. "You have it on your pants too. Do you have any more clothes here?" she asked, reaching for the snap on my pants.

"Hey, I've got this. I'm fine." I said, backing into the utility sink.

"You need to get that stuff off your skin before you blister," she said, reaching for my zipper.

"Tess, I'll handle it. You're not undressing me in public." I froze and fortunately so did she. "That came out wrong," I said, flushing scarlet.

White Eagle looked up and then went right back to work. She looked at my face and her hand fell away from the front of my pants. Thank goodness.

"Sorry."

"I'll just, um... bathroom," I nearly stuttered, sliding past her and into the bathroom where I could evaluate my damaged skin in peace. I could hear White Eagle murmuring so I moved closer to the not quite closed door.

"You know, my dear, he is only fifteen. He may be an exceptional fifteen but still only fifteen. You might want to take it easy on him."

"I only wanted to help. Do you have any hydrocortisone or something? My mom's a nurse. I'm no nurse but I know what I'm doing."

"I truly believe that you know what you are doing. Just remember he is a sweet boy. Try not to damage him. I have the cream and a pair of sweats you can give him."

Great! Now I had White Eagle being my nursemaid. I could handle Tess. Right? I stripped off my jeans. My boxers were unharmed. One of my thighs was turning pink and my abs had taken a beating but I didn't look too bad.

Tess knocked on the door. "Did you flush the affected skin with water?"

"Yes."

"You ready for hydrocortisone and dry pants?"

"Yah."

I thought she would hand it in. Instead she opened the door. She had on a nurse's professional manner but she didn't hide the look in her eyes. She tucked the sweats under her arm and opened the tube and squirted some cream onto her fingers.

"I really think I should do that," I said in a partially strangled voice.

"Sit and quit being a baby. I've seen less clothes on guys at the pool."

I bit my tongue – hard and kept biting until I tasted blood. She was quick and efficient but she still looked me over... a lot, as she smeared me with hydrocortisone.

"Nice boxers" she said, causing me to flush again. "Okay, tell me about this scar," she said, changing tactics as she pointed at my arm.

"I told you it's nothing."

"How about this one?" she asked running her fingers through my hair at the hair line. "Or this one?" she added as she ran her hand over the back of my head. "Or this one?" she said as she ran her fingers along the edge of my chin and looking into my eyes.

"Stuff happens."

"Why won't you tell me? I don't believe for a moment you're accident prone. Today was an exception, I'm sure. I've watched you move. You're... graceful... like a jungle cat, not a ballerina," she said with a laugh. "I really came today to watch you work out. I even brought my gear in case I could get you to spar with me. I thought I'd surprise you."

"Well you certainly did that." I said, snatching the sweats from under her arm. "Sure, I'll spar with you. I'm done with the bike for today."

"Is the bike for you or for White Eagle?"

"Both I guess."

"Wow. Your stock will go up with all the girls."

I started stuffing my feet into the sweats. "Yeah, right, look at me, I'm a mess."

"Yeah, you're a mess alright. You don't even see it, do you? You've got humble down. I just wish you would confide in me."

"I try," I said, wishing I could tell her but knowing I couldn't. "I guess you'll have to take what I'm willing to give," I said, trying to send her a double meaning.

Instead she shoved me out of the bathroom so she could change.

"She's a hot tamale, alright but be true to yourself," White Eagle said with great sincerity.

"Thanks Mother, I've got it handled."

"Sure you do."

I tied the sweats that were hanging from my hips. I put my shoes back on and got out some practice gear. Tess came out of the bathroom dressed like she often did to run. Sometimes she wore shorts but as the weather had cooled, she had shifted to ankle length running pants. She often wore a fitted workout top and had added a jacket when the weather called for it. On rainy days she wore a ball cap. Today she had opted for either two overlapping sports bras in aqua and violet or one was a crop top. I had no idea. I just knew that she showed off lots of tanned abs. She was tough to run with – I wondered what she had in store for me today.

"Well, what did you have in mind?" I asked. It was her show, she was the surprise visitor.

"I've done some boxing and kickboxing but I've never worked with a live person. What do you know how to do?"

"White Eagle has taught me boxing, wrestling..." Tess' eyes lit up but I ignored her and moved on, "karate, some kung fu, aikido, hapkido and other miscellaneous forms of fighting that we refer to as street fighting."

"Do you have any belts?"

"I haven't taken the time to compete or to focus on one style."

"How about if we start with boxing? Maybe you can teach me some other stuff later."

"Okay, let's get you gloved up and I have a helmet for you."

"No helmet. Anything you damage you have to kiss and make better."

"Tess," I hissed, flipping my head at White Eagle. His back was to me but I saw his shoulders shaking.

"I've got it handled, Mother," he murmured.

"What did he say?"

"Nothing. Okay, Tess. Let's see what you've got. Try to hit me and I'll block you."

Try nothing - she was tough. She really had been to boxing classes. I could tell by the way she moved she was used to working with a bag and not a person. My blocking threw her off at first but she quickly got the hang of it and got a couple of good hits in on me. I was reluctant to hit her back.

"Come on Owen, don't be a girl, try to hit me. I can take it."

Maybe that is what I was afraid of. I came at her a few times but held back and made my punches soft. As she got better at blocking I got a little more aggressive with her.

"Can I try some kick boxing now?" she asked, barely panting.

"Sure, why not. Just no head shots."

Her side kicks looked pretty good. She even landed a good one that left a foot print right over my belly button. Her front and back kicks needed a little work. I guess that working in a kickboxing class is different than the real thing. I called a halt and took her to the bag where I worked on her form some. She was looking really good when Adrian showed up.

"You got anything left for me?"

"Sure," I answered.

"I'll take a break and watch," Tess offered. I tossed her a water from the fridge which she caught neatly. "Thanks, I had fun. Let's do it again sometime."

"Don't hold back," Adrian said to me, "I'm feeling like a good fight today."

Adrian wasn't kidding. He was pretty vicious. I had to really pay attention. He came at me fast and hard, using every type of mixed martial arts we'd ever learned and some we hadn't. White Eagle soon stopped his work and leaned on the counter near Tess. With a small part of my attention I hear him say, "Now that is what you came to see. Fun to watch, aren't they? Now Marlo has a completely different style. I encourage them to do what they feel comfortable doing. It was good for him to work with you today and see another style. It's smart to keep him guessing and thinking."

Sweat was running down my face and dripping in my eyes. Adrian was still going strong but I'd had a head start on him. I felt like he was taking out everything that had made him mad at any point in his life on me. I wondered if White Eagle would call him off but then he needed me to be my best so this was probably yet another test. I knew that in the end it all made me better. Maybe Adrian would finally get out of his system whatever had been bugging him this year. Back and forth across the mat we went. I finally tricked Adrian and knocked him flat on his back. I stood over him bent at the waist, sweating and panting. Adrian snaked out a leg and knocked me down too. White Eagle whistled a stop. Adrian and I just lay there gasping.

Tess must have taken a turn in the shower. I was glad I'd cleaned it this morning. She came and stood over us, looking down, and then busted up laughing. "You two bring a whole new meaning to wearing yourself out." As if to emphasize her point the dryer dinged, signaling the end of the load I had noticed Tess put in for me while I was sparing with Adrian.

I rolled my head to the side. It was all I had the energy for. "You still mad at me, Adrian?"

"I was never mad at you, Dude. Life just feels unfair sometimes. Some really good stuff has been happening to you and I wanted some of that. I just have to remember that my life is more… normal than yours. You get the really bad crap to balance out the good." Adrian looked at Tess seeming to realize his mistake.

"I knew it! What's his deal, Adrian? I know about the 'accident' at the mall last year. I also heard about him taking on a burglar in the neighborhood. There are rumors about a bully at the middle school and a pedophile, too. I know you are asking questions about the drug dealer that hangs around school and the gang rumors. These are your scar stories. This is why you fight, isn't it. You are teenaged vigilantes! I want in."

White Eagle, Adrian and I all gaped at her, speechless. Too bad it didn't make You Tube. I bet Adrian and I, collapsed on the floor head to chest with our feet in opposite directions and our mouths agape, looked really great. And this is why I'd told Adrian a million times that having a girlfriend was a bad idea. *Epic*ally bad! Now what?

"Well?" she said, and actually stamped her foot. Stamped her foot – I couldn't believe it. It made me laugh. And I couldn't stop.

"Owen Ryer! You will not laugh at me. I would be an asset to your team!"

I rolled onto my side and then onto my hands and knees. I tried to regain control. I was laughing so hard my eyes were watering. "I... I'm... NO.. NNOT... laughing... at... you." I fought for a deep breath and stood up. "I'm not a vigilante, Tess. I've been in the wrong place at the wrong time."

"Hogwash."

I busted up all over again. 'Hogwash?' Who says that? "Fine Tess, we don't like injustice but you really don't want to be involved in this. It's dangerous."

"We're kind of a guys only club, Tess," Adrian tried. He had risen up to his elbows so he wasn't his most convincing.

"I'm telling you I can help. I know about the drug dealer," Tess insisted.

I looked at White Eagle. He looked at her closely with his other sight and shook his head. No gift. Too bad. I had a flash of insight.

"Give us a sec, would you Tess?"

At her nod, I pulled the guys aside. "I can't tell her who I am, but maybe she could help with this. Then she will see that it's dangerous and lose interest."

"She might also learn even more about you," White Eagle cautioned.

"Then I will have to be really careful. If she is with us, she will know she needs to keep it a secret and we can keep her safe because we'll know where she is. We'll have to hide a bunch of what Marlo does though. No one else should know about that. It would be dangerous for him."

"I agree and I get the next shower," Adrian said, not even waiting for White Eagle's answer. Which was a grudging 'okay'.

"Okay Tess," I said, turning to her, "you can help with the drug dealer."

"Great. Now tell me why you have the topographical map of Mt. Hood all marked up." Geez, she was way too smart for her own good.

"We like to go camping and hiking," I said, hating to lie to her but not having a choice. "We are planning next summer's adventures."

"Fine, don't tell me. One mission at a time, right?"

"Yeah, one mission at a time," I said, resigned.

"You need a cool shower so you don't aggravate your skin anymore. Afterwards you should put on more hydrocortisone. You do look better. Maybe you sweated the chemicals out."

"I hope so." I wasn't sure I could handle any more of her nursing or the next cold shower wouldn't be for my skin.

"Are we still on for Thai food tonight?" she questioned.

"Sure."

"Are you about done here for today? Can I kidnap you now?"

"I could be done. I ran here and I was planning on running home so I don't have any nice clothes here. I need to go home before Thai food."

"I'm clean now, so I don't want to run and my car is here anyway so I'll drive you. I could help with the hydrocortisone."

"Thanks, but I'll handle it this time. Let me get my stuff together and jump in the shower and we can go."

I gathered all my stuff and was almost done folding towels when Adrian came out of the bathroom. I hurried on in and took the cool shower Tess had suggested. Good thing too because Adrian had used almost all the hot water. My skin did look better but it was a bit pink yet. I didn't seem to have any blisters, so far any. I put on the clothes I had run over in and stuck my dirty ones in the washer with my damaged shirt and jeans.

"White Eagle, would you mind putting this stuff in the dryer? I can fold it next time but I hate to take it home to wash with solvent on it. I think I'll leave them here as an extra set of clothes. That will guarantee me not to have any more accidents."

"Sure, I'll dry the load. Don't start the washer yet though, I have some rags and stuff to throw in," he said, then paused and turned to Tess. "You remember what I said about the other and be sure to tell Owen what you told us about our new friend Skimmer. I'll fill Marlo in. I look forward to seeing you again."

"I hear you," Tess said seriously to White Eagle.

We loaded up in Tess' car but she just sat there.

"Tess?" Still she sat.

"Tess what is it?" I asked, concerned. I reached out and tucked her still damp hair behind her ear – then I touched her cheek with the back of my fingers. We were a study in contrasts this afternoon. I wore a t-shirt with the sleeves cut off and some raggedy shorts. Tess looked amazing as usual. Today she wore a denim mini skirt, wedge sandals and a soft knit top that clung in all the right places.

Finally she turned in her seat. Her eyes were luminous and damp. "I'm so sorry! I forget. Most of the time you act so... old, so I forget that you're a freshman. You don't look like a freshman and you really didn't look like a freshman when I walked into the back room of the shop today. Max told me to go on back – that you were working on the bike. I wasn't expecting... I don't want to hurt you. Sometimes I look at you and ... want things I can't have."

She looked so sad. "Tess," I started, my hand was still by her cheek. I opened my hand and slid it through her hair to cradle her head. "I like you a lot. You're fun to be with and we like many of the same things. I like to run with you because you challenge me and I especially like that you eat real food. We have found several fun and new restaurants. I do love to kiss you but I can't see past high school right now. I don't know where I want to go to college or where I'll even be in five years, let alone ten. I can't make the kind of commitment to you I think you want."

"Maybe I'm not looking for commitment – remember I'm all about *fun*," she said softly.

"Tess, I'm not that kind of guy."

"Are you seriously going to wait until you get married?"

"I don't know, but I know now's not the time. If you can live with that – I'd like for you to stick around. There isn't anyone I'd rather spend time with."

"You know, what White Eagle said about you is true. You are a sweet boy. Probably too sweet for me, but I'm not ready to give you up yet," she whispered. She wiped at a lone tear and turned her face completely toward mine. She moved very slowly to the center of the small space inside her car. Her eyes never left mine as she moved in even closer. I leaned toward her. Her lips moved slowly over mine. She sighed and her eyes drifted closed. She leaned in closer yet and kissed along my jaw. She worked her way down the side of my neck and inhaled deeply the scent of my skin. When she felt me shudder she moved away. I looked at her. I wanted to tell her not to stop but I said nothing.

"Maybe we'd better talk about Skimmer," she stated as she turned over the ignition.

"Who?... Oh, yeah, the drug dealer."

She laughed, "Well, at least I know I get to you as much as you get to me."

"Tess, you get to me plenty. You make me exercise my willpower often but I know it's the right decision."

"I know what it is about you – it's the look you give me. You have a look that smolders," Tess said, twinkling at me.

"I don't smolder. I just look," I said with disgust. "*Smolder* – geez – honestly."

"Oh no, Bucko, you smolder. That's why the women follow you around. Next time Kirk bugs me about slummin' it with you, I'll tell him I couldn't resist the smolder."

"Super, Tess, that will make my stock go way up with him. He already hates me."

"Kirk doesn't hate you. He's jealous. You're adorable and he is... well, a big, dumb jock just doesn't seem to cover it, but I should play nice. He is my friend."

"You know that I'll be sitting on the varsity bench on Friday. Kirk hates that. I know it's only because Doug needs surgery and will be out the rest of the year. I'm back up, period, but if I do make it onto the field, guess who gets to protect me? Yep, your buddy Kirk."

"You deserve to be there, you have talent. Kirk respects talent. He doesn't hate you. In fact he asked me to invite you to his house for Halloween. He's having a party. Don't look at me that way... Please say you'll come."

"Okay, Tess. Now tell me about Skimmer."

"We can talk more at dinner but I have mostly rumors. I haven't met the guy. I figure we need to put out feelers and either try to meet him or find someone who knows and uses him, who is willing to talk. Mostly I hear that he's a graduate and he's doing some recruiting at the high school. He's making the activity look like 'gang' as the cover. Their real goal is selling drugs for money. Personally I think they're targeting the wrong audience if they want to make real money. Students around here don't have a lot."

"I don't think it's about how much they can make right now. I think they're looking ahead and building a business plan. If Skimmer recruits and gets more people selling, it will have a trickle-down effect. As his recruits graduate, they will go on to other places and start again, but still feed Skimmer. It's genius," I exclaimed, both hating and admiring him in that moment.

"You really don't think like a kid – you know that."

What could I say to that? When we got to my house I left Tess visiting with my mom in the kitchen and I ran up to change my clothes. I put on Tess' favorite shirt, a black button up, my black slacks and black shoes. I tucked in my shirt and finished with a belt. I knew that it made me look older and we had found that we got better treatment at restaurants when the staff mistook us for college age students instead of high schoolers. I looked at my sadly dwindling pile of cash. Between our dinner dates and bike parts, my funds were stretched. I needed to be putting money away for college, Christmas, birthdays, gas money, and car insurance but... Well, what can I say? Tess is fun and our restaurant forays had been gastronomically educational.

I rounded the corner into the kitchen and was verbally pounced on by my mother. "I guess you can go to the Halloween party next Saturday, but be sure you are home by midnight. You don't need to be running around later than that. You be sure that you open all your own drinks, be careful of what you eat and absolutely no alcohol." She gave me a firm, steady look. I had the feeling that the lecture was not just for my benefit.

"Okay, Mom," I said, deciding that less said was wiser.

"So, Thai food tonight. You two have fun. Don't stay out too late."

"Love you, Mom. Don't worry so much."

She had that mother look going again. Something was on her mind. For all I knew she was aware of what Tess and I had talked about. That was a conversation I *so* did not want to have with her. And please don't let her be reading my mind.

Dinner was fantastic. Tess really knows how to order. She loved food so much that she actually did research and watched the Food Channel. It kinda makes me laugh but I do enjoy her efforts. She can tell me about almost any dish from any culture. If I ever travel the world, I'll be set!

She didn't have a lot to add about Skimmer. White Eagle told Tess that he would have Marlo begin some computer research. We needed to know who this guy really was and what he was up to. Adrian would try to jazz up the social network that he had going, to get the latest buzz on the guy. We needed to know who was buying, where they were buying and when they were buying. Tess said that she would try to put her feelers out too. I warned her to be very careful. We didn't know how dangerous this guy was. I was half afraid that she was not taking me too seriously.

After dinner Tess wanted to see a movie. I had to tell her that as much as I would like to go, I didn't have enough cash left on me. No problem, this one was on her. Since our first date we had mostly each paid for our own. Tess was glad to have someone who was willing to try her crazy food ideas and she worked more hours than I did right now so she didn't need to worry about money so much.

Tess walked to her car with her arm around my waist and into the theater the same way. This time Tess sat with the arm rest up. She picked up my arm and put it around her shoulders. She kept ahold of my fingers. She was more interested in playing with them than she was in watching the movie. She seemed to be deep in thought.

"What?" I whispered in her ear.

"I'm trying to do what you asked. You look really good, you smell even better and you're warm. I'm trying to… behave myself."

"Tess."

"Sometimes it's very easy to be your friend and sometimes it's not," she said, forcing herself to look at the screen once again. She quit playing with my fingers and released my hand. She put her nearest hand on my leg just above my knee and left it there. After a few minutes she turned from the screen and watched me.

I turned and looked at her with my eyebrows raised in silent question. She moved closer so that her forehead rested against my neck. She was done watching the movie. "Do you want to go?" I whispered. She just shook her head and stayed where she was. I rested my jaw on the top of her head. She moved her hand from my knee to behind my lower back and rested her other hand on my chest. There was no way she could see the movie but she didn't seem inclined to move either. What was I going to do with her? Was she listening to me? Would she press me more? Was she giving up on me and preparing to move on?

The movie ended and she sat through the beginning of the credits. Finally she sighed and released me. She stood up and took my hand. She said nothing all the way out to her car. I was afraid the end was coming. We got in the car but she didn't start it. She turned to look at me instead.

"Thank you for tonight. I can't run with you tomorrow but I'll see you in Biology on Monday." With that she faced the windshield again and started the car. She said nothing on the way home.

"Tess, are you okay?" I finally asked as we pulled into my driveway.

She gave me an overly bright smile. "I'll be fine. I'll see you Monday," she said as she leaned over to kiss me goodnight. She didn't linger and seemed to be in a hurry to go.

"See you Monday," I repeated and got out of the car. Tonight she didn't even wait until I had opened the front door like she usually did.

"Hey, Owen, you're home early," Mom said, sounding surprised.

"Yeah, I guess Tess had some stuff to do."

"Are you running tomorrow?"

"She said she can't, so I thought I might go swimming instead. I haven't done that for awhile and then I'll catch up on some chores."

"We could make some time to drive tomorrow, too. Also, your dad called. He's coming home on Monday. He sounded a little strange on the phone."

"Mom, why would you come home on a Monday from a business trip? Why not come home on a Friday to spend the weekend with your family?"

"We'll piece all this together, I promise you."

"He must have remembered that we have conferences this week."

"I don't know, but we'll get through this together."

"I hope so, Mom."

EIGHT

Monday dawned foggy and cool. I was feeling pretty foggy and cool myself. I had tried to call Tess once and had sent her a text. She didn't respond to either. It had been fun while it lasted but it made me sad. I really liked her and I'd miss her. I realized that I hadn't thought much about Lucie lately. Tess had filled that particular hole in my heart. I was also worried about Dad. I never knew how things would be when he got home. It was all so frustrating. None of us could take the time off to follow him and we could not afford a private detective. Sadly, there was not yet enough evidence to bring in the FBI. Sarah knew everything but it wasn't enough to convince her boss. We would have to wait and collect all the data we could in other ways. Have I mentioned lately that I hate waiting?

Marlo met me at the bus and assessed my mood warily. "Tess trouble, huh?"

"I'm not sure, but I think so. She hasn't returned my call or text. We didn't run together on Sunday and she didn't say why. Mostly I'm worried about Dad and, well, Lucie just seems to be disappearing before my eyes. She avoids me almost all the time now. Whenever she sees me she goes the other way."

"I've tried to talk to Lucie. She barely speaks to me either. She seems nervous much of the time and withdrawn. She has pulled away from her other friends some as well. She's still pretty tight with a girl named Brenda. Now, for the big news... I've been using some of Sarah's resources lately. Nice job on her lawn on Sunday by the way – I came by to use her computer shortly after you left. Anyway... I was able to look at the activity on your grandfather's credit cards and check his bank accounts."

"You're a scary Dude, Marlo."

"I know, right? Anyway... It looks to me like your grandparents have not left the house. Everything seems to be coming in – you know - delivery. The security company has upped their fees. Your grandfather never goes to see your dad anymore. I also hacked into your dad's company credit card and we're watching the private airline. Your dad isn't going to see your grandfather either. Everything is being provided for your dad on the Atlanta end and his salary is going directly into your parent's joint checking account. They have your dad at a company owned condo and he's transported by limo. Judging by his credit card activity and based on how much is deposited, he isn't going anywhere except to work."

"My God, Marlo, how do you find all this stuff?"

"It isn't as easy as it sounds. Why do you think it's taken me so long? Sarah has access to some amazing software. I could never do this stuff without her FBI contacts. She's still keeping us a secret from her boss. I don't know how she gets away with it and I probably don't want to know. I'm just thankful for what she can provide us with. Did you realize that some of the cool gear we've been getting lately are actually castoffs from the bureau. I don't even want to know how she got her hands on them."

"When we went to the beach to check out Trevor's mom, she let us borrow some pretty sick electronic stuff. What's up with Willie Brown and Skimmer?"

"On the Willie front... that dude has dropped off the grid. It's really weird. We got all that stuff on him and even have his picture out there as a person of interest and now... nothing. He hasn't contacted his sister and there's no sign of him in Atlanta. He arrived and checked into a cheap hotel for one night and then, BOOM... he was gone. If he really is working for the security firm, Bauer Hays Securities, they are paying him under the table or under another name. At least I have the name of the security firm now. Also owned by... you got it, the umbrella company, Becker Hauer Affiliates. I'm going over all of their financials. If nothing else, we may be able to pull an Al Capone and get them for tax fraud. It's taking a lot of time to wade through it all but Sarah has gotten me some help from a guy named Rick. I've only talked to him over the phone. He works for Sarah's boss and she trusts him. He calls me Martin and thinks I'm a college student from Detroit! Ha!" Marlo laughed.

"Sarah is just trying to protect you, you know."

"I do know," Marlo replied more seriously.

A couple of more kids showed up at the bus stop so we stopped talking. We could see the bus just down the street anyway. After boarding the bus, Marlo shoved me into a seat far away from the other kids and sat down. "On Skimmer, I have zip. I need a real name or something... I can find no Skimmer references yet."

I was completely taken by surprise when Tess met our bus. I was a little worried that this was it and I was dreading the end. She threw herself into my arms, about knocking me down.

"Wow," was my intelligent response to her exuberance.

"I wanted to prove to you that I could help you and be of value to the team," Tess bubbled excitedly. Marlo started to edge away but I grabbed him by the collar of his jacket and held fast.

"I'm afraid to ask, but what did you do?"

Tess smiled at me hugely and then at Marlo. "I did some research on our *friend*," she ended with raised eyebrows to signal the significance.

"Oh-kay..."

"I went to see my sister and we went through her yearbooks. There was a kid in her year group who was a real troublemaker. He was caught smoking and even had some pot a couple of times, but he was underage so he got a hand slap. It looks like he has been getting smarter because I checked the local paper archives and he's not listed under arrests as an adult. I have a picture of him for you. It's his senior picture but it matches the description I had for you. I didn't know if I'd ever seen him myself. I mostly had rumor for you but now I also have a name. My sister confirmed some of the information we had and she's sure it *is* the same guy. It's where I was all day Sunday. See?"

I let go of Marlo and stared at Tess. "That was brilliant - asking your sister. After you acted so odd on Saturday and then when you didn't return my call... I thought... well, I thought you were done with me."

"I forgot my charger and my cell died. Besides, I told you I wasn't done with you. I wanted to help you and I wasn't sure how. I know you try to keep what you do under wraps and I know you were concerned when I figured it out. I promise I will never give you away – no matter what," she said crossing her heart with an index finger.

I had to laugh. Sometimes she does the funniest stuff. "Tess, I'm glad. I was thinking about how much I would miss you. I've really enjoyed our time together," I said seriously. I suddenly realized that Marlo had melted into the crowd and had left us in our own private bubble within the surging mass headed to class.

Tess reached for my hand and we began to walk. "We need to get to class but I have pictures to pass out to everyone. Let me give you some, so we can start watching for this guy. How about if we set up team captains so that people can report to them and then *we* captains can compile our information. I figure, you and I with Marlo and Adrian are plenty of captains. I don't know how big Adrian's network is though. I printed twenty pictures. I've gotta go or I'll be tardy," Tess said exuberantly as she simultaneously shoved some pictures into my free hand and lunged at me for a full body kiss, pushing me into the lockers next to me. A couple of kids hooted at us.

I caught up with Adrian and gave him all but one of the pictures. We would start watching and reporting Skimmer's movements and nothing else for now. We needed a picture and some proof, if we could get it, before we did anything else.

Between classes Marlo, Adrian, Tess and several of our friends watched for Skimmer. Tess had given us a verbal description at the pawnshop that we shared, along with the picture. Adrian had rounded up ten people to help us so far. The guy sounded strangely like the hated ex-boyfriend of Jesus' sister, Selena. Jesus got a little freaked out when I tried to pull him in for his help. He recognized the picture. We were definitely looking for Selena's ex.

"Jesus, Dude, you can't hide from this. We have to take care of this and then it will be done and he won't be able to bother you anymore," I told him at lunch on Tuesday.

"You don't understand. These guys are dangerous. I've been able to stay out of it as best I can but they've threatened Selena. She has done so much for me. I can't let them hurt her. They spy on her at the mall and take pictures to keep me in line. I've been trying to keep you away from this. It's my problem."

"It's not just your problem! Getting kids hooked on drugs and pulled into a gang that sells drugs is everyone's problem. If you don't want to get involved because of Selena, I understand, but I have to pursue this."

"They know they're being watched. Some of your friends aren't careful. I really shouldn't be seen talking to you. I'll try to slip you what I can without raising suspicions. Look for them after school today by the field side of the building. They'll be parked on the street. He drives a black Lexus sedan to make him look like a parent, I guess. Be careful."

I tried to question him more, but he shook his head and disappeared into the crowd. I found a quiet out of the way corner and began texting key people to be in place with cameras ready after school today.

Jesus was right; he'd done a pretty good job of staying out of trouble. He hadn't been pulled into the principal's office even once. I had to help my friend and any other kids unlucky enough to get involved with Skimmer.

Right after school I walked up the sidewalk next to the track. I spotted a black Lexus on the other side of the street. I promptly dropped the book I was holding and bent to pick it up, phone camera in hand. I snapped the car and the license plate. It was all I felt I had time for today. I didn't want to draw attention to myself. I quickly headed on up the street and turned the corner. Once I was out of sight I looked back and saw a kid stop at the passenger side window of the car, then move on. I snapped his picture too and then I ran around the block and to the locker room to get ready for practice.

After practice, I quickly met up with Adrian and Marlo before we headed out to be picked up to go home. I gave Marlo the chip with the pictures on it out of my phone. I hadn't had time to meet up with any of the kids assigned to me but I would see some of them in class. Adrian slipped me a note from Jesus with tomorrow's locations written on it. Adrian sent out the text that would start the information tree to the network and we headed out.

I was surprised when it was Sarah who picked me up after practice today. "What's up?" I asked, noting her worried face.

"I don't have details, but your mom gave me a quick call and asked for my help. Your dad is almost... loopy. My friend Saul will drop by tonight on a 'social call' to see him. Saul's a medic and your dad needs medical attention. You answer the door but be on full alert. He will say, "Hey Owen, remember me? I'm Saul." *Read* him before you let him in – White Eagle says he will look good or pure to you. Something is really wrong. Play everything cool and close to your vest. I have that feeling I get when I'm being watched. Turn your senses up to maximum. White Eagle will be by my house tonight. We're going to turn our scrutiny up to high. He will be around the neighborhood to keep a lookout for anything unusual. Pretend it's normal for me to drop you off. Got it?"

"Geez, Sarah, way to drop a bomb! You know I'll do what you say, but the timing sucks. Did you know we're trying to track a dealer at school?"

"Of course dear, Marlo and I are like *this* these days," she smiled, crossing her fingers and waving them under my nose.

"Well, it's a good thing that up 'till now I was caught up on my homework. I think tonight is going to be a busy night."

"I wouldn't normally offer this kind of assistance, but what is your homework?"

"I have some Geometry problems and a Biology worksheet due Wednesday. I also have a World History project due, but it's almost done.

"You do your best on the World History and leave me the rest. I'll have Marlo pick it up on his way to the bus. He comes by all the time, so it won't look out of place. He can pass it to you on the bus. Just this one time though, okay?"

"Wow, okay, Sarah," I said, pulling out the books and papers she would need. Call Marlo if you get stuck. Let Mar know too, that I may get stuck on the World History. We're on the same team so he might be able to pick up some slack."

"Will do. I love you, Trouble, be safe," Sarah said as she dropped me off.

"Thanks Mrs. Lando, you too," I said in a loud voice as I got out of her car - hoping that if someone was listening they were getting nothing exciting. I took a deep breath and went to meet my next problem.

Dad was sitting staring at the TV when I came in. Alex looked at him worriedly as he tried to play Uno with Lucas. I stood in the entry hall just watching. Mom must have heard me come in because she came to see me from the kitchen.

"Hey honey, how was your day?" She sounded overly bright and happy.

"Fine. Let me say 'hi' to Dad and then I'll come help in the kitchen," I said, concerned myself. Dad had not looked at me once. Mom put her back to Dad and held up a note for me to see. 'Sarah said that your dad may be bugged. Be careful what you say. Saul will check when he get's here. I'll meet you at the door at 7 to *read* him.' I gave her the o.k. sign with my hand and went to see Dad.

"Hey, Dad, how was your flight?" He slowly rolled his head in my direction. His pupils were too large for the lighting in the room.

"Oh... hi... Owen... I have... a bit of... a headache." *I bet you do!* I thought in my mind.

I reached out a hand and touched his skin. He felt dry and warm. He also looked like he'd lost weight. He'd gone back to staring at the TV and didn't even respond when I touched him. Now I was really creeped out. 'The solution to pollution is dilution,' I remembered from science so I went to the kitchen and got him a glass of water hoping it would help.

I took Dad the water and encouraged him to have a few sips. Then I casually went around and closed the blinds in the family room before I returned to the kitchen. I helped Mom put the finishing touches on dinner and set the table for her. She fixed a plate for Dad and poured him a big glass of milk. She wrote down everything he ate for Saul. After dinner Dad returned to the TV and the rest of us cleaned the kitchen and fed the animals. I helped Alex with his math homework and then Mom settled my brothers in to watch a movie in her room while Saul was here. If she thought Alex would stay and watch a movie she was a little delusional. I knew he would sneak back. He was getting more and more suspicious.

The doorbell rang at promptly at seven. I opened the door cautiously and looked at the man standing on our porch. He waited a beat and then said his line, "Hey Owen, remember me? I'm Saul."

Sarah and White Eagle were right – he felt like a good person. Mom came and looked over my shoulder and said, "Well, hey there, Saul, long time no see. Come on in." Mom flipped her head to the family room just as the door clicked shut. Saul handed her his ID and opened a small handheld device. He noted the closed blinds and smiled at us. He walked toward Dad while holding out his device. I walked near enough to him that I could see the readout on the screen.

"So," Saul continued, "I hear you're a freshman this year." I watched the meter and although I couldn't tell for sure what I was looking at, I would guess that the rapidly changing screen indicated a bug.

"Yep," I answered.

"Tell me all about it," Saul said, while rotating his hand in a circle in a 'carry on' motion.

So I began to rattle off all kinds of nonsense about school and football. I dumped out every boring detail and even mentioned my girlfriend but gave no names. The whole time I watched Saul, Dad was virtually oblivious. He helped Dad out of his suit coat and handed it to Mom with a look. At which point she interrupted my story to say, "Here, honey, let me hang up your coat so it doesn't get wrinkled."

Mom took it into the laundry room and turned on the dryer. Smart lady. I gave her a big thumbs up when she returned. I had resumed my boring story. Saul seemed to have found another bug in Dad's shoe.

Dad looked at Mom funny when she took his shoes off and handed them to me but said, "I'm really tired. Maybe I should go to bed." Saul had moved behind Dad's chair and was staying out of his line of sight. I hurried the shoes out of the room.

When I returned Saul was in full medical mode. He had a blood pressure cuff on Dad who was sitting docilely in the chair. Mom giving him a stern look probably helped. While in the laundry room I had checked Dad's coat and shoes. They had the mark of Willie on them. I refused to believe that two people would have the same gift and feel the same way. Mom had turned up the TV and everyone was keeping their voice down.

She began to tell Saul what Dad had eaten since he had been home and all his symptoms. Dad seemed confused and wondered why a doctor had come to see him. Mom told him it was because he wasn't feeling well to which he answered 'oh'. Saul took his temperature, drew some blood like a well practiced phlebotomist and set up plain IV fluids.

"He's dehydrated so the drugs are wiping him out. Lila, can you stay with him? I'll take Owen to go through his stuff, look for bugs and any oddities and take samples of any of his meds. I'll also do a quick sweep of the rest of the house. I know that Sarah checked it for you before and this room is clean, but it never hurts to do another check. Call if you need help or if he starts coming around," Saul instructed briskly.

"Okay," Mom answered, wringing her hands.

Saul took pity on her and placed a hand on her shoulder. "I've seen worse. He'll be okay."

Saul and I took the stairs two at a time and quickly headed for Mom's room, as I'd come to think of it. My brothers were watching their movie. I could tell by his body language and the look on his face that Alex had been spying so I simply held my finger to my lips so he wouldn't speak. I showed Saul where Dad's bags were in the closet and then went to whisper to Alex, "I know you're worried about Dad but this is one of those things that you need to not tell anyone about. We are trying to help him, okay?" Alex nodded and returned his gaze to the movie that had Lucas absorbed. I ruffled Lucas' hair then went over Dad's stuff with my *other sight* as Saul was finishing with his equipment. We found more bugs but were already working nearly silently. Saul indicated that we should leave them. I didn't know what Saul knew about me so I didn't let him in on what I saw – a whole lot of gray fogginess. Dad had brought his laptop this time so we decided to slip it into Saul's courier pouch and leave some of his equipment here. Marlo or some of Sarah's people could crawl through the computer. There was nothing else interesting in Dad's stuff except for his pills which were the same shape but a new shade – and I would bet my next paycheck, were a new chemical cocktail. I gave one to Saul for testing and he wrote down everything on the bottle.

He and I did a quick sweep-through of the whole upstairs and found no other listening devices. I hugged my brothers and we headed downstairs. We did a quick sweep of the main level and the garage. Saul said he would be in touch and to be very careful. He asked Mom if she felt comfortable pulling out the IV. She said she could handle it. Saul changed the IV bag. Dad was starting to shiver which Saul said was normal considering how fast he was having fluids put back into him. He asked Mom to get him some blankets and then to put him to bed when the IV was done. He left her gauze, tape and all the stuff that would not fit in his bag. He took Dad's laptop, blood sample and pill. He'd been with us for just over an hour and I already felt better. I felt like we were getting somewhere with Dad's situation at least.

I told Mom that we'd left the bugs and to be careful of what she said and did in her bathroom and closet – maybe even the bedroom as I didn't know what kind of range the devices had. We needed to give the bad guys stupid, normal family stuff. I also told her I would take the first 'Dad watch' and do a little homework. I settled in at the coffee table and Mom went off to do 'mom' things. Dad dozed in the chair. When the IV bag was nearly empty I got up and felt his skin which was feeling much better. I found Mom reading to Lucas and told her it was time to pull the IV. She hurried downstairs and I took her place with Lucas.

"Is Daddy going to be okay?"

"Yeah, Little Man, he'll be okay. He was sick but he should be a lot better by morning. Don't worry."

"If you say so, Owen," he said solemnly. His serious voice and facial expression made me sad so I hugged him tight. I wished once again that people would leave my family alone.

Alex wandered in and crawled into his own bed. He turned on his bedside lamp and pulled out at book without even looking at me.

"What's up Alex?" I asked, worried now, about him.

"I'm in fifth grade. I can handle it. I wish you'd tell me what's going on and let me help," he whispered, his voice angry. "You treat me like..." he looked at Lucas but did not say his name.

I settled Lucas in, told him I loved him and went over to sit on the floor by Alex. "Alex, I don't know everything. Something is going on with Dad. Remember when the bad people broke in here last year?"

"Yeah."

"Well, it's kind of like that. Sometimes we don't tell you things because we want you to have time to be a kid. This time we just don't know everything. What we do know is that someone is making Dad do things he doesn't want to do. To get him to comply they have poisoned him."

"That man was here to help, right?"

"Yeah, he was here to help. We may not be able to fix this until Christmas and maybe not even then. Please just hang tough and when I can think of something you can do to help, I'll let you know."

"Promise?"

"You bet. Now sleep good. Love you. See you in the morning."

"'Kay"

Yay, now my little brother wanted to help. Soon I would have a baker's dozen to manage and I could barely manage my own self. It was only Monday – heaven help me.

I went back downstairs to check on Dad. Mom was ready to put him to bed so I helped haul him upstairs. Once he was comfortable I rechecked all the doors and windows and moved myself to the kitchen table to finish my homework. By ten I'd fallen asleep on my books. At least I hadn't drooled on them. I wasn't sure what had woken me up. I looked around and found Beggar by the back door. She wasn't barking but she would periodically growl low in her throat and she looked at the back door as if it were sending her secret dog messages. I couldn't hear anything upstairs. Memories of last year washed over me. I remembered losing Buddy and I didn't want to relive that awful night.

Hugging the shadows and blind spots I hurried upstairs. My brothers were safe and asleep. I rechecked their window. Next I moved to Mom's room. Dad was sleeping peacefully and she had dozed off in the arm chair, her latest book clasped to her chest.

"Mom," I whispered as I gently shook her shoulder.

She was instantly awake. Dad snuffled in his sleep and rolled over. I tilted my head to the door, picked up her shoes and headed there to wait. Mom gave me one of her looks, picked up a sweater and followed me out. She said nothing until we hit the stairs.

"What is it?"

"Someone is outside the house," I replied, keeping a careful watch on the front door and regretting that there was glass to see through. Fortunately someone had turned off the inside entry light so the stairs were relatively dark. I pulled out my cell and quickly texted White Eagle.

'Still in the neighborhood? Think we have a prowler. Investigating w/ mom. Will use back door.'

"Should we risk letting Beggar out with us? She would alert us and we could stay close."

"Okay, Owen. I trust your judgment."

My cell beeped. White Eagle was still out there and headed our way. Mom and I did a silent sweep of the lower level. We peered out windows and checked locks. Nothing seemed to be amiss. We looped back to the kitchen where Beggar still sat at the back door, her head cocked to the side. I shoved Mom behind me and against the refrigerator – the pop-lock was slowly turning in the knob. I left Mom and silently rolled past the door, took a knife from the butcher block and waited, my back to the wall by the kitchen door. The dead bolt was beginning to turn. I glanced back at Mom, a cast iron skillet had appeared in her hand. Where did she get that from?

Beggar growled and whined. I felt the presence on the other side of the door... the signature foggy gray I'd come to associate with... Willie. Then everything exploded around me, literally, as the door blew inward with a flash and then smoke, Beggar barked, Mom yelled and I threw myself at Willie. I slashed, catching him on the arm. He howled with rage and pain. The smoke detectors went off. I grappled with him and plunged the knife into his leg. I heard the distinctive clang of the skillet followed rapidly by a second clang. I noted that Beggar had taken a bite out of Willie's pant leg. He and I went down in a heap. Beggar came in for another bite. I could hear my brothers thundering down the stairs.

"Mom, the boys!" I yelled. Clutching the cast iron skillet in front of her she backed out of the kitchen, her eyes streaming from the smoke bomb. Willie threw an elbow at my throat while my attention was diverted. I let out a strangled gasp as the blow hit. Willie struggled to free himself. I fought with every ounce of my being. I would not let him get to my family even if I had to sacrifice myself to do it. He tried to kick and punch at me but we were hopelessly tangled. He tried to pull the knife from his leg. I could hear a commotion in the entry way.

"Leave my brother alone!" Alex bellowed. Before I could extract myself to protect him – Alex was kicking Willie for all he was worth in the back and ribs. Willie finally yanked the knife free and took a swipe at Alex.

"Alex, NO!" I croaked, my damaged throat burning and aching.

Alex looked stunned and surprised as blood bloomed across the front of his thigh. I got a hand on the front of Willie's neck and pushed as hard as I could, my other hand going around the knife hilt still clasped in Willie's hand.

Alex sat down hard on the kitchen floor, whipped off his shirt and began to apply pressure to his wound. I whapped Willie's knife hand against the corner of the nearest cabinet and it clattered to the floor. When the knife dropped, I must have loosened my grip because Willie went for my throat a second time, smashing into it with his fist. I choked and gagged as he broke free and scrambled out the door, Beggar hot on his tail.

A beat passed as I tried to gulp some air - I could hear Beggar bark and howl her frustration. Willie must have gotten away. Moments later White Eagle burst through the open back door, panting but ready to fight.

"I'm sorry I was late," he said as if he had just missed dinner.

I rolled my eyes at him from my position flat on my back. "Alex," I croaked. Beggar continued to bark.

"I'm fine." Alex said bravely.

"I'll check the yard and be right back," White Eagle decided.

I crawled over to Alex, my breath still rattling in my throat. I had him lay back and I took a look at his leg. I was so relieved when I saw it, that more tears joined the ones already running down my face from the smoke which was rapidly clearing. Mom must have silenced the alarms. She cautiously rounded the corner, Lucas at her side, his eyes enormous. Dad staggered in behind her.

"What's going on here?" he asked groggily.

Mom just turned and gave him a look. "Another home invasion," she said matter-of-factly, her voice a little scratchy from the smoke, "and always in my kitchen. What is it with the kitchen?"

"You need to be more careful, Bro," I whispered to Alex.

"I learned from the best," he said proudly.

"Well, when White Eagle sees this it will be more practice for you. Trust me, I know from personal experience," I whispered as I hugged him. The bleeding had almost stopped. I stood and got the first aid supplies.

Dad was still leaning against the doorframe like he wasn't feeling well. "What's happening to us?" he asked of no one in particular.

"Dad, tell me about your bodyguard," I croaked, out of the blue, in a harsh whisper.

Mom rushed into the laundry room saying, "Just look at this mess. We've got to clean it up." I heard the dryer come on and about banged my head on the floor. Of course, the bugs, Stupid!

Dad seemed oblivious. I knew it was the drugs still affecting him. "Bodyguard?... I'm not supposed to talk about that," he said, sounding confused. "I'm here for information – not to give it." His eyes looked glazed.

"Tell me about the bodyguard. It makes you feel frustrated – being watched all the time. Why are you watched?"

"They will hurt you if I talk. They already have my father prisoner and... Mom. She never hurt anyone... you know? He was always harsh and didn't understand me and she was... she tried to protect me..."

Mom shut the door behind her. I could tell she overheard part of it. She looked at Alex with sad eyes and scooped up Lucas, who was still standing wide eyed and almost shocked in the corner. She exited one doorway as White Eagle came in the other, Beggar in his arms. I signaled him to be quiet. I gave Alex the same motion and finished his leg.

Dad continued, lost in his own memories. Perhaps he could see them better right now than he could real life. "He hurt her sometimes for protecting me. I felt... rage and helplessness. He can't leave the house now. I can go from the condo to work and back and that is all. They even cut my hair at work. I'm working on... an adhesive. It doesn't work right. I'm not working right. What have they done to me?" He nearly sobbed and then took himself back under control. "They will hurt my family if I don't do as they say."

Dad slumped into a kitchen chair and looked across the table to White Eagle. "When did you get here?"

"I heard the noise and thought I'd help," he said in his most soothing voice.

"Let's get you back to bed and then maybe White Eagle will help me clean the kitchen." I said, pulling Alex to his feet. "Come on Dad."

Dad followed me docilely. It was weird. He was more himself but yet not. It was a relief to not have him be angry as he had been so much of the time. Whatever drug they had him on now it was clearly too strong. I wondered how they got any work out of him like this. A better question was… Why had Willie tried to break in? To check the bugs? To drug Dad? To harm us? My life was so *not* normal.

Mom took Dad from me in the upstairs hall. I escorted Alex to his room. "I don't know what story you want to make up about your leg but what really happened – didn't happen," I said firmly.

"I know. What do you think? Broken glass? No wait, I know, we were cleaning the garage and I moved into a piece of a broken screen that was sticking out."

"Now that sounds good. Maybe don't mention it unless it comes up, okay?"

"Sure, 'night," Alex said, sounding proud of himself.

I could hear Mom and Dad's soft murmurs coming from their room. I walked on past and headed downstairs. White Eagle had the knife and the remnants of the smoke bomb in plastic bags. He was sitting back at the table with his arms crossed. Oh dear, now what had I done?

"Good job. Too bad he got away. You know he'll be back, right?"

"Yeah, I figured he would." I picked up the scrap of jeans that Beggar had removed for me. "You know," I said, as I weighed the fabric in my palm, "I wonder if whatever our gift is, we sort of *become*. I sensed Willie on the other side of the door. He was that same foggy gray that I've come to associate with him. This piece of fabric from his jeans tells me nothing although it was touching his skin. When I touched *him*, I got nothing. He did not drain me… He didn't even try. I wonder why? I also wonder why he was here." I fell silent, deep in thought. Then my eyes took in my damaged homework. Yay! That would make my teacher happy. Super. I hope I don't drag down Marlo's grade. There was no way I could let my teacher know about another break in at our house, so I'd have to let her think I was a hopeless slob.

"I don't know what to say. One thing at a time I guess," White Eagle said calmly.

"I have more than one ability, but I thought that was rare. Willie seems to be a *stalker* and he has a dark ability. I'd believed that *stalkers* were pretty much just around to drain *watchers* as part of the cosmic balance, like an ecosystem with predators and prey. *Stalkers* do it to gain temporary strength and conversely it weakens us so we are more easily beaten. I saw our abilities or gifts as an added bonus to help us do our jobs. You're a mentor and not a *watcher*, though you and I share many qualities. You can heal which I view as opposite of a drain. I guess I'm now seeing this like there are levels or tiers in ability. Am I on track with what I'm visualizing? Is Willie… a normal *stalker*?"

"I don't know what's normal anymore. I do think that his ability would be very useful to a *stalker*. Maybe he moved up a tier, to use your analogy. It's hard to say. Each person's story is so different. In the past all the *watchers* I knew had one ability and I taught them to fight much as my grandmother had before me. I'd always believed that one was a *watcher* or a mentor and nothing more. I always believed that we were called to be one or the other. We hunt the dark side in our quest for balance, so of course there are *stalkers* that prey on our side. They drain *watcher* powers and use it for themselves for a brief time, until it burns out. I've always thought of it as more of a mentor type ability, like how I know that you are good. I can see your power glow within you. I always assumed that *stalkers* could sense power much the same way. In the past, I've seen them go after the weak and untrained because they must be easier to get to. Why mess with someone like you? From what your dad said, it is definitely *you* they want, but it will take a whole lot more than someone like Willie to take you down. What I want to know is – who's holding Willie's leash."

There was a soft rap at the back door. White Eagle stood to let Saul in. "The cops were not called. I think your team needs to handle this. We have moved way beyond a local problem. You know this is one of Sarah's special cases. We need to treat this family like they're in witness protection. He picked the lock and handled the knife. His blood is on it but you'll find the little brother's blood on the tip. Check it for every disease while you're at it," White Eagle said quickly and quietly to Saul but looked at me while he ended.

I felt myself go cold. Of course. My God! Willie was a drug user. What if he gave something to Alex? I knew from school how dangerous blood born pathogens could be. I felt lightheaded and nauseous.

Saul was quietly printing the back door but looked over at me in concern. "If you cleaned the wound well, you did the best you could. I'll rush the labs and... well, if anything is not as it should be, we will start whatever treatment we can right away. Don't fret over what you can't control."

I nodded, still feeling sick. I pulled my homework toward me and tried to finish the little that was left but I couldn't focus. White Eagle came and put a hand on me where my neck met my shoulder. His hand felt overly warm and I began to feel calmer. "It will be alright," he said softly. I realized he had to be using his brand of magic.

Saul took the evidence White Eagle had bagged and left. We cleaned the kitchen, and then White Eagle secured the downstairs, while I forced myself to finish my homework. My work was nowhere near my usual standards but it would have to do. It was almost one in the morning. White Eagle was dozing on the couch and I fell into Mom's favorite chair, propping my feet on the footstool. I was out in seconds.

NINE

I awoke to the sound of cartoons and a blanket thrown over me. I stretched and rolled my neck. I looked at my watch – only seven. I turned to look at Lucas. "What's up?"

"Why did you sleep in Mom's chair? Lucas asked. He still looked a little bug-eyed this morning.

"I wanted to be sure you were safe. See, everything's fine now."

"Why do you sound so awful? And why is your neck purple?"

"I took an elbow and a fist to my throat last night. I'll be fine. Don't worry. Where's Alex?"

"Pigging out on cinnamon rolls and bacon. Sarah's here."

Well of course she is. If I would have paid attention, I would have noticed, that over the acrid smell of the smoke from last night, there was the pleasing aroma of homemade cinnamon rolls and real bacon. Yum! I threw back the blanket and rushed into the kitchen.

Mom was sitting at the table with Alex and Sarah was turning another batch of bacon. I noticed the dryer was running again and the laundry room door was closed. "Wow, Sarah, you may have just saved my life. That smells amazing."

Mom smiled at me over her cup of coffee. She was wearing her 'everything's going to be okay' look – whether or not she believed it was another matter. White Eagle came in from the powder room looking crisp and fresh. How unfair! I looked like I had been run over by a truck, I was sure.

"You sound awful," Mom commented.

"Yeah, but he looked amazing!" Alex crowed.

"He needs to be more careful," White Eagle and Sarah reprimanded in unison.

Time to change the subject. "Whoever threw a blanket over me – thanks. I'm gonna go take a shower. Save me some of that great smelling food," I croaked.

"You'll be alright. Tell everyone at school you are coming down with something and find a shirt that will cover your neck," White Eagle advised.

"Yeah, yeah," I said as I headed for the door.

"You're welcome," Mom said softly as I left.

Marlo must have smelled the real bacon all the way at his house because he was sitting at the table enjoying Sarah's efforts when I came back downstairs. I dished up and stuffed my face. Mom had left with my brothers to walk them to school for their safety. I had looked in on Dad and he was still sleeping peacefully, so I left him alone. Sarah walked out of the laundry room where I could now hear the washer going.

"Such a nuisance! I wish we could just smash them," I said with a scowl.

Marlo took a good hard look at me. "What happened to you?" he asked in a concerned tone.

"I was just starting to tell him when the dryer went off," Sarah supplied. Then she went on to tell the rest of the tale while I ate. While she talked and I ate, Marlo picked my homework up off the table and looked it over with a big eye roll.

"Is this a footprint?" he asked disgusted, "Did you fight with this too? Yeesh!" He made a couple of notes on it and then put it in my backpack. "It will have to do," he finished in an exasperated tone.

"I had a rough night. Maybe she'll take pity on me. I sound like I have a cold anyway."

"If only we could get that lucky. Well, while you were wrestling the wicked, I was busy. I have filled in Sarah and White Eagle. He's off trying to meet with Evelyn, on his way to work, to bring her up to speed and get us a little help with Skimmer. Don't look at me like that. He's fully aware that we want to bring down the whole thing and he agrees but Evelyn can't move mountains with the police. She has to sneak it in. This gives her time to contact the right people."

I had to give Marlo credit. Once he told his story, I was pleased and proud of him. While I was chasing shadows, 'depolluting' my dad, and drooling on my homework, Marlo had been hard at work too, compiling all we had on our 'friend' Skimmer. He discovered that Skimmer, otherwise known as Francis Fendike – *I'd have changed my name too* - sold everything from pot, cigarettes and alcohol to the harder stuff, to anyone stupid enough to buy it. No one turned him or any of his wannabes in. They had been able to keep it quiet for almost three years because of fear. I guess I was just too stupid to be afraid of a two-bit crook like him. I'd taken on a bigger, scarier menace than Skimmer last year.

I wasn't the only one who saw kids pause at the open passenger side window and move on, like nothing had happened. Skimmer seemed to be the only one selling, but he was clearly grooming the others who would occasionally make a delivery hidden in a binder or book. They would take money to Skimmer the same way.

We were figuring out the pattern, piece by piece. We would see if they changed it up next week. At lunch Skimmer hung out by the back side of the Fine Arts building on Tuesdays and Thursdays and was up by the track after school. Mondays and Wednesdays he did the opposite. The gouge, our funny name for gossip, was that he ran the same pattern on Fridays that he did on Mondays and Tuesdays. Unfortunately we had conferences so there was no school on Thursday or Friday this week. We made our plans to watch him today and tomorrow. We figured he would not be around with so many parents at conferences.

By next week we should have enough camera shots to turn in to Evelyn to get Skimmer in some serious trouble. I just wanted to be sure when he was taken down that the whole infrastructure fell with him and the next in line did not just pop up and take his place.

Today I took some cash to school so that I could walk off campus and get a sandwich at the deli. I wasn't supposed to leave campus as a freshman, but I would try to look old today and see if I could get away with it. I easily avoided the campus monitors by blending in with some seniors and then went down behind the auditorium to head to the deli. Sure enough there was Skimmer's black car. I about fell over when I saw who was at the window... Katie... No! I'd dated her briefly last year. She was a sweet girl and had been a good student. I had no classes with her this year and had lost track of her. I felt a sudden burst of pure loathing for Skimmer. How dare he drag in someone like her?

I watched from behind a pickup truck. Katie walked away from the window and looked around furtively. She was headed for the stairs and I was after her. There were things more important than lunch. I went in a different direction, hopping the wall to the parking lot and coming at her from the side. I caught up with her next to the auditorium and took ahold of her arm.

Images flashed before my eyes in rapid succession. Katie was staring at me open-mouthed.

"Owen, what are you doing?" she gasped in surprise.

"I think the better question is... what are you doing?"

Katie hung her head. She fidgeted and tears began to pool in her eyes. She looked dejected, forlorn, lost, hopeless and helpless. I pulled her toward the nearest low wall and sat her down. She leaned forward and put her head on my chest.

"I wish you could help me like you did those people last year. I'm not innocent though; I caused my own problem. I guess I'm the person you must have thought I was. I'm not good. Now I'm in too deep. I wish..."

I waited but she just sat with her head against me. It reminded me of all those times that Lucie had sat close to me to absorb a little warmth and friendship last year. I slipped my arm around Katie's shoulders. "Talk to me. Tell me your problems. I'll listen and not judge you. I'm still your friend."

Katie looked up at me with her huge brown eyes and I noted the dark circles beneath them. She was even thinner than before. She wore no makeup today which was totally unlike how she used to be. I watched her body language and knew when she had surrendered. I thought that I had most of her story from her favorite jacket but I knew it would do her good to tell it.

"Let's walk to the deli and split a sandwich. You can talk as we walk. I'll keep you safe."

"Okay, Owen. I remember last year after we... stopped seeing each other, you told me you were still my friend. You'd once promised me if I was in trouble you would be there. I was just afraid to ask. I should've come to you sooner. I felt... guilty and unworthy of you."

"Never feel like that, Katie. No matter what happened – you have a good heart. If you started down the wrong path, then let's forge a new one for you in the right direction," I said, putting an arm around her shoulders and guiding her off campus in the other direction, away from Skimmer. I hoped the deli would be fast today or we'd be late for class.

"Hey, you have a girlfriend now. Won't she be mad?"

"This isn't about her or me right now. It's about you. Tell me your story."

Katie sucked in a shuddery breath. She held it for a moment and blew it out as if she was taking a firm grasp on herself; like she had to prepare herself for the snatches of ugliness that I'd seen when I touched her jacket. "I was invited to a beginning of the year party. I thought it would be really fun. I was invited by a senior in my art class. I thought he liked me. He did like me but not in the right way. Anyway the party was really fun at first, just like I thought it would be. The senior, Eric, put something in my cola, I'm sure of it now. I was a mess by the end of the evening. I couldn't make a good decision to save my soul. I was dizzy and disoriented. I couldn't find my cell. The party wasn't so fun anymore – everything was distorted and scary. Eric took me in a back room to get me something for my head, which was spinning. The back room was a bedroom. He... did things he shouldn't have done. It's all warped with moments of total blackness..."

I could feel my body going rigid with fury and loathing for Eric and people like him. No wonder some of the images I saw looked so weird. They were thickly layered with self-hatred, confusion, fear and drugs.

"I had my phone back when I woke up the next morning and a text waiting for me. It told me to say nothing or my picture would be posted. I didn't know for sure what had happened to me so I went to the clinic and got a day-after pill just in case. I had some blood drawn and had a urinalysis done to find out what poison they'd put in me. I refused the rape kit but had them... you know, check everything..."

"What picture, Katie?" I tried to say it calmly but I already knew the answer.

"It's me topless but I look unconscious," she said with remorse. "I thought about fighting it but... I got another text. It told me if I talked there would be more pictures and they would tell my mom. They gave me a website to check. There are a lot of pictures. It's bad... Anyway to keep the pictures from being seen and to pay my bills, I have been running errands for Skimmer. Eric knows him and set it up. I swear to you – I'm not using. It was all a mistake."

I stopped and hugged her. "We will fix this. I need to have all the information you can give me. I need that website so that we can take it down and I need to know how often you run these errands for Skimmer. Trust me. Keep doing what you are doing for now so that you can keep a low profile. By next week this will all go away. You have my word."

Katie really did cry at that. She stayed to the back and I ordered us a lunchbox to split and I got an extra diet soda for her. Then we hurried back to class. I asked Katie if she would feel comfortable giving everything to Marlo. I explained that it was safer for her not to be seen too often with me but if she needed me – I would be there. Katie hugged me outside the building, whapping me on the back with her half a sandwich and cookie before she turned and fled into the building. I sent Marlo a quick text and hurried to English. He had saved me a seat like I asked. I whispered to him as much as I could that I hadn't take time to text. He would meet Katie after school before he went to soccer practice to get some information directly from her. He was furious and would make it his personal mission to wipe her pictures off the internet. Marlo told me he would have Eric's full name and school record ready for Evelyn by the end of the day. If we got Eric too, that was one more out of the way – soon the whole group would fall apart. Everyone was sending pictures to Marlo of Skimmer's activities and visitors. He was trying to break down who was helping Skimmer and who the victims were. We wanted to solve this problem and not cause more.

I did awful at practice. Between my worries about Dad, Willie, Skimmer, Katie, Lucie... well, my list is long and combined with not enough sleep I was far from my best self, so I got to run extra laps. I think the football hitting me in the helmet instead of my catching it was the straw that broke the camel's back on that one. If I didn't look better tomorrow it would be the bench for me. Fine! I thought in my mind. You have no idea what I'm dealing with and it's all more important than a stupid game. Two more weeks of football and then I could get back to work. I had learned from it but it ate a huge chunk of time.

White Eagle picked me up again. I was glad because I felt grouchy and didn't want to deal with my dad. White Eagle also had all the latest intel and could catch me up. Marlo would get back to us later tonight on the Skimmer front. He had practice today too. Willie had not turned up anywhere... yet. The police had been alerted and were watching for him. Sarah had found a way to share some of her information about our 'break-in' without giving everything away. She and Evelyn had forged an uneasy friendship but since we would make the chief look good by clearing cases... it all worked out. Since Willie's prints were taken from our house the police were a whole lot more interested in proceeding with the warrant for his sister's storage shed. Apparently the hint of cold cases had left them, well, cold. They had too many current things to clear. Now he was interesting again. The right people should have the warrant by next week. On the Dad front... Mom had stayed home today. He spent most of it sleeping. Saul had been back to check on him. Sarah had watched our house as best she could and Mom had been alert. When it was time for my brothers to come home, Sarah had arranged for Saul to take shifts with her and White Eagle to keep a presence in the neighborhood without alerting my dad or hopefully Willie.

Wednesday, Skimmer was still following the anticipated schedule. I went nowhere near him because I didn't want him to 'make me' yet. Katie came through with some great information for Marlo. He compiled everything for Evelyn and sent her the whole file, including pictures of visitors to Skimmer's car with as many as possible identified and their school records attached. We knew we didn't have all the players accounted for yet. Tess found another young freshman who had been tricked like Katie. She charmed him into telling his story which she recorded. Wow!

I was much more focused today at practice so my coach was much happier with me. The next few days I would have time to go to the pawnshop, work out and take care of things there. I just had football practice and my conferences with my teachers. I wasn't worried. My grades, although not stellar, were fine. What can I say? We can't all be Marlo, but then I have no interest in being our class Valedictorian. He can have it.

My time at the pawnshop was like a balm to my stressed-out mind. It felt good to get back into the rhythms of Tai Chi and Karate. The results came back on Dad's new med that Saul had swiped with my help. They were still trying to control him. That was clear from the cocktail of chemicals they were flushing through him. Knowing what was in him, between the information from his blood draw and the pill itself, Saul was able to detox Dad even further. He was in the best shape he'd been in since about last May – had we only realized then... well, we were fixing it now and hopefully there would be no permanent damage.

Dad would be going back to Atlanta on Monday. Now that he could think clearly, he was scared and finally willing to admit that they had tricked him and the only way to beat them was to fight back. Sarah watched my brothers while Mom, White Eagle and I met with him. He would try to act drugged and not take his pills. He also planned to get us any information he could. He didn't want to go back but he knew he had to, to protect us and his parents. We told him that we stood behind him but we gave him as little information as possible so that he would have nothing to take back to the other side. We let on nothing about Sarah and her contacts, nothing about my friends or Evelyn, nothing about my growing abilities or Mom's and nothing about the training my brothers did with White Eagle or that Mom had joined them. White Eagle just told him that he had friends and we would get him help. He would come up with a couple of flash drives and a prepaid cell that my dad could use to save information and communicate with us if he could get away from the people watching him.

Dad was now afraid to have us go to Florida for Christmas but White Eagle convinced him that it was the only way to finally put an end to this. Dad admitted that he knew on some level that they were after me after White Eagle said that he was sure that was what was behind all this. White Eagle said privately to me that he thought that they were thinking that it was easier to bring me to them and get me off my turf than to try to capture me here. Perhaps that was what Willie was trying to do. We would be studying maps and area information now as well as having tougher practices. I needed to be ready.

Dad said that much of his time in Atlanta and Miami was blurry and fuzzy. He remembered Willie through it all though. Willie, it seemed to him, was more of a warden than his guard and Willie was *always* around – *always* watching. Dad had never believed in special abilities, magic, or psychics but now he was beginning to see the light. He'd seen Willie do some pretty weird stuff. He knew Willie was out there watching us right now. He was appalled to learn that he was bugged. He had very little he could tell us about the man pulling the big strings but now he was aware and he would be watching. White Eagle warned him that if he was bugged here, it was likely he was bugged at work and at his condo. White Eagle warned him that he might even be under video surveillance.

Dad would be gone for three long weeks. He would come home for a few days at Thanksgiving and then he would have to deal with three more weeks before we could get to him. Dad was turning into a nervous wreck before our eyes. He was worried about my brothers trick-or-treating on Halloween. He was worried about people coming to our door for Halloween, and he was worried about me going to the Halloween party with Tess tonight.

Mom and I finally convinced him that I could handle myself and that she would find an alternative activity for my brothers. Dad felt that Willie would make a play for us soon. He already knew he would be stuck in a window seat with Willie next to him on the way back to Atlanta on Sunday. Not if I could help it, I thought. I must have had a certain look on my face because White Eagle caught my eye and shook his head. He pulled me aside and suggested that sometimes it's better to deal with the enemy you know. If we pulled Willie out now, then Dad would likely get someone much worse to watch him. White Eagle thought we could fool Willie. If the police nabbed him before Sunday's flight, so be it - at least that was his past catching up to him and had nothing to do with us.

With so much going on, I hadn't done much costume planning. All I knew was that I had to be able to move and not have my face covered, just in case. I shuffled through Miles' memories and saw a flash of him dressed as Waldo from 'Where's Waldo' with the hat, scarf and red and white striped shirt. Mom came up with Zorro or Sherlock Holmes, which I really liked until Alex suggested a zombie or Indiana Jones. Now there was a really good one! As much as I loved the Sherlock idea, the costuming would be more difficult. I could raid Dad's closet for most of the Indiana Jones costume and I already had the jacket.

I found a hat, suitable shirt and baggy pants in his closet. I had the brown boots, belt and jacket. Mom fashioned a whip for me out of some old rope and leather scraps from our garage. She also helped me with a little makeup to bring out my beard. I was set and better yet – if I came across Willie - I could fight.

Tess showed up right at seven. Perhaps we should have planned out our costumes. She showed up dressed as a Dallas Cowboys Cheerleader complete with tasseled boots, a starred vest and pom-poms. Her outfit was... spectacular. It also showed more of her cleavage than I had ever seen before and I had seen plenty on some of our dates. Now it wasn't just Willie I would have to watch out for but every guy in the room! Great. Mom looked a little stunned herself when she met her at the door.

"You look very... detailed," Mom finally choked out.

"Thanks, my sister made this last year. Isn't it amazing?" Tess answered, oblivious to Mom's awkward comment.

I hugged Mom, thanked her for her help and headed for the door before things got any worse.

"Wait! Let me get a picture of you two."

What did I say... things just got worse. Tess and I smiled and Mom snapped several shots. I will now have the moment recorded full body, waist up, head and shoulders, smiling and goofy. Yay! As we got in the car I smiled at Tess for her good humor and added, "Tess, you look spectacular. I hope my mom recovers."

"You look good too. Indiana Jones, right?"

"Yeah. Hey, I can't believe what you got out of that kid on Wednesday. How'd you do it and how did you know to talk to him?"

"I hate to tell you this but... I think some of my friends are involved. I haven't always been Miss Perfect and I'm still not. I've done some things that you wouldn't like but I'm trying to... I don't know, rise above it, I guess. When I was in eighth grade I went to my first party with my sister. I shouldn't have gone but my mom was working nights. My sister took me to lots of parties that year and the next. Anyway, I saw stuff I shouldn't have seen and did stuff I shouldn't have done. I don't want these guys to corrupt anyone else."

"What happened to you Tess?"

"Nothing like happened to your friend Katie. I saw kids drink and try pot. I saw kids being reckless and promiscuous. I looked old for my age and they accepted me. I thought I was cool hanging out with the older kids. I didn't realize then that I was hanging out with the *wrong* older kids. My sister drank too much one night when I was a freshman and got alcohol poisoning. It was horrible. I went looking for her. I can still see her crumpled body - passed out on the floor of a dirty bathroom with vomit in her hair. I had to help her because everyone else was bombed out of their minds. They laughed when I yelled for help. I had to carry her to the car; I drove home without even a permit and took her into the house. I put her in our tub, tried to clean her up and wake her. I should have taken her to the hospital. My mom came home early, thank God, and saved her. I had almost killed her by not getting her the help she so desperately needed. They forgave me but I... she almost died." Tess finished but her voice was thick with tears.

"Tess, you have to forgive yourself. You were young and you did more for her than anyone else at that party. She would have died for sure if you wouldn't have brought her home. You're helping now and she did too by identifying Skimmer. We'll get these guys because of both of you. You wouldn't be who you are if you hadn't experienced what you did."

"There you go again... sometimes you sound so... old. I am trying to forgive myself. At least you see why I wanted to join your *band of merry men*. I wanted to be a vigilante and wipe out these... you know it's some of the same people. I knew Skimmer from back then, he just wasn't as dangerous at the time.

I picked up Tess' hand and brought it to my lips. Then I just held it. I knew that it would probably seem weird and old-fashioned to her but I wanted her to know that I was there for her and that until she forgave herself, I would.

When we got to the party we had to park two blocks away and walk up. Tess gave me a big hug before we got to the driveway.

"Thank you for what you said. I'm glad you're here with me. I should've told you more and told you sooner. I haven't been fair to you and I think I underestimated you. I know I've put you in a really bad situation tonight. If you don't want to go in then we will turn around right now..."

"Tell me now, Tess, what's going on?"

"They're here, Owen. You'll be able to see it first hand. If we go in and we're careful, we may be able to save at least one person tonight. I think you can find a lot of information here if you aren't afraid to get it. I'm sorry... I should've... I'm the vigilante and I used you. I'm so sorry."

I pinched the bridge of my nose to hold off the pain that was beginning to pound in my head. I would have prepared if I'd known. I was frustrated with Tess, but I understood her motivation. I shook it off and did the best I could. I had to go in, but I needed Marlo and White Eagle. I looked at Tess, "I understand. Give me a minute here and then we'll go in. I would've preferred to do this in the car but we're here now and we've been seen, I'm sure."

She gave me a fierce hug as I pulled out my cell and called White Eagle. I quickly told him what was happening and that we would just collect information if possible and then send it to Evelyn after Marlo processed it. I told him that we'd let him know if we needed back up. Our team was already stretched thin watching our house for Willie. Knowing White Eagle – he'd come up with something. I texted Marlo while Tess continued to hold me like we were having a pre-party moment together. I sent Tess White Eagle's number and then I erased all my call and text records.

I took a deep breath and let it out, then I brought my face close to hers. "Ready?"

"I am – are you?"

"I sure hope so," I said, hoping it was true.

We headed up the front steps and the door opened for us into a dark hall. "Hey, Tessy," Kirk's drunken voice rang out. "I see you brought us fresh meat. If you wanted to play with him you didn't need to use the driveway – I would've given you a room. You have the admission fee?"

My gut tightened. I could smell the stink of alcohol and the sickly sweet smell that I thought was pot. I knew nothing about the fee Kirk was talking about. I hoped Tess knew – this one would be tough to bluff.

I put my arm protectively around her as Kirk leered. She just looked at him. This was not 'sweet' Tess – this was 'don't mess with me' Tess. I'd never seen her act so tough or brave. She pulled a bottle of whiskey out of her bag and shoved it into Kirk's chest. "You know what Kirk?... You're not half as cute as you think you are. Now this one... he's simply... mouth-watering."

I was shocked but quickly hid it. Kirk was so busy glaring at Tess that I don't think he noticed my reaction. She purposely bumped him with her shoulder on the way past. "Sorry," she growled, not sounding a bit sorry. I could feel fingers of dread run up and down my spine. I didn't want to fight enormous Kirk, half drunk, in his own narrow entryway with a house full of crazy drunk and high teenagers. Plus we didn't have any solid information yet. Kirk reached out a long arm and grabbed Tess' nearest arm. He leaned in and whispered in her ear, "He is... okay to look at I guess. Maybe we could use him. Get him ready, would ya?"

Tess shrugged in response to his demand while scowling boldly up at him and quickly disengaged herself from his grasp. Kirk continued trying to whisper in her ear but she stepped back. I could hear every word anyway because he was too drunk, high, or both to control his volume. He looked angry and spat at her, "You owe me. Pay me now. I like the idea. It's perfect."

Tess's face took on a sly look that was lost on Kirk's dim drunkenness, "Fine, Kirk, I'll see that you get what's coming to you. Don't you worry about it," she said, smiling sweetly as she showed off her cleavage to its greatest advantage, making me gulp. What had I signed up for on this gig? I needed my head examined. I could feel all my muscles tighten. I felt completely on edge. "Come on, Baby," Tess said, taking my hand. "I want to show you around."

Kirk let us walk away but I was left wondering... Who was this crazy woman? What happened to the Tess I knew? She led me deeper into the house. She seemed to be looking for something specific. I mapped as much of the house as I could in my mind as we went, but much of it was dark or oddly lit for Halloween. Finally Tess stopped in front of a door. She knocked and when no sound was emitted, she dove inside. Closing and locking it behind us, she flipped on a light. We were in a windowless utility room and storage area. She let her bag fall to the ground and lunged at me, wrapping me in a tight hug. Her bravado melted away as she stood there shaking and holding me tightly.

"Tess, that was... reckless and probably dangerous. What did you just agree to and what do you owe him?"

"You were listening, I actually promised him nothing. What he is hoping I will do, is drug you and take pictures of you like happened to your friend Katie. It's how they suck them in. As you know from football, Kirk has anger management problems. I knew if I pushed the right buttons he would say things he shouldn't – besides he's had enough social lubricant to have his tongue loosened. We're lucky we caught him before his pants are around his ankles, he's unconscious or both." Tess blew out a breath and stepped back. Kirk has kept me out of this world. No one ever drugged me or took my picture because of him. He's only one year older but my sister was always nice to him and even dated him for awhile. He looks at me like a little sister or a pet. In a way I hate to do this to him. I was afraid he was involved but I wasn't positive until just now. He's not the brains behind this. I bet Skimmer is. What he has on Kirk – I don't know. How's my costume?"

"You look fine. What now?"

Tess moved some clothes on a rack to expose a full length mirror. She twitched her costume a bit and then messed up her hair. "We need to look our part. Then we'll go out there and pretend to get wasted. We need to take as many pictures as we can. I'll show you where the worst stuff happens and try to cover so you can snap some shots with your phone. First rinse your mouth with this and I'll clean you up before we take you home. I think your Mom will have a heart attack if she sees what I am about to do to you – just remember it's all a show. You're now on stage, Handsome."

Tess handed me an airline sized bottle of vodka. She had me rinse and spit. She did the same and then she put some on me like cologne. Fantastic! I thought sarcastically. She unbuttoned my shirt two more buttons and rumpled it up. Finally she took some lipstick out of her bag and put it on. "Pucker up. You need to be labeled so that no one else tries to take advantage of you tonight."

"So this is not going to be one of the top ten on our date scale, huh?"

"I don't know, I think it may be quite memorable for you and if we're successful, it will be the last of its kind for a really long time. I want you to know that I appreciate this. I'm doing it for my sister, for me and for people that should never have been hurt. I didn't mean to hurt you. Any innocence left in you will be viciously murdered tonight. I'm sorry for that but I need you. White Eagle told me you're a sweet boy. You won't be sweet anymore." For a moment I thought she would cry but she pulled herself together and moved toe to toe with me. She took ahold of the front of my shirt, then pressed her lips to my neck and chest *and then* she kissed me. It was one of her more spectacular kisses and for a moment I lost track of why we were here or where we were. There was a knock at the door. Tess took a moment to answer. "Just a minute," she half panted in a husky voice. She winked at me, laughing silently and made some rustling noises. She checked her look in the mirror and pushed the hanging clothes back over it. She looked me over with a critical eye and made a couple of adjustments. "Ready?"

"I hope so," I replied.

The knock sounded again. "Keep your shirt on," Tess said in that same sultry voice and then she giggled a very convincing giggle. She squeezed my hand and opened the door. We were faced with two drunken teenagers I didn't know. They moved quickly into the room, their beverage cups slopping pungent alcoholic drinks. The boy shoved us out and slammed the door. I heard the girl giggle and squeal. Gross. I heard fabric rip and more giggling before Tess could pull me away. Clearly I'd descended into a den of...what? Ill repute? Iniquity? Miles' memories came up with a few words – personally, I thought I'd descended into hell. What was happening in there had nothing to do with loving someone. I wondered if they would regret it later.

I pulled Tess close and whispered in her ear, "People want to be here and come for fun? This is not my idea of a good time. I feel nervous and on guard." I made it look like I was nibbling on her ear. I held her close and slid my hands over her. It would've been totally awesome except, well... It smelled like sour alcohol and sweat overlaid with that awful sickly sweet smell that was giving me a headache. Tess gave as good as she got which was pretty distracting.

We broke apart when someone suggested we 'get a room'. To which Tess rudely snapped back, "We just did. Jealous much?" She shoved past him and led me upstairs to where kids were making out in various rooms. We paused in the deserted hall so that I could *feel* the house. I told Tess I needed to listen for a moment. What I heard was not what my parents would want me listening to. My mom would die if she ever found out. I let Tess lead me on but I knew that I needed to look in the last room on the left. She had to actually look in all of the rooms or listen at the doors. She was doing it the hard way but I couldn't let on about my gift.

When we reached the door I'd identified we could hear soft sobbing within. Tess slowly opened the door so we could slip in. A girl I recognized but didn't know was huddled on the bed half dressed and holding what remained of her costume around her. Tess pulled a bottle of water from her bag and then flipped me a small case and two surgical gloves. "Look for cameras and swap out the cards. Look for anything else that seems off." She leaned forward and began talking to the girl. She gave her the bottled water and held her hand.

I watched in surprise for a moment. Tess was tougher than I thought and a whole lot better prepared than I'd given her credit for. The camera on the tripod was obvious. I gloved up and then quickly ran through the pictures to see if the card was worth taking. I was sickened. How could people be so cruel to each other? Well, that was why I was here, right? I swapped out the card as Tess asked and then I began searching the room. I found a hidden video camera and checked to see if it was working. I stopped it and switched out its card too. I checked the window. I didn't know how we could get her out of here and I didn't want any more harm to come to her.

"What's under this room?" I asked Tess.

Tess rolled her eyes to the ceiling as she thought. "We're at the front of the house, right?"

"Yeah."

"She should be okay here for a bit. They'll think that they got what they wanted – some material to sign a new recruit. They only do one or two a party. They aren't completely stupid. Someone would take her home after the party. We'll come back and tonight it will be us who takes her home. We'll check the den that I think is below us before we come back up and then do you think we could lower her down?"

"Okay and yeah, I think we could. You first, to catch her and then I'll cover our tracks and follow you out."

Tess wrapped our victim in a blanket and stuffed her in the closet with the water bottle. She told her we would be back. The girl was pretty out of it and closed her eyes like she was going to take a nap.

"Is she okay?" I asked, worried.

"She will be. Come on." I peeled off the gloves and pocketed the chips. We closed the door behind us and headed downstairs again. Tess took me to the family room where much of the action was happening. Some were watching a horror movie in one corner. The bar was in full service swing with none other than Skimmer serving as bartender. Tess sashayed over and ordered us drinks while I snapped some pictures. When you're twenty-one you shouldn't be serving minors.

"What are you doing, Bitch?" I turned, it sounded like someone was speaking to me. Oh yay, Kirk. I turned back around without comment. Kirk put a hand on my shoulder. "I'm talking to you."

I flipped his hand off my shoulder and turned to face him. "What do you want?"

"I want you out of my house, out of my life and away from Tess," he snarled.

"We can't all get what we want," I said and turned back around. Tess was walking toward me. Kirk grabbed my shoulder and shoved me into the wall. I gave him my best stink eye but refrained from hitting him.

"Kirk!" Tess hissed, "Stop it, right now."

"I was just straightening out a few things. You need my help?"

"I'm fine but you will not get what you want if you don't stop it. I mean it!" Tess handed me the drink which I pretended to take a sip of. It smelled sickly sweet and 'alcoholy' with something bitter in the background. Tess caught my eye and gave her head a slight shake. She returned her gaze to Kirk. Tess stuck her finger in his chest and pushed him into the same wall where he had just smashed me. "Do you want me to do something for you?" she asked him sweetly. She pushed her chest toward him and his eyes glazed over. While he was distracted she switched cups with me without even looking. "Here, drink my drink for me and we'll go set up."

Kirk slurred an "Okay" at her cleavage. He took a big swig of the drink that had been meant for me.

"I'll just be a few minutes. You drink that," she said to me, with the slight 'no' head movement again. I put the cup to my lips and drank none. This one lacked the bitter undertone. Tess led Kirk back toward the stairs. I saw him take another big gulp. I leaned against the wall to wait. Two kids were talking next to me and I eavesdropped shamelessly. One set down her cup. Noting it was much emptier than mine, I quickly switched. She picked up my cup a moment later and did a slight double take before shrugging and taking a sip. I wandered over to get a better view of the bar. Skimmer was watching everyone so I pretended to watch the movie until his attention was diverted to the other side of the bar. I slid along the darkened wall. I found a nearly empty cup along the way and traded again.

At the end of the bar a girl sat on a stool facing another guy I didn't know. Her legs were on either side of him and I was starting to wonder if they would ever come up for air but they were a good cover. I tried to hide behind them and watch Skimmer but they noticed me. So I moved. There was a window in the corner that should have a good view of the bar. I was getting a little worried about Tess but keeping busy always helps with my worries so I moved outside.

It was just as bad out here. I was somewhat surprised that the neighbors hadn't called the cops. It was loud and the smell of pot was pungent. I could see them lighting up and sharing. I kept to the shadows and moved over to the window. Skimmer wasn't paying any attention. I suppressed my flash and took around twenty shots. I moved on around down the side of the house and quickly sent them to Marlo and White Eagle. Then I wiped my phone again. I moved the chips from my pocket to my boot.

I looked at my watch. Tess had been gone for almost fifteen minutes and I was getting more concerned by the second. I thought about where I was and realized I was on the same side of the house as the bedroom we'd found the girl in. I moved silently in the shadows until I could look up at the window in hopes of seeing Tess. What I saw sent my heart into my throat. Tess' silhouette was struggling with a much larger one.

I ran for the back door and headed inside. I threw my hand over my mouth and hunkered down as if I was sick. Only Skimmer watched me head for the hall. One boy caught sight of me and laughed. I made it to the hall and flew up the stairs four at a time. I could now hear the noise of a struggle mixed with other noises. No one else was bothering to check. I pelted down the hall. At five feet from the door I took a flying leap and hit it with both feet near the latch. The door slammed back into the wall startling Kirk. I landed, crouched on my feet, just inside the door as it jumped back from its smack into the wall, narrowly missing me.

I took two seconds to evaluate the situation, sprang from my crouch and kicked Kirk in the chin. I used my momentum to flip on over and back away from him landing in a crouch again. Tess stared at me, her top ripped open and hanging from one shoulder, her nose dripping blood and one eye starting to swell. The closet door was ajar and one bleary eye peeked out at me.

Kirk shook his head and growled. Geez, was this guy a tank or what? The fact that Tess was still standing was a credit to her skills. Kirk looked a little glassy-eyed and dim but I had angered his inner bull. He was preparing to charge. Kirk came at me with fists swinging. His belt was undone and his pants unbuttoned and partly unzipped; the rest of Tess looked fine so I assumed she was okay, just threatened. I ducked under his fists, shouldered him in the stomach and at the same time grabbed a handful of his pants on each side and yanked. He sank to his knees and stumbled trying to get up and free his legs. I kicked him again in the stomach. I caught a flash of movement and turned just in time... Tess, having had enough, jerked the bedside lamp's cord from the socket and smashed the whole thing down on Kirk's head. Tess was right behind the lamp. She jumped on Kirk's back, wrapped the cord around his neck and pulled tight.

"I... said... NO!" she screamed at him.

I convulsed momentarily with laughter. She looked like a mad cowgirl – the lamp cord her reins and Kirk her unlucky steed. I quickly sobered when I saw Kirk's color and heard him choke.

"Tess, enough... Tess. STOP." I took hold of her wrists as Kirk collapsed beneath her. With a whoosh the remaining air in his lungs burst out. Tess lost her grip on the cord and hung her head.

"What took you so long?" I held up a finger and then peeked out the door. Un-*freakin'*-believable. No one – not one person was coming to investigate. Did they care nothing about each other? I checked Kirk's pulse. He was passed out but breathing on his own. Tess had moved off him and flipped him over.

"I'm sorry I was slow to help you. I didn't know you needed me and I thought you were coming back. Let's get out of here and talk about this later. She looked down at her ruined costume. "What am I supposed to do about this?"

"Um, well, your bra is... blue. You could put the shirt in your bag? Or I can give you my shirt and just wear my coat?"

We both froze when we heard footsteps. Tess hopped back on Kirk, waved me away and then put his hands on her hips and bent over him. When the door opened I dove behind the dresser and she moaned, "Oh, Kirk," and moved a bit. The door clicked back shut. Tess turned and looked at me and we both started quietly laughing. Kirk moaned a little and looked at Tess with bleary eyes. "Hey Baby, you want some Kirk?"

Tess clenched both hands together and swung, smacking him right in the temple. I stared at her with my mouth hanging open. "Reflex," she said hopping to her feet. "Help me get him on the bed. We tossed him onto the bed and Tess positioned him. She took a pair gloves, snapped them on, put Kirk's hand in his boxers and snapped several photos with the camera on the tripod.

"Tess!" I hissed as she snapped away.

"What? He deserves it. Besides I won't post them on the internet like he deserves." She had me open the window and remove the screen. She tied the top sheet to the bed post and flung it out the window. Then she went over and coaxed the girl out of the closet. Tess climbed out the window and told the girl to follow her. I helped the girl out and Tess caught her. I untied the sheet, took pity on Kirk and tossed it over him. I checked his pulse and breathing to be sure he would live to regret tonight. I hung from the windowsill with one arm and closed the window with the other. Then I released and rolled.

Tess had tucked the ragged ends of her shirt into her bra. The girl was still a mess. Tess said that her mom was working tonight so we headed to her place. I called Marlo. "Hey, Mar, did you get what I sent? I have a video for you too... No I didn't get a sample."

"Yes we did!" Tess interrupted.

"Hold on, Tess says we did... I'll tell her, oh, and we have an errand to run first. Thanks, Buddy," I finished with Marlo and turned to her. "He wants us to meet up at Sarah's."

"Fine, but her first."

"How did you get the sample?"

"Later." Well, alrighty then. I kept my mouth shut the rest of the way to Tess'. We took the girl up to her apartment, headed straight to the bathroom and sat her on the closed toilet. Tess had me wait with her while she ran and got some clothes, then she shooed me out and shut the door. I'd never been to Tess' home before. She always came to mine. It was a smallish two bedroom with one bath. There was one eating area and one living area. I could see it all by standing in the same place. It was tidy and neatly furnished. I wandered over to the photos decorating the wall around the fireplace. The three of them looked happy. Tess' mom worked hard to take care of her girls. I saw baby pictures of Tess, every year of school and graduation photos of Tess' mom and her sister. I closed my eyes and felt the apartment. It was happy and calm except for... a music box sat on the end table near the couch. I picked it up. I opened it and there was a pair of earrings inside. When I touched them, I knew that Tess did feel guilty about what happened to her sister. She blamed herself. She did have vigilante tendencies and had been trying to bring this gang down ever since the night her sister nearly died. She liked me but she'd used me to get to them. She saw me as a tool to get what she wanted.

I felt hurt and anger well within me. I put the earrings back and returned the music box to its home on the end table. I sat down hard on the couch. Was I mad at her or me? It had been fun. I still had her in Science until at least January. Should I say something or should I wait? I shouldn't know what I knew. What a mess.

Tess came out of the bathroom, her outfit held with safety pins. "What?" she asked a little taken aback. I needed to work on my poker face.

"Is it me or the services I can provide that you're interested in?" Oh crap, did I really say that. I guess the hurt won out.

"Can't I have both?"

"I don't know, Tess, can you? I don't think I'm what you *really* want. I think that getting revenge for your sister meant more to you than I ever did. You didn't think I would help you unless you dated me. Tess, you're so much more than that! Use your brilliant mind, hang out with me because you like me, or don't, but you know what? Stop using me and treating me like all I could want from you is what you could *do* for me physically or by showing you off because you look good. You may be gorgeous but you're smart, funny and have a real spark. Don't sell me short – don't sell *you* short either." I was frustrated to find my hands shaking so I crossed my arms over my chest.

Tess just looked at me. Several different emotions drifted across her face. I could see hurt, anger, fear, guilt and relief. The relief stung. "I do like you. You're cute, funny, smart and handy to have around. I could not have done what I did tonight without you. Don't hate me. You're different, I should've treated you differently but I treated you like all the other boys at school... I'm sorry," she ended with a whisper.

Tess didn't even wait for a response. She walked to the kitchen and dropped her bag on the table. She pulled out a permanent marker and some plastic bags. She neatly labeled the bags and put several items from her bag inside each of them. She put them all in a bigger bag and handed it to me. "Do one last thing for me, would you?"

"What is it, Tess?" I asked in a tired voice.

"Turn this in to your cop friend. I'll drop you off at Sarah's and take her home," she said indicating the bathroom with a flick of her head. "If you're still speaking to me on Monday, save me a seat in Biology. If you aren't... I'll understand."

"Put an icepack on your eye, Tess," I said, instead of answering her.

She gave me a sad look and headed back to the kitchen. She took some frozen corn out of the freezer and wrapped it in a towel. She'd cleaned up her nose but now her hand was swelling where it had connected with Kirk's head. I leaned on the kitchen counter causing her to jump.

"How'd you get the evidence?"

She sighed and watched me. I'd pushed my anger and frustration as far down as I could. She measured me with her one-eyed gaze. "I had Skimmer make the special cocktail for you like Kirk wanted. I knew you wouldn't drink it but at least Skimmer could vouch that I had asked for it. When Kirk was messing with you again it made me mad so I got the idea to switch the drinks. I thought I'd give him a taste of his own medicine. Literally. Kirk is a big guy and the drug was not enough. He'd already had a bunch to drink. We went to set up the room for you. He drained the cup and set it on the dresser. I picked it up and put it in my bag. He couldn't figure out why the video camera was off. I tried to distract him but it didn't work out. I kept waiting for the drugs to take effect. Kirk decided that a different kind of payment from me would be fine. I went with it for a bit to see if I could find any of the drugs in his pockets or if Skimmer had it all. I found one pill so I took it. He caught me and tried to make me take it and we fought. I put the pill in my bra and he tried to take it back; that's how my costume got ripped. He began to realize that I'd turned the tables on him. I don't know what he'll remember tomorrow. I don't know what Skimmer will remember."

"Do they know where you live?"

"I don't think so but even if they did – I'm safe here. I have a nice elderly neighbor who will call the cops if he hears anything. The manager lives across the hall and my mom will be off at two. She also has the next couple of days off. By Monday this mess should be about cleaned up."

Tess' rescue came around the corner holding her head. "I'm ready to go home," she murmured like it hurt to talk.

Tess dropped her makeshift icepack on the counter and began rummaging in cupboards. She pulled out a couple of pills and a caffeinated beverage from the fridge. She sat her down at the table and then pulled together a quick sandwich and a glass of milk and made her eat it. She also pulled out another bottle of water. The girl looked at Tess like she was nuts. "You gotta flush it out, sister. I know - I've been there. Eat up and I'll take you home."

"My parents are gonna kill me and I think I left my purse there."

"Nope, it was in the room with you. I snagged it. I hope nothing's missing," Tess told her as she pulled the purse from her never-ending shoulder bag. The girl looked like Christmas had come early. The first thing she checked was her cell. She told us her ride had called looking for her. She called back and said she had walked home. It didn't sound like her friend had pressed her. She needed better friends.

Tess cleaned up the kitchen and sent us out the door. She locked up and we headed for the car. I got in back. Tess gave me a sad look in the rearview mirror. She took me to Sarah's. "You gonna be okay?" I asked.

Her smile was overly bright. "I'm nearly always alright," she said, her smile turning sad.

"Well, call me to let me know you got home okay and call if you have any problems between now and when your mom gets home," I said earnestly.

She reached up and touched my cheek as I leaned on the window frame. "Sure, Indy. Cute costume. You did great tonight and I'm... truly sorry." She put her car in gear and pulled out nearly running over my toes. I watched until she turned the corner and was out of sight.

TEN

I walked up to Sarah's door. Marlo met me there before I had a chance to knock. "This one had a steep price tag, huh?" he said, catching my mood.

"Yeah."

Sarah appeared behind Marlo and ushered us into her office. I couldn't believe it when I saw Evelyn sitting in the visitor's chair in front of the desk.

"Don't look so surprised, young man. We've been working with the school and trying to catch that son of a... gun for awhile. Let's see what you've got." I handed her the bag without even looking at it. I'd totally lost interest for now. I wanted a shower and sleep.

"Owen honey, you smell... awful," Sarah said with a worried frown.

"I know. Tess had me rinse and spit some Vodka and then she doused me with it. Some people were also lighting up and I don't mean cigarettes. I bet I smell... fantastic," I scoffed with a mocking tone.

"We'll get you a shower soon but Evelyn has some questions first," Sarah said in a gentle worried tone. I looked at Marlo but he was madly typing on two separate computers at once. What was with that guy? He was so not normal.

"Did you label all this?" Evelyn asked me with raised eyebrows.

"No, Tess did. Why?"

"Well..."

"Oh shoot, Mar, I have some video in my boot, too." I quickly pulled it out and handed it to him.

"Owen?" Evelyn tried again.

"Huh?"

"Well, there's a note in here for you and a signed confession from Tess."

"What?!?"

"There's a flash drive, too. Marlo, would you be so kind as to check this out please," Evelyn asked, as she handed it over and passed me the letter from Tess.

I looked at her beautiful loopy handwriting. I was half afraid to open it but it was free of darkness, it just held sadness. I looked up as sound emitted from Marlo's laptop.

Tess had left us a video cataloging all her evidence. She'd been watching, waiting and tracking Skimmer from the day her sister had nearly died. That party had been at Skimmer's house. She had his parent's address and his current one. She had makes and models for every car he'd ever owned. She had pictures of all the kids that had been recruited over the last three years, which she showed us and gave names for most. She listed who she thought the number two guy was and that she suspected that Kirk was now the number three guy. She hated to get Kirk in trouble and ruin his chance at a football scholarship but he had to pay for his crimes. She repeated that he'd tried to keep her out of it to keep her safe. For Skimmer she held no remorse. She felt bad for all the kids that had been trapped and tricked. Skimmer had started out with willing kids – the ones who would work for drugs. When his business grew too fast and he couldn't convince enough of them to join, he'd come up with a new scheme to recruit them. Tess was ashamed she'd kept it quiet so long but she didn't know who would believe her and then she heard rumors about me. She got switched into my Biology class to meet me. She worked as a waitress for none other than Skimmer's mom so that she could gain more information about him. All of her high school time to date had been dedicated to the fall of Skimmer. Skimmer was her obsession. She would have justice and revenge for her sister, herself and all the people Skimmer had hurt.

The rest of the flash drive held charts, graphs, documents and photos. I looked down at my letter again and finally stuck my finger under the flap to open it. I felt thoroughly played.

"Tess' confession is a list of all the things she did that she thought might be illegal. She begs for forgiveness and hopes her evidence will help but she is willing to face the music," Evelyn stated as she looked up from the paper in her hand.

"You have to help her," I found myself saying. I might feel betrayed but I understood her and held a grudging respect for her. "One of you should probably hire her. She played me well enough."

Sarah and Evelyn made eye contact but I ignored them and finally opened my letter.

Dear Owen,

I'm not who you think I am. I'm not a good person. I didn't meet you by chance, I picked you. I heard rumors about you and felt I had to meet you. I got changed into your science class. I picked you out right away from the group in the room and I decided it was fate that the seat next to you was empty. I set about recruiting you to help me and I used every skill I had to do it. It broke my heart that you were such a nice person and seemed to genuinely care about others. I'd gotten to where I only cared about bringing Frances Fendike down. He pushed too much alcohol on my sister and then wouldn't help her. He laughed – laughed when he saw her passed out on his bathroom floor. He was mad that she had thrown up in there. He said it was too bad she was so weak. He kicked her. I'd already been watching his cruelty for six months and I was done. I swore I would get revenge that night. I used you to do it. I'm so very sorry. I came to really care about you. I didn't plan on that. On the bright side, we saved one tonight if nothing else. You may not feel that it was worth it but I do. Please try to find it in your heart to forgive me and I will try to forgive myself like you said, but not just about my sister – I will try to forgive myself for what I did to you. Despite what life throws at you, keep standing up for what you know is right!

Love, Tess

I slumped in my chair, suddenly exhausted. I handed the letter to Evelyn. "I'd like it back when you're done with it. I'm going home now." I started to stand but Sarah put a hand on my shoulder.

"I texted your mom. Your dad is asleep. There's no sign of Willie. White Eagle is on his way. He'll walk you home just in case."

"Okay, Sarah," I sighed and rested my chin on my hand. Next thing I knew White Eagle was tapping me on the shoulder. Marlo was already gone and so was Evelyn. White Eagle and Sarah walked me to the door. Sarah hugged me and suggested I let White Eagle take my clothes to air-dry somewhere safe. I nodded and we walked home in silence. I quickly showered, dressed in an old pair of sweats, handed White Eagle all my costume pieces, thanked him and fell into a deep dreamless sleep.

My bed wiggled, annoying me. I opened one eye to glare at the offender. My room was brightly lit with a new overcast day. Seeing Mom, I wiped the scowl off my face. "Your dad is leaving soon, honey. White Eagle told me all he knew last night but if you want to talk, I'm here for you. You know that." Mom bent forward and kissed my forehead. "Don't forget, you're my favorite."

"Yeah, I know Mom, and don't tell the others, right?"

"I'm glad you still remember the drill." She smiled at me and left the room.

I rolled over and stretched. My bedside clock read almost eleven. Wow! I checked my cell but only Marlo had texted. I hurried through my morning rituals and threw on a t-shirt over my sweat pants. I put on a pair of socks and went downstairs.

Dad was nervous but trying hard to hide it. "Owen?"

"Yes, Dad."

"I just wanted to say that I am sorry for the pain I have caused you. I didn't understand. I didn't believe you and that got all of us into trouble. I wish things were different." He smiled a half smile. "I guess I'll pay for that now."

"I'm sorry too, Dad. I wish things were different as well, but we can't change what is behind us – we can only move forward and make the next best choice when given the opportunity."

"Wise words – when did you get so old?"

Now it was me who smiled the half smile. "Over the last year I guess. I'll tell you about it sometime."

"Look, Owen, I'm really worried about when you come to Florida for Christmas with your mom and your brothers."

"I know, Dad. Have faith in all of us. We have time to plan and strategize. We won't come in there blind. Trust me."

"You can't plan for everything," he said nervously.

"We know that – you have to trust us."

"I know Willie. Honestly, he scares me. The people he works for can be no better, in fact I know they're worse. I've met a few and what they did to me without my fully realizing it..." Dad looked ashamed and he looked old. I reached out and hugged him. He looked like he needed it.

White Eagle came quietly in the back door. He gave Dad four things – a prepaid cell to call us if he needed to (with the warning that it might be discovered and taken), a personal GPS tracker and two of the smallest flash drives I'd ever seen. "I promise you, we'll do what we can. We need some solid evidence to go after these guys. Just taking out Willie means we've removed the one nemesis we know about, but he might lead us to more information unwittingly."

Dad nodded looking more resigned than anything. He walked into the laundry room where the dryer was once again doing its 'white noise' job and put on his bugged sport coat and shoes and picked up his luggage. A black car pulled into the driveway and White

Eagle melted into the shadows. Dad hugged my mom, my brothers and finally me. He whispered to me, "I hope it's all worth it."

I wanted to ask him what he meant but he was already heading out the door. Was he wondering if taking out our adversaries was worth it or if I was worth it? I knew he was trapped in a bad situation but he was partially to blame for being there. We all make choices.

As Dad approached the car, Willie got out. I knew I would see him eventually but this was too much. It was like salt on an open wound – a taunt – a slap in the face. Our eyes met for a moment as we measured each other. There was a moment of understanding. We would meet again and only one of us would walk away. Many emotions crashed through me at once, freezing me to the spot with my hands fisted and my jaw clenched. Dad looked sullenly at Willie, loaded his gear into the back of the car and got in. For a brief moment I wondered if I would ever see my dad again. I needed to forgive him and myself before it was too late and it ate at me forever.

The car pulled out – the moment passed. I stepped inside. White Eagle reached out and grasped my arm. "We have a lot of work to do."

I nodded. White Eagle made eye contact with Mom in some pre-arranged signal. He threw his truck keys to me. "We're picking up Marlo and heading for the shop. You drive."

White Eagle worked me hard. I couldn't remember when I'd been this physically and mentally exhausted. Marlo brought me up to speed on Skimmer. Evelyn would get the information and evidence to the right people. Kirk would be in big trouble too, but he was underage. All of the players in that big mess were falling into place. The innocent were being separated off. I wondered what would happen to Tess. Her only real crime was breaking and entering into Skimmer's house last year, but she had taken nothing but pictures. She was brave and reckless and foolish. I hated that she'd used me but I didn't want to see her get hurt. She was being questioned today. Part of me wished I could hold her hand.

Still feeling guilty on Monday, I saved a seat for Tess but she didn't show up. I'd decided to forgive her but our friendship had taken a serious blow. She would have to re-earn my trust. The teacher droned on and I drifted off. I was worried about Tess and hoped she was okay. I was startled when the bell rang at the end of class. I'd lost nearly an hour. I quickly wrote down our assignment from the board and flipped open my cell. No news from anyone. I sent Tess a text to let her know that I'd saved her a seat, gave her the assignment and said I hoped she was okay.

I headed for the commons, having missed most of the crowd. In the nearly empty hall I was hit by a wave of fear, dread and hopelessness. I heard my name whispered softly like a protective ward or a prayer. I looked around and saw no one paying attention to me. I closed my eyes for a moment and felt around me but the wave had rushed on by. I headed on wondering what had just happened. It wasn't my dad, but whatever it was, it didn't feel right.

The commons was abuzz with gossip. I ate alone and eavesdropped. I wondered where Jesus was but I wasn't worried. He had other friends he hung out with sometimes. I heard snatches of conversation about Skimmer's party but one conversation stopped me cold. Someone had been so badly beaten that they were in the hospital. I sat with my full attention on the speaker, my lunch forgotten. It sounded like some of Skimmer's thugs and it happened at Jesus' apartment building. I was ready to tap the speaker on the shoulder when my cell vibrated in my pocket.

I looked at the read-out, Tess. She thanked me for saving her a seat. She'd given her statement and right now she was at the hospital with... Jesus. He would live. He was sleeping. He was able to identify his attackers. They blamed him for the leaked information about Skimmer. Tess was there because she felt guilty. He had a police guard. A friend of Tess' mom, who also worked ER, had called to let them know that a fellow student had come in. Tess knew immediately who it was because Jesus had been assigned to her team. He'd been giving his Skimmer information to her so she knew there was a connection with his beating. She called the detective assigned to her and they had met Jesus in the ER.

I felt empty inside. I hoped he suffered no permanent damage. I hated it that people had to get hurt. How could humans be so cruel to each other? For a moment I wished I was oblivious to the ugliness in the world. More texts came in that day. Tess updated me on Jesus and Adrian's social network was still tracking Skimmer and his known associates as they were taken down.

Skimmer and nearly all of his gang were in custody by Thursday. They ratted on each other faster than the detectives could type. Rumors flew around school like gnats in a summer swarm. Tess had me email her assignments for the rest of the week. There was no news from my dad. It was strange to play football without Kirk and one of our defenders. Much was officially hushed up but the students still talked. Adrian's social network rerouted all gossip to credit mainly Tess. Due credit was given to Katie, Jesus and a couple of other kids. Our part was made to look very, very small. I was proud of Adrian because even he was hip to keeping a low profile on this one.

I wanted to protect the innocent as much or more than anyone else but sometimes I wondered if getting more information out there and exposing a few good guys wouldn't be the key to preventing much of the ugliness from happening instead of covering it up and hiding it away.

Football ended and all my free time became pawnshop time. I now knew more about Florida, and Miami specifically, than I ever wanted to. I read all the research Marlo could find on my dad and my grandfather. I knew more about the companies than was probably necessary. I studied maps of important buildings and of the streets around them.

The warrant came through on Vivian's shed. She was very cooperative and let the authorities take anything they wanted out of there. She called White Eagle two days later to see if he wanted to buy the van. She was done with her brother, Willie, and didn't even want to look at his any stuff. The police let her know that he'd been spotted in town.

Lucie still avoided me. She gave me long unreadable looks frequently and seemed to be followed by a dark cloud. Sometimes I thought I could almost hear her mumble to me but that was crazy because she was across the room. Just before Thanksgiving she ran into me, literally, giving me some crazy flashes of images. Her head had been bent and she had no idea where she was walking. I put an arm around her to steady her. "Lucie, let me help you," I said as I started to reach for the book she'd dropped. She gave me a stricken look and rushed off without her book. I slowly bent and picked it up. I caught an image off of it and was just focusing on the self-help title when it was snatched out of my hands and Lucie was once again running down the hall. Later I got a text saying thanks and she was sorry but she was late.

Things weren't much better with Tess. 'Awkward' was the phase our relationship had fallen into. She was frequently busy and so was I. Biology was the only time we had together and we were drifting apart. It was odd to have both Lucie and Tess look at me almost longingly and yet none of us did anything about it.

Jesus only missed a few days of school. I signed up to help him get caught up. Once Skimmer was in custody my buddy's whole world seemed to brighten. In just a couple of weeks he was a new man and was nearly always in a good mood and joyful, which made everything else in my life seem a little better. He got several more kids that no one knew about to turn in evidence on Skimmer and his gang. Tess and Jesus became good friends and I really didn't mind so much. I felt like a chapter had closed.

It was a shock to find my dad at home the Tuesday before Thanksgiving. I knew he was coming but not what day. The bigger shock was seeing him sitting at the kitchen table with my mom and Willie. I took in the scene and slowly let my backpack fall to the floor. Mom was holding her coffee cup clutched in both hands. She was practically vibrating with suppressed anger and fear. Dad looked awful. He was grayer than I had ever seen him and his skin looked dead and tired. Willie looked menacing. How had I missed…? Willie was using his talent on me. He was making himself invisible. I should have noticed.

"Owen, this is Willie Brown. He's my personal bodyguard. He'll be staying with us for my visit. He'll have your room and you'll camp out with your brothers. Please go move the things you need from your room into your brother's room. Willie will be staying with you after I go back to work and someone else will be assigned to me. Isn't that... great?" Dad must have paused too long because Willie sent him a warning look.

"Yes, Dad, I understand. I'm just wondering why we need so much security."

"Do as I say," Dad said through gritted teeth.

"Yes, sir," I answered, trying to figure out what was really going on. "Mom, I see that dinner isn't going. Shall I order some pizza? I'd like to help."

Strangely she looked at Willie before she looked at my dad. He gave a slight nod. Mom looked at me with frightened eyes. "Well, wouldn't that be lovely. I would love to have your help. Pizza sounds nice."

I turned the corner and headed for the stairs. I heard the click of a safety going back on. I blew out a breath as I lightly ran up the stairs. I used my cell to call White Eagle.

"Yah," he barked after only one ring.

"I need to order some pizza and I need it here right away."

"What?!?" Why hadn't we ever come up with a prearranged emergency signal?

"I need some help... with a pizza order," I repeated hoping he would get the message that we were in trouble.

"What do you need?"

"Let me check."

I walked to my brother's room keeping the line open. They were hunkered in their room playing very quietly. They looked up at me, saying nothing. I tried to give them an encouraging smile. "Everything is going to be okay, guys... I'm ordering pizza," I said aloud and then I mouthed 'White Eagle' and put my finger to my lips warning them to be quiet. To White Eagle I said, "My brothers like Canadian bacon and sausage. Let me go downstairs to see what Mom, Dad and our guest want." Trying to give information and not alert Willie was exhausting.

White Eagle interrupted. "Got it... But wait. Dial the pizza place on the corner and hang up. Then if Willie looks at your phone you're clean. Erase your call to me. I'll call in pizza and be your delivery boy. It's Willie, right? Your parents are downstairs and your brothers are in their room?"

"Yep, that's our order, Gun. Thanks and please hurry." I quickly erased the call and dialed the pizza place. I left the line open for as long as I could and then killed the call. I quickly took my most important stuff out of my room. I keep very little on my actual hard drive but I quickly took the auxiliary unit I keep hidden. I moved that to my brother's room. I had Alex take Lucas to get a load of my clothes while I quickly stashed my portable hard drive in the wall of their closet. Willie would never see it unless he stepped into their closet and looked back and up over the door. Who does that in a normal closet? If it's not a walk-in closet, you don't generally walk in so I should be good.

Mom hollered up from the foot of the stairs. "What's taking so long?"

"I'm doing what you asked. I'm moving my stuff and I ordered the pizza," I replied innocently.

I heard a faint scrabble sound and a hiss from Mom. "Would you come down here, please?" she asked stiffly. I moved to the head of the stairs. Willie was right behind her. I couldn't decide if she was more angry or scared. I moved slowly down the stairs.

"Let me see your phone," Willie snarled, his small dark eyes nearly slits.

"Why?" I asked, playing stupid.

"Because I said so," he said, moving the gun into my line of sight and holding it to Mom's side.

I was still four stairs from the bottom. I thought I could take him but I'd have to be quick. "What do you want?"

"Well, you of course. I know you went to see my sister. I smelled you there. I know that all of my treasures have been removed from her shed and I'm sure you had something to do with that. You know just a little more about me than I'd like. I don't know how you got on my trail but you won't ruin this job for me. You're going to have a little accident. Your whole family is going on a nice little vacation. Too bad you won't make it back. I won't miss you. Now give me the damn phone."

With his attention fully on me, Mom stomped hard on his instep and rolled away. I leaped straight at his chest connecting with both heels. The blow sent him right back into the entry door, the gun flying from his hand on impact. I didn't give him time to recover but jumped right on top of him, fists flying. Dad came around the corner and kicked the gun toward the kitchen.

Mom came over, fireplace poker in hand. Willie was fighting hard. He reached for my chest but I knocked his hand away. He tried again and connected. It felt like I imagine being hit with a taser would feel. I clawed at his hand, fighting to free myself. I began to feel weaker and disoriented as pain shot from my heart to my extremities, my back arching in response.

"Back off Lila, or I hit him again," Willie snarled.

Mom held the poker like a baseball bat. I could tell she was at war with herself. Dad had slumped to his knees.

"Brad, get me my gun," Willie barked and then added a thunderous, "Now!" when Dad did not move quickly enough. Dad put his foot to the gun but instead of kicking it to Willie, he kicked it even further away. Willie just stared at Dad for a moment. It was all I needed. I leaned back and rolled off him as mom swung down. Willie screamed on impact. I knew that sound – Mom had broken his rib.

Dad leaned heavily against the door jam. "Now what? They'll send someone worse."

Willie crawled to his feet. "You'll pay for this," he snarled, holding his side. Mom held her weapon aloft but Willie reached for her instead of me as expected. He swung her around and reached inside her shirt to touch her skin near her heart. There was a sizzle and a crack. Mom slumped to the floor before I could move. "What a neat little gift to find more than one of you in the house. No wonder they watch you. No wonder they want you."

"Who wants me?"

"Why the company, of course. They have spent plenty to collect you. Wait until they find out you're a matched set."

"What company?"

The doorbell rang and Willie lunged at me again. He picked me up by my neck, pushing me into the wall, my feet four inches off the ground. I tried to punch him in the side where I thought the broken rib was but he only laughed. I brought both hands together to whack his arms down and I tried to knee him. Mom struggled to her hands and knees as the front door burst open, pizzas flying. White Eagle kicked Willie in the side sending us both onto the stairs. White Eagle landed on top of us, hands around Willie's neck. He banged his head twice on the step and then continued to squeeze until Willie stopped moving. I lay next to Willie, panting. White Eagle pulled himself up and then extracted me.

"We need to tie him up until the cavalry arrives," White Eagle instructed. Mom nodded and left to find some duct tape as Dad fell into a kitchen chair. White Eagle began to pick up the pizzas he had thrown out of his way when he entered. I stood watching White Eagle, breathing hard.

I felt the air around me surge, as if the air pressure had suddenly changed. I froze to listen and *feel* the room. I was hit from behind and sent flying out the door - Willie right behind me. I landed heavily on the front porch and tumbled down the steps. Willie's big feet came stomping after me trying to connect. I rolled to my feet. Willie got a good hit to my cheek before I was ready. I jerked away, but not fast enough. He brought his other hand across my face and hit me full force, snapping my head back and to the side. I could hear the grunts of exertion as he hit me. He was wearing down. I could see the bulging of his eyes. White Eagle was coming down the steps. Willie snapped a leg around, catching me in the side while my attention was on White Eagle. The impact threw me sideways into the flowerbed below our front porch. Willie completely ignored White Eagle. I put my hands behind my head and used my legs to flip myself back to my feet. White Eagle landed a forceful kick to Willie's back, sending him head first into our porch railing. I paused, ready. He'd already fooled me once. When he twitched, I landed a kick to incapacitate his knee. I looked up to see Sarah running up our driveway as a car pulled in. I stepped from the flowerbed and fell to my knees. I hadn't felt the pain at first but it all hit me in a tsunami wave. Voices exploded around me, pain slashed from temple to temple and down the back of my neck. It caused me to drop back again onto the grass. What in the world? I filled my lungs and tried to steady myself.

I was amazed to see Evelyn pop out of the car and walk up to me in a flak vest followed by a young officer. "Another home invasion? You do know how to have fun around here, don't you? Guess we shouldn't have let him get away the first time," she said evenly. "Frank and his partner are getting suspicious of you so I thought I'd bring in someone new. Willie will be caught trying to break in here. You all fought him off. There is going to be some jurisdictional mud and then Sarah's people can have him. I can't have him shooting his mouth off about *you*. You're cleaning up more stuff than I've ever seen done by one of your kind. I appreciate it. I like living in a safe town."

She led her young officer off and went to work with Sarah right behind her. They cuffed the unconscious Willie, carefully searched him and dragged him to the police car, locking him in the back. Evelyn had the officer watch the car while she took our statements. She corrected them to fit with her version of the story as she went. I could have kissed her if my head weren't pounding. She left the company car and Willie's belongings for Sarah to go over, saying that she planned to play 'the dumb card' and not realize they were Willie's, so to be quick just in case.

Mom and Dad and I sat on the couch, all in a row, while Evelyn was there taking statements and 'fixing' our story. 'Hear no evil, speak no evil, see no evil' kept running through my mind. White Eagle sat in a straight-backed chair from the kitchen.

Sarah had ushered the inquisitive Alex back upstairs and then kept my brothers up in their room. Evelyn let Sarah know when she was about ready to leave. White Eagle looked the three of us over and began making repairs. He was surprised to find fingerprints on us where Willie had touched us. Mom and I each described what it felt like. We both had awful headaches. He switched his attention to Dad when we heard footsteps on the stairs. Lucas made straight for me and climbed onto my lap. Sarah pulled some equipment out of her bag and began to scan for bugs again. Alex sat in Mom's chair looking furious. Sarah noted his attitude and quickly put him to work with another piece of equipment. He brightened immediately. She signaled that the room was still clear and moved on with Alex in tow. Mom took Lucas from me and left to salvage the pizza and pull out leftovers while holding her head.

Once the room was cleared, White Eagle questioned Dad extensively about everything. Dad told him that he was not taking any obvious drugs but that he could still feel the weird effects. He thought they hid some in his food. Dad had kept the GPS and the flash drive hidden. He had been able to sneak a little information onto the flash drive. They'd found the cell phone and were angry; that is why we had received the gift of Willie. He'd become furious when Vivian had called him on the way from the airport, to bitch him out and tell him never, ever, to come back. He hadn't smelled me after all – he'd learned of our visit from his sister. He was trying to scare me. Dad thought that Willie was supposed to just watch us but he'd gone over the edge. In the end, we hadn't had a choice about Willie; we had to turn him in, but the scary question was... now what?

We hoped that because the warrant at Vivian's had come through first, there was a record and 'the company' would think it was a rotten coincidence. We were concerned about what we'd need to look out for next. Dad turned the flash drive over to White Eagle.

Mom called everyone to dinner. Sarah said she wanted to check the upstairs and call in Willie's car first. Alex, her sidekick, went with her – some things, apparently, are more important than pizza. Who knew?

White Eagle pulled me aside. "Willie knows for sure what you can do now. He touched your power. He also knows what your Mom's gift is and I think he used it to heal himself, though it's possible he just transferred the pain to your mom, both of which are scary skills. What I don't know is how he got them. He seems so multi-talented. Perhaps he's found a way to keep a bit of what he steals. I haven't seen a draining leave a mark before. I'm afraid. I can't decide if we should rush in and take them by surprise or surprise them at Christmas as we'd planned. We aren't ready yet but... neither are they."

"For the moment, I think we need to let Evelyn and Sarah do their jobs. I can't believe I'm saying this. I'm usually the one to rush in but it feels... wrong. We're not ready and for once I think we need to be. I also feel really weird and weak. I feel like I'm back to the early days."

"He definitely sucked some of your power away. He did it really fast. I wonder if that's why he left a mark... Your mom's is worse but he touched her skin. Yours was insulated by your shirt..." White Eagle left me behind, to wander into the kitchen as he did sometimes when he was deep in thought.

My head still pounded but it was dull now. I went to bed early, but I had trouble going to sleep. My life was a disaster. My thoughts churned and the more I tried to shut it all off, the worse it got. My sheets were tangled and twisted, much like my mind. I finally ran through some yoga and Tai Chi at about one in the morning. I fell asleep soon after.

My eyes snapped open. It was still dark. My clock read just after three. I listened with my whole body. Wind roared as rain pelted the windows in a staccato rhythm. The few remaining leaves I could see out my rain-drenched window, twisted helplessly on branches, dancing wildly as if they were hanging on for dear life. It was both beautiful and terrifying to watch the trees wave frantically like seaweed under a storm-tossed sea. A branch must have hit the house, I thought, but I walked the house and checked every window and door anyway. My heart was still beating fast as I walked through the living room. I felt again the strange wave I'd felt at school. There was an impatience and hunger to it. The fear, frustration and hopelessness was... calling to me. Suddenly I was looking out another rain smeared window that was not my own and then it was gone. There was a faint ringing left in the air as if someone had just said my name... I spun in a circle feeling like I'd lost my mind for a moment.

I sat in Mom's chair and waited for it to come back or for something to happen. After an hour I was cold and shivery so I slowly took myself back to bed. I hugged a pillow to my chest, rolled onto my side and was gone.

ELEVEN

I awoke to Lucas sitting on my bed watching me. He told me that Mom and I had overslept and that we had missed plenty. The biggest news being that Willie's company car had been loaded onto a flat bed and taken away by Sarah and some other people. He had watched every moment with relish. Sarah, ever popular with my brothers – well, all of us - had brought orange rolls with her. When the woman had time to bake, I had no idea.

Dad was only with us for five days. He was picked up by a new man in a black suit and mirrored shades. He gave me a long hard look when he came to the door. I could feel the waves of darkness roll off of him. This was the quietest and most refined 'bad guy' I had yet to meet. He seemed to be emotionless - which in some ways was a whole lot scarier than the people I'd dealt with up 'til now. His arrival and Dad's departure were both a big surprise to us all, but Dad had been prepared just in case. He left with none of his usual gear – just the clothes on his back, the mini flash drive hidden in his shoe and the new GPS unit hidden in his belt.

My life fell into a hectic pattern. Marlo, Adrian and I were at the pawnshop every free moment of every day we could get away. For me that was literally every day. We did all our usual work for Max and worked out and studied like never before. White Eagle had me swimming three times a week, running and practicing every fighting style we had ever learned. He also added rock climbing and a new style of martial arts similar to what the Marine's teach. It was a blend of hand-to-hand and close quarters combat including unarmed, edged weapons, and weapons of opportunity. I started losing weight so Marlo got back to work on my diet, logging my every move and every morsel I ate.

Tess was almost back to normal by the second week of December but things still weren't the same. I made time to go to a movie with her and we tried some Arabic food one night. She wasn't running with me anymore because she had a new job and worked on Sundays, she said. I missed her company but I was afraid to let her get too close again. We'd never officially broken up - we were just drifting apart.

Lucie seemed desperate to talk to me and afraid to do it at the same time. I wanted to scream from frustration. She seemed to sense that things had changed with Tess. A few times I found her startlingly close to me. When I did manage to touch her, I still got strange fleeting images, none of which seemed particularly dangerous, just odd. Once she even went so far as to open her mouth to speak. The words seemed to clog in her throat. She ended up shaking her head and walking away after putting a hand to my cheek.

Adrian and Marlo were dying to go with us to Miami after they had worked so hard on this mission but of course their families wouldn't let them go. Christmas is family time. Marlo and Sarah worked extra hard to have us technologically prepared. She also carefully mapped out a Miami contact. She and White Eagle left three days before Mom and I packed up the boys to go. Time had gone so fast and as much as I'd trained, I didn't feel ready. I had two types of clothes with me, one to fool my grandparents and my usual work attire of plain t-shirts, cargo pants and boots. I packed the boots but wore running shoes to the airport. White Eagle had insisted on a new type of foot gear just in case. I now had black rock climbing shoes. I had cargo pants in beige and black and all my t-shirts were now plain. My favorite rock band shirts would have to stay at home for this adventure. I had nothing to make people notice me - nothing to make me stand out. I would be using urban camouflage.

Marlo's dad took us to the airport in a jolly mood, which was pretty darned amazing considering that it was four in the morning. Again, morning people – gross. He gave us big hugs at the departure drop-off area. Marlo was a lucky guy. As we waved goodbye I wondered if it was the last time I'd ever see him. I quickly pushed the thought away.

I carried much more cash than I normally would. Just in case we got separated, I needed to be prepared. The only weapons I carried were my mind and my body. Mom and I were on full alert. We watched everybody and noted every surveillance camera and security guard. Lucas was all about the excitement and adventure. Alex slid back and forth between that and wariness. He was much more sensitive to how Mom and I were acting.

Our flight was on time and everything went smoothly. Lucas charmed all the flight attendants. I felt that same sense of doom, wondering if this was the last fun we would have together. Marlo was watching our pets at his house. Our house had been secured and was being monitored by Sarah's team. As the plane crossed the tarmac I had another one of those waves hit me. It caused me to suck in a surprised breath. This time there was a feeling of worry and... need. The wave passed with a whisper of disappointment and again I swear my name was said.

As soon as we deplaned I took my brothers to the bathroom and quickly called White Eagle to give him an update. Dad was not the only one with a GPS unit. We all had them hidden on us. My normal phone was locked up at Sarah's house. I had committed to memory all the important numbers I'd need. I had a cheap disposable on me and had another in my suitcase. I only had my DMV issued permit as identification. They would get nothing from me if I was captured. What a great thought.

We were dressed a little warm for Florida so I helped my brothers unzip the bottoms off their pants and helped them stuff their pant bottoms and sweatshirts into their back packs. Alex and I reset our watches to local time, now almost four in the afternoon with the time change. I had a nervous moment when my mom didn't appear right away.

"Line," she said by way of apology. She took Lucas by the hand, held her head up high and led us to baggage claim. A woman was waiting for us by our assigned baggage carousel. I hadn't seen her before but she felt like a clone of the man who had picked up Dad. She was just as coldly silent. She wore dark glasses so I couldn't see her eyes – which really upped the creepy factor. She held a sign with our name on it.

As we retrieved our baggage, I took my lock picks and knife from the hidden compartment near the wheels of my rolling duffel bag and quickly stashed them in my cargo pants in the confusion. We loaded into a black limo that Lucas thought was pretty cool. He had no memories of the last time we visited our Ryer grandparents. I already felt like a prisoner. It was a relief to know that Sarah and White Eagle were out there but I still felt that my priority was the safety of Mom and my brothers. As we drove, I thought about White Eagle and his special addition to my duffel. He had designed it so that when it passed through the airport machines it looked like supports for the wheel mechanism. I didn't know if it would really work and had put a few items of clothing in each of my brother's suitcases, just in case mine got confiscated. I should know better than to doubt White Eagle.

Lucas and Alex looked on in awe as we pulled into a fantastic waterfront neighborhood and then up to a wrought iron gate set in stone. The greenery was tropical and lush. The gates swung slowly open and the car moved in. So far everything looked just like the satellite images I'd studied. It is amazing what you can get off the internet these days.

We were ushered quickly inside. Alex and I manned the luggage. Lucas looked like he was having a great time. "Mommy, look. Is this our hotel?" His words came out slurred from a combination of excitement and no front teeth at the moment.

"No honey, this is Grandpa Ryer's house."

"Really? It's so big. He must be spoiled."

"You have no idea," Mom muttered under her breath. I hid a smile.

We entered under a two story arch and the front door swung wide. Our chauffeur followed us to the door but didn't come inside. The door was locked behind us, with what felt like finality. If this was prison, it was a gilded cage. The entry was huge and included a magnificent staircase that went up and then curved back on itself to both sides. Beyond was a sitting area and past that a sparkling pool.

A worn housekeeper asked us to leave the luggage in the entry and invited us into the parlor to our left. Alex and I set down our load and followed Mom. I snuck a peek back over my shoulder and saw a code entered into a keypad by the door. I quickly turned my head before the operator turned his attention back on me. I did notice that he had a chair by the door and was wearing an ear piece.

"Welcome, welcome," my grandfather said stiffly, from his position by the hearth. "Dorothy, some refreshments for our guests." No one said anything. Grandma Ryer sat huddled and submissive in an arm chair. They were both grayer, smaller and more wrinkled than I remembered. My grandfather may not have been the greatest guy but now I almost felt sorry for him. From our research I knew that he was rich and powerful. He was good at making money and making things happen. Not long ago he'd gotten involved with the wrong people. Marlo had read all the corporate reports. New people started flowing in when Grandpa's umbrella company took on the Atlanta branch. Now he was not the puppet master but a puppet himself. Dad's brains and now my gift were unexpected bonuses. Marlo's theory was that some smart lowlife had started banding others together, those that could be paid off or manipulated. This person needed money to make it work. The more good guys they sucked dry or converted, the better for their bottom line. There had been a rise in disappearances in Atlanta since the new folks moved into town. Last year the same thing had happened in Miami. Sarah and White Eagle agreed with Marlo. They'd formed a pack to hunt good *watchers* and Grandpa had gotten involved because of greed – he was now, unknowingly we hoped, their chief financier.

"Thank you for having us," my mother replied just as stiffly formal.

Lucas broke away from my mom and walked right up to Grandma Ryer. "Are you my grandma?" he asked her with sweet innocence. The whole room froze and watched. Grandma looked at Grandpa;

a look passed between them. Then she opened her arms as if to invite Lucas onto her lap. "Yes I am, honey, and I'm glad you're here. I've missed you. You must be Lucas."

There was a knock at the door and shortly after, Dad was ushered into the room. His eyes slammed into each of ours and he seemed to relax. Suddenly I felt my internal warning signal go off. Mom seemed to feel it too. She has grown to have a relatively powerful sixth sense; the others in the room clearly lacked that ability because no one else turned. From the moment I'd stepped into the house I felt that strange pull I feel sometimes just behind my bellybutton. Today it combined with a vibration along my skin, a traveling current that moved up my feet, to my legs, my spine, down my arms, pulsing in my head like I had a headache coming on. It was as if my very molecules were humming. Mom and I were feeling something that we could not yet see. I wished I knew what my body was trying to tell me.

The whole house had things to tell me too, which was very distracting. The house itself and several objects were all shouting for my attention. My head began to pound harder. I felt almost seasick. I needed to sit. I hadn't felt this overcome even in my early days. I suddenly felt alone in the middle of the crowded room. I closed my eyes and took a deep breath. And then I knew... I was being *scanned*. This was nothing like when White Eagle did it or even Emiline Clairmont.

I took another breath and shook myself mentally. I focused on a single thought: Get out of my head! The pounding began to recede. My mom looked at me with worry on her face but no one else seemed to notice my lapse. A new man entered the room. I *looked* at him and knew he was the one who had *scanned* me. He looked right at me and smiled like he could sense what I was doing to him.

He was strangely young and old all at once. He was neatly dressed in tailored immaculate clothes. He was tanned and blond like a wealthy playboy. He slowly removed his dark glasses to show startlingly blue eyes.

"You must be Owen. We've been waiting a long time for you." His voice was silky smooth. It was that same combination of young and old. I was hit with a realization as he looked at me. He *was* young and old. That was his power. When he drained others he took some of their life away. He kept young by feeding off of *watchers*. He was the one who was banding them together. He trained others like White Eagle did but he fought for the side of darkness. How old was he? He must have years of wisdom. He seemed to realize he'd let me see too much. He quickly looked away from me and proceeded into the room where Grandpa Ryer was introducing him. I switched my gaze to Grandma Ryer and saw her tighten her grip on Lucas for a moment. Grandpa was fooled and sucked in but she was not. He wanted to believe this slick son of a gun. Grandma saw right through him. I had an advocate. Now I just had to get her alone.

Grandpa couldn't say enough wonderful things about Stephan Kraeghton, the CEO of Atlanta based Frederick, Cooper and Niles. When I couldn't stand it anymore I burst in, "So you must be some sort of adhesives expert then?" I had been staring at the back of Mr. Kraeghton's head for long enough. My words had come out a little aggressively, I knew, but I was done with the charade. He turned and looked at me for the first time since entering the room, his eyes slitted and his mouth in a hard straight line.

"You'll find I'm good at many things," he hissed, barely sounding even polite.

So I had gotten under his skin a little, good to know.

In an effort to make peace, my grandfather interrupted our impromptu staring match. "You have not been here for awhile, how about a tour? I'm sure you young ones are bored."

"First some ground rules, I think," Kraeghton interrupted.

"Yes, certainly, how... irresponsible of me... The ground rules or maybe we should call them the 'grounds rules', ay?" Grandfather Ryer tried to make a little joke but it fell flat. He nervously cleared his throat and continued, "Our safety is a top priority, so you are not allowed off the grounds. You have access to almost the entire house and we have a magnificent pool and a game room I know you boys will enjoy. You have access to the inner part of the backyard but do not go past the fence. We have a wonderful chef on staff. If you need anything you may ask Dorothy, our housekeeper. Dinner will be served at six sharp. We dress for dinner here. Do not be late."

"Why all the security," I boldly asked. "Has someone threatened you?"

"Powerful people always have enemies," Kraeghton answered for him. He was trying to make me feel afraid but I wasn't having any. Kraeghton scowled harder in my direction and I badly wanted to tell him not to pop a blood vessel. He quickly gave up when he noticed my grandfather looking at him and turned to give him a slimy smile.

Dorothy gave us the basic tour. She was very reluctant to answer any but the simplest of questions. She seemed nervous as hell and worried too. She was another one that I would have to get alone. I got the chance to touch her sleeve when she slipped on a palm frond near the pool. The images I got were frightening. She would have to be handled delicately – Kraeghton had threatened her family - a trick I knew well and it sickened me.

Dorothy ended our tour by showing us to our rooms. We were given a suite of our own. There was a sitting room that was almost as big as our family room at home. Mom and Dad had a room to share that was bigger than their room at home, complete with their own bath. My brothers and I would share a bathroom but not sleeping quarters. I was alone. Alex and Lucas had a smallish room with two twin beds. There was a large flat screen TV and stereo system in each room. In addition, my brothers and I each had the three most popular game systems complete with games in our rooms. Our luggage sat open and had clearly been searched. My second cell phone was missing. Super. I would have to keep all the most important stuff I had with me – on me.

I checked in with my brothers and discovered that they had been left their Play Station Vitas, their small handheld game systems. I hid a smile. You gotta love grownups; most of them don't know a thing about kid's toys, specifically the electronics. It was disappointing to have my cell phone confiscated but we were expecting that. I would bring it up at dinner. My new roll seemed to be that of an agitator. Well, everyone else could rest but I for one was going on my own tour of the house. We had pretty well mapped it out at the pawnshop but I wanted to check a few things and figure out what was off-limits before I was further restricted as I sensed I would be.

I'd have plenty of time to investigate our own quarters. I gave Mom the prearranged signal and let her know I would be on the prowl for fifteen minutes. She knew that if I was not back by then that she should come looking for me. She and Dad were having a quiet conversation with the stereo system playing for cover. Dad looked at me with concern but Mom put her hand on his leg and gave a minute shake of her head.

"I need a snack," I said, for any bugs listening.

"Don't ruin your dinner," Mom said in reply.

"I'm a teenager, I'm always hungry." Provided our food wasn't drugged or poisoned, I thought in my mind.

I had seen no obvious surveillance in our room but I was sure it was there. I paused at the door to our suite and listened. Hearing nothing, I opened the door and looked both ways as if deciding which way to go. I already had in mind that I would search the house one level at a time following the 'right hand rule' backwards. I would go left and check every room along my route, always keeping a wall on my left hand side.

Our suite took up the left front corner on the second floor. The wide upstairs gallery was lined with doors also widely spaced. What a house or should I say estate. My grandfather, yeesh, there were years he could have sent us money to help out but all the fancy opulence here? I would never trade it for the life I had. Who needed all this? The upstairs hall was empty of people, but held plenty of huge potted, tropical plants; perhaps suits of armor would have been more appropriate. The plush off-white carpet silenced my feet. Across the way were floor to ceiling windows overlooking the pool.

I passed a circular staircase that I remembered from the floor plans went down to a breakfast nook overlooking the pool and near the kitchen. I continued on through the semi-open game room. We had our own sitting room so why this was necessary was beyond me. It had tables ready to play cards or board games. There were shelves filled with every board game imaginable as well as a number of books. There was a bar with stools and the extravagance of a built-in soda fountain and a theater-worthy popcorn machine. There were several chairs with side tables with lamps. I could see my mom reading here overlooking the pool if things weren't so... scary. The room even contained a second staircase that I thought ended near the kitchen. I looked up at the ceiling. This room had been part of the old house but had been expanded to be part of the new section as well. These stairs must come down behind the kitchen.

The first real door to the left I tried was unlocked. I saw no one and stepped inside. It held a fully equipped gym. The house curved or angled so this room still overlooked the pool. Looking out the window I could see that there was more of the house to my right but Dorothy had not shown us this section. I saw movement so I pulled back from the window. It was a fourth black suit. I recounted in my head - Stephan Kraeghton, the female driver, the man at the front door and now this new guy who was a balding red head. I bet he hated the Floridian sun. I wondered if he was Dad's new guard. I didn't have a clear enough view to be sure. I went out the door on the other side of the room.

The next door was locked. I'd have to check it later so I moved on. On my right was now the gym and to my left the big entryway staircase we had come up. Just past the stairs was the media room Dorothy had shown us. It had stadium seating like a movie theater but with huge armchairs all connected. It was even set up for split-screen gaming but was also empty. Just past the media room was a small hall I hadn't noticed on the way in.

I eased down the hall still not seeing any internal surveillance. The hall opened to an area three times the entry width. I was on a covered bridge. I could see over the front driveway where our driver lounged under a palm tree while another man detailed the car. That guy looked and acted like a servant and not one of the suits. I looked out the other windows and could see Dad through his window sitting in a chair with a remote in his hand, probably watching TV. I moved on and reached another closed door. I was almost out of time.

From the floor plans I knew that this crazy house, no wait, estate, right?... had two separate multi-car garages. I must be over one of them. The door was locked. I looked around and seeing no one, pulled the lock picks from my pocket and had the lock undone fast enough to make White Eagle proud. I opened the door slowly and cautiously moved into the huge open space. The room had a low sloped roof and few windows. It was warm and muggy. There were stairs going down, an empty closet and a small bathroom. I peeked over the edge of the stairs but they turned, blocking my view. I was out of time and didn't want Mom to worry so I quickly relocked the door and went back over the indoor bridge, turned left and checked the one remaining door on this level.

The door was unlocked. There was some Cuban music playing softly but no one was present so I stepped inside. It was a laundry room that was more like a hotel laundry than one you would see in a real home. There were three sets of washers and dryers and tons of storage. There was also a dumbwaiter that I figured went down to the garage attached to the house. I checked the specifications that were neatly adhered inside. It had a five hundred pound capacity. Good to know. There was no obvious surveillance in this room but I was sure that I'd missed some on the rest of this floor. Marlo had done a search of every permit ever filed on the house and his research told us that there was more here than met the eye. Aren't public records great? If you know where to look, that is?

I hurried to our rooms and was relieved to find nothing had changed, though Mom looked like she was ready to head out the door. "Get your snack?" she asked innocently.

"Nah, I just wandered a bit. I forgot where the kitchen was but I found a nice gym," I answered.

Her eyebrows went up a bit. "You know, I believe they've remodeled since I was here last. The place seems bigger. I think this whole side is new. The garage used to be detached and the house ended at the kitchen."

I gave her a slight nod to indicate that I was with her and that she was correct. Mom moved in and gave me a hug. "Be careful. Also, I saw Sarah in the bathroom at the airport. We need to check in again tonight or first thing tomorrow at the latest," she softly whispered in my ear. "Time to dress for dinner," she added in a normal tone.

All of us got ready in our 'finery'. It seemed silly to me. Mom dressed my brothers in slacks, button up shirts and ties. Dad and I wore suits and Mom a nice dress. I let Mom know I'd meet her at dinner. I wanted a ten minute head start to explore the main level.

I decided on the stairs in the media room that came out behind the kitchen. I could hear a muffled argument from over near, or possibly in, the gym. I was afraid to get too close. There was no good place to hide in the game room so I edged on down the stairs. They opened into a large empty space. I could hear kitchen noise to my right. To my left was a short hall that curved back under the stairs. It ended in a huge pantry and utility area that rivaled the one upstairs in sheer volume and ridiculousness. At the far end I could see through the open door into the kitchen. I turned around and headed back. I'd missed it coming in but on my left was the dumbwaiter. I looked at it again. It also served as a pass-through into the garage. Now hey, that was something to keep in mind. The normal door to the garage was locked so I walked on by and angled left. Down a long hall that went across the back of the garage I found an unoccupied guest room. It had a walk-in closet and its own bathroom. It was mostly under my brothers' room upstairs and our shared bath. I went back the way I'd come and entered the first door on the left. It was a huge ugly behemoth of a billiard room. I'd only seen them in magazines and on the game board for Clue. I mean seriously, who has that in their house?

Next to the billiard room was a bathroom and dressing room area that you could enter from the pool or the hall. There were several stacks of towels in there. Looking out I could tell that the upper level overlapped the lower level creating a covered patio between where I was and the pool. Out by the pool was an outdoor cooking and eating area. Well, of course! Geez.

Since no one was out by the pool I snuck around the backside of the circular staircase and moved on to a huge sitting area that opened onto the pool deck. The room sat between quadruple sets of French doors and the backside of the grand staircase. I could see through to the entryway. The overweight door guard was dozing in his chair. The room was filled with overstuffed white sofas that looked like you could fall into them and never get out. On a raised platform sat a white grand piano and a beautiful blond harp. I moved on past the French doors.

There was a plain door near the harp that opened into a small hall. I could hear soft sounds coming from my left. I took a peek into the doorway and saw my grandmother. She was sitting in an armchair with her back to me. The room was a perfect octagon. Half of its wall space was filled with floor to ceiling windows overlooking the pool and a hint of a sitting room could be seen through the windows to the right. This side of the pool and the sitting room beyond were thick with tropical plants. I noticed the half of the room that wasn't covered with windows was covered by pictures of my family. Many, I could tell, my mom had sent but others looked like they had been taken from a distance – as if a private investigator or the paparazzi had taken them. I stood too long torn between amazement, shock and wonder. I heard her soft intake of breath...

"Owen," she whispered, "You shouldn't be here."

I walked over to her and knelt in front of her chair. "What's really going on here? Who are all these people? Are you okay?"

Her eyes welled with tears and she reached out to cradle my cheek in her hand. "I have missed you so. You look so much like your father. I'm glad you're here and I'll do everything I can to protect you. Do not trust Stephan Kraeghton– he is a dangerous man. He keeps us trapped here. He says it's for our safety but I don't believe a word of it. He's using your grandfather. They're making money together so your grandfather ignores what he doesn't want to see but we don't need it. Mr. Kraeghton is from Atlanta. He brought our new guards and chauffeur with him. Even your father has been different since he went to work in Atlanta. I don't know what they have your father working on. You know how intelligent he is but sometimes he lacks wisdom. I think he was fooled and now..."

I heard a noise and she must have too. "Go quickly," she breathed. She stood and walked over to a built-in bookcase and returned the album she had been looking at and picked up a camera. I didn't wait. I checked the hall and hurried out the door and then headed back to the door by the harp. All along the family room wall on what was now my left side must be the rest of my grandparent's suite. I moved toward the entry keeping tight to the wall. I found a powder room and silently moved on. The guard in the chair snored a thunderous snore. I froze. I could pretend I was just coming out of the bathroom. He snuffled and let loose another loud snore. How could he sleep through that? Would his head explode? Seeing that no one was coming and that he wasn't waking himself up, I decided to try the last door. Locked.

I pulled my picks from my pocket and had it open between snores. I wiped the sweat from my upper lip and ran a hand across my forehead. I hoped my antiperspirant was up to the task. I couldn't be sweaty at dinner and I only had about two minutes left. I slipped inside the room. It was empty. I blew out the breath I didn't even realize I'd been holding. I sent a quick text to White Eagle on my remaining phone and wiped the call record clean. This room had a second door that must go back into my grandparent's suite. It was fully lined with bookshelves everywhere that did not have a window. I quickly looked out front – the chauffeur and outside guard was still at her post. My grandfather had an enormous desk. I closed my eyes to see what in this room most needed my attention.

On the wall behind the desk was a family tree chart. All of us were on it going back many generations. I'd never done much family history research and was surprised to find that our Ryer name came from Ireland like my mom's background. I silently snorted - so Ryer was Irish. Hypocrite. Grandpa was about one thirty-second Irish. So an Irish lad once fell in love with a Cuban lass and the name had travelled down to me. Huh? Grandma's side was no better in Grandpa's eyes, I was sure. She was one quarter Choctaw, one half mixed breed American and one quarter Cuban. What was the deal with Mom's name? I looked closer - her name had been covered another name.

A file lay under the chart on the credenza. Dad was to marry a full blooded Cuban girl and he had refused. It looked like Grandpa thought she had an excellent pedigree. I flipped the page and about dropped the file. He now had plans to set me up. What? I would pick my own wife, thank you.

Below that file was another all about me. I spun in place until my eyes landed on a tall cabinet. I was out of time but I didn't know when I would get in here again. The cabinet was unlocked and held a nifty three in one printer, copier and fax unit. I quickly texted White Eagle that I needed to send them a fax. I could feel my body temperature rise as I waited impatiently for a reply. Sweat again beaded on my upper lip. A reassuring snore sounded from the entry but I knew that at any moment folks would begin gathering for dinner. I tried to calm myself but my hands were starting to shake. My phone vibrated, making me jump. I quickly stuffed my file into the fax and punched in the number White Eagle had sent. As soon as it was read, I grabbed the other file and sent it as well. I put everything back and watched with horror as the chauffeur started to enter a code by the front door. Crap. I was trapped. My eyes darted to the windows. I could tell right away that they were alarmed. I scanned the room and my eyes fell on the other door. Should I? I erased my phone log again after memorizing the fax number. As I pressed my ear to the door into my grandparent's suite, I heard the front door open and a loud slap.

"Bill, you lazy son of a... grrr, you're going to get us all in trouble and you know what that means!"

I didn't wait for Bill's reply. I cracked the door and eased into... my grandfather's... closet? Many items screamed for my attention. I touched as many as I could on my way past and would have to sort through the images later. What they showed me, scared me so badly that I wanted to hide in the closet forever but I couldn't. I had to save my family. Grandpa might not recognize the danger but I had a glimpse of what I was facing.

I kept to the darkened closet – its one window shuttered. It was up high and didn't look like it was alarmed. I watched Grandpa wash his hands at the sink, dry them and turn away from me.

"Maela, its time to go meet our guests for dinner."

"Yes, Richei, I'm ready," came Grandma's reply from the master bedroom.

I watched Grandpa exit the bathroom and turn left at the bedroom. He was headed out. I quickly hopped up on a built-in bureau with a marble top. The window was not alarmed. They missed one. The drop to the ground would be about ten feet. I had dropped further at Kirk's house.

I listened hard as I walked through the bathroom and passed Grandma's closet. Nothing here called to me. I looked both ways before entering the master bedroom. I took a quick look at the sitting room beyond the bedroom then turned left toward Grandma's octagonal gallery. I listened at the door but the voices were moving away. I pushed the lever and cracked the door. My grandparents were walking away from me and moving to the main staircase. The guards were still at the front door participating in their argument which now took place at a whisper. They stopped when my grandparents came into their view. I moved soundlessly behind the harp and piano and then made straight forward over a couch so that view of me was blocked by the stairs.

I could hear my parents and brothers coming down the stairs so I made a dash for the kitchen. I entered by the circular stairs surprising the chef, sous chef and a waiter.

"Hey, I'm Owen, I'm..."

"We know who you are, sir," the waiter said formally.

"I just thought I would pop in and see if I could help."

"Thank you, sir, but that is not allowed."

"Really?" I couldn't help it. It just slipped out. This was so far from what I was used to. "At home it's my night to clean the kitchen."

The chef gave me a huge grin and let out a jolly laugh. "Do you realize that we have prepared a dinner for twenty? Have you ever cleaned up after more than five?"

"Well sure, but I bet we don't serve as many courses," I replied with a big smile.

"Hey, you come on back then if they'll let you and you can try your hand in a bigger show." The chef laughed her happy laugh again.

"Mary, you're gonna get us in trouble!" the waiter hissed.

"Relax, Ralph, I'll take the heat. I don't have anyone to threaten and they won't fire me. I'd be challenging to replace."

Ralph, the waiter, looked at Mary, the chef, with concern, then quickly looked at me. I was already moving toward the opposite end of the kitchen like I hadn't heard the last part.

If I played my cards right, I had another ally. I would bet that she wouldn't poison my food intentionally. I waved at the three of them and left through the kitchen door that went to the dining room. My grandfather looked at me sharply, but no one said a word as I found my seat. Mom and Dad were prepared to sit along one side of the table with my brothers between them. I started to sit between my brothers but my grandfather had me come sit next to him at the head of the table and across from Kraeghton. Yay?

I felt pretty confident that tonight's dinner was safe but I carefully watched everything that happened in the dining room, especially Ralph, the waiter, and how people reacted to the food. I ate very slowly tasting each bite to detect any odd flavors. I also drank slowly for the same reasons. If things went South, at least I had gotten some information to Sarah and White Eagle. I imagine things were even worse for them because they would be worried and were helpless to do anything for us right now.

Dinner conversation was long and boring. My brothers were soon fidgety. My grandfather scowled at them but let them go when my mom politely asked if she could take them upstairs. I started to rise also but my grandfather bade me to sit. Oh boy. Alex sent me a look as he left the room. It was a combination of, 'I'm sorry' and 'I'm glad it's not me'. It was creepy to have Kraeghton follow my every move with his eyes. He was waiting for me to screw up. His eyes lit up a bit when he watched the interaction between Alex and me. A new worry. Goody. We had just handed Kraeghton a tool by mistake.

My grandfather put a hand over the one I had resting on the table. "Well, my boy, I have some exciting news for you!" he began in a pleased tone. "Since your father has not done as I have asked, I have decided to groom you to take over for me."

All conversation at the table stopped. My dad's dessert fork dangled half way to his mouth. The piece of coconut mango cake fell with a plop back onto his plate – strangely loud in the now silent room. I glanced at Kraeghton who quickly hid a secret smile as my grandfather continued, "You will start school here after the holidays and you will be trained in all that I know. You will be sent to the finest universities. You will travel abroad with me..."

"No," I said firmly without giving him the chance to go on.

"Father, I will not..." Dad tried to interrupt.

"You will not what? Get yourself involved in things that don't concern you? You had your chance. You are no longer valuable to me," my grandfather cut in over his attempt to seize control of the conversation.

"Richei!" my grandmother said fiercely.

"Why not be blunt? Abelardo Bradley Ryer is not doing a good job of raising his son." I winced hearing Dad's full name, knowing how much he hated it. "Owen will stay here and become what Ablelardo should have been," my grandfather said, like he had no idea how wrong it all was.

Grandma, Dad and I all spoke at once. Kraeghton rose and walked out of the room. My grandfather slammed his hand onto the table. "Enough," he roared.

"No," Dad answered defiantly, "I think that is quite enough out of you. We are leaving. Thank you for your hospitality. Mother, it was lovely to see you." Dad rose from his chair and said to me, "Come, Owen. This was a mistake."

"I'm so sorry you feel that way," Kraeghton said from the archway into the parlor. The chauffeur was at his side and the other two men blocked the way to the kitchen. "But it is too soon for you to leave. I have some special... lessons that I plan to teach Owen. I would hate for him to miss that." His handsome face took on an evil smile turning it ugly and frightening. I felt a moment of panic. I didn't know what fighting skills Dad had, if any. How would I protect my grandmother who sat silent, tears streaming down her face? Could I even take on four? I had a flash of inspiration. I focused all of my attention on Mom and called to her with my mind. I didn't even know if I could do it.

I felt her reply and got a glimpse of her being locked into our suite and of her rattling and kicking at the door in frustration. No help. No help for any of us. Well, I would NOT go meekly!

I lunged and picked up my steak knife on the way. I did the unexpected. I grasped my grandfather roughly and held the knife to his throat. "Let my family go or he get's hurt," I snarled in my most menacing voice. I pressed the knife in firmly making a white mark from the pressure and causing my grandfather to wince.

Kraeghton laughed. "Go ahead, Owen, I don't need him anymore."

"What?" my grandfather gasped and my grip lessened a bit.

"Silly old fool. I used you to get Owen here. I tapped into your crazy obsession about gene pools and lineage to get what I wanted. I've trapped you in your own home. You've been working from here for months. No one has seen you. You've taught me much and let me take over so much. I can now run both companies without you. I even got you to remodel and add the security system. Except it holds you in - it doesn't keep buglers or thieves like me out. We are... already here!" Kraeghton laughed and nodded at the chauffeur who moved toward me.

I stepped back from my grandfather. I tried to watch all four of them and Dad who was trying to get in the chauffeur's way. I threw the knife at the fat guard from the front door. I missed my mark and it imbedded harmlessly in his arm. I followed quickly behind the knife. I ran straight at the fat man who was struggling with the knife and blocking the doorway to the kitchen, the red-haired man behind him. I used his body like a ramp and ran straight up him, knocking him back into his partner. He grabbed futilely at the doorframe. With a crack he broke off part of the molding from the doorway on his way down taking his partner with him. I landed a well placed stomp on his stomach forcing the air from his lungs. I kicked at the jaw of the redhead when I heard a loud, extended ZzzzzzAaaaaaP and a double thump behind me.

"Owen, stop! Or the next jolt will kill him," shouted Kraeghton. I spun, ready to face what was next but stopped short. The chauffeur was down on one knee next to my father with a taser held right over his heart. Dad was out cold - the side of his head already swelling. The chauffeur smiled a sickeningly sweet smile at me - daring me to move.

"It was so nice to see you in action. You're in better shape than I'd hoped. It shall be a shame to break you but it must be done to remake you," Kraeghton continued with his own sick smile.

My grandparents hunkered listlessly in their chairs looking at their feet. My gaze left them and moved to my dad. I could see the rise and fall of his chest. He was okay for now.

"Don't look so disappointed, Boy. You may have lost this round but together we can win the war. We can get rid of all the goody goodies out there and rule the empire."

"No." I would die before he would turn me. I knew there were others out there. He might be wiping us out as fast as he could but it would now be my mission to take out this little cell of darkness – starting with Kraeghton. Miles had never faced anything like this. He had taken on many men and women working for chaos and disorder, fear and submission. Never, to his knowledge, had they banded together like this. Miles felt that there was 'no honor among thieves', so to speak. What did Kraeghton have on these guys or what was he willing to pay to keep them working together?

Kraeghton and I still stared at each other. I could hear sounds of the men in the doorway coming around. The kitchen was silent. I felt trapped.

"You will not turn me," I said, sounding braver than I felt.

Kraeghton just smiled. "Take him to the back, boys. Then come clean up this mess," Kraeghton said to the men. He turned to me, "You go nicely now, or one of them dies. It could be any one of them... your grandmother... your father or maybe one of your brothers. I'm not finished with your mother yet. I see that she is a little more than meets the eye."

Fear and revulsion rolled through me. Sweat ran down my back as icy fingers ran up my spine. The man I had stuck the knife in shoved me hard sending me to a knee. He followed it with a punch to my cheekbone. "You're fast, kid, but don't expect to get the upper hand with me again." He took ahold of my suit jacket and hauled me to my feet. The redhead took a painfully firm grasp on my arm and then they wrenched me into the kitchen. The staff watched in fascinated horror from a corner as I was dragged by.

TWELVE

I was thankful that I'd explored the house earlier. I was unceremoniously dumped in the empty room past the billiards room and locked in. I looked around the room again searching it thoroughly. There was nothing here that would help and I was locked in tight. I went to the closet and quickly concealed what I did have on me. The closet was not finished on the inside. I put my back to the wall and faced the door. I slid my money, lock picks and knife into the space between the drywall and the wood of the closet door frame. I pulled out my phone and started to text White Eagle. I'd gotten no more than a few words when I heard the door handle rattle. I quickly hit send and then erased the call. I tossed the cell into the closet and shut the door before the door to the room opened. The waiter, looking totally scared and worried sick at the same time came in the room with a metal straight-backed arm chair. The chauffeur watched his every move. His eyes begged my forgiveness. He set down the chair and left. The door was relocked behind him. A few minutes passed. I went back for my phone and sent more of the text. This time I had less warning. I sent and barely had it erased before the phone was snatched out of my hand by Kraeghton himself. He blasted me across my face with his open hand. Stars burst behind my eyes. He took ahold of my neck and squeezed before I had time to move or recover. The side of my face burned and my eyes watered.

"I think we are done playing games here. You know who I am and I certainly know who you are," Kraeghton said, sounding pleased with himself. He threw me into the wall hard enough to damage the dry wall. I slumped to the floor and lay there stunned. I saw a flash of Lucie reaching toward me. The red-haired man and the chauffeur roughly yanked me up by the arms and stripped my suit coat off of me. "This time search him carefully," Kraeghton said in an angry, silky voice. The redhead used my tie to hold me up as the woman slowly unbuckled and pulled off my belt and then tossed it aside. Kraeghton pushed me into the wall face first, the redhead still holding my tie, like a noose. The woman removed my shoes one at a time and tossed them onto my coat. She patted down my back, sides and arms. Then she tore my shirt free of my pants, carefully felt my waistband and patted down my hips and legs. They flipped me over slamming my head into the wall. She started again on the front side, her hands raising goose bumps on my skin and making my stomach roll with revulsion. She seemed to be having a lot more fun than I was. "Take his tie, check the shoes and the jacket. Come back with the serum," Kraeghton said in that same silky voice.

He and the redhead wrestled me into the chair and zip-tied my arms and legs to it. I'd never been so scared. Not even when I was in the trunk of the car last year, hurt and bleeding, zooming away from the mall and into the night. I thought I would die that night as I lay on the bank by the river. I'd made my peace. Now I felt that I had work left to do. I wasn't ready to go because I had to save my family. I sat silently, saving my energy and thinking. I am not alone, I reminded myself. Kraeghton watched me. I wondered why he didn't try to drain me. All of these people were dark - they exuded that dank almost oily, creepy feel that I'd come to associate with bad things, but they were different from Willie and the *stalker* I'd encountered in DC. Maybe that was it – they weren't *stalkers*. Maybe Kraeghton was like White Eagle but opposite. He had *looked* at me earlier but he didn't seem to have any other power – well, that he'd shown me yet. I still wondered if he drained people to keep himself young.

Tied to a chair in a locked room with two monsters... what were my choices? My lip and face were starting to swell from his vicious slap. My head throbbed from being thrown into the wall. My neck was stiff but I had no severe damage. My dinner seemed to have been fine. I had no adverse effects that I could sense. I used the time to watch Kraeghton and the redhead but they were giving very little away.

The woman returned. She was putting a fluid into a syringe. My stomach clenched and I broke out in a sweat. I took a deep breath to calm myself but all I inhaled was terror. Fear swooped over me and my skin superheated. My heart hammered against my ribs and I could feel myself begin to shake. "I have something for you," the woman leaned over the back of the chair to whisper and then she licked my ear. A shudder ran through my body.

"Don't," I said in a pathetically weak voice.

"You aren't afraid of a little needle, are you?" Kraeghton asked curiously.

"I would have to say that what is in the needle is of greater concern," I said, channeling Miles. My fifteen-year-old self was about to have a heart attack so I pulled out Miles.

The woman moved toward me and I put up as much fight as I could. The red-haired man came up behind me and put me in a choke hold so that she could roll up my sleeve, slip the needle in and depress the plunger. She tossed the syringe aside and laughed. "Easy," she said, "but then my gift is instinct. I know what you are going to do right before you do it."

"Claudia! Don't give things away!" Kraeghton roared and slapped her. She snarled in response. I was beginning to feel the chemicals in my body. A shiver ran through me. My vision blurred. My heart was racing but I didn't know if it was the fear or the drugs.

"Lock down the house. Leave him to me." Kraeghton was still angry. His voice was no longer silky smooth; it was rough and grinding.

"I wouldn't mind some alone time with him," Claudia smirked, running her tongue over her lips. I gulped. Gross!

"Maybe later, for now he's mine," Kraeghton replied firmly.

Claudia gave me a long look and then she and the red-haired man left.

Kraeghton circled my chair. "Feeling a little more mellow, are we? Perhaps a bit more cooperative and less aggressive? You know I shouldn't have sent Willie. I thought he could control himself. Control is so important. I don't know what set him off but I feel a little frustrated with you for depriving me of one of my better tools. Claudia, Bill and Shawn have their gifts, its true, but Willie was... well, what a gift he had! He had you confused and fooled for quite awhile. Such a wonderful talent – being able to conceal what you do. You'll make a wonderful addition to my collection though."

"I can't help you," my words came out slurred despite my best efforts to form them. I tried to shake my head to clear the fogginess.

"Sure you can. Our gifts are neither inherently good nor evil; they are, what they are. It's all in how we use them. You, I'm looking forward to exploring more fully because I suspect that you have more than one ability floating around in there and I intend to find out. Willie may be a loss but I have others. Did you think it was just the three that are here? Too bad for you. They're only the tip of the iceberg. I find that there are lots of people out there who want to make money or can be otherwise convinced. I do try to find their weaknesses and I think I'm coming to a conclusion about yours. You would hate to have something happen to your family. I'm so glad we got you here in a neat little package. Do you even realize how well this all worked out? I sought out your grandfather for his money. I was so happy when I needed a really good chemical engineer that I could manipulate and voila, your grandfather provided one. I did need to do a little prodding. I'm not beneath using someone like Darren to drive what I need. Too bad he got caught. I bet you helped. You do remember Darren, don't you? He took such wonderful pictures of your brothers last year at school. He even left that note for your father at his work. After that your father was happy to come to work for your grandfather. It was luck that I was around when your father blabbed a crazy story about you. He didn't believe a word of what you tried to tell him and then he got to be such good friends with Willie. Now he believes you, but it's a little too late. Oh dear, Owen, did we give you too much?"

I was trying my best to keep track of what he was telling me and thought under normal circumstances I would've been really freaked out, but whatever he gave me was not only making my vision blurry but making me weak and sleepy. Darren and Clive? Kraeghton had his hand in that pie too? Kraeghton bent forward and lightly slapped my face. I let my head loll to the side. He was mad at Claudia for talking and now he was telling me lots... why?

"Claudia!" Kraeghton bellowed. "Damn big house." He snarled and stomped off.

I heard a sound and slowly rolled my head around to look out the patio door. It was dark and I couldn't see much. The handle twisted in the French door and it slowly opened. The little sous chef came in holding a bottle of water in one hand and a kitchen knife in the other. "I'm so sorry," she softly whispered. "I'll cut you free."

"No wait. Can you get something off the property for me?" I asked in a raspy voice.

She merely nodded.

"Then take the syringe over there. Call my friends and someone will meet you. Tell them I was injected at about eight pm. Please," I begged her. I told her to leave me behind and then gave her the number. I could hear her mumbling the number under her breath as she gave me a sip of water.

"Hurry," someone whispered from the door. I rolled my head back that way - it was the chef. The sous chef picked up the syringe and made for the door. It clicked shut and I turned my head from it and feigned sleep.

"Claudia, you idiot, you gave him too much. I will not tolerate mistakes. I can get five more as good as you in as many days. Show me you are worth keeping around," Kraeghton snarled from the hall outside my new room.

"Seriously? After Bill got himself knifed you are giving *me* a hard time?" she whined.

"Get him upstairs and lock him up. He is useless like this. One of you is to stay on duty outside their door tonight and listen to what they're saying. Turn on the listening devices," Kraeghton snarled at her again.

"All night?" The tone of her voice made it clear to me that she was trying to find a way out of it.

"Yes, all night! Take it in shifts if you need to and make sure the senior Ryers are locked into their area as well. Give the old lady another hit of Barbital if you need to. I don't care what you do to the old fart. I've put up with him long enough. The boy we need to keep alive – the estate is going to him. Cut out his own son and bragged about it. A part of me admires the old man," Kraeghton said as he came into the room, thinking that I was completely out or trying to fool me, who knew.

It was difficult not to hiss or flinch when Claudia was careless with the box cutter and cut into my already damaged skin as well as the zip-tie. I let my body go completely limp so that I fell naturally to the floor as I was released.

"How are we going to get him upstairs?" Claudia asked.

"Throw him in the dumb waiter and hoist him up. His dad is still out of it and the mother will give you no trouble. She'll be worried about her baby boy here. Threaten her if you need to. We'll start again tomorrow," Kraeghton sighed.

"What about the hired help? Have they seen too much?" Claudia asked.

"Their silence has been purchased. Lock them up in the servant's quarters for the night. I don't care. They talk and someone near and dear will die. No problem. Take that chef for example. Her mother's in the hospital – a medicine mix-up would be... unfortunate. Besides I don't want to cook and I know you can't," Kraeghton replied.

"I have other talents!" Claudia answered fiercely.

"I am fully aware of your... talents. Now clean up this mess!" Kraeghton was back to barking at her. I was glad that I didn't work for him.

Kraeghton helped Claudia lift me into a fireman's carry. Painful as it was I remained limp and listless. She staggered a bit under my weight and Kraeghton steadied her. They made their way to the pantry area behind the kitchen and tossed me unceremoniously into the dumb waiter. The doors clanged shut and the system began to move. I heaved a sigh and settled myself a little more comfortably. It lurched to a stop. I had about decided that they were going to leave me there for the night when the door slid open and I was lifted out. Now Bill was helping Claudia. He held my shoulders and Claudia my feet. She shifted my feet to one arm and keyed into the room. They shuffled in and threw me on the floor.

"Owen," my mom screeched. "What did you do to him?"

"Stay back or we zap one of the little boys!" Claudia said aggressively.

I heard the door click shut. Mom must have rushed to me because I felt her cool hand on my forehead. I could hear my brothers whimpering nearby and Dad's low moaning. As fast as I was able, I snatched Mom's wrist. She hissed in surprise. I pulled her down next to me. "They can hear us but they can't see us," I whispered softly into her ear. "They think I'm unconscious. Go warn the boys. I'll be there in a minute."

"You're bleeding." I could hear fear and concern in her whispered words.

"Not important."

Mom rose to her feet. "It's okay boys. He's breathing and his heart is beating. It's like he's sleeping."

"I'm scared Mommy," Lucas said in a wobbly voice.

"I know, Angel Boy, me too. Let's find you a movie."

While Mom was settling my brothers in their room with a movie, I crawled over to my dad - it was all I could manage. When he saw me, he started to speak so I quickly clamped a hand over his mouth. "They can hear us," I whispered. "Are you okay?"

"I feel awful. She stunned me with a taser and kicked me in the head. How did I get up here? Last I knew we were in the dining room."

I didn't know if I should laugh or cry. Mom came into the sitting room and turned on the other TV to the same channel the boys were watching. She noted that Dad was awake. She raised her eyebrows at us. I waved her over and asked her if any of us had a cell phone left. She shook her head so I asked for one of the boys' handheld games. She looked at me oddly but went and got one and brought it right back. Alex followed her. His eyes lit up when he saw we were conscious. I quickly put a finger to my lips. He nodded and came and hugged us. Mom went in to keep Lucas busy.

"Alex," I whispered, "have you gotten onto the internet here?"

"Sure, it was easy," he whispered back.

I was glad that Kraeghton's crew had not figured out all the things these game devices could do. If they had, they would have taken the handheld games away from my brothers. Alex knew how important it was for us to communicate with White Eagle. I wasn't surprised that he had figured out how to access the wireless internet by spying on the grownups. He'd turned a horrible situation into a game. I really admired his way of coping. I was amazed to learn he'd already hacked into the wireless internet and used his PS Vita to Skype White Eagle. We might be trapped in a gilded cage but we had help on the outside and smart people on the inside.

Mom came back with Lucas. She reminded him to be quiet. She turned up the volume on the TV. Alex logged on and told me the password. It was 'Owen1', creepy – but then you could count on the older generation to not be real original. Still I would've expected Grandma's name or Dad's over mine. White Eagle came on at once but Alex was smart and had the volume way down. It was fortunate because White Eagle was clearly ranting. He was obviously relieved to see all of our faces but his worry and fear were a living, breathing entity. We all had our fingers at our lips so he clamped his lips together.

Alex turned up the volume a little and asked in a very soft voice if White Eagle could hear him. He just nodded so Alex passed the Vita to me. I gave him all the information I had, including the names of our captors and what I thought they could do. I told him about what I'd seen in Grandpa's closet and Kraeghton had confirmed it. Grandpa was only guilty of being selfish and spoiled. He wasn't evil and he didn't realize he was funding evil. He wanted Dad to follow in his shoes and when that didn't work out he thought he would use me instead. From the images in the closet I knew he had early dementia and the paranoia and lack of reasoning was starting to show. He was too absorbed in his own world to realize that Kraeghton and his crew were drugging Grandma much as they had Dad. It was hard on her heart and she hadn't been allowed to see her regular doctor. The doctor I had not yet seen, but the same one saw both Dad and Grandma. The doctor was all for banding together if it meant more for him. He was part of Kraeghton's collection of *dark watchers*. The scariest news was that Stephan Kraeghton was not top dog. He was just top dog here.

White Eagle and Sarah were ready to pull us out but I was reluctant to do that yet. "They won't kill me and if they think I'm cooperating they won't hurt anyone else. I could learn more if I stay a bit longer. I'd like to learn enough to take them out. They'll only get stronger if we leave them intact. We have to wipe out this cell. They'll come back for us when we least expect it otherwise. Like you said before... the devil we know. Maybe Alex could snap some pictures to... wait, Grandma had pictures all over her room and I saw her fiddling with a camera. I know she has more information for us. If I can't do it, then one of you needs to get the information to White Eagle. Let's get him pictures of the captors and see what we can turn up and use. We also need to protect the staff. They're being emotionally blackmailed. I need to know about the alarm system here as well." I knew in the state I was in I was forgetting things. My vision was still a bit out of focus and I felt groggy.

The door rattled and I severed the connection. I loaded the game Alex had installed on his PS Vita and handed it to him. I dove for the spot on the floor where my blood marked the location they had dropped me earlier and lay there motionless as the door opened. I heard the soft whoosh of fabric hitting fabric and the double thump of my shoes hitting the floor. I took two slow breaths and the door shut again. I waited, listening hard.

Mom came and patted my leg. The coast was clear. My head was starting to ache. I pulled myself up and walked slowly to the bathroom. Mom kicked my suit coat, belt, tie and shoes to the side out of the way and followed. "The redheaded man just peeked in and said nothing. He just looked at you for a bit," she whispered close to my ear. I nodded and started drinking water. My attention drifted to my wrists. My skin was damaged from my struggle with the zip ties and I had a cut on one wrist where Claudia had nicked me with the box cutter. I washed my wrists and checked my ankles. They had taken much less abuse, thanks to my socks and slacks. I rummaged for first aid supplies. There were none. I went back to drinking water. I was pretty sure they'd given me what they gave Dad so I needed to flush my system. I drank water straight from the faucet until I thought I'd throw up. I figured I had about fifteen or twenty minutes until I'd be peeing like a race horse.

I flopped onto a couch and watched the movie. I was afraid to sleep, or maybe we should sleep in shifts? My body was tired and my mind churned in slow, viscous circles – like hardening cement. How big was the fireplace chimney between the dining room and the skyway over to the garage? Could Alex get through? I needed to get my stash back. I'd love to get the layout of our captors' quarters. I knew the floor plan at least. I realized that I hadn't carefully checked our quarters.

I got up and drank water until my stomach hurt again. Mom watched me closely. My nice white dress shirt was ruined. What was new? Always the nice clothes – oh well. I practically ripped off the buttons trying to get out of it in my anger and frustration. I threw it angrily against the wall. I pulled on a black t-shirt and cargo pants. My slacks looked okay so I hung them back up. Treat a suit well and it will last a long time. With my luck, I'd be fortunate if this one, that Sarah had altered for me, would even last the time we were here.

I started my search of our quarters in my room. I hadn't really looked at it earlier. There was a set of French doors leading out to a deck just like the sitting room had. Every door and window seemed to be alarmed. I did a careful inspection of our shared bathroom and my brother's room. I looked over Mom and Dad's room and their bathroom. Then I inspected the sitting room. I'd found a few listening devices and I was sure there were more. They hadn't bugged the bathrooms as far as I could tell – how thoughtful.

While I was in the bathroom I emptied my bladder and drank another mega dose of water. A guy could grow to hate water. They must have filtered water here though because it didn't taste too bad. My stomach was not happy with me but my head was feeling a bit better. I walked back into the sitting room and Mom and Alex smiled at each other and then each held up a number on their fingers. Mom was showing nine and Alex twelve. My brain was churning... nine and twelve... big grins. It clicked into place with what felt like an audible sound. I smiled back at them. Once again Alex was making the most of a bad situation. I pointed at our mom and dad's room and held up a three. Alex nodded. Mom showed a two. I pointed at the master bath and showed a zero. Alex shook his head and gave a one. I raised my eyebrows and he crooked his finger at me. He turned on the faucet and then opened the tissue holder and sure enough there was one. I drank more water while the faucet was on.

We walked back to the sitting room and I held up a four. Alex and Mom both nodded. I pointed at Alex's room with two fingers. Nods from both. My room was where we all disagreed. Mom showed a one, Alex a two and I showed four. I held up my hand for them to wait and made sure that my drapes were drawn like they were in the sitting room. Then I showed them the lamp by my bed, the frame of my canopied bed up near the top, the mirror over the dresser and one over on the side of the door trim where the drapes covered the area. We gave each other a silent high five. Alex's game system pinged in his pocket. We moved over by the TV to see what White Eagle had for us.

"What've you got?"

"A little lady just gave us a syringe and a bunch of information. The staff isn't at all happy. Looks like they're getting locked up tonight but they have no alarm system. Your alarm system is monitored by Baur Hays Securities, the same folks that Willie worked for."

"That I knew. Any good news?"

"The number of windows alarmed does not match the number of windows installed during the remodel."

"I think I know which one they missed – though I'd visualized climbing out of it, not in it. Right now I need to get out of here – any ideas?"

"You feel okay? We don't know what they gave you yet but we think it's a type of hypnotic and sedative."

"I'm pretty sure it's what they've been giving Dad, but in a different form. Kraeghton asked if I was feeling more mellow and cooperative after he gave it to me. My vision is nearly back to normal but I'm still a bit groggy. Did you find anything on Grandma's heart condition? What am I dealing with?"

"She suffers from an irregular heart beat. She also has a weak valve. They didn't feel that she was a good candidate for surgery and that's all we know so far. Yes, I have an idea about how to get you out of there. We went over the plans. There should be an entrance in one of the closets. Once you're in the attic crawlspace you have access to the new section. It's unclear whether you can get through to the older section. If you can't, you can get out onto the roof from the vent on the center of your side of the house and then drop down onto the deck. What are you thinking?"

"I'm thinking that I'm glad you sent climbing shoes. I think we should put a fake in Alex's bed. Put Alex in mine. Put one parent in each room for the safety of my brothers. While they pretend to sleep, I'm going to see if I can communicate with Grandma."

"It's as good a place as any to start. If things change we want you to know that we can be there in about ten minutes."

"I'll send you information as soon as I can."

"Good luck."

I shut down the Vita and looked at each pair of eyes circled around our new favorite 'toy'. "I can tell by the look on your faces that you don't like it, but we have to be proactive. Keep thinking up ideas and hang tough. Keep Lucas' Vita handy and I'll contact you every thirty minutes if I can. I need to keep Alex's off so they don't hear a ping in the ceiling."

"Okay boys," Mom said loudly, "time for bed."

We shared a group hug and then my brothers started hamming it up for the listening devices by complaining about going to bed. I'd now have plenty of noise to make my escape. I knew where the access was from my earlier exploration of our suite. I ran to the bathroom first but drank no more water. I then put on my climbing shoes and a pair of weightlifting gloves I had stashed between the layers of my duffel. I hurried back to my brothers' closet. Dad was already there, balanced on an arm chair, opening the access for me and looking around up there. He gave me the sign for 'wait' and hurried out of the room. He came back moments later with the mini flashlight from Mom's purse. I gave him a huge grin. Dad gave me another hug. "I hate to let you do this, but I don't see another choice. You're in much better shape than I am, though it pains me to admit it." Dad moved the chair out of the way and boosted me up into the opening.

I swung my flashlight around. I spotted the vent to the outside right away. I couldn't see if I could get through the other way. It was horribly hot in the small space. I was really hoping I wouldn't meet any wildlife up here. I like nature fine... out in nature. I don't like it when it sneaks up on me. What was poisonous around here? Did Grandpa spray for insects? Show some backbone!

I carefully moved the insulation just enough to determine which way the joists ran. The last thing I needed to do was step through the drywall and into a room from up here. That would end my adventures for the night for sure. I made my way over to the old section of the house. Sure enough, White Eagle was right. It was blocked off by a stucco wall. Being older it probably had a completely different kind of roof. I remembered from this afternoon looking up at the house, that this new section had a higher and more peaked roof. I carefully reversed my route and made for the vent. I noted that Dad was back to watching. I pointed behind me and shook my head and then put the beam of the flashlight on the vent. Dad nodded and then closed up the panel.

The vent was nailed shut but they'd only used enough to tack it in. I would have been quicker if I could've used my knife but I was able to get it out after a few tries. I scared myself when I almost dropped it. The noise would surely have caused a disturbance. I clipped the flashlight to my belt loop with its carabineer. I cautiously poked my head out the opening and looked around. Please let the tiles be secure. I eased out and grasped the tiles above my head. The roof was not far above the opening so I could pull with my arms and push with my legs.

I took a moment to breathe the outside air. Freedom. Well, sort of. I pulled up onto the roof. My movement startled some kind of critter in the nearby trees and it took off. I froze. To me, the noise was deafening. I waited a beat and heard nothing further. It was relatively dark up here but much of the house and many trees around the property were lit from below. I decided to check out the roof first. The moon was bright and the air warm after the air conditioning in the house. I crawled along the old section which was relatively flat. I stopped to check out the chimney. It had a grate at the top to keep out wildlife. It wasn't easy to remove so I left it alone for now. By the time I reached the far side of the house I knew that White Eagle was right again – all sides went straight down to the ground except for the back of the house where a deck or veranda ran the whole distance from my room and our sitting room over to our captors' quarters. Which gave me an idea – since I was over here anyway... I hung my head out and listened before I lowered enough to peek down at their French doors. It looked like a mirror image of our side from what I could see. Claudia sat on a sofa, channel surfing. The red-haired man had headphones on listening, I had to assume, to my family. Occasionally he would make a note on a pad. Kraeghton was out of sight. I wouldn't be able to lean over far enough to see in a window and check.

While I was up here I scoped out the best route to the servants' quarters that would keep me away from the lit pool area. They had a small one story bungalow at the back corner of the property. I'd save that for last if I had time.

I made my way back to our end. I was just ready to lower myself onto the veranda when I heard a noise back on the other side. I froze and made myself as small as possible. Kraeghton came out on the veranda to have a smoke. I was surprised. I hadn't smelled it on him earlier. He leaned on the railing looking out over the pool. Great. Claudia came out and took the cigarette from him. She took a long drag and handed it back. I soon saw what some of the other talents she had mentioned earlier were. He took one last long drag and sent the butt of the cigarette over the edge to fall near the pool deck. Fortunately for me, they didn't stay outside long and decided to take their activities inside. At least they would be busy for awhile.

I quickly hung off the edge of the roof and dropped onto the veranda, going down into a squat to silence my landing. I'd kept my eyes to the other end of the curved deck the whole time so when I glanced back at my own French door I about fell over backwards. A figure was standing on the other side of the glass not three feet from me. I froze in shock for a brief moment until I realized it was Dad tracking my progress. I rolled my eyes and gave him a thumbs up. He shook his head and turned away with a half smile tugging at his lips.

I quickly climbed the railing and dropped to the ground below. I changed my mind about the servants' quarters because the way to my grandfather's closet window would take me past the servants' quarters if I wanted to stay in darkness. I made my way along the barely lit path to the back corner of the property. My senses were on full alert. I walked around the perimeter of the building looking for a way in. It wasn't alarmed, I'd been told. I about laughed - they couldn't even truly lock them in. The bungalow was not air conditioned so the windows were thrown wide and ceiling fans were beating the helpless air into submission. There was a nice breeze off the water. I bet in the morning there would be a nice view of the water off the back deck. I also bet I wouldn't get to enjoy it. I decided on the back door, went up and gave it a gentle knock. The door popped open and the chef stood filling the doorway and looking defiant. When she saw it was me, she threw a hand over her heart. She let out a puff of air and then yanked me inside.

"What in the world are you doing?" I was frantically trying to shush her. "You're fine, honey, they don't pay any attention to us. We're the invisible class. They think we're beneath them. They just use us to run the house and do their odd jobs. We know about the bugs in the house. They had Ralph install them. He can tell you where they all are and there're none out here. They haven't had a chance to put them in. One of us is always here and I think they're too lazy anyway. We all have worked for your grandfather for years. He's a little odd, no offense, but he was generous to us. Things were fine before, but these new Blighters stink. They fired the gardener. Now Ralph does that too. He used to be the chauffeur and your grandfather's personal assistant and butler. Now he keeps the cars running and the grounds neat and serves when we need a waiter. Dorothy should have retired but they won't let her go. She's the head housekeeper and it's getting to be too much for her. You know I cook and Lena helps all of us. She's a 'Jill of all trades'. Kraeghton has dirt on all of us but we're sick of it and we don't like what they're doing to your family. We want to make a stand with you. What they're doing ain't right." Mary had kept her voice low just in case any other folks were out wandering around in the night to check on them.

"I heard him say your mom was in the hospital. I'm so sorry to hear that. Aren't you worried about her?"

"She's had a great life and made her peace. She's terminal anyway. I bet she'd thank Kraeghton if he ended her life early. She's a feisty old gal so maybe she'd take him with her and good riddance to him. Slimy devil."

"I wanted to thank... Lena... for taking the syringe and some information to my friends."

"You're welcome, honey. We're so relieved you're okay. Like I said, we want to help. We like how you stood up for yourself and your family and we're done being bullied. Your granddad just can't see what that Kraeghton fella's like. He's bad news. I don't understand what he wants from you but it's not good. Now how can we help?"

"Tell me where all the bugs are. Is there any visual observation that they do, like cameras? And how about food allergies?"

In no time at all Ralph had drawn up a crude picture of the house. We had found all the bugs in our quarters. He showed me where five had been placed in my grandparents' quarters and three in my grandfather's office. He knew of no video surveillance and they really did have him install most of the equipment. He was quite the handyman and fixed more than just the cars around the house. He had no family and lived here full time. Dorothy also had nowhere else to go. Grandpa had promised her a spot in the retirement home the umbrella corporation owned but Kraeghton had taken that away. Lena stayed too, she was trying to work and go to school and tonight Mary got the privilege of staying. She did sometimes but usually went home to her husband who was on the road right now anyway.

As soon as Ralph was done talking, Mary jumped back in. Dorothy and Lena mainly listened but occasionally put in a comment. The red-haired man, Shawn, was allergic to shellfish. So for breakfast we were having shrimp omelets. One down.

Dorothy was most concerned about my grandmother. She'd worked for my grandparents the longest and remembered my dad as a young man. She'd watched my grandfather become stranger and more demanding over the years and she had watched my grandmother decline – most severely lately.

They told me that my grandmother loved us all very much but my grandfather was the one who had spoiled the relationship with my dad. He was very stubborn and wanted things his way. Recently Kraeghton had been feeding his paranoia and strange superiority complex. Just like the picture gallery told, my grandmother had been watching from afar for years. She was very proud of us and talked about us all the time, just not in front of my grandfather. She even knew I'd been helping people. She was very concerned about Kraeghton and his interest in me. She confided in Dorothy and because she cared about my grandmother, she spied Kraeghton and his crew. She was very afraid of them and for good reason. She knew that drugs were slipped to Grandma, my grandfather and my dad. She did what she could to help but she constantly lived in fear. Kraeghton threatened to throw her out on the street, in a foreign city with nothing.

"Kraeghton thinks that he can get me to work for him. I won't do it willingly but he is of course threatening my family. I have to stop him," I told them defiantly.

"No, we do," Ralph said firmly. "So, Mary poisons the redhead, then what?"

"I know the window into my grandfather's closet is not alarmed. I plan to sneak in tonight and look at my grandmother's photos and see if she has a small camera I can use to take pictures of our captors. We need full names and anything else we can get on them. At the least we can get them on kidnapping. I wonder if there's a malicious intent charge they could be brought up on too."

"I know your friend Sarah works with the FBI. She will help us, right?" Lena asked nervously.

"Sarah will do everything she can. She's out of her normal area so I don't know what all she can do but she's like family – she is family. She won't let these guys get away with this."

I pulled out Alex's PSP and sent a message to my family. Alex came on right away. "All clear here," he whispered. I could hear a radio in the background. I told him he was doing a great job and to keep at it.

Next I put in a 'call' to White Eagle and had the staff tell him everything they knew that would help. Sarah came on and thanked Lena again and complimented my ingenuity for reaching out to the staff. I told her that they had reached out to me. They briefly told her their stories and how they were being blackmailed. They also talked about my stand in the dining room with pride. They'd appreciated my offer of help in the kitchen.

We decided that breakfast would be served at eight and by eight thirty we would stage a coup. Ralph would tamper with the car so that it broke down in the open gate. Shawn, the redhead, would be caught in the car with an allergic reaction to shellfish. "Oops," Mary threw in with a grin. His epinephrine would not be working. When Kraeghton's crew came down to breakfast Dorothy would go up to clean their rooms as usual and she would tamper with it. She knew where he kept it. They were the invisible after all and Kraeghton's crew liked being served and took advantage of the staff regularly. "Oops," Dorothy added with a wink at Mary. We had a plan. I told Sarah that I'd to break into my grandparents' quarters, get a camera to photograph our captors and get the pictures back to her. Ralph said he would help get me in the unalarmed window. I signed off and Ralph and I left through the back door.

Ralph led the way to the window. I had failed to unlock it earlier and now I felt disgusted with myself. Our captors were right above me. It wasn't alarmed but now what? I looked around for an idea – my brain still slow. I spied the floodlights shining on the trees near the fence.

"Would it be totally out of character if you changed some floodlights out at this time of night?"

"Are you kidding? They keep me working round the clock. They'd think it was great if I did it for security."

"Do you have some extras? I think that maybe you could drop one in time with my breaking the glass. If they notice the noise, you say 'oops, sorry. I was trying to change the light out here'. What do you think?"

Ralph's face lit up like a Christmas tree. He waved for me to follow him. There was a small shed in a dark corner up against the stucco fence. We stepped in and he closed the door behind us. He then turned on a small shop light and pulled out three flood lights, a sturdy crate and handed me a rag and a hammer. He wrapped the rag over the hammer's head and gave it a little swing, then raised his eyebrows at me. I smiled back at him. "Just drop it in the flowerbed and I'll hide it, okay? I'll pretend I used the crate to carry my supplies. Try to tip it over with your foot when you pull yourself in but I should have a moment to grab it if you can't."

I shook his hand and we turned out the light and proceeded with our mission. I set up the crate and made sure the hammer's head was wrapped tight. Ralph took a rag from his pocket and unscrewed two lights across from my position by the closet window. He nodded at me. I held up my hand with the flashlight pressed against it which made my fingers glow red from the illumination. Three – two – one – crack – crack and the sound of shattering glass. Ralph had dropped a bulb at the same time my hammer struck. Muffled by the rag my window breaking was even quieter than I'd imagined. I didn't hear our captors so I quickly knocked out as much glass as I could reach.

"Hey!" hollered a voice that I thought was Shawn's. "What's going on out there?"

"So sorry to disturb you sir, some of the floods were out and I thought I'd replace them but I dropped one."

"You need to be more careful. You were told to check in if you were going to be out of your house."

"Yes, sir, my apologies. I thought that since I was working..."

"Well next time check in. Now hurry up and get back to your house. I don't want to see a one of you before seven. I'll lock you in if I have to."

"Yes, sir." I swear I heard him say 'ass' under his breath. It made me smile. I dropped the hammer into the flowerbed and heaved myself up and in. I'd missed some glass in the darkness and snagged my shoulder ripping through my shirt and the skin beneath. My shoulder burned and hot blood ran down my back. At least my gloves had protected my hands. I squatted in the broken glass on my grandfather's built in dresser. I could hear nothing inside and Ralph was moving around in the bushes outside. I shined the light on my hand again and gave him a thumbs up. He looked up at the windows above me, mumbled 'good luck' and began cleaning up outside. I carefully broke the last piece of glass out of the window. I brushed off my gloves and checked my shoes. Then I went to find a wastebasket. I found one and an extra hand towel in the bathroom. I closed the bathroom door and I lined the can with the towel and swept the glass inside. I figured the longer it took them to discover the broken window the better. If there was no obvious glass or broken pieces it would take longer. I wrapped the towel over the glass, returned the wastebasket and closed the shutter over the window.

I checked my wound in the mirror with the flashlight. The bleeding was already slowing but I could use at least a butterfly bandage over it in about four places. Oh well. I returned to the closet and *felt* the room. I'd already gotten everything here worth learning. The office didn't have anything else to tell me either. I checked grandma's closet and sensed a journal hiding in a shoebox. It was small so I stuck it in my cargo pants pocket. There was no other new information to be found here so I silently moved to my grandparents' room. They were both snoring softly. There was nothing here or in their sitting room. I moved on to my grandmother's special round room and *felt* all the things that had called me earlier. I went around touching them and absorbing the images both good and bad. Everything Dorothy said was true. Grandma loved us very much and thought of us everyday. She missed us desperately but she loved our grandfather more, so she respected his wishes. She was very glad that my dad had come back to see them more and more and she was so happy about this Christmas visit but she was very worried about Kraeghton. She didn't realize just how bad things were until we were in the air and it was too late to warn us.

If she said anything to us, Kraeghton told her that he would make her watch while he hurt us. *Nice*. I thought sarcastically.

I thought about going for my lock picks, knife and money but decided against it. I figured, given the chance, they'd search me again and I might be able to use them to get out of the room if things didn't go as planned. I looked at Grandma's cameras and was drawn to the one she had been looking at earlier. She was trying to tell me something. I looked through the digital images. She had photographed each of our captors as well as some other people who'd been to the house. I didn't know the significance of the strangers but I would give the whole thing to Sarah and White Eagle. There were also some documents on the memory card but they were way too small to make out on the camera's viewer. I powered down the camera and took the memory card. I quickly checked the other cameras but nothing jumped out at me. I *felt* the room one last time. A photo on the wall called to me. It was a picture of my family that was taken last Christmas. I knew my mom had sent it to her. I kept looking at the picture and wondering why it was calling to me. On a whim I took it off the wall to take a better look. I realized that the back felt lumpy. I turned it over and found taped to the back, a small envelope with my name on it so I pulled it off. I heard a noise in the other room, I popped off my flashlight and dropped down low to put myself in shadow. One of my grandparents was up. I heard bathroom noises and waited. I heard feet shuffle back into the bedroom and I waited some more. I decided to try going back through the house instead of out the window but the door really was locked. I felt disappointment wash over me. This was why I was supposed to have my lock picks. I heaved a silent sigh and turned around. My grandmother stood motionless in the hall watching me. Soft light from the pool washed over her in a pale glow making her silver-streaked hair shine. In her long white nightgown and bare feet she looked like an angel. She held out her arms to me and I walked forward like I was in a daze. She wrapped me in a gentle hug. I was surprised by how tall she was. I hadn't realized it before but she must be close to five feet ten inches which is surprisingly tall for her generation. Tall as she was, she felt fragile in my arms. "I knew you would get my message. Do you have the memory card?" she whispered. I nodded. "Did you find my note?" I nodded again. "I'm sorry about earlier. Use what I gave you to hurt them. I'll do what I can to keep them away from you."

"Be careful. Don't do anything reckless," I found myself whispering back.

"I'm sorry I've missed so much of your lives. Please forgive me. I should have done things differently."

"I forgive you. I know you did what you thought you had to do. Forgive yourself." I wasn't sure why I added the last, I just felt I needed to say it.

"Forgive your father and your grandfather. They were... misguided. I should have... I wish I would've done more sooner. I do love you all. Don't forget." She gently pushed me away from her and walked back to bed.

I quickly darted into the closet and hopped up on the dresser below the window. I felt like Peter Pan for a moment and then, silent as a shadow, I moved to the window. I carefully looked around. No one was about and everything was pristine as if Ralph and I had never been there. I looked up and saw a light on upstairs but caught no movement and heard nothing. I eased myself down out of the window, closed the shutters as best I could and landed lightly. I found a palm frond right next to me and figured it was a gift from Ralph. I brushed out my footprints as I moved further into the shadows. I continued to brush them out until I hit the darkened slate and gravel path. I tossed the palm frond near the shed and moved soundlessly around the outer perimeter of the property.

THIRTEEN

All the lights were out in the servants' quarters so I kept moving. I finally made it back to our corner of the house. There was still a light on in the sitting room of our captors' area but I could see no movement. I was thankful that the back of the house had fancy pillars supporting the arches of the veranda. I leapt up and grasped the 'leafy' upper edge of the corner column and pushed myself up with my feet. I pulled up with my arms, my fingers straining against my weight as I heaved with my fingertips. I pulled myself up enough that I could grab the edge of the veranda.

I heard a noise and froze. Crap. The changing of the guard had begun. It must be midnight. I remained frozen, feet on the smooth pillar supporting part of my weight and my fingers holding the edge of the decking. I was on the side away from the pool so I was in semidarkness. I held my straining body still and kept my breathing slow. My shoulder burned. I could feel that the wound had reopened a bit and my shirt was stuck to it in other places. Bill was out on the veranda rolling his neck and shoulders. He finally went back inside. My arms were shaking from the strain. Dad looked out the corner of my French doors. I barely had the strength to pull myself up and onto the veranda. I waved limply at him, then used the upper pillar to stand on the railing. As he let the curtain go, I swung myself back up and onto the roof and lay there for a moment panting. I made my way over to the vent and lowered myself in. I wedged the vent cover back in place and worked my way back to the closet opening. Dad had it open by the time I got to it and I practically fell into his arms, exhausted.

He hissed when he saw my shirt and shoulder. Alex was asleep in my bed. Dad and I moved into the bathroom. He went and gently tapped Mom on the shoulder to wake her from her doze. I sat backwards on the edge of the tub, pulled my shirt over my head until it caught on my wound and then leaned against the wall in exhaustion while they fussed over my shoulder. Mom had to work a bit of the fabric of my shirt loose with a warm wet washcloth. It wasn't one of my better moments. My wrists were raw from the zip ties, one was cut from Claudia's carelessness and now my shoulder had a gash. I wanted to laugh when Mom came back with Band-Aids from the small first aid kit she kept in her purse because I really needed so much more.

I pulled out the PS Vita, the memory card, Grandma's journal and her letter from my pockets and handed them over. Dad sat down hard on the edge of the tub next to me, but facing the opposite way, and ran his hand over the outer envelope as if he were feeling her handwriting. Memories must have been flooding his mind. He sat for a moment lost in his own thoughts, then slid a finger under the flap and began to read.

Mom finished me up and then moved to read over Dad's shoulder. "How did she know you would find this?" Mom asked softly.

"I saw her today when I explored the house. She's been watching me for a long time. She knows a lot about me; she just doesn't understand what it all means. She hoped I would come back for the camera that she brought to my attention. She's been very busy. We need to get this stuff out to Sarah and White Eagle. I think my best bet is to sneak out again and throw it over the back of the fence. It's dark and quiet at the back of the property towards the water. I just need to stay away from the front of the house and the pool."

"Owen, you're about dead on your feet. There's got to be another way," Mom pleaded.

"Unless you think we can overpower Claudia and her taser without alerting the others, I don't think there is. Contact White Eagle for me while I get ready, okay?"

I had them leave so I could use the bathroom. I washed my hands and looked at the damage. Cuts, scrapes, broken nails (good thing

I kept them short) and aching muscles. Not to mention that I still felt goofy. I threw my ruined t-shirt back on and opened the door. Mom had taken the Vita and set up the meet at the back gate. She was reading Grandma's letter to Sarah. It sounded like grandma had a safety deposit box. There was a key in the letter and authorization for me to open it but it wasn't safe to keep any of it in the house where it might be found.

I stretched and put my gloves back on. Dad reopened the hatch in the closet and I retraced my route. This time as I headed straight back to the far corner of the property, past the servant's quarter and into the darkness beyond, I found that my body was shaking from the strain. I could hear the rush of the ocean and wished this were a normal vacation. I had now been up for about nineteen hours during which time I'd been beaten, drugged and mentally manipulated. Tomorrow I'd be a mess in more ways than one.

Mom had put all the important pieces for White Eagle and Sarah into a Ziploc bag she had in her suitcase. She's super organized and packs everything in Ziploc bags. I had always thought it was kind of funny. Today she was looking really smart. I leaned against a palm tree by the low stucco wall at the back of the property. The moon shone on the waves causing long white stripes to ripple across the water as the waves rolled in. The sound was soothing and under other circumstances I would've loved to have stood here and sucked it up.

I sensed the change in the air and knew I wasn't alone. I waited... I didn't want to give myself away to the wrong person. I reached out cautiously to see what I could sense... White Eagle. I moved away from the tree and leaped onto the wall.

"Owen!" White Eagle hissed at me.

I hid a smile. I had startled him. Tired as I was, I was getting better. I handed him the gallon sized bag with its precious cargo. "We need this out of here so they can't get it but we have not thoroughly explored its contents. I hope the journal and photos will help. My grandmother took pictures of the people who are holding us and some documents I can't make out. You know the plan? We hope to attack at eight o'clock. The cook will serve shellfish to one of the allergic *dark watchers*. His antidote won't work. It will be taken out by the housekeeper. They haven't shown us any guns, just tasers. What have you got?"

"Preliminary results look like the drug they gave you is mainly a Flunitrazepam derivative."

"In English?"

"On the street it is known as the 'date rape drug' because of its hypnotic properties and in higher doses can cause semiconsciousness and memory blackouts. Its pharmacological effects include sedation, muscle relaxation, reduction in anxiety, sleepiness, impaired psychomotor and cognitive functions as well as the prevention of convulsions."

"No wonder it made me groggy and I feel like crap. So far I've been drinking water like a camel just in from the desert. I figured the solution to pollution was dilution like Saul did with Dad. I didn't figure it could hurt anyway."

"This will help." I felt a sharp jab into my upper arm.

"Ouch! Damn it! What did you do?"

"I thought if I warned you, you would resist. Nobody likes needles. We ran the pharmacology by Saul and it was his recommendation that I inject you with what we believe to be the right antidote. The drug they gave you can take eighteen hours to completely metabolize and possibly longer. Saul thought we could give you a boost and slow the stuff down if they give you anymore. Just avoid grapefruit juice; it makes it harder for you to break down the drugs. Something happens with the absorption."

"Too bad I don't have chemistry this year," I said sarcastically. "So, I'm on the right track? I should keep drinking water?"

"Like you say, it couldn't hurt. The drug is removed from your body using your renal system."

"Renal... kidneys? I pee it out, in other words, right?"

"Correct and you know they'll be at you again tomorrow, right?"

"Yeah, I hope all goes well at eight."

"Owen, if it doesn't we'll be in by noon. Sarah found a contact here and we've been working with her this week. Activity in your grandfather's businesses was looking suspicious. People were starting to notice. Stephan Kraeghton thinks he's so much smarter than everyone else. Be careful, I think there's more to him than meets the eye. The housekeeper was pulled and interviewed just before you got here. At first she wouldn't talk because of the threats made by Kraeghton but she eventually caved when they showed her the pictures of some of the missing *watchers*. She just thinks that they're missing kids. She also said that she thought your grandmother was being neglected by being denied proper medical care. She thinks they're here to kidnap you boys. If Kraeghton is involved in a black market slave trade we haven't found it yet but it wouldn't surprise me. He's been... very careful over the years."

"We can't let the FBI or anyone else come blazing in here. They can't find out about me. We need to shut this down ourselves."

"Owen, trust me. You'll like this agent. She works for the same type of people Sarah does. She won't expose you. She knows the value in what you do. Her sister was a *watcher*."

"She told you that?" I was truly surprised. Our secret is not let out lightly.

"Sometimes like speaks to like. She recognized in me the qualities of her sister's mentor. She put two and two together when she found out that Sarah works for the FBI but I don't. We've been using her lab and equipment."

"I better get back. Good luck with the raw data. I hope you find lots of good stuff in it."

"We'll be ready at eight."

I gave him a quick hug and melted into the shadows. Whatever he'd given me was beginning to make me feel better, but I could still feel exhaustion weighing down on me. I looked up at the house from the sheltering darkness of the many plants in this part of the yard and dreaded my climb back up onto the roof. I edged my way back to the corner column and listened. All seemed quiet and I saw nothing. I leapt for the top of the column with its decorative leaf-like carvings and took ahold once again, pushing up with my feet and pulling up with my arms. I pulled myself onto the first level of the deck. I stopped and listened again. I silently jumped onto the railing and pulled myself onto the roof. I was tired enough to curl up here and go to sleep but I moved back to the vent and slipped inside.

This time Dad was not waiting for me. I slid down through the opening and into the closet. All I wanted to do was go to bed.

"Too bad you weren't here for bed check. Have a nice adventure did you?" Kraeghton said in his silky smooth voice. "I did warn you that you would pay if you didn't behave."

Mom was shoved in from the bathroom by Claudia. Her eyes were enormous. Fear and dread seemed to roll off of her in waves. I could almost taste it in the air. Shawn pushed into the room with a piece of plywood, some screws and a battery operated screwdriver. He shoved me out of the way from where I stood motionless, taking in the scene. He sealed up the opening in the closet.

I finally found my voice. "Where are my brothers?" It was eerily quiet, I realized, feeling sick.

"So I guess Claudia didn't overdose you after all. Too bad. What I will do to you now, is much worse, I'm sure."

"Where are my brothers?" I ground out much less worried for me than for them.

"I told you earlier that patience was important," he snarled, turning to my mom. Claudia had a taser to her neck. I could already see one burn mark near her shoulder from the previous zap she must have received. Kraeghton put his hand on Mom's chest over her tank top and pressed. Mom hissed in a breath through her teeth. Her eyes rolled up in her head and she sank to her knees.

As she began to fall, Kraeghton let his hand move from her body. I lunged forward as he turned toward me striking me in the chin with the heel of his hand. I dropped to my knees in front of Mom but caught her as she fell into me.

"Owen." Just my name. It came out as a sob. "I'm so sorry," she ended in a choked whisper before her eyes closed.

I looked up at Kraeghton with death in my eye and a snarl on my lip. The last thing I saw was his foot approaching my head. I tried to block him but Claudia got me with the taser at the same moment and everything froze and then went black as pain coursed through my body.

The next thing I knew I was on the floor of the room downstairs. I looked around slowly. I was alone. They had stripped off my shoes and watch. The loss of the watch made me angry, though I no longer needed it to communicate with Miles. All that he was, while he owned the watch, I'd absorbed and incorporated into myself but it was a reminder and I viewed it as a gift from him and from White Eagle.

The sun was up but the light had that bluish early quality to it. As I looked out the French doors to the east I could see it just cresting the horizon. I listened carefully to see if I could determine the time by the activity in the house. I could hear nothing. I sat up slowly and took a moment to evaluate the condition of my body. My neck hurt right where Claudia had zapped me, my arm hurt and was sporting a fantastic bruise from the kick I'd received trying to protect my head. They must have tried to drug me again because I had that weird groggy feeling and my arm showed a bruise where Claudia had injected me last time plus a new spot. White Eagle had gone for my upper arm, which had its own separate sore spot.

I climbed unsteadily to my feet and staggered into the bathroom. I made use of the facilities, washed my hands and took a long drink from the faucet before I examined the nice burns on my neck from the taser and ran cold water over my head. I checked my shoulder. It didn't look so hot either. Basically I was a mess.

I heard the door unlock so I opened the bathroom door and leaned against the frame. I wasn't sure what to expect, but a defiant looking Alex sporting a black eye was not it. He was carrying a breakfast tray and a bad attitude. I'd never seen him like this. He was like a dangerous animal, silent and tense. I could tell he was afraid but he was also pissed off.

"Here's some food. It's probably rotten," he said in a voice thick with scorn. "Claudia made it. The cook has just started the real breakfast, but I hear you don't get any because you weren't behaving last night. I'm allowed to tell you that Lucas is fine. If you're good you can see him later. They have Mom somewhere and left us with Dad." He looked like he wanted to say more. I knew I didn't want him to go.

Claudia came in and looked at Alex with contempt. It was then I noticed than she was walking with a limp. I looked from her to Alex and he smiled a knowing smile at me. The black eye must have been worth it. I winked at him as she barked at him to set down the tray, then grabbed his arm and hauled him roughly out of the room. Alex made to trip her but I gave my head a slight shake. He scowled at me but complied. I knew if he antagonized her she would just retaliate and she was a lot bigger. I did admire his courage.

I looked at my breakfast – a piece of bread and grapefruit juice. Nice, Claudia. The juice I dumped and refilled the glass with water. The bread I ate – I figured they couldn't hide much in it. It looked and smelled fine. I noted that I had no eating utensils and the 'glass' that the juice had been in was plastic. I left my lock picks alone but stuck my knife in my sock. If I was correct it must be just after seven. I was thankful once again for all of White Eagle's training. Who else would have made me learn sunrise and sunset times for an area I was visiting, along with the all the topographical maps and facts about the area. Sometimes I questioned his methods but the guy knew what he was doing. He would want me to always question though. He'd be the first to admit he didn't know everything. Five hours until he pulled the plug and came and saved us. I hoped my plan would work. I drank more water and waited.

I made use of my time by stretching and meditating. Kraeghton wandered in at what I figured was about 7:30. "Good morning, my boy."

"I am not *your* boy."

"Maybe not yet, but you will be. I'll own you like I do the others."

"I don't think so."

"So, how are you feeling? A little tired, sleepy, groggy, and weak?" He drew out the last; trying to scare me I was sure. "You'll tell me what you were doing last night."

"No."

He just huffed at me as his lips curled up slightly. The air had blown out like a quiet snort or almost laugh. "The drugs should loosen your tongue. If they don't, I have other means."

I just looked at him. White Eagle had talked about torture one day and Miles had training from the military. I could do this. Lie and tell the truth. Mix them together. All I had to do was hang on until noon. Just hang on.

"You're looking a little defiant yet. I think we need to up your dosage and bring in a little incentive. Last chance, what were you doing last night?"

I tried to look weak and small. "I was looking for a way out."

"Really." He said it like a statement, not a question. "I'm not buying. Try again."

"I was looking for a way to get us and my grandmother off the property."

"Warmer. Now I wonder, how *is* old Grandma this morning?"

I just stood there. What more was there to say? I was sure he would hurt us either way. Hold on until noon.

"Claudia!" he bellowed as he stared at me.

She came in with another syringe. I looked at her and rolled into my fighter's stance. I was not going willingly into this one. She carefully set the syringe down in the bathroom and looked at me. Kraeghton moved in from one side and Claudia the other. I relied on instinct. Kraeghton was bigger so I went for him first. They were far enough from me that I started with a kick. I brought up my right leg, twisted my body around, and lashed out. The back kick I released into his abdomen should have dropped him like a stone. His eyes bulged and his mouth half opened in surprise but I only pushed him back. Claudia was on me with a savage snarl.

She was fast. She didn't have her taser on her but seemed to relish her fist pounding into my flesh. She came in with a second swing but I leaned back and her fist sailed past my jaw throwing her off balance. I helped her on her way with an elbow to the back of her neck. She hit the ground with an angry growl. Kraeghton was back and almost on me. I stomped on his foot to slow him, spun and kicked him in the chest. I was wearing down but they kept coming.

Claudia tried to rise but I put a foot in her back as I vaulted over her. She was quick and was able to get a hand on my leg as I passed her, dumping me on the ground. I quickly rolled onto my back and sprang to my feet. Kraeghton was right behind me. He swung but I grabbed his fist before it impacted – twisting it as I dropped to one knee, throwing him off balance.

Claudia screamed as she charged, tackling me while I was still down on one knee. She quickly put a knee into my stomach and a fist to my jaw. She moved back and sat on my hips and Kraeghton stepped on my hand. If not for the thick carpeting I would've had broken bones again. He left his foot on my hand and put the other on my chest. I struggled but couldn't get loose. Claudia bounced once on my abdomen then went for the syringe. Fear and adrenaline surged through me. I twisted my leg up so that I could reach with my free hand and pulled the knife from my sock.

I jabbed it into Kraeghton's calf. He screamed and fell off me. Claudia dropped the syringe and came at me again. She pulled off her outer shirt and wrapped her hand and lower arm as she glared into my eyes. "You better hope I don't get that away from you. I'm about done with your family. If he doesn't turn you, I swear I'll torture you for the rest of your short life!"

I could keep them off me and at a distance but we were at a standstill. They didn't want to get close to the knife but I was exhausted. Kraeghton just smiled. "I had a good night's sleep and I am chemical free. How long do you think you can hold out?"

I didn't bother to answer. I saved my energy. They both converged at the same time. This time I went for Claudia. I came in under her guard and plunged the knife into her chest but too high to hit anything vital. She screamed and tried to pull the blade free. Kraeghton didn't even flinch. I held up my arm to block but between the kick last night and his standing on that hand today it was next to useless. He used both fists to knock me back and then picked me up and slammed me into the wall.

I tried to fight but this time I couldn't get him off. Claudia had pulled the knife free and plunged the needle in my arm before I could put up any more of a fight. She angrily pulled it out, drove the empty syringe into the wall and left it there to vibrate right next to my eye. I tried to gulp. Kraeghton released his grip and I fell to the floor. Claudia delivered another kick to my abdomen, making me cough and gag. She laughed and limped out of the room, blood running bright red down her chest. Kraeghton gave me one last look. "I do admire your tenacity," he said and left the room.

I lay on the carpet panting. My vision was out of focus and the room was taking a slow spin. I crawled to the bathroom, drank some water and cleaned my wounds. I tried the door. It was locked, so I listened. I could hear nothing. No kitchen noises so they must be eating. Please let them be eating. I lay on the floor in front of the door and pushed the carpet back. I couldn't see much but it looked like I was unguarded.

I staggered to the closet and retrieved my lock picks. Reaching up made me dizzy. I had to lean on the wall for support. I finally retrieved them and took down my money too, just in case. If I lost it now, so what. I leaned against the wall to keep the room from spinning as I made my way back to the door. I sank down onto my knees and checked under the door again. I gave it a soft knock just in case but heard nothing from the other side so I went to work.

My hands were shaking and I had to keep wiping at my eyes that would not focus. I dropped my picks and had to start all over again. I wanted to cry in frustration but I wouldn't allow myself to give up. The lock finally gave way. I opened the door a crack and saw no one. I put my back to the billiard room and crept down the hall using the wall for support. The hall was no longer square but strangely canted to one side. I chanced a glance around the corner. I heard a tremendous crash and a commotion from deeper in the house. I heard yelling voices and pounding feet.

I eased around the corner and headed for the pantry area behind the kitchen. I could now make out some of the voices coming from the kitchen and dining room. It sounded like all hell was breaking loose as planned. I peeked into the kitchen in time to hear Kraeghton in the dining room, "Bill, get his medicine. Claudia, subdue our guests and the staff. I'll hold the boy to make sure they comply."

I slipped back into the pantry. Claudia led my family and the staff through the kitchen. They were all strangely compliant. I silently moved to the other end to see where she would take them. I saw her shove the last, all but Lucas, into the billiard room. I moved back through the pantry as fast as I could. Claudia half walked, half ran back through the kitchen and I followed her as she entered the dining room. Bill came huffing in the other door and knelt by Shawn who I could see laying on the floor gasping for breath. Bill struggled with the epinephrine.

"What's taking so long?" Kraeghton barked, causing the suspended Lucas to whimper.

"It's damaged, it won't work!" I could hear the panic in Bill's voice.

"Claudia, get the car." Kraeghton snarled. He looked at Lucas, unsure what to do with him. He shook him once and growled at him in frustration and rage. I was about to intervene when he came marching toward me so I quickly melted into the shadows.

I watched Kraeghton lock my brother into a broom closet. Lucas was too scared even to cry. He sank down onto the floor as the door slammed in his face.

Kraeghton sprinted for the dining room where I could hear him and Bill struggling with the limp Shawn to get him out the front door to the car. I moved over to the broom closet before they were even out the door. I unlocked it and Lucas fell into my arms in relief. I didn't even have to warn him to be quiet. I took his hand and made for the billiard room.

Lucas kept a lookout while I picked the lock. There was a crash and the scream of distressed metal out front. All of the staff had clearly done their parts. The door popped open and Dad almost struck me, mistaking me for one of Kraeghton's crew.

"We have to hurry!" I gasped even as I fell to one side as the walls moved yet again. Dad, Ralph and Alex jumped over my legs and ran for the front of the house. Mary was behind them but puffing hard, through the pantry, to get another angle on them. Lena was right on her heels. Lucas had been trying to work his way into the room as everyone else ran out and he kept getting pushed aside. He finally made it in as I regained my own footing. I was starting to sweat and my stomach rolled.

Dorothy and my mom had Grandma lying down. "Relax Maela, help is on the way."

"No!" I cried. My grandmother's skin was gray. She turned slightly at the sound of my voice.

"My Owen," she whispered.

I staggered to her side. Her pulse was weak and fluttery – her breathing shallow. It was then I saw my grandfather hunkered in a corner with his hands over his face.

"Do something!" I barked at him harshly.

"It's all my fault," he mumbled.

"Then do something now before it's too late!"

"I... can't."

"Look at her!" I screamed, snatching a hand from his face. "Do you have an AED?"

"A what?"

"You know, an automated external defibrillator. The portable machine that diagnoses heart problems and can deliver a shock if needed. Do you have one?"

"I... yes. In the kitchen."

"Go get it."

"Owen," Mom called frantically. Dorothy had her head bent over my grandmother listening. She looked my mother in the eye and shook her head. I moved over to my grandmother but her pulse was gone or so weak I could no longer feel it.

"Did you call for help?" I asked as I began CPR.

"Kraeghton cut the phone lines this morning and they confiscated all our cells," Dorothy answered grimly.

"Then run out front and see if you can get a cell phone or take Alex his Vita," I instructed.

"Is Grandma going to be okay?" Lucas asked in a voice I never wanted to hear again. It broke my heart just to listen to it.

"I don't know, honey, we are doing our best. Do you want to help?" Mom asked.

"Yes," he whispered in that same sad tone but I could hear an edge of hope and courage.

"I'm going to switch out with Owen and he'll show you how to hold her head so that it's easier for her to breathe."

I nodded at Mom and we switched out. I tilted Grandma's head back and listened for a breath. I shook my head at Mom but she kept circulating her blood. I blew a breath into her while Lucas held her head.

Grandpa came in with the device and I set it up while Mom kept pumping on Grandma's chest. Lucas had taken to whispering to her. He told her to hang on and that he was there and that everything would be okay.

The machine ran through its program and suggested a shock. We all moved back. I watched the lights, blurry from tears and drugs, and listened to it give its warning powering up sound. mmmmMMMMMMM!!!!! Thwap! Grandma's body arched in response and the machine checked her again. We set it up for a second shock. She wasn't responding.

Tears were running down my face unchecked. I looked at Mom and she was in the same state. Lucas huddled by my Mom's side and my grandfather stood staring at Grandma as a lone tear ran down his cheek. He turned his back and walked away, his shoulders hunched.

White Eagle came careening around the corner, Saul right behind him. They screeched to a halt and took in the scene. The pause was brief, then Saul was at my side and went to work. White Eagle assisted and Mom and I fell back, waiting, hugging Lucas between us.

They worked on her for the ten longest minutes of my life. Saul finally shook his head. White Eagle put a hand on his shoulder and turned to us. "I'm so very sorry," he said in a deep husky voice. I knew that voice.

I looked up at the ceiling and then walked over to the door. I tried to open it to walk out to look at the ocean but it was locked. I pulled out my lock picks but I couldn't focus. I threw them on the floor and hit the door as hard as I could with both fists, shattering the glass.

I turned back to White Eagle. "Tell me we got them."

"Kraeghton got away. When the gate would not open, Claudia tried to drive the car through it. When the car hit the gate the airbags were deployed. Bill was in the backseat with Shawn and tried to run but we got him. Kraeghton was in a separate car behind the first one. When he saw us swarming the gate, he made a break for it around the side of the house. Your dad nearly had him but all he got was a broken nose for his trouble. You'll be proud of Alex. He's the one who caught Bill. Shawn didn't make it but the other two will be hospitalized under guard."

"Why aren't we still after Kraeghton?"

"An APB has been issued and agents are on his tail. I thought I could be of more use here and Sarah is cleaning up with the locals out front. You're in no shape to go after him right now, but we will. I promise."

I looked down at my bloodied hands and sank to the floor. Saul moved over to me now that my rage had burnt out. "What did they give you?" he asked, his concern vivid and strong.

"I don't know. Too much of what they gave me before or something else? I don't know. The syringe is still in the room next door. You'll find it stuck in the wall. Saul nodded at White Eagle who bolted from the room and set me up with an IV much as he had my dad earlier. Mom and Lucas crept over to hold my hand. I noticed that Mom had laid her outer shirt over Grandma and was down to a tank top again. She had a faint mark on her where Kraeghton had touched her and another where Claudia had zapped her. Saul was still checking me out but he was drifting away from me. I looked at him and tried to tell him to take care of my mom but no words came out. The world faded to gray. I saw Lucie reaching out to me again – a light shining behind her. I tried to lift my hand toward her but she evaporated with the rest of the room.

FOURTEEN

The first thing I noticed was the horrible taste in my mouth. The next thing I noticed was that I was no longer sitting slumped against the shattered French doors in the billiard room. The third thing I noticed was the pounding headache. I cracked open one eye. I seemed to be in the main sitting area of the house. With so many rooms who knew what this one was actually called and more importantly who cared.

"Owen?" Sarah's soft voice reached out to me in gentle caress. I rolled my eyes in the direction of her voice. "Hey, honey. Lay still, okay? Saul still has you hooked up to an IV."

"Grandma?" I tried to ask but it came out as a croak.

"I'm sorry, sweetie, we couldn't save her."

"Kraeghton?"

"Still out there, but we'll get him."

"Where is..."

"Your family is packing. We'll celebrate Alex's birthday and Christmas at home."

"How did Saul get here?"

"I sent for him yesterday. I knew we'd need him to keep this as quiet as possible. I also want you to meet the newest member of our team." Sarah helped me to sit up and gave me a sip of water. She held out her hand to a beautiful young woman with long dark hair swept up in a simple pony tail. She was wearing navy slacks and boots. On her hip she wore a badge. She wore a blouse of light blue with the sleeves rolled up. I was surprised to note as she came closer that her eyes were a surprisingly bright blue. I'd expected brown.

"Hi, Owen. I'm Mica. I'm so sorry for your loss. Your grandmother was a nice person. I talked to her a few times."

"You did?"

"I was assigned to this case when things began to look... Well, you know Sarah, we deal with the stuff normal people shouldn't know about. Bob, Sarah's boss, put her in contact with me. We've been working together and sharing information this week. We'll protect your grandfather as much as we can but he'll still have to pay for some mistakes. Your grandmother has been sending us information. You got the last of it out to us. We have enough on Kraeghton now that we'll have no problem bringing him down. We're afraid that he isn't the biggest fish in the ocean, however."

"He's not..." I tried to remember how I knew that. Had he told me or had I sensed it? I tried to think back but my head was still fuzzy.

"Don't stress about it right now. Rest and we'll talk later. I'm going to be part of Sarah's team now. You're my key to Kraeghton."

I wondered how this tiny girl was going to take on someone like him but my body had other ideas. I needed a bathroom and food and more water, though not necessarily in that order. I pushed everything else out of my mind.

Sarah helped me to the small bathroom off the kitchen but stayed outside the door. Saul met us when I came out. He led me to a seat in the breakfast nook near the circular stairs and checked me out again. He removed the IV and told me I was recovering nicely. It didn't feel like it. Mary brought me eggs, toast and a big glass of milk. She hugged my shoulders and moved back to the kitchen without a word. Sarah sat next to me the whole time. After a few bites I put my fork down and just looked out the now open French doors.

"Come here," Sarah said, putting her arms around me. All my anger, frustration and grief welled up inside me and overflowed. I sobbed. I rested my head on her shoulder. She was the grandmother I never had - the one who really loved me. I would never know Grandma Ryer like I knew Sarah. I'd just a few small glimpses of Maela Ryer's life. Sarah's gentle hug was like being swept under a mother bird's wing. We sat there for a while, rocking back and forth with me tucked under her protective wing, her soft soothing words washing over me.

I sniffed and wiped my eyes and nose on the napkin Mary had left. "Thanks, I didn't know her well but the whole thing just seems so wrong and unfair. Why did she have to pay? A mean part of me is glad that Grandpa had to watch. It should've been him." Sarah leaned over and pressed her lips to my temple. Her comforting arm was still around me. She knew enough to stay quiet and just listen. Eventually I continued, "This isn't the best part of me. I need to put that ugly part away."

"There was nothing more you could've done. It isn,t fair and it's okay to be angry, just don't let it eat you."

"Yeah, let's go home. I don't want to be here anymore."

Sarah's boss got us a private flight home. It was the last allowable flight out but not one of us wanted to spend one more minute at my grandfather's. It was hard to believe that we'd been in Florida for such a short time. If I never saw Florida again it would be fine. There were lots of loose ends to tie up but none of it had anything to do with me. Agents would keep Grandfather company as they went through the whole house and his businesses in a major audit and searched for evidence. Agents would also crawl all through the firm in Atlanta.

Bob had even sent a limo to take us from the airport home. As we approached our house I thought about my life – I felt like everything had changed but I knew that what had happened was worse. Everything here was the same - I was the part that changed. The person who went to Miami was different from the one who had just come home. Things would never be the same. In a couple of days my whole world had turned upside down and backwards.

I was amazed to see our house all lit up with Christmas lights. Beggar was so happy to see us that she ran in circles and did fantastic leaps. I could barely even make my face smile. Adrian came over with Marlo's family. Both families and Max had pitched in to decorate our house. We hadn't done much before we left since we thought we would be gone for Christmas and New Year's. Our wonderful friends couldn't stand to have us come home to an undecorated house after what the story they had been fed about our trip. My boys and I retreated to my room where I told the true story. I was sad to see them go at bedtime but I knew that our family needed some time to... heal.

That night I had another of those strange waves. This one felt different. The need, fear and confusion were all still there but this one had a touch of relief in it. Like for the moment everything was... not okay, but good enough.

On Winter Solstice we celebrated Alex's birthday. Mom always says that Alex is the best Christmas present she ever got. He had a right to celebrate – he'd done amazing things in Florida. He also let me know that he was on to me. He didn't know what all Mom and I could do but he was certain we were *not* normal. Yay. Keeping him safe was now a top priority. Dad didn't complain at all about having Sarah and White Eagle around. He now knew their value. After my brothers had fallen asleep on the flight home, he and I and White Eagle had finally had our long overdue discussion about me, my abilities and what I had to do. He didn't like it, but at least he was willing to make an effort.

Christmas was quiet at our house but pleasant. Thanks to Marlo's and Adrian's families we had a tree. We hung out, watched movies, played games and cooked together. Sarah and White Eagle were with us most of the time. We even called my Arizona grandparents and pretended to act normal. The story was, we came home early because we were in a car accident – to explain all the damage to us and the loss of my other grandmother. Every free moment I had, I spent back at the pawnshop and in training. We kept up to date on Kraeghton. No news was not good news... it was frustrating.

School was just as it had been except all the leaves were down and it was colder and even rainier. Tess was friendly but distant. She still sat by me in Biology but I didn't see her at all otherwise. We'd both stopped asking. I probably wasn't that much fun to be around right now. She didn't even ask about our Florida trip. It was just as well - I didn't know what I would tell her anyway. Lucie looked at me from across the room in the classes we shared with a look of relief and sadness. She wouldn't talk to me either.

Things remained on edge at home. Dad was gone a lot to help Grandpa settle things in Florida. The old curmudgeon was retiring, selling nearly everything and moving to Oregon. Yay – not. I didn't know what to think of that. Luckily for my Grandfather there was a great nibble on his estate to be used as a high end bed and breakfast. It looked like he'd be able to get out of all his IRS and legal worries but it would cost him. Dearly. He'd turned over all he had on Kraeghton and could basically prove that he'd been tricked and held hostage. He helped his staff find other, even better, employment. Dorothy got the retirement package she was promised.

Kraeghton had completely vanished. He had turned a corner during the chase and had disappeared. He could be hunting us or out of the country, who knew? The Atlanta firm was collapsing under the close scrutiny and lack of its leader, Kraeghton, so it was being sold. There was no sign of Dad's work on the explosive adhesive and it was believed that it had disappeared with Kraeghton. The mysterious doctor who had 'treated' Dad and my grandparents was also gone. The only bright spot was that Kraeghton had Dad so confused when he worked for him that he hadn't been able to finish the adhesive. It still didn't work right and hopefully never would. Dad was on paid leave until June when he would get another job at the affiliated Oregon company he'd worked for previously, thanks to pressure from Richei Ryer. Dad still didn't like what I did but he agreed, grudgingly, that someone had to do it. He even agreed to take some self-defense classes from White Eagle.

Before he was to come to Oregon, Grandpa Ryer was going on a month long cruise with some of his retired buddies and then he would be moving into a place near us. It would be a much smaller house but it was still much bigger than ours. His new neighborhood had groundskeeping included and he would have a household staff of two to manage him. Good luck to them and I hoped I didn't have to visit often or ever actually. I needed to be a better person but I still felt angry and resentful.

At the end of January, Tess made it official and broke up with me. She wished me well and said that she would be in a different section of Biology next semester. I knew the end was coming but it still made me sad. I was a little relieved, too. Tess had been a big adventure. I was glad that she didn't get in any trouble from the whole Skimmer thing. In the end, she had gotten her revenge. She and her sister would have normal lives and Skimmer and his gang were gone from our school. She earned every bit of the credit she got.

New classes began the first week of February. Tess really was gone from my Biology class but then my schedule had changed too. I was in a different section of Biology as well. I now had it with Marlo and Lucie. Marlo was thrilled – Lucie was resigned. They'd been lab partners but they absorbed me into their group. We sat three in a row at the back of class but Marlo was always between us and Lucie avoided talking directly to me as much as possible. All of us, including Adrian, had a computer applications class together. Much to Lucie's chagrin, she had to put up with the three of us in English, too. She would sit mainly by Marlo but sometimes Adrian got her. She never sat by me.

Lucie seemed to have a new boyfriend but it didn't last long. I didn't pay a lot of attention. I didn't pay much attention to anything. I was back to flying under the radar. Marlo and Adrian were frustrated with my quiet. Not even bubbly Jesus could put up with me for long. Marlo found me to be overly focused which truly is an irony. In the quiet, before our next big thing broke, I tried to learn as many skills as I could. I was determined to be on top of my *watcher* game as school drifted to the side.

To keep my mind occupied and off Lucie, I worked out or focused on *watcherly* things. I didn't know what the deal was, but I was more drawn to her than ever, no matter how weird she acted or how I tried to resist. I kept finding my mind drifting to her, so in response, I ran every other day. The days I didn't run, I swam. I squeezed in some snowboarding and skiing as well as indoor rock climbing. I was seriously considering learning how to parachute and fly a plane. I continued to work out in White Eagle's gym for a little over an hour five days a week. I did all kinds of chores and odd jobs at the pawnshop and kept *reading* items. Only petty small problems came in. When I felt like it, I solved them but mostly they weren't worth messing with.

Lucie tried out another new boyfriend the end of March but since she couldn't keep her eyes off me, he quickly went his own way. I saw them having a... discussion in the commons that included lots of hand waving in my direction. Marlo noticed it too and sighed heavily next to me. "Look, you're the brother I never had, but I'm about ready to put you up for adoption. You've got to snap out of it. You're losing weight again. You do your school work but all you really care about is that bike you work on with White Eagle and working out. Watching you fight is scary and amazing both, but you're becoming a machine. I miss my friend."

I looked at him for a stunned moment but quickly realized that he was right. "I'm sorry Marlo. You're right, but I just can't seem to shake it. I have this weird thing going with Lucie. We can't take our eyes off each other but she won't talk to me. She only dated that guy for two weeks. Why does she bother? Why won't she talk to me? And then there's my grandmother... It's crazy, but I miss her and I never really knew her. And then of course Kraeghton has vanished. Maybe if you feel up to it, we could hang out and game. Maybe I just need some of your mom's lasagna and waffles the next morning for breakfast. What do you say, Mar?"

"Deal! I don't have a girlfriend to impress right now so how about Saturday?"

"Deal!" I said with the first real smile I think I'd had in weeks.

Marlo was right. Goofing off on Saturday night and Sunday morning did leave me feeling better. It got my mind off Lucie, Grandma and the fact that Grandpa and his stuff were arriving soon. We were expected at a house warming once he was settled. I just wasn't feeling the joy and good will. In my mind he was responsible for my grandmother's death. For my dad, I would try to behave myself.

My grandfather finally was settled in over spring break. I couldn't believe how the time had flown by. Fortunately he'd waited long enough that I'd cooled off quite a bit. Our relationship was still a bit rigid and formal but I tried to be somewhat friendly. He and Dad seemed to have repaired much of their relationship.

The beginning of spring break White Eagle and I spent finishing the bike. We even took it for a few test drives but it reminded me that Trevor was still waiting for us to find his remains and to give his family peace.

The last weekend of spring break White Eagle, Adrian, Marlo and I went camping up on Mt. Hood. We hadn't given up on - or forgotten about Willie. He'd rolled over on Kraeghton but wouldn't disclose any information about his victims. The boxes had been removed from Vivian's with all the items I'd found being linked to his victims but no remains had yet been found. Marlo had worked at it constantly since September. On this campout we planned to photograph all our likeliest spots for the mysterious cabin that Willie was linked to. We'd waited until now so that the snow had a chance to melt off and we could explore more easily.

Friday night I had one of my weird episodes. I hadn't said anything to White Eagle. I didn't purposely avoid telling him. The moment either wasn't right or I didn't think of it. This time when I was swept up in the current of worry, despair, helplessness and need, he saw it.

"What on earth was that?" he asked as he looked at me over our campfire.

"It happens sometimes," I said and described the wave and the feelings that washed through it. Marlo and Adrian stared at me.

"I know there's something that I'm supposed to be doing and this 'wave' is calling to me but I'll be darned if I can figure out what it means. Other, more urgent, things just kept popping up so I haven't focus on it. Now I guess I better get serious about it except I can't grasp it. I try to follow it but it just evaporates."

"Geez, Dude, sometimes it just sucks to be you," Adrian said with feeling.

"That, my friend, is the understatement of the year, but then, that is why he has us – the *dynamic duo*," Marlo added to lighten the mood.

"Someone is calling to you, Owen. They need help. We have to figure out who it is," White Eagle said, looking serious.

Marlo jumped up and rushed to the truck. We all just watched for a moment. He came back carrying his ever-present laptop. "Let's record every event you can remember and see if there is a pattern."

We spent the next hour logging all my episodes and looking for those patterns. At the end of the hour I could only see one thing in common. Lucie. But that just wasn't possible. I felt stupid even saying it out loud.

We set that problem aside and looked at the photos we had managed to take today. Marlo pulled out the big map that we had up on the board in the shop. He had every known lake marked and a list of who owned all the properties around each lake.

"I wish Willie would give us something," Adrian finally said in frustration.

"I don't think he ever will. He knows he's never getting out. What incentive does he have?"

Adrian looked at me. "Is there nothing he wants?"

"What he wants - we would never give him. He wants to drain *watchers*. If not that - then drugs. Which, of course we wouldn't give him either. By the way, I heard his rehab is not going well."

"It couldn't happen to a nicer guy," Adrian added under his breath.

"There you go! It couldn't!" Marlo threw in with a grin.

More photos of some new spots would need to be taken tomorrow. We hadn't found our sweet spot yet. I slept the best I had since... Maybe it had been last summer. My dreams were filled with Lucie. I had flashbacks of all the good times we'd shared. My dream shifted to me dancing with her in the commons last fall. I knew the part was coming where Tess would approach me and kiss my socks off, but she didn't appear. I was happy dancing with Lucie but a part of me kept looking around... waiting. It was like someone was calling my name but I couldn't quite hear. I scanned the room once more and there was Trevor – watching me from the raised section. He was leaning on the railing. He looked up over his head as if he could see the posters that hung there. I looked up too. Everything around me swirled away as the posters transformed into a picture of the mountain. I felt myself zoom forward to the mountain side. I was both scared and exhilarated as I raced forward – the mountain coming ever closer. I could see Highways 26 and 35. I zoomed in closer yet. The images changed faster than I could register and then I was rushing through the trees to land by a lake. I had a clear view of the dock I was looking for. I turned and saw the cabin. Trevor stood near it and beckoned to me. I followed him through the trees until the lake was out of sight. I reached a tree that stood out from the others. I looked back at the lake as it called to me. I turned to ask Trevor about it but he was gone and then the whole thing swirled to gray. I was underwater and I couldn't breathe.

I awoke with a yelp, fighting for breath and to get the covers off me. Adrian rolled over and opened one eye. "What's your deal?"

"Nightmare," I whispered as I slipped on my boots, threw on a sweatshirt and left the tent. I took my coat from the cab of White Eagle's truck. The chill in the air surprised me. I should've known it would be cold in the mountains. I took some deep breaths of the crisp mountain air and pulled out the map. We weren't in quite the right spot. I still didn't know where but I knew we were getting warmer. I found a highlighter and circled the area we should focus on.

Marlo crawled out of the tent, his old glasses askew. "Hey," he said, by way of greeting.

"Hey."

"You thinking about your grandmother?"

"Nah, I was thinking about Trevor."

"I just thought... I heard you say her name last night after you fell asleep. I know you didn't have a service... Look, I know things are rough and I'm here for you, Buddy, okay?" Marlo finished awkwardly.

"You're the best, Mar. Just so you know, she didn't want a service. She wanted to be cremated and my grandfather has her urn. She set up college funds for each of us boys. She wanted... She wanted us to go on. She didn't know what I was doing but she knew I was helping people. She wanted me to keep doing that." Marlo put his hand on my shoulder. We stood there for a moment and then his attention was drawn to the map.

"What are you doing?"

"Either Trevor contacted me or my subconscious gave me a kick last night. I don't have GPS coordinates but I have narrowed our search down."

Marlo cocked his head to the side and studied my crude circle. He squinted at it some more and then turned it sideways. He dove into the cab of the truck and pulled out his laptop. He started mumbling and punching keys which led me to believe that my presence was completely unnecessary. White Eagle crawled out of the back of the pickup and I went to restart our fire.

I could hear Marlo and White Eagle quietly conversing. Periodically, Marlo would wave his hands around dramatically, but I ignored them and started breakfast. Adrian poked his head out when he smelled the coffee brewing and the bacon sizzling.

Marlo couldn't even wait for breakfast. He was practically bouncing as I was dishing up. He still had bedhead and his glasses were crooked. He rarely wore them anymore because of his contact lenses but they were awkward on a campout so he reverted to the glasses. He looked like his younger self for a moment.

"Eureka!" he exclaimed, as he bounced on the balls of his feet. I knew he was waiting for it so I caved.

"What did you deduce, Einstein?"

"I've narrowed it down to eighteen properties." I could feel his excitement but Adrian was our resident bucket of cold, mountain lake water.

"Gee, only eighteen, what a deal. I can hardly contain my excitement."

"Adrian, it's better than looking at the whole mountain," I said in Marlo's defense.

I was feeling more like Adrian by dusk on Saturday when we'd made no real progress. 'Not true', Marlo, the optimist, had said 'We've eliminated half'. I just hoped my dream was real and not craziness. One thing was clear – we'd have to come back. We spent part of Sunday searching but we still hadn't found anything.

Adrian finally snapped in frustration. "Can't you just turn on your... your... power or whatever and locate the spot like radar or sonar or whatever?"

"I wish I could but it doesn't work like that. I just don't have that kind of range. I imagine when we get close I will be able to sense it. If he really did bury the bodies there, it will have a dark residue. I just can't do it from here. I'm sorry."

"I'm sorry too. I shouldn't have snapped. It's not your fault. This running around just feels... dumb."

Marlo and White Eagle remained positive. We could meet up at the pawnshop after school on Monday and strategize.

Monday dawned dark and dreary with huge clouds and much misty rain. My day at school felt much the same way. Lucie was in a foul mood. I'd never seen her so distressed and on edge. She refused all offers of my help. By Tuesday she looked small, scared and had circles under her eyes. I tried again to talk to her, I couldn't help myself, but she ran from me. I looked at Marlo who just shrugged.

By Wednesday I had to resist the urge to kidnap her and beat out of her whatever her deal was. Even when I managed to touch her I got weird mixed messages. It was like love and hate or need and revulsion and fear – always fear. Toward the end of Biology Lucie packed her bag, popped up the minute the bell rang, and practically sprinted out of class. "I don't even want to know what that was about," I said to Marlo.

"Yeah, she does that sometimes. Hey, I'm hooking up with Adrian and heading to the pawnshop. Wanna join us?"

"Thanks but I'll be there in a bit. I finished my History at lunch and I want to turn it in. I'll see you there."

"Sure."

I watched Marlo go and then I finished putting my stuff away. I slung my backpack onto my shoulder and wandered into the nearly deserted hall. I turned left to head out of the science hall but stopped. The strange wave I felt sometimes was rolling over me again. This was the strongest I'd ever felt it. Anguish – remorse – guilt – and that strange need. I turned slowly – today I would track it down. I realized that this wave didn't just roll past; it had been coming from behind me continuously this time.

Scrunched up with her back to a locker... was Lucie. I walked slowly toward her with my palms out in a gesture of peace. She had her head in her hands and was softly crying, not paying any attention to me. I knelt beside her and put a gentle hand on her shoulder. As my hand connected, I was zapped with a strong electric shock and a vivid image.

"Lucie, do you see a girl in saddle shoes, bobby socks, a poodle skirt, and a sweater with a matching shirt thing?" I asked, astonished. I'd never gotten an image from this hall or had anything around here speak to me. In fact, I'd never gotten an image off of

Lucie that didn't pertain directly to her either. What in the world was this?

"A sweater twin set? And pearls? With her hair in a pony tail? Do you hear her sobbing?" Lucie asked with a gulp.

"I... do." I realized Lucie was right. I could *hear* this image but she wasn't real – she had the wispy ghostly look that most of my images did and I do not hear my images. Sure, my watch had almost whispered to me but no other items did. Even the watch, or Miles, didn't really talk to me; the pictures were just so vivid that it was like hearing them. This was... amazing.

"Oh my God, I'm not crazy. If you hear her too, I am not crazy! All year I've been hearing things. I thought I was losing my mind. Every time I tried to tell someone or ask for help, they thought I was nuts. So I stopped saying anything. I didn't want you to know I was nuts, so I never told you," Lucie said, as tears began to well anew in her eyes.

I peeled her away from the locker and held her close as sobs of relief began to shake her body. What she had said had come out in a rush. I was still processing it.

"Is everything okay here?" a teacher asked, coming out of her classroom.

"We're okay. She had a bad day. I'm helping her. I'll get her home now. Thanks."

"Well, if you're sure," the teacher said with a mix of worry and relief.

"No problem, thanks anyway. Come on, Luce," I said as I pulled her to her feet and turned her to head her toward the exit.

"Owen, can't you help her? You help people, I know you do. Help her. I can't... I can't listen to her anymore. She's breaking my heart even more now that I've seen her. Please, Owen," Lucie begged, still sniffling. She tried to turn in my arm to go back but I kept a firm hold.

"Luce, let's take care of you first. That girl felt bad sixty some years ago. We'll worry about her next." I was due at the pawnshop but they'd understand and my paper could wait. Lucie didn't live too far from campus so we could walk. "Come on," I added as I led her down the steps, turning right to head down the street. "Do you have everything you need to take home for homework and stuff?"

She nodded. I guided her along. We walked three blocks before she stopped me. "Owen, I'm so sorry. I was afraid. I was afraid of the stuff you get involved in and then I started hearing things I shouldn't be hearing. I've missed you so much!" she said, as she turned and hugged me. She just stood there holding me like she was afraid to let go. She buried her face in my chest and breathed in deeply. "God, you smell good. I forgot how good you smell."

I wasn't sure what to do with this Lucie. She was like my old eighth grade Lucie but so much had happened. "Um, Luce, are you okay?" It was wonderful to have her this close but it had been almost a year since she had been. I guess I just don't shift gears that fast. I kept expecting her to shove me away, or yell at me, or run.

She surprised me instead. "Nope. I'm crazy, remember?" she giggled, taking another deep breath and squeezing me tight. We stood there in the mist as the cars whizzed by and no one paid attention. "Wait a minute... you heard her but together we saw her. How is that?"

I opened my mouth to answer but she was quicker. "You... *you* can do that. You did it last year. That's how you find out about these... problems you solve. You *see* them. Why didn't you tell me?" I was astounded by what had just come out of her mouth.

"Lucie, you don't know how many times I tried to tell you. I just... couldn't. I really wanted to, but I couldn't. We can't tell people what we do – it's dangerous for us if people know. It's also dangerous for the people who find out."

"But Marlo knows and I bet Adrian does too. Why not me? You never felt about me the way I felt about you – I knew it," she said indignantly, as she slugged me in the arm. There was my old Lucie.

"That's not true, Luce. It wasn't that I didn't want to – I couldn't. Why do you think I was always so... awkward around you? Many times you saw the emotions travel over my face. Remember what I sang to you at graduation? Remember the dance in the fall? It has always been *you* that I saw – always *you* I wanted but couldn't have. I couldn't tell you, but I wanted more than anything for you to understand."

"Why?"

"What I do is dangerous but I'm driven to do it. If you're like me, then part of the craziness you feel is *your* need to fix what you are *hearing*. Now I have to tell you about me and teach you about what we do. In the fall you were afraid of my secret. You only knew half of it. Now you have another piece. I think we need to see White Eagle. He can help you."

"I don't want to go my house anyway. Let me text my mom that I won't be home until late."

I whipped out my own phone to give White Eagle some heads-up. I wondered and worried why Lucie's mentor hadn't shown up sooner. I knew White Eagle would help her but it was either very rare or impossible for a mentor to have more than one protégé at a time; though Kraeghton seemed to work with more than one. I'd never heard of it happening and White Eagle had already promised to help Mitchell, the *watcher* we met in Nevada last year, if the need arose. On the other hand, the *dark watchers* were banding together so why not us? I argued with myself.

Lucie and I walked to the pawnshop. We caught up on what we'd missed in each other's lives this year and she bombarded me with questions. Could I help her? Yes. Would I help her? Yes. Where should she start with the stuff she heard? I couldn't say but she'd learn like I had, to sift through it all to get to what was really important. Yes, I would go with her and walk around all the locations where she'd heard things and try to meld with her to get more information. And yes, Adrian and Marlo knew about me. Absolutely, Marlo would help us do research because he hates injustice and he's incredibly talented. Yes, Adrian would help too;

he's good at getting information out of people. He can charm anyone. When it comes to a fight he's a good wing man. Would she have to fight? Yes, she probably would, so why not get trained just in case. I told her we regularly got into situations that required us to fight our way out. We're here to balance the bad so we 'fight' the evil in the world, sometimes literally.

Lucie was giddy with relief, excitement and nerves. She didn't walk next to me; she bounced most of the way to the pawnshop. She'd been so distressed for so long that her response to the news that she wasn't crazy was almost an overreaction the other way. It was like she was bipolar and unmedicated - super happy after being almost desolate.

Just before we reached the door Lucie grabbed me by the hand and yanked me back. "Hey, wait. Remember our first day of World History? I wanted to talk to you and fix everything. It was my first urge to tell you that I had heard things over the summer." I started to speak but she put a finger to my lips. "Remember when you put your hand on mine and looked into my eyes?" I nodded, her fingers still on my lips. "I *heard* you and then I was really scared. I thought I truly was crazy and I thought it was a sign not to tell you... the one person who could've helped me. In my head, you said, 'Everything will be okay and I'm still your friend.' You wanted me to know that I could still count on you."

"You *heard* that? Wow, that was pretty much what I was trying to tell you. I remember thinking those words. Did you see anything?"

"I thought I was just remembering... sitting by you in Science and leaning my head on your shoulder and the time you saved me from Calvin and kissed me or the time we watched the people at the mall as we looked over the railing and talked. I kept seeing us walking around the campus at the middle school and my blue scarf fluttering in the breeze. Mostly I saw us smiling."

"That's pretty much what I was remembering – the good times that we'd shared. I knew you were afraid of me and I wanted to send you some good will."

"Owen, I wasn't ever really afraid *of* you. I've been afraid *for* you. I was afraid that if something happened to you... I didn't want the pain of losing you, so I pushed you away. In December, over break, I had this horrible... I thought I was going to lose you forever; a part of me nearly died. I remember dreaming that horrible things were happening to you." Lucie paused and gave me an odd look, then she took ahold of my wrist and turned it over to trace the scar that Claudia had left. "I tried to reach out to you but you were always just out of reach. I tried to call your house but you were gone. I finally called Marlo. I figured if something was wrong he would know. He thought everything was fine. I didn't hear another word and then you came back. I knew you were okay before I even saw you. I didn't know how I knew. I just... did. I should have... I was stupid. You're the best friend I've ever had. You've always been there for me. Always. Why didn't I trust that you would be there for me this time? I'm so sorry," Lucie's voice ended hushed and broken. She had slid back to sadness. A tear slipped out and I automatically wiped it away.

"Lucie, I *will* always be here for you," I said, taking both of her hands in mine.

"I'm glad," she sniffed, pulling herself together. She plastered on a nervous smile, "Shall we go meet your famous mentor? Will he be mine too?" she queried.

"I hope so. We'll see. No matter what, he'll help us."

Max greeted us with a bit of surprise. In the year and half that I'd been coming to the shop, I'd never brought in anyone except my family. Tess did find her way here once on her own and I hadn't had anyone here since. He had, of course, heard of Lucie but was amazed to be meeting her in person. He kept watching her as we made our way into the back.

White Eagle looked up from his latest project on the workbench. Adrian quit boxing and Marlo gaped over the top of his computer screen. By looking at their faces White Eagle had not told them what my little surprise was. There was a beat of silence as White Eagle assessed Lucie.

"Um, hello?" she ventured quietly.

"Hey, Lucie," Marlo said regaining his composure. "What brings you here?"

"Hey, Lucie," Adrian added.

"*She* is one of us," White Eagle said, using his calm, soothing voice. "Lucie has found her talent."

"No! What? Not fair!" Adrian griped, as he swung a fierce punch at the bag.

"Amazing," Marlo added, his eyes huge over the top of the monitor.

White Eagle stepped forward and took ahold of both of Lucie's hands and looked deep into her eyes. She seemed to go into a trance as the rest of us just watched. Maybe it had been like this for me too. It was so long ago and I was watching it from the other side this time.

"Wow," Lucie breathed.

"Huh," White Eagle said.

"What does she look like to you?" I asked, unable to control my curiosity.

White Eagle took ahold of my hand and Lucie's and closed his eyes. She flared with a beautiful violet burst of color with blue and fuchsia streaks. Her image shimmered like she'd been dipped in pearlized paint. It was amazing to behold. I'd never before seen what White Eagle saw. I wanted to look at Adrian and Marlo too.

"Owen, you are beautiful," Lucie said in a dreamy voice.

My head snapped around to look at her and White Eagle's eyes popped open. "You *saw* Owen's talent? What I see as light? I can't believe it. What does this mean?"

"It means that now that I know you can do this, I want to see what Marlo and Adrian look like," I tossed in to lighten the mood.

White Eagle obliged and took my hand and Marlo's. A soft blue light surrounded him. Marlo looked at us like he was waiting for the show to happen. Next we tried our experiment on the reluctant Adrian. His light was weaker than Marlo's and was a greenish color. He too looked disappointed that he didn't see anything happen.

"Before you two get too disappointed I would have you know that most people look like nothing at all when I use my *other* sight on them. Most people are not good or evil; they're neutral. When I look at them I see nothing but what you all see when you look at someone. You two are exceptionally good so I see a little spark of color about you. Now, back to work boys," he added for Adrian and Marlo. Adrian grumbled a bit but got right back to it. Marlo sat and stared, clearly deep in thought. Lucie was looking overwhelmed.

"So you hear things do you? Do you hear objects or is it locational?" White Eagle asked, turning his attention back to Lucie.

"Umm," Lucie hesitated and looked at me. Then she nervously reached for my hand. I suddenly realized that she was still wearing her backpack so I helped her out of it and got her a stool, then I took the hand she seemed to need me to hold.

"I think she's locational. She's been hearing voices in the hall at school and a few other places. There's one voice in particular that seems to reach out to her. It's a young lady from the 1950's. We were in the old part of the building today. I saw that Lucie was upset. I reached for her shoulder to comfort her and suddenly I could hear weeping and we saw a ghostly image of a girl in a poodle skirt."

"Hmm," White Eagle breathed as Marlo said, "Wow." Adrian perked back up and stopped boxing long enough to add, "Cool."

"Why didn't her mentor find her?" I asked concerned.

White Eagle looked at me intently, then at our joined hands and then his eyes lost focus as he looked at us with his other sight. Finally he spoke slowly and deliberately, "Her mentor did find her, Owen. He's been reaching out to her since last year in preparation. He didn't realize what he was doing and she wasn't ready for him yet. I think that she was trying to deny her gift and that complicated things."

"Who's her mentor? Maybe we can help him," I said with mixed feelings. I felt so protective of Lucie that I really wanted to check this guy out and keep tabs on him. I wanted to be sure he did things right and...

Marlo was laughing. That should have been my first clue. White Eagle was smiling at me and waiting expectantly...

"Oh – My – God... It's me? How can that be? I can't be both? Who's both? Has there ever been someone who's both? How do you know it's me?" I stammered.

Lucie looked from one to the other of us completely perplexed.

"Owen, I don't know what to tell you. I've been telling you the whole time that you're different from anyone I've ever worked with. Now I know why. Now I get it and I think you do too. Don't worry though, we're a team. We'll work together. I've got to get your mom and Sarah in on this though. We all need to meet and talk."

"Owen, what's happening?" Lucie asked, sounding scared.

"Well, you aren't going to be able to run away from me anymore. You're stuck with me for the next couple of years at least. *I* am *your* mentor. We're now linked. You know that *comfort and trust* feeling you used to get from me when you leaned on me in Science last year? Well that was your gift calling to mine. In those moments, I *was* comfort for you physically and mentally, we just didn't understand it yet."

"I understand that you have things to teach me, but this is a lot to take in."

"As I was once told by my mentor, be patient – everything will become clear with a little time. You'll know in your heart what to believe. It'll all come to you."

Lucie slumped on her stool and rested her elbow on the workbench, then placed her head on her hand. She sat unmoving for a bit, doing nothing but blink. I remembered doing that too. I let her be.

"So now you train me to be a mentor too?" I asked White Eagle.

"Yep. No help for it. We're called, not asked. We'll all help you, right guys?"

Marlo was an enthusiastic, "Yes."

Adrian was a little more hesitant, "All our guy time is gonna change drastically. We'll have to share the bathroom and make sure we're dressed properly," he said, sighing.

"You should be happy, Adrian. You love women. You should be thrilled to have one around more," I said with a mischievous smile.

"But she's never liked me like that. She's always resisted my charms. Now I'll be around her all the time and it will be pointless to charm her. Why waste it?" he moaned.

Now that got Lucie's attention. "Ugh, Adrian, you're like a brother. I've never been interested in you!"

"I know – it's tragic," Adrian said with a smile as Marlo added, "Ouch."

Lucie turned her back on them and looked at me intently. "Owen, tell me more. I'm ready to listen now."

"First of all we need to set a practice schedule. I don't know what your family will go for. We meet here every day after school and on Saturdays. If something comes up, we let each other know. We keep tabs on each other for safety. We try not to go anywhere alone. So lesson one: Always be either with one of us or let one of us know where you are."

Lucie gave me a small nod. "After school won't be a problem. No one is home until at least six. I'll have to think about the weekends and figure something out."

"We'll jump off one bridge at a time, okay?" I said trying to reassure her. "Don't worry about everything at once. It'll come and we'll help."

"Tell me more about what we do and how this happened to me, please," Lucie said, her concern returning.

"Let me try something that White Eagle once showed me. If it works, it'll be faster to show you instead of telling you. I took ahold of her hands and looked deep into her eyes. I could feel that light electric arc I felt sometimes when White Eagle *looked* at me and tried to communicate with me. I thought of all the things I'd done over the last year and a half. I started with the day I found out who I was - I could once again see White Eagle's and Miles' face overlapping each other. More images flashed past quick as a blink and I hoped that Lucie would be able to recall them all like I did. I watched her eyes as her pupils slowly dilated. I could tell that she was seeing something. Her eyes were a bit overly wide and her mouth was set in an 'o' of wonder.

I began to speak, "I'm a *spirit watcher* or *vision watcher*, so that would make you a..."

"*Whisper watcher*," White Eagle supplied in a soft tone.

"We're a type of guardian. You'll be driven to right wrongs. Evil things that have happened or are about to happen will appear to you and you'll feel the strong need to fix them. Sometimes bad things happen to good people and they should not. Sometimes a good person contemplates doing wrong and that will change their true path. It will be your job to help these people. White Eagle has been training me and now I'll train you," I told her – saying nearly the same words that White Eagle had once said to me.

"Your power, your gift, comes from within you. White Eagle once told me it's like trying to find a station on an old radio with broken knobs. Now you're receiving the station, loud and clear - now you are aware. It can also be compared to waking up. You can *hear* beyond the doors that covers other people's ears," I added. I smiled at my use of words. I had twisted and reused what White Eagle had once told me about *seeing* behind the curtain. Lucie had closed her mouth but her eyes were still wide.

"After much research by Marlo and after many discussions amongst us and with the few other *watchers* we know, we still believe that *talent* is cosmic chance and not necessarily genetic, though my mom also has a gift so in my case it may be genetic. Every gift is unique, just as each person's brain is. We all think in our own way so our gifts all work in their own way. Most importantly we need to keep what we do a secret. Are you doing okay?"

"Yes," she whispered.

"White Eagle, can we shut her power off until we have a chance to work with her and help her to control it?"

"No!" Lucie said firmly.

White Eagle and I looked at her in surprise. "Now that I know what it is – I'll be fine. I kind of think I might know how to listen and what to ignore. I've been trying to tune it out for awhile. Sometimes it just feels like people are shouting at me. Those are hard to ignore. The crying girl in the upstairs hall is the worst. She needs me. Once I help her – I won't hear her anymore, right?"

"Yeah," I said reluctantly. Then I took a breath and dove in. "Well, let's get started then. Do you ever feel a pull at your bellybutton, kind of a tingle and kind of like a hit of adrenaline?"

"Yeah, I think I do. Like the upstairs hall at school - I always feel weird right before I hear the sobbing. I also feel drawn to that spot. It's almost like I can't resist standing in front of the locker where we saw her sitting on the floor. We need to go look at that locker, don't we?"

"Yep, we do but I wanted to know about the feeling. Do you feel it other places but maybe not as strongly?" I asked, trying to get her to focus on my point.

"Yes, I do. The big Douglas fir out front calls to me, but I've been afraid to get too close after the hallway thing and some other stuff."

"You truly amaze me, Luce. Since we don't need to shut it off for you, let me teach you how to relax and breathe. It will help you focus and it'll help you shut off your own gift if you need to. Eventually it'll be second nature and you won't have to think about it. Ready?"

"Yes," she whispered.

I still had held her hands. I asked her to close her eyes. "Just pay attention to your breathing for a minute but still listen to what is happening in the real world around you."

"I can hear the hum of Marlo's computer and Adrian hitting the bag. It's quiet up front and I can faintly hear street noise."

"Good job. Now practice breathing in and out through your nose. Just relax. Feel the rhythm of your breath."

"Can we move to the mat?" she asked, cracking one eye open to look at me.

"Sure," I smiled. We sat on the mat with our legs crossed, knee to knee. Lucie took my hands again. I watched her settle in and relax. "Now, as you inhale, think of filling your belly. Really open your diaphragm. Don't breath with your chest. Put one hand on your belly if that helps." She didn't move so I released one hand and did it for her. I felt her relax into me. "Relax your face, your neck, your shoulders... breathe. Now focus on the stillness. When you're ready, open your eyes."

Slowly Lucie opened her eyes. She looked deep into mine. I felt the arc again. I saw all the places she'd been and heard the voices. It probably happened in seconds but it felt like we'd sat unmoving for days. I had no idea how much time had just passed. Marlo cleared his throat.

"I hate to interrupt the moment, but it's about time to go and Lucie isn't wearing her running shoes. White Eagle said he'd give us a ride."

"Where's Adrian?"

"He left with Max a bit ago. He didn't want to interrupt the... moment either. Amy broke up with him, which you may not have noticed, so he can't stand to see you two... umm." I realized that I still held one of Lucie's hands and the other still rested on her belly. I blushed and she laughed.

"Okay, time to go... so tomorrow then. Let's get recorded what you're hearing and where you hear it and then we'll start some Tai Chi. Do you run, Lucie?"

"Only when chased," she answered with a twinkle in her eye.

"Well then, I think I'm going to have to start chasing you. You never know when you'll need to run to get away. You want to be in better shape than the other guy."

"Yeah, but Marlo doesn't run, right?"

"Wrong, Marlo does run and Marlo hates it but Marlo is getting much better at it," he grumbled at her, making me laugh.

"Bring gym clothes and running shoes tomorrow. We'll all run to the pawnshop after school. If it's too much, you'll run as much as you can and walk the rest until you build up some stamina."

"Geez, Owen, if I wanted a training Nazi I would have gone to the gym."

"Sorry, Luce, it's what we do."

"What do I get if I make it the whole way? I work much better for carrots than I do for the stick," Lucie commented, her twinkle back.

"Tell me you didn't just compare yourself to a mule," Marlo moaned.

I just laughed. For once it felt like everything was right with the world. I knew it wouldn't last so I better enjoy it while I could.

I took Lucie's hand as we headed out of the shop. She looked at our entwined fingers and slowly pulled her hand away. White Eagle was locking the shop and Marlo was waiting by the passenger door of the truck. She looked from one to the other and sighed.

"We have to make a pact to be friends – just friends. Things will get complicated if we are more than friends. Promise me."

"If that's what you want Lucie. I'll try."

"It's what I want," she whispered as White Eagle climbed in the truck.

FIFTEEN

Our life shifted into a new and unusual pattern. Lucie was back to sitting right next to me in all the classes we shared. Hip to hip and knee to knee, we sat just like the old days. She seemed to be touching me all the time yet holding me at a distance. If I tried to hold her hand she shook it off but if she could lean on me or brush against me she would. She was sending more mixed messages than a political campaign. I knew that I'd rather have her as a friend than not at all. I was willing to take what she was willing to give. I guess that made me pathetic but there has always been something about Lucie.

Classes were going well for all of us. Adrian was doing a good job of accepting Lucie into our 'club'. We ran to the shop every day after school. Lucie was better than she'd let on. The four of us took to racing to the shop. Marlo's trick was to research new routes, looking for the best advantage. Lucie would try to distract and trick us and Adrian and I would just power on.

Lucie picked up Tai Chi in a week. I guess all those years of learning gymnastics routines paid off. She sucked at boxing but her karate was coming right along. She taught us a thing or two as well. She improved all of our flips and floor work. She and I worked well together when we team-fought for fun. It was almost intuitive with us. She did pretty well with Marlo but she and Adrian together were comical and she was reluctant to hit any of us.

White Eagle worked with me, with Lucie and with both of us. It was so strange to be both student and teacher. All those things that my mom used to tell me about how you learned things better when you taught them to someone else finally made sense.

Marlo was working on Lucie's task from the 1950s. We scoped out the other places where Lucie heard voices and logged them all with Marlo. Sometimes we got pictures to go with the voices and sometimes we didn't. We'd have lots to keep us busy for quite a while though. Most interesting to me was that the Skimmer echoes had disappeared. One of the first things we were able to solve for Lucie was voices she'd heard related to Skimmer, but didn't know what they were at the time. Guess when they disappeared? Yep, when Skimmer went away, so did they. I was fascinated by the fact that most of Lucie's problems had to do with relationships. They didn't seem to be as dark as the stuff I tended to come across but they were still important. She'd heard the cries of people used by Skimmer and snatches of conversation around where he parked his car regularly.

Lucie was taking to her new job with us like a duck to water. She seemed to be learning so much faster than I had. It was almost scary. I was completely frustrated with her unwillingness to hit me. The only thing I could get her to pound was the bag – not people. I was wondering if I needed to push her into a corner. Well, figuratively at least.

I was afraid that Lucie would be involved in a fight and freeze. What if one of us wasn't with her to protect her? She'd attacked the guy in DC last summer but I couldn't make her believe that hitting me for practice was okay.

The last Saturday in April, I snapped. It was just White Eagle, Lucie and me. Marlo was helping his mom cater a wedding and Adrian had a new girlfriend. I'd been so busy training Lucie that we had postponed any more Mt. Hood adventures until the first weekend in May, so my guilt over Trevor was building up and I couldn't get her to fight like I knew she could. I backed her into a corner as we sparred. She blocked but wouldn't hit back. We were both drenched with sweat and panting.

"I know you can take a hit from being in gymnastics and from what I saw today but I need to be sure that you can give one. Come on, hit me," I growled at her, showing my frustration.

"I can't."

"I can take it. I'm ready. Come on – hit me!"

She made a feeble attempt to hit me but it was nothing. She'd hurt me worse by mistake on occasion.

"Think of every time you've ever been mad at me, bundle it together and send it to me through your fist. Get mad and hit me, darn it. MEAN IT!" I ended with a shout.

Whump. Lucie finally landed a decent jab to my midsection.

"Much better. Now do it at least that well every time. You won't hurt me with the gloves on. Treat me like the bag, channel your anger, control it, use it. Now hit me!"

Sometimes you get what you ask for. Beware of those times. Lucie swung in a perfect uppercut. I had taught her well. I overextended and left my face unprotected from the girl who never hit people. She connected with my jaw, snapping my head back and making me see stars for a moment.

"Oh man, Owen. I'm so sorry. I knew that would happen, that I would hurt somebody. I'm so sorry."

I ran my glove over my jaw and smiled at her. "Much, much better. Do that all the time."

"You're kidding, right?"

"Not even a little bit. Hey, did you figure out a way to come camping with us? I could really use you. You might pick up something I miss." I started taking off my gloves and then began to help her with hers.

"Sorry, Buddy. My mom's not having any. Unlike you, I can't tell my family what I do."

"We'll figure this out eventually. We've fixed worse problems than this."

"I recognize that look – you're thinking about your misadventures in Florida. I get goose bumps when you talk about that. You're so brave. I don't think I'll ever be as good as you. I'm not worth either Marlo or Adrian right now and they don't have any extra abilities."

"They do though; you have to appreciate them for who they are and what they can do. I couldn't do what I do without them. We're a team now. Each piece is important. You are important. Don't underestimate them and don't undervalue what you add."

"You say the most incredible things sometimes. Now that you have told me about Miles, I understand you better but you always have been different – better than most people. I admire you, you know that?"

"I'm not better than anyone," I said, as I wiped off my face and neck with a towel and handed a clean one to Lucie.

"But you are," she said softly, as she stepped right up to me – toe to toe. She slowly rose up on her tiptoes, deliberately leaned in and kissed my lips softly and immediately withdrew. "I can't seem to help myself. I shouldn't have done that and you shouldn't have let me."

She was kidding, right? I tried to laugh but I failed miserably as I reached for her and pulled her back toward me. She didn't resist, falling onto my chest. I held her tightly and for a moment time stood still. I looked into her beautiful eyes and moved toward her slowly giving her the chance to run.

"No," she whispered but I didn't listen because the rest of her was saying, 'yes'. I brought my lips down on hers and I felt her shudder. I thought she was going to pull back but instead she wrapped her arms around my neck and kissed me back desperately. All thought and reason fled. I held her in my arms as I had not intended - she was right, it was safer to be friends, except that I knew deep down neither of us really wanted that.

I pulled back a little as reason began to return. "No," she whispered again as she held me tighter. Her lips returned to mine and then traced my jaw. She moved to my neck and for a moment I thought

I would die. She held herself there, breathing against my neck, her breath coming in soft puffs. I just held her, torn between knowing it should end and not wanting it to.

"You have to be strong." Was she talking to me or to herself? "Friends. We need to be friends. We decided. It's best to be friends. I'm the student and you're the teacher. We are friends. Say it, Owen. 'We're meant to be friends.'"

"If that's what you really want to hear, then I'll say it. I don't think I believe it but here goes... We're meant to be friends."

She thought she wanted to hear it, but I knew she really didn't. She looked so sad as she pulled away. "I get the first shower," she said in a somewhat shaky voice. I reached for her but let my hand drop instead. I turned my back on her and started picking up our workout area, lost in conflicting thoughts.

After Lucie and I got cleaned up, we helped White Eagle close up the shop. He had me drive, as he often did when he was taking me home, to provide more practice hours for my permit. Five months until I could get my license. After we dropped Lucie off, I had to ask, "White Eagle, when you first met me... how did you know I was the one? You said you'd been watching me... that you felt something. What did you feel?"

"The connection, you mean?"

"Yeah, that's it I guess."

"First I could tell early on that you were good and just. Later it felt like you were important, like you would come to mean a lot to me, like a son or a brother. Are you thinking of you and Lucie?"

"Yep, our situation is... difficult."

"It would feel different to you. The person will feel important, but it can manifest in different ways. Miles was like my brother but Miranda - she was my... everything. I loved her deeply and wondered if I could go on. She was a *watcher* too. Her death was an unfortunate accident. I've mentioned her before. We were engaged. Then I met Miles and that helped. You know what happened after I lost Miles. What we do is dangerous. You have to live your life to the fullest and enjoy it. You may live to be as old as our friend Emiline Claremont in Nevada or... not. The same may be true for Lucie. I understand her wish to keep your... situation a work-only relationship but I think she'll lose that battle. I've seen the way she looks at you."

"So what are you saying... go for it or respect her wishes?"

"I think her heart is telling her one thing and her head another. I'm telling *you* to be patient."

Yay, and I was so good at that. The rest of the week I tried to respect Lucie's wishes. Did she know how hard she made it when she sat so close? The gossip mill at school had already labeled us a couple. Fortunately no one asked me outright – I did not deny that we were a couple. It was a lie of omission but it kept the other guys away. For now.

Our campout that weekend narrowed down the spots but we still had two places that were possible. One did not look quite right and the other was occupied so we couldn't just walk around and *feel* the area. Something was telling me that I needed Lucie there anyway. Thinking of Lucie made me wonder. The bike was an object – I hadn't even tried to have her *listen* to it. What if we took the bike to the bar parking lot to see if she could get something? I'd been trying to prepare her for some of the ugliness that she might come to *hear* but unfortunately no one could really be prepared for some of the awful stuff out there.

May was almost half over and Kraeghton seemed to have fallen off the face of the earth, we were only marginally closer to helping Trevor's family, and we had narrowed the field to three girls that might have been crying in the hall. I tried to curb my frustration and impatience. Marlo and Lucie had been hard at work going through old yearbooks and reading microfiche newspaper articles from the time period as well as files on students from the poodle skirt era. They looked for girls who left and other tragedies that could've moved a young lady to such deep despair. Now that Lucie was narrowing in on who the girl might have been and what her problem was, she was settling even better into her job as a *watcher*. It was becoming so effortless for her so fast that I almost felt jealous. She also continued to do better with the friend thing. I kept trying to tell myself this was better than in the summer, fall and winter but it was still a difficult life to live – to let her take what she needed from me and to always remind myself not to take anything she did for granted.

Frustration was the keyword for me at home too. We were all trying hard to work Dad back into our lives. He was going stir crazy at home and had begged to go back to work. He and my brothers had started therapy after Christmas break. Alex was the first one out. He was done before Valentine's Day. Sarah had arranged for a special therapist who would be careful of our unique situation if anything came out about us that shouldn't. He also worked with people in witness protection. Lucas was done by spring break but Dad lingered on. Going back to work seemed to be the best medicine for him. They were able to transfer the person early who had taken over his old job. Dad was still busy with my grandfather as they settled everything and he worked things out with the IRS and various government agencies. Dad was placed back as heir so he got to attend a bunch of bored, I mean board meetings. There was no way I could run Grandfather's empire, or what was left of it, with what I did anyway.

It was strange now, after so much togetherness, to have Dad travel out of town again. This time he was only going up to Seattle. He could drive and with no sign of Kraeghton, he'd convinced himself that Kraeghton was out of the country and our lives. Dad had even taken some Saturday classes on self-defense. He ended up taking them at the gym instead of with White Eagle. They still had an uneasy relationship but at least Dad had taken some lessons. He felt confident but the rest of us worried. He left on Wednesday and would be back a week from Sunday.

Our Saturday practice at the shop had gone really well. Lucie was getting better all the time and had a unique fighting style that made good use of her gymnastics training. Her flips and kicks were the best of all of us. I made a point to tell her so. The fact that Lucie's parents virtually ignored her existence was a huge benefit to our group and our time at the shop but it still ate a hole in my gut. It was their incredible loss to not appreciate their beautiful, talented, smart, funny and gifted daughter.

I finally was able to convince Lucie to try *listening* to the bike. I was right, the bike alone had told her nothing. Max was working this Saturday so White Eagle could take us and the bike to the bar that Trevor was kidnapped from. Max thought we were taking the bike for a practice ride. For his safety, we still kept him in the dark about us – which wasn't always easy, but we all loved Adrian's Uncle Max so we did our best. The bar parking lot held too many jumbled sounds for Lucie to distinguish between, but when we put the bike in the right spot in the bar parking lot, we hit gold. Lucie did pick up voices from locations. Together with me and the bike she could narrow down all the sounds she *heard* and focus on Trevor.

Lucie gasped as we stood by the bike, each of us with our hand on it. We had gone through our breathing exercises and I'd tried to warn her. We linked our hands to focus and the images with sound this time slammed into us like a tidal wave. Lucie nearly let go but I held tight. We needed more information and she was providing an added element.

Lucie stood open-mouthed, her eyes wide with horror as the images flew past. Some things you just don't want to see or hear – when they happen together it can feel like a building was dropped on you. Lucie closed her eyes to shut it all out, but I knew from experience that would only make the pictures more vivid.

As the images came to an end, Lucie's hand dropped from the bike and she moved in to hug me and bury her face in my chest. She didn't have to say anything – I'd experienced it too. Right now she just needed my presence to know that everything was okay and that she was safe. White Eagle looked at us from where he sat on the tailgate of his truck but when he made to hop down, I shook my head at him to let him know that we didn't need him. Lucie needed me. Just me. I guess I needed to have my head examined but I lived for these moments. I could pretend that Lucie was just mine and it was my right to hold her like this.

She plastered herself against me like she wished she could crawl under my skin. She must not have been close enough because she unbuttoned my outer shirt and dove underneath it like she needed a place to hide. She wrapped her arms tight around me and rested her face against my t-shirt and neck breathing deep and slow. I could feel her shaking a bit. I knew she was trying to regain control but she was still holding on like a barnacle.

"Relax, you're safe. I'm so sorry you had to go through that. I was afraid it would be rough. I've seen it but adding sound was... I'm sorry. I need you to help me find Trevor."

"I... just needed a moment to let it all wash over me. You forget that you don't just see things – you feel them too. This was worse than watching a movie. When I closed my eyes the visions became more solid and vivid – not less, and I could *feel* how Trevor felt. I felt his fear and confusion. Worse I felt Willie's... rapture? I don't know what the best word is but when he drained Trevor's... power, gift, talent or whatever, he felt good in a sickening way. How can someone's pain and suffering make anyone feel good? I feel like I need another shower. Yuck!"

"White Eagle has compared it to a high from drugs. His theory is that *stalkers* like Willie sort of feed off people like us. They get a rush when they do it. They have a love of chaos and disorder. They feel that only the strongest should survive. It's our job to bring back balance, to return a sense of happiness or peace and order."

"I know Willie is locked up and that you promised Trevor's mom that you'd help her but how does this help us find Trevor's remains or prove that Willie did it?"

"I guess it doesn't directly but I had to try. It does give me an idea."

Lucie had been gently running her hand up and down my back as we talked. She finally lifted her head so that she could look at me.

"What *is* it about you that makes me feel better? When I touch you, I feel... safe, peaceful and calm. It's like you're my own personal drug. You're better than I hear Valium is. Is it something you do consciously?"

"I do want those things for you – the calm and sense of safety and peace. I want to protect you and I want you to be happy but I'm not *trying* to do anything but hold you right now."

"Huh, well, maybe it's just an Owen thing. I remember you made me feel this way in eighth grade - it just wasn't as strong. Maybe you're just what I need. So, what was your idea?" I had lots of ideas, most of which she wouldn't want to hear right now.

"I don't think you'll like it but we need to take the van White Eagle bought from Vivian up to Mt. Hood."

"Vivian is Willie's sister, right?"

"Yes, the police went through the van and her shed. They confiscated a bunch of stuff and know there are more victims based on what they found. They just haven't worked it all out – they need more evidence."

"Willie's souvenirs call to you. You saw the victims didn't you?"

"Yeah, we gave them the tip. At first we went only to talk to her and see if the van was there. We found part of his stash while we were on the scene. Marlo has it cataloged if you want to read it. I just thought... I wasn't trying to hide it. I don't want to scare you by putting you through too much, too soon, but I really needed you today. Willie won't tell anyone a thing about any of his victims. He won't give details or let on where they are, except that I know there's a link to that cabin. I can't prove it. It's only something I have *seen*. I can't give the police that but if we can even find one set of remains I believe the rest will turn up. We can give the families peace and they'll know Willie has been caught and will pay for what he did. I can't figure out if Willie thinks he can escape or if he knows someone will break him out. Or possibly he just doesn't care. Having no access to *watchers* or even drugs has got to be hard for him but..."

"Wait – hold on – all his victims were *watchers*?"

"Yeah, Luce, I think so."

Lucie dropped her arms from me and marched to the truck. She got in, slammed the door and laid her head against the back of the seat. White Eagle and I just looked at each other. As I mentally kicked myself for handling Lucie so badly, I wheeled the bike over to White Eagle so he could help me lift it into the back of the truck. We secured it and he got in the driver's side while I opened the door to the other side. Lucie scooted to the middle so I climbed up front with them. As soon as I was buckled, Lucie surprised me by picking up my arm and moving under it. She buckled her own belt, rested her head on my chest and closed her eyes. It seemed like she wished all the badness would go away.

"I don't know what I was thinking," she mumbled so that I had to lean down to hear her words. "I thought this would be easy. Most of the locational things I heard at school were small problems or at least not dangerous. I thought we'd solve mainly small problems... okay, so Skimmer wasn't so small but... what you do is... dark and scary. I'm not tough or brave like you."

"Lucie, we're called, not asked, to do what we do. I for one think you're very brave. Don't fret, you're right where you're meant to be," White Eagle told her calmly before I could reply.

"He's right Luce, you *are* brave – besides, no one said you had to be just like me. You're part of a team now, each member plays their part. It isn't easy but I know you can do this and I need you."

Lucie began to play with my watch. "I'm surprised every time you say that. It must be the Miles in you, the grown-up side that isn't afraid to admit you need help."

"What makes you say that?"

"It just doesn't seem like a guy thing... 'I need you' sounds like more than most guys would admit."

"It's true, Luce. If something is true, I'm not afraid to say it."

She gave me the strangest look but then she stayed where she was, holding onto the arm that she had wrapped around herself. *Just friends*, I reminded myself for the hundredth time. Lucie looked long and hard at my watch and at our fingers twisted together, light skin and darker. For all I knew my watch and Miles were now talking to her.

SIXTEEN

White Eagle and I spent all week getting the van ready including installing bench seats so that all of us could ride. We also got around to adding some shelves and compartments so that we could haul gear if needed. We weren't quite done but it was coming along. The next Saturday all of us piled into the van to drive up to the two remaining locations. Marlo checked out the one I felt was the better choice. It was now a rental property and it didn't seem to be booked this weekend. It was no surprise to me that it wasn't because it looked somewhat run down judging by the website.

Adrian thought we were wasting time but we checked out the least likely first. I was right, the first site was a bust – which made Adrian crankier. As soon as we neared the second spot, Lucie began to shake. She turned pale, her eyes wide as she gripped the armrest, her knuckles going white.

"Pull over, right away... please," I said urgently.

Marlo whipped around from the front passenger seat where he was navigating. White Eagle quickly pulled over and he too turned. Adrian leaned forward to look as well. I touched Lucie's face and was washed into what she was experiencing. It took my breath away. I broke contact with her and she whimpered in response.

"Marlo, pull up your list or however you record stuff but brace yourselves... its bad." I unbuckled as Marlo started madly typing. I knelt in the narrow space behind White Eagle's seat and unbuckled Lucie. I took her face in both my hands and looked deep into her eyes. I swirled back into her nightmare of voices. I was dimly aware of Lucie reaching out to take a fistful of my shirt in her hand. She'd begun to pant and sweat while tears ran from her eyes and splashed on her sweatshirt. I reached one hand toward the zipper thinking that if I couldn't make her feel better mentally, the least I could do was make her more comfortable physically.

I took a breath and tried to force the sounds into order instead of them all screaming at us at once. I dropped one hand to the floor of the van for balance and **wham**... I had some images I hadn't taken the time or energy to notice or process before. Trevor's message was now the strongest but I'd had contact with him before – he was... familiar.

What we knew about Trevor and a few new bits flew by in a flash of images and sound. I spoke aloud as I heard and saw things. "Start with Trevor...They're in the van. He's tied up in back but not secured so he's bounced around and taking a beating from the trip. Willie takes delight in the cries of pain he occasionally makes. They're on the road we're on now." I broke contact for a moment to give some directions, "White Eagle, pull forward slowly please, toward the cabin. I think we'll get more as we get closer."

As soon as the van was back in gear, I turned to Marlo, "Ready?" At his nod, I turned back to Lucie, who still had ahold of my shirt like a drowning man holds a life preserver. I placed one hand on her cheek and the other on the floor of the van again. "We're still on Trevor - I can see the cabin and the lake. They were there for a few days, I still think four. I can hear screams coming from the cabin. Now it is silent. I feel Willie's anger - it has ended too soon. On day four, Willie hauls out Trevor's body, turns right off the porch and walks behind the cabin. He isn't gone too long and then he drives away." Marlo looked at me over the top of the laptop and gulped, much as he had the first time he heard the story back at the shop.

Adrian stared at us, looking completely ill. White Eagle drove on down the rock-strewn road, his eyes on the track before him and his thoughts kept to himself. Lucie was damp with perspiration but she was no longer shaking and a bit of her color had come back. I helped her out of her sweatshirt. "Ready?" I asked her gently, knowing how much it hurt to experience someone else's pain, especially when you knew the ending was not a happy one.

"I don't know what you're doing but when you touch me, the sounds seem to separate out into distinct messages instead of being all jumbled. Adding the pictures sucks but we have to do this. We have to get rid of the *dark watchers* before they get rid of us, right?"

"Yeah, that's about right, it's another part of our job," I said softly. "Deep breath, re... lax, breathe," I continued slowly as I looked into her eyes." I felt the swirl begin again and then the voices came. I focused again on separating them. I talked to them in my mind. 'Help us'. It didn't seem to make any real difference so I focused on the items I had found in Vivian's shed, Willie's souvenirs. I wished again that I'd found more.

I saw the coin and remembered its story. I tried to dismiss it but it had taken hold. Back in eighth grade, I thought that sitting next to Lucie for sex education in Health was embarrassing; this would be... painful by comparison. Poor Lucie, in a van full of guys, nowhere to hide and she was about to experience something I would've liked to have spared her. Her life should be clean and sweet. She'd already seen too much ugliness. I cleared my throat as the sounds and images began to roll past. Lucie's eyes widened and her cheeks flushed from too pale to bright pink. Then a flush of color began to move up her neck but she kept ahold of my shirt and kept looking into my eyes as the sounds and images flashed past.

"We're seeing the young woman with the 2009 dollar coin. Willie picked her up at the same bar where he kidnapped Trevor. She's laughing in the van. Willie is being charming and funny. He's smoother with her; she's one of the recent victims. There are so many voices. He may have nine or ten victims in all trying to speak to Lucie."

I could also hear in our present, Marlo clicking away on his computer and road noises as the voices talked all at once. Adrian and White Eagle continued to remain silent. So I went on, "The young woman is still enjoying Willie's company as they pull up at the cabin. She turns to look at Willie, her decision made before she even got in the van. She thinks coming here is a good idea – she wants to have fun. He kisses her, then he comes around and opens her door for her. The atmosphere is playful but I can sense the darkness in Willie – she doesn't see it. They laugh, their arms draped around each other as they go into the cabin. It's quiet. Now we can hear..." I cleared my throat again, "they're... doing what they came here to do. Now it's changing. She isn't making the same kind of sounds. We can hear her fear as she says 'no' and 'stop'. Willie feels... euphoric." Gack, I thought as bile rose in my throat. "Now... a final terrified scream. I wonder why he killed her so quickly or if it was an accident. He also took her body the same way he took Trevor's but he was gone longer. She was one of the last but he killed her so quickly..."

White Eagle interrupted to speculate. "This one was different. Willie is getting worse – he needs a higher high. Perhaps it was more than the girl could take. I wish you didn't have to go through this so young. I wish you weren't exposed to the underbelly of society. I'd do it for you if I could. You deserve the chance to be children away from such ugliness. It isn't right or fair but I can think of few people who could handle it better."

"White Eagle, it's our job – we're tough and we want to help these people. We also know that relationships should never be like that," I said. Lucie gave me a crooked smile and put her hand on my shoulder.

Adrian had unbuckled and pulled his feet up onto the bench seat, almost curled up in a ball like he wished it would all go away. Marlo was turned sideways in his captain's chair with the arm flipped up. He was completely focused on his work as he clicked away, but I knew Marlo, he was listening and thinking. White Eagle pulled to a stop at the cabin about where Willie had usually parked the van.

"Aid, you okay?"

"I forget... I put out of my mind what you guys have to do. I'm sorry. I need to get out... I can't..." Adrian fumbled with the door latch. It finally gave way when White Eagle unlocked it for him, causing him to almost fall out of the van. White Eagle looked at Marlo.

"I'm good. You can go fix Adrian. We'll handle the rest of the cataloging," he said with calm authority. White Eagle said nothing more. He put his hand on Marlo's shoulder, then left the van to walk behind Adrian and give him some support and advice, I was sure.

"I've seen stuff like that in movies but knowing it's real... I feel like I'm invading the privacy of these people."

"I know, Luce. Just keep in mind that if we can really get rid of Willie, it's worth it. If we can bring peace and closure to the families of the victims it's also worth it."

"I know, it's just... That was worse than going on a first date and being surprised by a sex scene in a movie that you weren't expecting. I feel embarrassed and sick."

"Yeah, I know what you mean. Are you ready to move on or do we need to stop?"

"Move on, I guess."

"Hang in there, Luce. I'm proud of you. It will be okay in the end. We'll help these families and get rid of Willie and then it will feel more like it was worth it."

I didn't wait for her reply but moved right on to focus on the headband I'd seen in Vivian's shed. Lucie had let her hand drop from my shoulder so I reached for it to connect with her gift. I knew that this girl had been taken from a family picnic. This had nothing to do with the van and it was not at this location. I could still see Willie sneaking up behind her and cutting off her air by wrapping his hands around her neck. I could see her struggle. She'd walked out of the bathroom and didn't see him leaning against the wall nearby. He quickly dragged her into some nearby bushes. He tried to clamp a hand over her mouth as he put the other over her heart. There was no sound with the images but I could tell she was trying to make noise. I sensed someone was coming because Willie noticed – he snapped her neck and it was all over. As her body went limp her headband snagged on his jacket – he took it on a whim as he ran away and has collected souvenirs ever since. I relayed the information to Marlo who dutifully compared it to my earlier account. I thought I'd gotten a little more with the boost from Lucie. She wiped tears from her eyes, then reached out and touched my face.

"I'm so sorry," she whispered. I wasn't sure what she was sorry about but I took it and answered her with a half shrug. I started to move forward toward her, forgetting myself for a moment, but Marlo cleared his throat and I caught myself and pretended that I was just changing position.

"That girl could have been me. I don't think she knew who she was yet. She didn't have you." Lucie was now looking at me in a way that made me think that she was forgetting the *just friends* thing. Her gaze shifted and she quickly added, "Or you, Marlo." I turned my lips in and bit back a smile – literally.

I waited until I had Lucie's gaze again. I took a deep slow breath and watched her do the same. Then I closed my eyes and focused on the last item I'd found, a comb. I pulled up the young man's image. Willie had tried to befriend him like Trevor. It still felt like this one happened near the middle of Willie's reign of terror, but before Trevor. I began to speak for Marlo's benefit, "This is the comb guy. They were going camping together up here. The ride in the van is happy. They're chatting about motorcycles and movies and stuff. The sounds from the cabin are happy initially. They must have gone to bed. The comb guy is scared awake. Willie was trying to drain him while he was asleep. He fights Willie off. Now I can see him running through the woods and that is the last I see of him," I sighed, then pulled myself together for Lucie.

"Okay Luce, let's see what's left."

"Wait, I... I wanted to say that... It's still bad even when you just see what happens to these people and there's nothing you can do to stop it. You know what's coming and you can't... do anything. It makes me feel so... helpless."

"I know. Keep reminding yourself that we're doing something to help. We just can't save them all."

She rolled her neck and looked at me again. I touched her with one hand and the floor of the van with the other.

"Marlo, I can tell there are many voices here but they overlap. I can't distinguish between them. It's so weird. I guess I'm used to looking at pictures where people look different so even if the images are mixed I can tell who's who. But this... I need another link." Sensing what I would ask, Lucie was already shaking her head. "You can't tell them apart either, right?"

"No, sorry."

"I think that we need that extra piece. We need to know something about them to hear them. It's like how you can hear a conversation in a crowd because you are focusing on that piece in all the noise. Come on then, let's go check out the cabin and the surrounding area to see if there are separate pieces we can peel off and then we can check on Adrian."

We all piled out. I looked toward the dock, where it looked like Adrian and White Eagle were having a heart to heart conversation. Lucie and Marlo followed me to the cabin.

We only had to get within about fifteen feet of it and Lucie's eyes went wide. She'd been walking a bit away from me but the voices in her head drove her to me. She came up behind me and wrapped her arms around me as if the voices were coming from live people in the cabin. As soon as she touched me I was bombarded by a cacophony of shouting voices.

Just looking at Lucie had caused Marlo to look a little pale and shaky but he soldiered on. We had to do this. I slowly moved toward the cabin with Lucie clamped to my back and Marlo and his laptop bringing up the rear. As soon as I hit the porch I was slammed with images to go with the sound. I fell to one knee and Lucie still holding on tight, came with me. We landed in a heap, Marlo nearly tripping on us. I sat on the porch – my arm around Lucie and let the whole horrible mess bombard us.

Pain – suffering – abuse and fragile moments of hope, as a few victims broke loose or even got away, crashed over us, flooding us like the mudflats at high tide. I felt like I was drowning in the muck of events that lurked here. I tried to ease my heavy breathing and pounding heart. I needed to calm down for Lucie – she was new to this, she needed me to guide her. Breathe – relax – focus.

I began to speak to Marlo in a distant voice so he could record all the 'clips' of the final moment of these poor people. I used to see pictures or even a silent movie reel in my head – now it was like YouTube. Names began to come to me because of Lucie. Sound and pictures together made for a powerful combination. It made all my previous work seem weak and lacking.

"Becky Welch was the first victim here; she's a voice from the van. Karl Henderson, Nancy Comber and Sasha Clark were also brought here in the van, but I didn't find their souvenirs yet. Rich Tanner was the young man with the comb. I hear Trevor Vance's name. It's like Willie taunted them. He said their names and Lucie can hear it because of the darkness and pain here. Natalie Delmont is the name of the young gal with the coin. There is also a John Ricker. There are eight people here. Eight people who suffered and likely died. We have to end this," I choked out.

White Eagle and Adrian walked up as I finished speaking and looked at us with solemn eyes. I was limp, exhausted and sweaty by the time we were done. Lucie leaned heavily on me. Marlo saved the material on his laptop and backed it up to a flash drive which he slipped into his pocket as he slumped down on the step next to us.

We all stayed where we were for a beat before Adrian nervously cleared his throat, "I feel I owe you an apology. I know this isn't all fun and games – sometimes I push too hard – I want to get to the fun stuff. I don't have much patience. I've done pretty well in the past pretending this part of your job wasn't real. But hearing it today when you use *that voice* – when you describe that horrible stuff – I guess the guilt all piled up and... I'm sorry."

"Aid, its okay – it's really okay."

Lucie looked up and smiled at Adrian. "I, for one, am glad you're here. I could never take on someone like Willie – we need you, Adrian."

I was proud and impressed that Lucie seemed to know just what to say to make him feel better. She was doing a much better job than I was. I gave her arm a squeeze and smiled at Adrian myself.

"I think we need to explore a little more while we're here. We could break into two teams to cut down on the time it will take. Lucie could *listen* for one team to locate other hot spots and I could *look* for the other team. We need more information. We have very little the police can actually use. So how about if Adrian goes with me and White Eagle takes Lucie and..."

"I need to walk up the road," Marlo interrupted. "I can't get a signal here. I want to get into the missing persons database and see if I can get some of this to Sarah."

"Okay Mar, but when you're done, head on back so we can record more data from any locations we find."

"kay," he said absentmindedly, already opening his laptop and moving down the road.

"Meet back here in forty-five minutes whether or not you're done," I hollered for everyone's benefit but especially Marlo's. "I saw Willie take Trevor to the right so I want to start that way. I'm familiar with Trevor, so his images will speak the loudest to me, so to speak," I laughed at my own pun. Lucie and White Eagle just gave me a sidelong look but Adrian smiled.

Adrian and I stood on the porch and watched Marlo disappear up the road as Lucie and White Eagle headed toward the lake and off to the far side of the road.

"Adrian, I appreciate what you said earlier but it's really okay – we can't all be strong all the time and I totally get the impatience thing!"

"I know... come on, let's finish this, then afterwards, I think you owe me pizza!"

Adrian and I walked into the trees – he watched for our local nasty plants like poison sumac, poison ivy and poison oak. He also kept an eye out for stinging nettles while I *felt* my way, looking for darkness.

"Too bad you can't speak to the dead, Aid."

"That would completely freak me out!"

I just smiled as I stretched out my other *sense* by closing my eyes and focusing on Trevor. And there he was... I walked forward, eyes closed, feeling my way toward the darkest thing I could find nearby. I looked at the Douglas fir that marked his shallow grave. There was no object here for me to touch but I could feel the residual darkness seeping from the earth. Adrian and I snapped pictures with our phones and he marked the spot with some plastic marking tape, which he tied around the tree. I was afraid to dig and disturb anything more than we had too.

"Do you suppose he buried them all here and if he did, why?"

"Lazy? Or maybe it's something about the cabin. Maybe something happened to him here and so he's drawn to it."

"He's sick. I'll be glad when we can pin these murders on him. I wish I was more helpful."

"Adrian you are. I need you to watch my back. When I focus on the darkness or images I'm not fully in the present. I need you to watch out for me."

Adrian sent me a small smile. Maybe I didn't thank him enough. Marlo's work was so much more tangible and obvious. Adrian faded out sometimes but he was no less valuable. I needed to tell him more often.

I turned in a slow circle looking for the next dark spot in the woods nearby when something whispered past causing me to shiver. There was a change in the air. What *was* that? I wondered. Then, though, as I froze where I was – Adrian holding still but alert at my side - I got my answer. It started with the feeling that something wasn't right, but escalated to creepy as I realized I knew that sensation. Worse – I knew where I knew it from.

"What is it? Another body?" Adrian hissed.

"No – worse – a *stalker* – here... and I'm sure it's Kraeghton."

I started to run but only stumbled two steps before I halted, Adrian slamming into my back. It was definitely Kraeghton. I remembered well the last time he had *looked* at me and the effect that it had. Right now he was focused on someone else...

"Marlo! Aid, come on, he's in trouble..."

I didn't need to say anything more. Adrian took off with me hot on his tail. I quickly passed him as I pushed myself harder than I ever had before. My fault... this was my fault. I should've kept us together. I should never have let Marlo go off alone! I likely ran through every poisonous plant known to man but all I could think about was Marlo... alone. As I sprinted through the trees and dense underbrush, getting slapped and scraped by branches, I pulled my phone out... to find… I had no signal.

"Aid, signal?" I barked at him.

"No," he panted frantically, once again passing me.

Crap – I pushed on, scratches covering my face and arms. We hit the road and quickly scanned both ways. I could barely make out the lake in the distance but there was no sign of Marlo. I pelted up the road, away from the lake, swinging my head from side to side in frantic search. I could see no sign of Marlo. Adrian and I stumbled over the uneven surface of the rock-covered road. Fear and dread twisted my gut. Sweat and a bit of blood ran down my arms and face. I glanced at Adrian and he looked no better. He looked beaten up, dirty and raggedy.

Finally, when I was about to lose hope, I caught a flash of blue amongst all the green, gray and brown. Marlo's crumpled form was face down in the ditch that ran along the rocky road. I skidded to a halt next to him and felt for a pulse.

Adrian fell at my side as Marlo let out a low moan. "Mar, buddy, are you okay?" Adrian gasped.

Marlo groaned and rolled onto his side. "Some dude came out of nowhere and BOOM, he hit me in the side of the head and swept my legs out from under me. Am I in a ditch? I was watching the laptop for a signal. I wasn't paying attention... Where... where is my laptop?"

"Umm?" was my intelligent reply as I looked around frantically.

Marlo's eyes seemed to focus on the crushed laptop before mine did as if drawn there by instinct. "My laptop," he moaned. Marlo tried to rise but fell back down clasping his ankle. "My ankle."

"Aid, you got this?"

"Yep, we're good."

"Stay together, I'll get the others."

I hated to leave them but I knew Kraeghton would be more interested in Lucie than either of them. We were all safer if we were together. I put my senses on high alert and sprinted back down the road toward the lake. As I neared it the sense of 'wrongness' returned. I slowed my steps and moved into the cover of the surrounding vegetation. The closer I got to the lake the stronger the feeling became.

Suddenly I had a wisp of a thought reach me. I wasn't sure if it was real or my imagination – Lucie – but then she'd reached out to me before. Kraeghton – Kraeghton was with Lucie. It was then I realized that I could hear shouting through the trees. I had to halt my mad dash to stop and listen so that I could get a direction. It sounded like Lucie. *Hold on Lucie, I'm coming - please hold on!* The shouted words were coming more clearly now. The trees were thinning and the dense darkness around me was lightening. I took a deep breath of the crisp spring mountain air. The lake was coming into view through the trees. He stood alone on the dock – no, not alone – he had Lucie trapped at the end. Where was White Eagle?

I reached out for White Eagle and felt... nothing – no, wait – not nothing... but a faint signature. He was okay but... frustrated? Worried? Trapped? Reaching out to White Eagle was not something I normally did but we were so connected that I *could* feel him. He would be no help for now. I was on my own. At least for the moment he was safe.

Lucie, on the other hand, looked like she was torn between two impossible choices. She was clearly afraid of Kraeghton and she was thinking about jumping into the lake. *Don't do it Lucie. I'm here.* I hid in the foliage and felt the area. Was there anyone else around? The only evil I could feel was coming from *him*. All the danger was on the dock. My stomach pinched in response. Lucie's eyes were wide and I could see her hands shake a bit even from here. She was in a hopeless position at the end of the dock with nowhere to go. She crouched, ready to fight, her eyes wide and her hands held defensively in front of her.

Kraeghton's words came to me clearly, "Tell me where he is or I'll make what's left of your life miserable. I know he's close. I can sense him. He got away in Florida. He won't be so lucky today. You can't protect him, Tiny Girl. I got more energy out of his mother than I'll out of you but you do look delicious."

Lucie said nothing, giving nothing away. She changed position. She must have seen something in his face. She either knew or had figured out who he was. I'd told her a bit about Florida after she joined the team. She'd been horrified but she had to know. I knew that she understood what she was dealing with but I was afraid she wasn't ready and I was more afraid that she knew she wasn't ready for someone like Kraeghton.

I had nowhere left to hide but I hoped Kraeghton was distracted enough that I could take him by surprise, despite the fact that I'd have to move out into the open. He moved forward. Lucie focused completely on his movements, like I'd taught her. She rushed him then, jumped up with both feet to plant them in his sternum. The move was unexpected and I'm sure took him completely by surprise. He staggered backwards but didn't fall as I'm sure Lucie hoped.

I hit the beach at a dead run, but I wasn't as fast as I should've been - not nearly fast enough. Lucie landed too close to the edge of the dock and teetered. She windmilled her arms to catch her balance but he grabbed one and hauled her up against him. She punched him in the face with her free hand. I heard a bone break from the edge of the dock. She shook her hand like it hurt as he turned and spit blood. He growled at her, shook her and ripped open her sweatshirt with his free hand. She tried to push him off but he got a hand over her heart. I was half way down the dock but her scream of agony dropped me to my knees. I *felt it* as if the scream was torn from my own throat and I felt like my heart was being pulled right out of my chest. Lucie tried to claw at his hand and kick at his legs but I could feel her body going weak. This was what he'd done to my mother in Florida.

I forced myself to my feet and staggered a few steps before I broke into a run. I didn't stop but aimed my elbow right at Kraeghton's temple as I ran past him. He should've dropped. Instead he now held Lucie by one arm as he turned his head toward me and the nauseating smile slowly faded from his lips. His upper lip went white, a vein pulsed in his forehead and I thought he was about to explode.

"You!" he snarled as he threw Lucie aside, where she crumpled in a heap.

"I was paid to track you after you left Florida. Too bad about Grandma. I've been watching your pathetic little life for months. I'm good. You didn't even know I was around. Watching and waiting. Then you decided to come to Willie's favorite place. He hates it here. Lots of bad memories. You could say he's trying to bury his past. My boss wants you but you're just too tempting. I want your power for myself. This one is satisfying, I can see why you like her, but *you*..."

I felt nauseous. "Who's paying you?" I wanted to kill him but I needed information more than I needed to fulfill my own urges. He looked awful. I wondered if he had been living out of his car since December. Kraeghton needed a shave, a haircut and he was horribly rumpled. He looked nothing like his former self in

Florida. Life on the run must be tough. Add in the cut Lucie had inflicted and he was a total mess.

"It doesn't matter. When I'm done with you – you won't care. Hmmm, easy way or hard way? Fast or slow? Slow and painful I think. You should suffer like I have. You ruined all my Florida plans and I won't have it. No child will make me look bad."

"Who hired you?" I tried again.

He only gave me a strange half smile and moved toward me. I could see the insanity in his eyes and in the way he held himself. I backed up hoping to get him further away from Lucie.

"You're not afraid, are you, Little Man? You felt it when I pulled her power from her – you're connected somehow – I can tell. It feels so gooood when you pull their power from them. You should try it." His eyes lit with a strange glow. "It's better than... anything. Though you wouldn't know - you still have much to experience. Last chance to join me. If you won't, I'll take everything from you like you did from me. It will be different with you. Slow and painful – mmm – so tasty. And then I will finish her. Your little friends cannot help you and your mentor is... busy."

To keep from gagging I put my full focus into my attack. I ran straight at him as Lucie had - he thought I was trying the same move and turned to the side at the last moment - right where I wanted him. I put one foot into his hip, pushing down to lift my body up and kicked at his chin with my other foot. He fell onto his side with a crash as I fell back, carried by my momentum. I landed on both feet and sank into a crouch. I spared a glance at Lucie who lay unmoving. Damn.

He surprised me with his quick movements. I couldn't believe how fast he was back on his feet and on me. He was desperate and maybe he now had Lucie's energy. He reached for my shirt but I punched straight up through his chin, knocking his head back and his arm to the side. He shook his head and growled at me. I quickly followed the shot to his chin with a kick to his side. I had him at the edge of the dock so I kicked again trying to send him over. No luck. He absorbed the kick, grabbing my leg and dropping me to the dock. I rolled as he tried to stomp my head and then flipped to my feet once more. He advanced again. I leaned to the side to avoid his fist, grabbing it with both hands and twisting as I dropped to my knee to flip him over as I had in Florida.

He was taken by surprise just like last time and landed with a thud that shook the dock. Before he could recover, I kicked him in the side of the head hoping to knock him unconscious. I didn't even check my work. I ran to Lucie who was pulling herself into a sitting position.

"Lucie! Are you alright?" I could already see blisters forming on her chest where he'd touched her. "Let's get you out of here," I said, not even giving her a chance to respond. I pulled her to her feet. I turned and put an arm around her and took a step forward only to have a blur of movement knock Lucie right out of my arm and off the dock with a tremendous splash.

I looked for a split second, in stunned silence, at the empty dock – at my empty arms. A flood of silence filled the emptiness. I turned, knowing I'd have to dive into the water after Lucie. I heard a roar in my head filling the silence - Stupid – How could I have been so stupid?

"No!" burst from my lips without me even realizing I was speaking. I knew, with a sickening sense of despair, that she wouldn't make it. I ripped off my flannel shirt and t-shirt. I kicked off my shoes, stripped off my socks, watch and cargo pants. I ran at the end of the dock and just had time to snatch a quick breath before I jumped out past where Lucie had fallen so as not to hurt her. I hit the surface and passed through, down into the freezing, dark gray-green water. I felt around frantically and tried to see. I couldn't so I closed my eyes and just felt for Lucie. I used our strange connection to *call* to her. She was panicking and out of breath but her heart was still beating. I swam down toward her where she was pinned under the dock. I tried to loosen her but she was held fast.

I felt the evil before I saw him. He was delirious from the kick to the head. He'd tried to drain Lucie again under the water but his need for air was driving him to the surface. The water would prevent me from doing much damage hitting or kicking so I tried to prevent him from surfacing. My own lungs were screaming. I wrapped myself around him and squeezed. I used him to push myself to the surface for a breath. I grabbed a quick one, fighting Kraeghton all the way. He tried to put a hand on my chest but couldn't get a grip on me without my clothes for leverage. I kicked him as hard as the water would allow then pushed him down and away from me. He finally went limp.

The water bubbled and swirled as I made my way to the surface for another quick breath. How much time had passed? I immediately dove back to Lucie who had mostly freed herself, and dragged her to the edge of the dock, the water pulling at her greedily as if it didn't want to release her, but I was more determined. I would not release her to the water. I knew I was too spent to lift her onto the dock so I pulled her until I could stand. When the dock was at waist level I rolled her onto it and jumped up behind her. I didn't see Kraeghton or anyone else.

She was ghostly pale and her lips and nail beds were blue. I blew air into Lucie frantically. "Don't you dare leave me! Luce, come on, breathe." I checked for a heartbeat - it was still beating but it was far too weak. I blew in more air. How long... how long? I blew another breath and watched her chest rise with it. She finally coughed. I rolled her onto her side and let her gag and wretch. She coughed some more. I vigorously rubbed her back. I needed to restore some warmth and help her expel the water. She finally reached for me limply with one hand and pulled my hand up under her chin as she coughed some more. I was beginning to shiver. I could feel the hit of adrenaline wearing off and I was beginning to worry about the others.

Lucie coughed again and began to struggle so I helped her to sit up. She looked at me - her beautiful eyes red from the water. She wiped at her running nose with her sleeve and leaned forward to hug me. She was soaking wet, freezing cold and bedraggled, yet she was still beautiful to me.

"Don't cry, Owen," her voice came out scratchy and hoarse. "It's okay."

I hadn't even realized I was crying. She was right, it was more than just lake water running down my face. I bent my face close to her and gently kissed her reddened eyes. She sighed and coughed once more. Then she moved closer and touched her lips to mine. At first her kiss was delicate, like the wings of a butterfly, then her mouth opened and pressed in on mine at the same time her arms went around my neck. I let her do what she wanted, holding her gently. Her kiss turned from gentle to hungry. She tasted like the lake. I held her tight against me and the kiss went on and I let everything else go. I told her everything I'd ever wanted to say to her in that kiss. I hoped on some level she was listening. Being *just friends* was crap. She pulled back a bit and whispered in her raspy voice, "Thank you for saving me."

She tried to kiss me lightly and move away but I wasn't having any of that. "Don't stop," I said raggedly.

"We have to stop Owen. You promised to be my friend. We made a pact. If we're going to work together we can't do this." Her eyes showed her mixed emotions. I could see her need, her uncertainty, and then her resolution.

"Just today, please. I thought I lost you," I begged.

"You don't know what you're saying. I'm right here and I'll be okay. I won't let you change my mind. You might break my heart or yours. We can't do this. It will ruin everything."

"You started it," I said with a wicked glint in my eye.

She shoved me backwards onto the dock. "You saved me – now I'll save you from yourself. Don't ever quit being my friend. Just be my friend."

Somehow I strongly doubted that she was saving me from myself. When it came to Lucie - I was hopeless. I longed to hold her so badly it hurt. She mattered to me so deeply and after today I knew how much. I thought for a moment, "Okay, I'll always be here for you. I'll always be your friend." Please let me mean it and don't ask me what I'm holding back.

"I'm f...f...freezing. Where are your c... clothes?"

I stood and walked back to the end of the dock. I pulled on my pants and looked over the edge. No bubbles rose from the water. I really didn't want to fish him out. Lucie first and then White Eagle and the guys. I pulled on my t-shirt, picked up my shoes, socks and watch and walked back to where Lucie stood shivering.

"He's s s s still down there isn't h he?" she asked with a shudder.

I nodded and started pulling off her sweatshirt. She slapped at my hand. "What are you d d do doing," she asked through chattering teeth.

"I'm trying to warm you up," I said going back to the sweatshirt, but she shoved me away again. "Look, take off your shirt and put on my dry one. It will help."

She nodded and shrugged out of her sweatshirt. Then she turned her back to me and pulled off her t-shirt. I could see the delicate bones of her spine and her ribs. She half-turned, her arms crossed over her and reached for my flannel shirt. I wrapped it around her shoulders. She poked her arms into the overlarge sleeves and wrapped the body of the shirt tight around her and then slipped out of her shoes and pants so that she could wring them out. I pulled out my cell - I had a weak signal so I tried to call White Eagle. She moved close and hugged me, trying to warm up. White Eagle didn't answer but as I looked up I could see Adrian helping Marlo limp down the road toward us.

Lucie grabbed her wet clothes, wrung them out, slipped on her shoes and we moved off to the van. She was just laying her stuff over the hood when Marlo got a good look at us.

"What in the world happened to you and where is White Eagle?"

"Kraeghton tried to cut down our numbers. He took Lucie into the lake with him and I didn't want to share. White Eagle's nearby. We need to rescue him. Mar, I know you're hurting but I hate to leave you alone, just in case."

"It's just a sprain or strain. Right now my head hurts worse but I'll make it. Lead on, Captain," Marlo said with quiet dignity, pulling himself up.

Adrian stayed on one side and I took Marlo's other side. We moved off in the direction that Lucie and White Eagle had taken.

"Luce, before you ended up on the dock... what happened? Do you know where White Eagle is?" I asked.

"White Eagle and I were walking around the edge of the lake. He'd moved a bit away from me and away from the lake. I haven't been in the woods much and he wanted me to always keep the lake in sight. I was *listening* and he was doing whatever it is that he does. After awhile he froze like he heard something, but I think he actually *felt* something. He told me to go ahead and reminded me to keep the lake in sight – then he turned and walked purposefully into the woods."

"Do you know the spot where he turned?"

"I think so – Geez, I'm cold – Thanks for the shirt and at least we're moving."

"I'm sorry, Lucie, Marlo, I wish I could leave you in the van or take you home but one, I think we need to stick together and two, guess who has the van keys?"

We walked, or in Marlo's case, hobbled, toward the spot Lucie remembered White Eagle leaving her. She did a good job of narrowing the field, then I spied some broken branches and knew we were on the right track. We entered the woods together. I felt for White Eagle and my connection felt stronger. We moved on, trying to get closer to White Eagle but also keep the path as easy as possible for Marlo.

"Luce, what happened after White Eagle left you?" I asked.

"I kept walking and listening. When I *heard* something I stopped but very little had anything to do with Willie. He attacked someone near the dock once, a Marvin Coltrain, I think. He took the body into the woods. Someone once brought their cat here and drowned it. There were a couple of other really small things. I was focused on my job. White Eagle had been gone for maybe fifteen minutes and then I saw this guy walk out of the woods. He didn't feel right. I tried to edge back toward you guys. He would speak to me but I barely answered, all the time edging away. Finally he got frustrated and closed the space between us faster than I expected and grabbed my arm. I broke loose and started running. I'm glad you make me run three times a week by the way. He still caught me. He was driving me toward the lake. I jumped for the dock thinking I could jump off the other side and keep running but he was so unexpectedly fast... I'm mad at myself for letting him catch me."

"You think you feel bad? Kraeghton hit me in the side of the head and swept my legs out from under me before I even realized he was there. I was so busy with the laptop that I was oblivious," Marlo grumbled, clearly disgusted with himself.

"Both of you, quit with the beating yourselves up. Learn from it and move on," Adrian popped up with some sage advice – usually Marlo's department. I smiled but added nothing further.

Up ahead the forest seemed lighter. Sure enough, we soon broke into a clearing. It was another cabin. I *felt* again for White Eagle. He was very close. I could see an old-fashioned outhouse off to the side. A minivan was partially obscured by the native brush. We approached it first. I touched it and found that Kraeghton had driven it here – his unmistakable dark signature was all over it. I knew within seconds that he hadn't lied – he had been watching us for quite awhile. I had to respect his skill, much as I hated him personally. I could learn a thing or two about surveillance from him. He was good – I'd never been aware of him, which would really freak me out, if I thought about it too much. The van was stolen. There were only the two captain's chairs up front. It was clear that he'd been living in it.

I sensed no one around except for us and White Eagle so I took a small risk and called out to him. We looked at each other in confusion as we all heard a faint, muffled yell and some distant pounding.

We approached the cabin. It was small, empty and *told* me nothing. Fortunately it was unlocked. It was a two-room arrangement of an all-in-one eating, dining and living area and separate bedroom much like Willie's cabin. I could hear White Eagle faintly in the cabin but he wasn't here. Suddenly I got it. He was under the cabin. Lucie stayed in the cabin to search for a way under it and Marlo stayed on the front steps to keep watch. Adrian circled left and I went right. I met Adrian at the back where he had beaten me to an old-fashioned storm cellar and was working to unlatch it. It broke loose as I reached Adrian's side. The doors popped open to reveal a furious White Eagle armed with a shovel.

He squinted at us, like the light hurt his eyes and barked, "Took you long enough!" He crawled up the ladder-like stairs and sat on the lip of the opening rubbing a golf ball sized lump on the back of his head. "Where is that son of a motherless goat?"

"What?" I laughed.

"The bugger who hit me, where'd he go?"

"Kraeghton?"

"What!?!"

"I'm pretty sure it was Kraeghton. He followed us and was trying to peel us off one by one. I'd guess he got you first, then Marlo and finally Lucie before I stopped him." White Eagle's eyes had gone wide in a panicky kind of way. "They're going to be fine. Don't worry. They're no worse off than you are."

"Where is he?"

"At the bottom of the lake?"

"You sound... uncertain."

"With him, who knows? He hasn't turned up and I saw no bubbles but I'll feel better when we see the body. I was more worried about Lucie at the moment. He tried to drain her and drown her before I pulled her out. Which reminds me… I wonder if her hand is okay. I thought I heard it snap." Adrian shivered. "I know that's pretty grim. I'm sorry, Aid."

I turned back to White Eagle. "We found Trevor by the way. I think it's time we called Sarah and let her handle the jurisdictional garbage. We can try to find a few more in the next couple of hours until she gets here but this time we all stick together."

"I agree about calling Sarah but I'm worried about Kraeghton and Lucie. I know why he would drain her. It would give him strength to fight you but why try to drown her?"

"He seemed to know that we had some kind of a link. Maybe he thought he could weaken or distract me. When he drained her… I *felt* it."

"Did you? You have a more powerful bond than I realized. That will be a gift but it can also be a weakness. Be careful."

"I didn't get a name but he is or was working for someone else and now they'll be after us. I just don't see why I'm so… interesting."

"You're powerful, Owen, that is enough. Though… back in Florida, what did Kraeghton say? Something about you being an added bonus. They used your grandfather for funding and found your dad. Then I think that you were an added surprise. They know about your mom now, as well. If Kraeghton lives, they'll know about Lucie. Our friend, Emiline Clairmont in Nevada is having a birthday soon. I think it's time for a visit so that we can check in on young Mitchell Knight. We may be in need of their help," White Eagle said in a worried voice.

I didn't know what to think or feel. How would I protect and defend all these people that I loved? I decided that the best course of action for now was to stay busy and we had *plenty* to keep us busy.

I checked Lucie's hand and it seemed to be undamaged. Kraeghton must have broken a bone, not her. We spent the next two and a half hours, it turned out, tramping around in the area near the cabin I thought of as Willie's, and the lake. Marlo spent part of the time with Adrian for protection while he let his ankle soak in the cold lake water. Lucie was a real trooper and hardly complained at all but I knew she felt awful because she continued to cough and clear her throat. When she spoke her voice was rough and her throat sounded sore. I would've liked to have gotten her home, dried out and warmed up. She was determined to be tough and be 'one of the guys'.

We found three of the victims in all. I knew there were more but my team was a mess and I hoped cadaver dogs could find any others. I felt sure there were more concentrated in the area because I could feel the darkness all around me. This was Willie's place. I had suggested to Sarah that she also contact a diver to look for Kraeghton. We'd still seen no sign of him and I wasn't sensing him, but to be honest I hadn't really put much energy into *feeling* for him. I certainly didn't want to jump back into that freezing lake to pull his remains out if there were any. I couldn't shake the feeling that... this just wasn't over.

Sarah showed up with the two members of the team she was part of that I was getting to know, Saul and Mica. I introduced them to Adrian, Marlo and Lucie. Saul looked us over and made suggestions for each of our recoveries. Marlo turned over his flash drive to Mica to check out on her laptop while Adrian and I showed Sarah and Saul the plastic flagging. Then Sarah rushed us out of the area so that no one else would see us. They'd cover for us and say that it was a tip. We left everything in their capable hands and loaded up in the van to head home.

Marlo again sat up front, the remains of his laptop in a bag beside him. Sarah promised him a rebuilt, faster, better and all-mighty laptop with hardened case to replace it. How he would explain that one to his folks I had no idea. Marlo never got in trouble so he had a lot of trust built up. He also saved nearly all of his money so I supposed he could sell them on the idea that he'd bought it with some of the money he earned at the pawnshop and with the serving help he did for his mom's catering business. I hoped that he had all of the data on his laptop backed up somewhere but knowing Marlo, I was sure he did.

Lucie was another story. She sat sandwiched between me and Adrian for the trip home. It had been a draining day. As she got comfortable, she oozed down to where her hip was wedged against him on one side and her head flopped on my chest, with her arms tight around my waist. I'd draped my arm over her to help warm her up. Sarah had been gracious enough to pick up a sweatshirt for me and sweats and dry socks for Lucie, who still wore my flannel shirt. She said it made her feel better. Who was I to argue after the day she'd had. I slid down some on my part of the seat so that Lucie would be more comfortable.

Adrian just looked at me and rolled his eyes. He grumbled some on the way home but overall was good natured about his cramped position. He'd ended the day in the best shape of all of us so he knew it was wise to keep his mouth shut.

Even in sleep Lucie coughed some and cleared her throat. Occasionally she would frown, jerk and whimper in her sleep. Once she even woke herself up on a choked, strangled cry. She quickly realized where she was and snuggled back into my side to soak up more warmth. I just wished that I could fix everything for her.

SEVENTEEN

Fortunately for us, Lucie's folks were out of town for some kind of baseball thing for her brother. They wouldn't be back until tomorrow and there was no way I was leaving her in that big house alone. Lucie would be coming home with me. Mom was expecting us.

We dropped Adrian off first. I would've loved to have heard the story he would fabricate about our day today. He was a master storyteller and weaver of truth and lies. Adrian had mad skills when it came to dealing with people, that was for certain! Sarah loved to tell him that he had a great future as a politician, an attorney or as an elicitation expert working with her. "A what?" we'd asked and her reply, "You know, someone who's good at getting information." Yep, that was Adrian, no one was better at getting information out of people.

The rest of us headed to Lucie's house. We turned Marlo loose in the home office to find all the information he could on the family's cell phone account. We needed to get Lucie a new phone and we didn't want to share that information with her folks. Marlo was still the most amazing technology wizard I'd ever met. Even Sarah was impressed by what he could do and she used him frequently. I knew he had more than earned the laptop she was 'acquiring' for him.

Lucie filled Marlo in on all the passwords she knew. She also told him that the cell phone, like most of the family bills, were on auto pay. She doubted her parents even looked at the bill. Marlo would work something out for her just in case so that they would never know she had gotten a new phone. He was also going to recover all of her data and secure her line in some way so that she was more protected. I for one didn't want details. His hacking freaked me out. I lived in constant fear that he'd get caught. Sarah swore to me she had his back whenever I got that worried look in my eye.

I carefully felt the house before I let Lucie leave the entryway. I'd thrown out an arm, right across her chest to stop her. I was rewarded with a dirty look. "Geez, Owen, I'm not a baby. I can take care of myself," she said, exasperated.

"I know you can, but it makes me feel better to check." In my mind I was busy thinking, 'sure you can' but I didn't want to start a fight. I followed her upstairs and leaned against the doorframe as she packed a bag.

Lucie blew out a sigh and looked at me in *that* way she does when she's disgusted, right down to the wrinkle between her eyebrows. "Really?" she asked, still exasperated.

I just smiled at her. I held in the laugh I felt threatening. "Yes, really. I want to be sure you're safe. I worry. It's my job."

Another big eye roll. "Seriously, you're worse than my mother. Not that she was ever much of a one, but still, you get my point."

"Luce, I care about you, get over it."

"Just friends!"

"Whatever you say, Lucie. Whatever you want." I held up my hands in a placating gesture. I continued to watch her and wondered again if she was really trying to convince herself or me.

She finished packing her bag and gave me a hard look. "Let's go."

"Okay," I said but I didn't move. She pushed by me. "I know how I make you feel."

"Owen, don't… please," she begged. I felt like I was winning but I knew to quit when I was ahead. I stepped out of her way and followed her downstairs.

White Eagle was still in the entryway standing guard. I could tell by the look in his eye that he was still reaching out and sensing the area around us. We made eye contact and he nodded at me. We all turned and headed into the family office where Marlo was hard at work on the computer but broke to look up at us. "Almost," he said and dropped his eyes back down to the task at hand. With a flourish he hit the last key and exclaimed, "Done." A huge smile lit his face.

"Your new phone is ready for pick up. Let's roll."

Lucie locked the front door and we loaded up. Marlo directed us to the store where Lucie's phone awaited. He looked at Lucie expectantly. "Um, thanks, Marlo?" she said guessing that was what he wanted to hear.

"You're welcome. Wanna know how I did it?"

"Sure?" she said, like she really wasn't sure she did.

"The phone is prepaid and all set up. Your folks will never know. I took the money out of your savings account. You can shuffle your money around later. If you need extra work to make up the difference, my mom could use you at a wedding she's catering next week. Owen and Adrian are working too. What do you say?"

"Um, sure. It's the weekend before my birthday. I might as well be with you guys. My parents will probably forget again anyway." Lucie looked a little sad but resigned. I reached over and tucked some hair behind her ear and gave her a soft smile.

Our next stop, the cell phone store. Marlo had negotiated Lucie an amazing deal. He showed her the phone he'd picked out for her. A salesman tried to help us but it was clear that Marlo knew more than he did so he quickly backed off. Marlo went right up to the manager and got Lucie's phone that was waiting for us. We were out of there in record time and Marlo even had a job offer.

They had charged up Lucie's cell so it was ready to go. Marlo truly was amazing. Next time I need electronics Marlo is going with me! Lucie had missed a call from her folks. She called back and played the 'my battery died' card. They bought it. It seemed to me that Lucie did most of the listening. From her end I don't think they even asked her how her day was. It made me mad and I tried not to show it. I reminded myself that at least she had us. We dropped off Marlo and headed home.

Mom wrapped Lucie in a big hug. Both of their faces lit up. Since Lucie's family was pretty much a bust the least I could do was share mine. Alex and Lucas came stampeding down the stairs to greet her. She got way more attention than I did but she needed it a whole lot more. White Eagle shared a quiet goodbye with me and promised that he would call with any news.

"Did you get some lunch?" Mom asked in that classic concerned mom voice."

"No, we worked right through," I told her. "Why don't I show Lucie to my room and let her get a shower while I help you figure something out."

"As soon as I heard you were coming I changed your sheets for her," Mom said with a smile.

I smiled back, "Of course you did." That was my mom – she might not be able to fix everything but she fixed what she could. Lucie looked back and forth between us like she was trying to figure out if we were fighting or spoofing. Mom gave me a big hug – giving Lucie her answer.

"I'm glad you're all safe. I wish I could've been there to help but..." She looked into the living room where my brothers were picking a movie to watch with Lucie.

"Mom, its fine. They're the priority. We make do. I can do my job because I know you guys are taking care of each other." Suddenly I had an epiphany. "Sarah called... and here I thought you were reading my mind again. I keep telling you one day you'll find things in there you don't want to know."

"So far what I see... I... admire. I respect your choices." She glanced at Lucie and then back at me. "I love you and I know who you are. Don't worry so much."

Lucie had an interesting look on her face as I took her hand and led her upstairs. She said nothing until we entered my room. She looked around, then moved to look out the window. I was reminded of the times I'd viewed glimpses of her before I knew I was her mentor. She looked so sad. I wanted to wrap her in a hug. I could feel waves of sadness and uncertainty rolling off her and surrounding her like fog.

"What is it?" I asked, concerned.

Lucie turned slowly - her eyes were downcast but gradually moved from my feet up to meet my eyes. They were an amazing shade of blue in this moment, in this light. I know we all think we know what blue is, but do we really? If we are asked to describe it, can we? I figured our definitions would be as different as we are. I did know one thing – Lucie's eyes were my favorite shade of blue. At the moment they held a hint of green. They made me think of tropical waters – which made me think about how much I'd like to be with her on a tropical beach. She must have seen all kinds of emotions flit across my face. She still had not answered.

Lucie swallowed and reached up to wipe her damp eyes. "Nothing."

"Tell me," I begged.

The two words – tell me - so easily said, but apparently they were hard to answer. Lucie looked at me with such sadness and grief. "I just don't know," she finally said, her voice sounding bumpy and rough. "I'm... jealous and... thankful, I guess. Your mom is so... wonderful. I wish she was my mom. I'm thankful to know her. Can she really read your mind?"

"Yeah, sometimes. It used to scare me but it was really helpful when we were in Florida."

"Sometimes I wish I could... read your mind, but I'm afraid of what I'd find. You must be so disappointed."

"Lucie, no! Why would you say that?"

"I let you down today."

"Not even a little bit! We couldn't have done what we did without you. You *are* an important part of this team. I'm proud of you. You've been doing some tough stuff and you're handling it all so well."

"I'm not... I'm completely freaked out. I'm afraid to get in the shower. It's water. I don't think I'll ever willingly go swimming again. I..."

I took five measured steps toward her, reached out and pulled her into a hug. She rested her head on my shoulder and curled into me. I knew the memory of her near drowning was close, even I could see every bit of it – like it was happening all over again. I purposely called it up, forced her to look at it and fed into the memory all I saw and heard and felt. I showed her how courageous I thought she was. I showed her how desperate I was as I stripped to dive in after her. I showed her how scared I was when I couldn't find her and had to *feel* for her – I had to sense where she was because I could see nothing in the cold murky darkness. I was ready to die to save her. I could feel her shuddering in my arms. I was afraid I had shared too much. That was why I should have left; it was also why I had to stay and make this right.

I lifted my hand and rested it gently on her chest, right over where I'd noticed her skin had blistered from Kraeghton's touch. She closed her eyes and leaned into it. It was a relief to feel her warm, safe and alive. I slowly pushed my flannel shirt aside to look at the handprint. It was already fading. It looked no worse now than a sunburn. I don't know what I was thinking in that moment – clearly my brain shut off. I brought my head forward and placed a kiss on her overheated, damaged flesh.

She inhaled sharply but didn't pull back. She looked into my eyes and moved closer. She covered my hand, where it still rested near the burn and squeezed it. She tilted her chin up, and then she was kissing me like she had on the dock, sudden and intense, as if trying to push away the bad memories and everything that had prompted them. Her kiss was hungry, so good and very un-Lucie like. I moved the hand from her chest up to her neck. My other hand found the skin at her waist.

Lucie froze at the light caress, and I was aware of the conflicting emotions that were tearing through her. Her eyes grew large and dark as a light flush bloomed on her cheeks. Her breathing hitched. I could tell that the bad memory was receding. The knowledge would remain, though. I would have to help her tackle the fear. She now held the knowledge that Kraeghton had attacked her but hadn't been content to just drain her. For some reason, he'd wanted to torture her further. He wanted to watch her pain. He had hated her in that moment or maybe he just hated me enough to hurt the people I care about.

Lucie was my greatest temptation. I would fight to protect her; I would give my very life for her safety. She was becoming my greatest strength, and I knew she would be my greatest weakness. She broke off the kiss and tucked her head under my chin. "I want to climb under your skin and soak up your warmth. I want you to make it all better, to make the demons all go away, and to erase the pain. Is that wrong?"

"Whatever you want," I whispered, my voice thick and rough.

Lucie pulled back a bit to look at me and she almost laughed, but the sound seemed to stick in her throat as her gaze slipped to my lips again. Her breathing was uneven. Her eyes told me that she didn't understand all the sensations suddenly running riot through her. Her fingers played along my neck and then they were twisting through the hair at the back of my head. Her nails scraped lightly along my scalp bringing thoughts I shouldn't have.

Think of something else. Something completely innocent. For a moment I couldn't think of a damned thing outside the need to touch her. Then I felt saved by the bell or more accurately the feet racing up the stairs. I pushed Lucie back from me by her hip bones and began babbling about the location of towels and stuff. At which point she did laugh.

She scooped up her bag and I lead her to the bathroom. "A warm shower will be good for you. You'll be fine. Call if you need... Mom... I guess."

"I'll be okay. Just don't expect to see me at the pool for awhile."

"Yeah, I kinda feel that way about being tied to a chair and needles right now."

"Aren't you done yet? Don't you want to watch the movie?" Lucas asked.

Alex just looked from one to the other of us and rolled his eyes. "They weren't done. We interrupted."

"Thanks, Alex. Come on. Let's leave Lucie in peace."

Lucie put a hand on my arm as I turned to go. Alex and Lucas bounded ahead and on down the stairs. She looked at their retreating backs and then back at me.

"I don't know what I would do without you."

"Considering I'm the one who seems to get you into trouble, it's my duty to get you out of it."

"Don't joke, I'm serious. You're my... best friend. You always know how to make me feel better. I like the way you smile at me with just your eyes. I like the way they light up with amusement, with warmth. I see it when you look at your brothers, too. You're... like a flash of summer in the middle of winter."

Lucie put a hand on my chest to shove me back so she could shut the bathroom door but seemed to change her mind. Instead she took a handful of my shirt and pulled my lips down to hers one last, too brief, time. Then she closed the door in my startled face. I placed a hand on the closed door and could imagine her leaning against it on the other side. I knew I was right a moment later when I felt the pressure change as she lifted herself from the door. Apparently she had found her courage. I listened for the water to start and then I headed downstairs. So she thought I was like summer in the middle of winter. Wow, that described her kiss better than it did me. She tasted like summer - addictive, powerful and scary. How was I going to be 'just friends' when she was all I thought about?

Mom had hauled meatballs out of the freezer and had them baking while she made sauce. She took one look at me and shook her head. "Remember the rules."

"I know, I know. Lucas is the youngest child who will live in this house. Trust me, would you?"

"You, I trust. Your hormones – not so much."

"Mom!"

"I'm just glad she didn't drown. You saved her life. Remember you have to work with her. Go slow."

"I know. I can take a relationship forwards but not backwards. Trust me. And get out of my head. It's creepy the way you read my mind."

"Fine. Get out the noodles and the big pot would you please. I shouldn't tell you this because it gives away my secrets but... I don't really read your mind. I can't hear exactly what you're thinking. I just know you well and I can *read* your face and body language. For some reason I'm just more in tune to you than anyone else. Other people's body language almost whispers or speaks softly to me; with you it's loud and clear."

"Super," I added sarcastically, but then I smiled at her. I knew that no matter what, Mom *always* had my best interests at heart. Someday, I hoped, we would be past these awkward conversations about girls. Knowing my luck I would still get advice when I was married and had kids of my own.

Mom and I worked silently side by side for fifteen minutes, knowing what the other needed without words. During which time, she looked at the ceiling no less than fifteen times. "Mom, she's fine. I can tell."

"Can you really?" she asked, fascinated.

"Yeah, I can *sense* her. It keeps getting stronger. Kind of like your ability to read my mind. When she's in our house... I can sense her even more. She had trouble getting in the shower." I closed my eyes to focus on Lucie's energy. "She's out now. Listen, you can tell the water's off. She'll be down soon. She just feels a little... awkward? Unsure?..."

"Tell me you can't literally see her!"

"No, Mom, geez... It's more like I can kind of sense how she feels. It's not really clear. I can do it with you and with White Eagle some. Maybe I get it from you?"

"Oh, it's sort of like what I do with you?"

"Is it?"

"I think so, but it's different too. I have to see you to *read* you and then I can sense how you feel. Maybe it has to do with your new job as a mentor?"

Lucie moved shyly into the kitchen. She had on fuzzy socks, jeans, a t-shirt and my flannel shirt over the top. My lip twitched as I tried to fight a smile and failed. Mom gave her a big smile and told her it was ten minutes to dinner. She swatted me with a towel and told me to hurry.

I squeezed Lucie's hand on the way past and sprinted up the stairs. I figured it was best to get them both out of my head and wash off the blood, lake and dirt from the day. I knew my mom would take good care of her. I snatched up some clean clothes and hurried into the bathroom. As I stepped in, I took a deep whiff of Lucie's shampoo or body wash or whatever she used that smelled so fantastic. I tossed my filthy clothes into a pile, adjusted the water temperature and stepped in. The hot spray felt fantastic and I finally felt some of the tension in my muscles melt out of my body. As much as part of me wanted to linger I was anxious to get back to Lucie. I snapped off the water, toweled off and quickly dressed in jeans and a t-shirt. I ran my fingers through my hair instead of combing it, slapped on deodorant and ran down the stairs two at a time. I leapt over the last five or so.

Mom and Lucie were in deep conversation as I rounded the corner. Lucie had an almost embarrassed look about her. My mom was... warm and fuzzy – just what Lucie needed, I'm sure.

"There you are," Mom said looking at the clock, "call your brothers in to dinner and then we can talk about what movie they want to watch but homework first of course."

Of course, I thought in my head as I turned to get my brothers. What else could you expect when you lived with a teacher?

Dinner was... good, fun, easy, friendly and pleasant. Pick a word. It was very comfortable and just what Lucie needed. My mom was good at putting people at ease and making them feel welcome. I wondered again why my grandfather had never connected with her. He still preferred the company of just my dad. He... tolerated the rest of us. I figured that was kind of the way Lucie was with her family. Her brother they loved, Lucie was tolerated. Now that she was no longer famous, she wasn't worth their energy and time. It was crazy. What she did now was so much more important cosmically than being a gymnast – even an Olympic hopeful.

Around our dinner table we joked, laughed and just enjoyed each other's company. Mom told stories about some of the jobs she'd had subbing so far this year. Her funniest story involved a kid throwing up right on her shoes while she was trying to take attendance. Guess that one should have stayed home. Lucie laughed until her eyes watered. When she laughed she coughed a bit but Saul had promised she would make a full recovery in no time. Her heart was strong. I could have told him that!

Lucie and I had done most of our homework on Friday at the pawnshop. It was nice to get out of school earlier this year. We all got our chores done at the shop, worked out and still had time for some homework most days. Having so many classes together and with great brains like Lucie and Marlo – it was easy to keep up. We had a bit left but it was easy to convince Mom to let us watch the movie first. We'd had a rough day after all.

The five of us piled into the family room and got comfy on the couch, loveseat and chair. I would have liked to have sat by Lucie but what can I say? She is popular. She had Lucas on one side of her and Alex on the other. Lucas had wormed his way under her arm and up to her side like he sometimes did to me. A part of me was a bit jealous but it was pretty cute at the same time.

"Lucie, why are you wearing Owen's shirt? It's too big for you."

"You're right Lucas, but after my unexpected swim in the freezing lake today, I can't seem to get warm and I guess it makes me feel better."

"My stuffed dog makes me feel better so I get it. Owen makes me feel better too." He ended in a whisper but I could still hear him.

Alex just smiled. Over the last year and especially since our Florida fiasco he had gotten much better about keeping some thoughts to himself, especially the not so kind ones. I sent him a wink to let him know that I admired his restraint.

My phone vibrated in my pocket startling me. I hoped it was good news. All eyes left the flat screen, a gift from my grandfather at Christmas, and turned to me.

"Owen? Sarah."

"Hey, what's up?"

"Good news and bad, I'm afraid."

"Great," I said sarcastically. "Let me guess... You found more remains and some good evidence but the diver found no sign of Kraeghton."

"How do you do that? You're getting as bad as Earl. Why did I even bother to call?" she grumped.

"Because you love me and you want to give me details. Is it my fault he got away, Sarah?"

"Not in any way, sweetie! Lucie was, most certainly, your priority. I can't imagine what you could've done differently. How exactly he was able to get away we can't discern. He shouldn't have been able to. I wouldn't want to take you on."

"Seems to me that last time you did, I needed stitches in my chin. I think I should be afraid of you," I said playfully.

Sarah laughed out loud at that and then gave me the scoop. I looked up to see every eye in the room still on me and the movie paused. I held out one hand and then tilted it side to side in a so, so motion to indicate good and bad news.

"It looks like you have found plenty here to put Willie away for a long, long time. Even though you know who the victims are we still need to prove it officially through DNA. When we have it, the families can be notified."

"I want to go with you when you talk to Trevor's mom. I owe her at least that much," I said, feelings of regret filling me.

"Are you sure you want to do that? It won't be easy but it is part of the job. It's the part I always hated the most. Notifications always tear me up inside."

"You are a kind-hearted person, Sarah. I want to go – I need to go. What else did you find?"

"They have found six sets of remains and the diver found nothing. He searched all around the dock and then moved into a grid beyond it for several feet until he ran low on air. The cadaver dogs are still working. They're expanding their grid. The state police are just now breaking out the lights for the forensic scientists. Mica will stay since Kraeghton is her case and he is linked to Willie but I'm tired, I'm headed home. I don't know what Saul has decided. Mica will keep me informed."

"Sarah, thank you... for everything. For keeping us out of it... for being there. You know."

"I do know, dear. What you do isn't easy. I'm so glad that I can help you do your job. I've never been this close to someone like you. I've always been kept at a distance. Now that I know about *watchers* – beyond suspicion, I'm amazed. I should be thanking you. I wouldn't be here to help you if you hadn't saved me first. Don't forget that but do stay humble."

"Okay." Sarah ended the connection but I stared at my phone for a moment before I looked up to meet first Lucie's eyes and then Mom's. I looked over at Alex and then at Lucas.

"He got away, didn't he." A statement not a question. Alex always seemed to get to the root of a problem. He was scary intuitive and too smart for his own good.

"Yes, Alex. He got away."

"He isn't going after you though. He knew if he hurt Lucie he'd hurt you worse than if he hurt you himself. He wanted to turn you in Florida. He wanted to make you a *dark watcher* like him. Now he wants to destroy you."

"Alex," Mom tried to interrupt.

Alex turned fierce eyes on her. "We're not dumb, Mom. We know that Owen is not your average teenage boy. We're all in danger now. Kraeghton will come after us to hurt Owen. We have to stick together and be ready."

"Alex, we don't want you to worry. It isn't... well, it isn't good for you to worry. White Eagle, Sarah and the rest of us will..."

"Will what, Mom? Kraeghton lied to us, he hurt all of us and he used drugs on Owen and Dad and Grandma. It's his fault she's dead. She tried to help us... I hate him. I plan to be ready when he comes back. I'm gonna be like that kid from *Home Alone*. Lucas and I decided. We want to be ready. We want to see White Eagle every day."

"Alex..."

"Mom, he's right." All eyes jerked in my direction and all of them looked surprised. "We need to be done with the lying. We are a family and a team. No more tearing us apart like Grandpa unintentionally did. We need to build. We need for Lucas and Alex to know what is going on and they need to be prepared. They will feel better and safer if they feel like they can defend themselves. It's time."

Lucas and Alex crowed a happy "Yes!" and pumped their fists in the air. Mom and Lucie looked startled by my words.

"I know first hand that working out, sparing and practicing makes me feel better. No one likes to feel out of control. The things we can't control are what scare us the most, both kids and adults. Alex has shown over and over again that he is ready to help. We need to let him do that."

"Yeah and I have the scars to prove it."

Great, I was creating a monster. My brothers couldn't even wait for the movie to end. They pressed me into sparring with them. Mom sighed but handed me the keys to back the car out of the garage and then she helped me, Lucie and Alex set up the mats. We'd already hung a punching bag in the garage for when I needed to blow off steam. All five of us stretched and ran through a Tai Chi routine. Then we moved through a series of Karate stances. I worked with Mom and Alex and Lucie helped Lucas. Each of us focused on form and function. My brothers lasted for almost fifty minutes. I called it quits and we went back to our movie. Lucas helped me make popcorn to share.

Lucie was back to her funny standoffish behavior. Either I made her nervous or she was doing that to herself. I really liked her but sometimes I almost wished to have Tess back. Somehow things with Tess had always been simpler. I liked her but I had never felt about her the way I felt about Lucie. Why were things with Lucie always so complicated? Alex was already sitting next to her and Lucas reclaimed his spot on her other side. Mom was in her chair so once again I flopped onto the loveseat by myself. Loveseat... what a misnomer.

The movie ended and Mom hustled my brothers off to bed. Lucie looked uncomfortable so I pulled out my backpack and started rummaging for homework. She said nothing, just kept watching me. I could tell that there was a lot going on in her mind. I smiled at her and pretended to focus on the book in my hand. I was really watching her with my peripheral vision. She opened her mouth as if to speak and snapped it shut. She leaned forward and then back. She was making me crazy.

"What?" I finally asked, exasperated when she opened her mouth a second time without speaking.

"I..." Lucie closed her eyes and cleared her throat. "I'm very grateful that you saved me. I suppose it's kind of your job. That's not really it though, I'm not..."

I had never known Lucie to be at such a loss for words. I stood up and purposefully set my book in the chair before I slowly walked over and knelt in front of her. She looked like she was going to cry. I reached out to touch her face. I wanted to make her feel better.

"Why are you so... nice?"

"I'm not sure how to answer that... I care about you. You know that."

"I don't deserve you. I'm not... ready for you."

"Luce." She held up her hand so I stopped talking. She still seemed to be struggling for words.

"What I feel for you scares me. You're my best friend. What if everything gets ruined? I couldn't stand it if you weren't my friend. You're always there for me. I don't know why. What do you see in me? I'm not... I'm not like you. I'd like to be though." I started to speak again when I saw a tear spill over. Lucie put a finger to my lips. "I know that I still need to practice with you and work with you but I think I need to spend some time with my girl friends. You and I need to be friends, not more than friends. I'm going to bed. You... you stay. I just need ten minutes and then you can have the bathroom. Just... stay... please."

I gave her a bewildered look. She rose from her seat on the couch and virtually ran up the stairs. It seemed so weird to have her push me away right when she needed my protection the most. Who knew where Kraeghton was but then maybe she just had a lot to think about. I continued to sit where she left me. I had a lot to think about too. Like what was I going to do with her? Could I work with her and ignore this thing between us?

I gave her exactly ten minutes. I headed up the stairs, checked on my mom and brothers and noted my closed door. Dang and I forgot to get sweats to sleep in. I slumped into the bathroom, brushed and flossed and went looking for Mom.

"Hey," I said in a woebegone voice as I leaned on the door frame to my brothers' room.

"Hey, what's up?" She asked softly. She kissed Lucas who promptly rolled over and got cozy, curling up into a ball with his favorite stuffed dog. Then she kissed Alex and reminded him not to read too long. Mom tilted her head to the side as she looked at me. I knew she was reading me.

Mom walked toward me and took a gentle hold on my arm and pulled me into her room. "You seem... conflicted."

"Yeah, that about says it. Also I let Lucie go to bed before I grabbed my sweats and stuff. Can I borrow from Dad?"

"Of course." Mom headed to the closet and tossed a pair of sweats to me. "You can sleep here or are you hitting the couch?"

"Couch I think. I feel the need to patrol the house first and I have the feeling that I won't sleep much tonight. I don't want to keep you up."

"It is going to be one of those nights, I feel it too. The way people break into our kitchen, maybe you and Beggar ought to sleep in front of the fridge."

At the sound of her name Beggar looked up from where she had made herself comfy on Mom's side of the bed, her head on Mom's pillow. But then, the cat was on Dad's side – so there you go. My mom, the Pied Piper or Doctor Doolittle, take your pick.

"If I thought it would do any good I would sleep there. I'll be on the couch. I need a pillow and a blanket."

"We'll get those from the hall closet. You wanna talk?"

"I really don't know what to say. I just feel so... weary and frustrated."

"Owen, you did at least two really good things today. You saved Lucie and you helped Trevor and some other people."

I felt my throat constricting. "Why didn't I... Why didn't someone help those people before it was too late? I wasn't even a *watcher* when some of them disappeared but I feel responsible. I feel like I didn't do my job. I... I just... hurt, I guess." I could feel hot angry tears around the edges of my eyes. Mom pulled me down onto her bed and we sat side by side, shoulder to shoulder.

"I'm not White Eagle, but I feel obligated to tell you that you are but one human and there is no way that you can fix everything. So quit trying. Do your best – that is all anyone can ask and you do that every day."

"Mom, I feel so... overwhelmed. I'm trying to do what I know I should here as a family member, I'm trying to keep up with school and I'm trying to do my job as a *watcher*. I'm still learning to be a *watcher* and now I have a *watcher* to train. Am I a cosmic joke? Is God laughing at me? I can't juggle all this. The least He could have done was send me a male *watcher* to guide but instead God, the forces of good, or however this happens, sent me not just a girl, but Lucie of all people. I have liked her forever. Do you know how difficult..."

My mom put her arm around me and rested her head on my shoulder. "God is not laughing at you. He knows how special you are. Your road is not easy but I know you are up to the task and I'm here. White Eagle is here for you too and so is Sarah and your dad. You need to refill your inner well. Let me try something. Just relax and breathe. Mom had me turn sideways and she sat with her legs crisscrossed. She took both my hands and closed her eyes. I just watched her for a bit and then I tried to match her slow breathing. Slowly I became aware of how warm her hands were. Soon it was travelling up my arms. I closed my eyes and misty images began to form out of the darkness.

I saw my mom holding a small baby, her head bent over... me. I saw the soft, sweet look on her face. I saw her dancing with a tiny me. I could see myself standing in a crib as she cleaned my room. I saw me sitting in a highchair playing with toys while she worked at a table. I saw me washing tomatoes while sitting on the counter and her singing to me while she made a salad. I saw her take me to preschool, all smiles and proud and then sit in the car and cry. She did the same thing when I went to Kindergarten and again when I graduated from sixth and eighth grade. I saw her sitting with five-year-old me next to her and baby Alex on her lap. I saw her playing with Legos, Bionicles, blocks, coloring, painting, reading, cooking, gardening and doing stuff with and for the animals – all of it for my entertainment and education. Time warped forward. I had grown up fast from her perspective and she was proud of me. She saw more good in me than I did in myself. I felt... humble. I slowly opened my eyes and looked at her. She leaned forward and gave me a hug. "I thought it would help if you remembered where you came from."

"It does help. Thanks, Mom."

I picked up the sweats, changed in the bathroom, grabbed a pillow and blanket and started to head downstairs. For some reason I paused at my closed door. Oh Lucie, I thought, why do you make things so difficult? You don't have to hurt. I could fix it – if you'd let me. I was afraid pushing her would make it worse so I did what I usually do when it comes to Lucie – I walked away, but like always... I would be waiting.

I patrolled the house, checking windows and doors. I *felt* the house and purposely stretched my ability as far as it would go, sensing for Kraeghton as I stood in the living room with my eyes shut. I moved into my fighting stance and then I raised my hands up by my head and imagined pushing my ability out. I could feel my muscles strain as I pushed away from my head. A small part of me was pretty sure that I looked ridiculous but I could feel it working. I visualized my house and then worked my way into our yard and out into the neighborhood. I got as far as Sarah's when I felt a fantastic snap. I had stretched my ability as far as it could go apparently... At the outer edges I had begun to shake and sweat. When it snapped back it knocked me to my knees. I didn't know if I should laugh, shout or cry. I felt horrible, my whole body was shaking and my head was pounding but I had done something I had *never* done before. I had not felt Kraeghton anywhere, or anything in the area that needed my attention. Wow!

I stretched out on the couch and tried to relax into sleep. I think I must have stared at the ceiling for hours. The next thing I knew, I sensed... something. I flipped the blanket back and jumped to my feet all in one motion – ready to fight.

Lucie let out a squeal and dropped low, anticipating my attack. I jerked my body back from her, afraid I couldn't pull myself back in time.

"Jeez, Owen, It's just me. You about gave me a heart attack."

"Yeah? The feeling's mutual," I said as I flopped back down onto the couch. I really looked at Lucie who apparently hadn't slept either. And my flannel shirt was optically mind-bending in combination with her pink bunny pajamas. Still with the shirt - well at least she didn't hate me. Lucie wrapped it tighter around her and looked at me uncertainly.

"I'm really sorry I scared you but I'm thrilled that you didn't hit me," she said with a small smile. "I... um... couldn't sleep. I thought I'd just... ah, sit here and... I should go."

Lucie turned to go but I was faster. I jumped up and took hold of her arm. "Luce, wait. Talk to me." At the almost frantic look in her eye, I added, "just talk to me."

"It's stupid... Look, I would be a total, freaked out mess if I was at home alone right now. It was nice to be in your room. It was... calming but it's not as good as you are in person." Lucie looked down at her feet and mumbled, "I thought I could sneak down here and just watch you sleep and be with you. I didn't mean to wake you up." She turned again to leave.

"Luce, its fine. Sit." At her skeptical look, I took my hand off her arm and waved it to Mom's chair. She gave me a defiant look and sat on the couch. I picked the blanket up from where it had fallen to the floor and offered it to her. She wrapped it around her shoulders and held out half for me. I sat down slowly next to her. We sat there for a beat both looking straight ahead, not talking. Then Lucie unbent a bit, sighed and rested her head on my shoulder.

"I still want to be just your friend but do you think you could just... maybe... hold me. Please?"

"Yeah, Luce, I could do that." I leaned back onto the arm of the couch with my arm draped around her. She stretched out, wrapped her arms around me, rested her head on my chest and closed her eyes.

"I like to listen to your heart beat."

"Luce, for now, I'll just have to be happy with what you are willing to offer. Even if it's not what I want right now, at least it's something, and I don't want there to be nothing. I would happily stay here, covering you like a blanket forever, but I don't want you to live in fear. You're allowed to be scared today – tomorrow we practice fighting. I squeezed her with the arm I had around her, before she could even answer, to let her know that she didn't have to answer. I wondered if she had ever been held when she had cried or been scared. Was she ever held, period? I guessed her gymnastics coach had hugged her. I knew they were still friends but Lucie's family? I would say that some people shouldn't have kids but then I wouldn't have Lucie. Her parents didn't deserve her. Who leaves a not quite fifteen-year-old, especially a girl, alone for a night so they can go to a baseball thing? My dad and I still had some issues but not even he would do that!

I realized that Lucie's breathing was steady and even. Against my warm body she had finally relaxed into sleep. I eased out from under her, causing her to grumble. She was so exhausted that she didn't wake up. I knew Mom would flip a biscuit if she found her down here with me so I carefully picked her up and slowly made my way back upstairs. She wasn't much heavier than Alex. When I reached my room I saw that she had flipped the covers back up to the pillows. Great. I reached out a toe as I balanced on one foot and moved the covers back. I eased Lucie down onto the bed but she reached for me before I could move away. I was warm and the bed had cooled I guessed. I knelt on the floor next to the bed, covering her with my chest. The position was making my back ache. I pulled the covers up and waited. As soon as she relaxed I moved away. I watched her sleep for a bit and then I turned and went back downstairs.

I tried to go back to sleep but now my blanket smelled like Lucie. Fabulous. Mind off Lucie – plan a workout routine to build her skills and confidence. I finally drifted off, my plan for tomorrow set.

EIGHTEEN

I awoke to Lucas sitting on my feet watching silent cartoons. I could hear soft voices in the kitchen. I kept my eyes closed. It was Mom and Alex making waffles. Yum.

"I know you're awake, Owen. Your breathing is different." I cracked one eye to look at him.

"Were you supposed to let me sleep?"

"Yep, that's why the sound's off."

"Uh huh, and you are sitting on my feet because?"

"I can see the TV better from here and I know where you are."

Well of course. Who could be mad, looking at that great toothless grin? I untangled myself from the blanket and stretched, feeling my muscles and tendons pop. Lucas moved into the spot I had warmed up and hugged my pillow. I smiled at him and made for the upstairs bathroom.

I ran into Lucie, literally, as I left the bathroom. "Hey," I said as I steadied her with a hand. "Since you're out of my room, I'm gonna get some clean clothes."

"Okay," she breathed. "Was I... Did you bring me upstairs last night?"

"Yeah, I'll see you downstairs for breakfast. Mom and Alex are making waffles." I moved past her and headed for my room. I would honor the friend request but I wasn't going to make it any harder on myself than I had to. She'd hate me plenty after the workout I had planned for her today.

I dressed in workout gear. I stopped in the kitchen to check the status of breakfast and to tell Mom my plans. Workout – homework – workout – lunch and let Lucie go home... after I was sure her parents were there. My mind was busy trying to figure out everything I needed to do to keep everyone safe. I needed Marlo. I could use a little technological help. I realized that Alex was looking at me really hard.

"What?"

"I asked if I could workout with you?"

"Oh, sorry, I was thinking. You can, but could I have some time with just Lucie first? I need to work with her on some stuff, then we could spar." Alex lit up like a Christmas tree. I took that as a 'yes'.

The practices and sparring went well. I taught Lucie every move I could think of to take down an opponent. She is one scary fast study. She would have to be quick with Kraeghton around. In a fight it isn't always about size – lucky for Lucie. Lucas even joined us for awhile. I stayed on my best 'friend' behavior. I could tell that Lucie had mixed feelings about it.

We took her home after her parents arrived back in town. They still didn't like me. I could feel it. I gave them all the good vibes I could but it seemed to be hopeless. I bet my stock would go way up if they knew who my grandfather was. I, however, would NEVER play that card.

On the way home we stopped at Marlo's so that I could do some planning with him. Mom had let me drive but took the boys on home from Marlo's. Either I or we would walk home later. I felt like the parent when I reminded Mom to be careful. I wanted her and Alex to check the house and if there was any doubt to just leave. I was counting on Beggar to let them know if something was wrong. Dad would be home soon and that would be another adult in the house. Kraeghton better bring reinforcements.

Sarah called while I was at Marlo's to let me know that eight sets of remains in all had been found around the cabin. Some were identified based on the bits of clothing and personal items found with them. It was a work in progress and would take time to clear up. Mica was in her element. She was asking to be attached permanently to the task force that Sarah worked for. She would be hot on Willie to get information about Kraeghton.

Kraeghton. Great. We would all be on edge until he was out of the picture - which brought me back to Marlo. He had lots of ideas to keep us in contact. He wanted to upgrade our phones to be like Lucie's new one so he'd be able to track us by GPS *all* the time. He insisted that our phones be programmed with each other's numbers and he wanted us to be better communicators. The safest place for us was at school but I worried about the rest of our family members. Marlo reminded me to not 'borrow trouble'. Man that was a tough one. My headache was back and I felt the need for an antacid.

"Would you relax?" Marlo griped at me. "You won't do anybody any good if you go nuts on me now!"

"You're right. I'll try."

School was a good place to be. I could keep my eye on Lucie, Marlo and Adrian. It was distracting too. The pawnshop after school was better, but sadly we couldn't stay there all the time. I set Lucie up to spar with Adrian while I worked on my abilities with White Eagle and the two of us strategized with Marlo.

I asked Lucie about her birthday plans to which I received a steely-eyed glare. The only thing that saved my life was Marlo. He quickly distracted her and then pulled me aside to plan a party which would include a cake made by our favorite caterer. He added that after last year, Lucie felt guilty about my family doing anything for her birthday so this year Marlo would take the heat. What a guy! Now I just had to find the perfect gift.

Lucie and Adrian were a little nervous Saturday morning as Marla inspected us before we left for the wedding catering job. She had outfitted us in black slacks, black shoes, black ties and her signature dark red shirts. She completed our outfits with neat black aprons with her Marla Saggio Catering logo! She was very precise and gave excellent instructions. Being Marlo's mom this was no surprise.

The first thing we did was help her set up the wedding cake. I was surprised to find that I had the steadiest hand, so Marlo and I helped her. She shooed away Lucie and Adrian to start the coffee before the wedding cake had a whole new look. They were so nervous about goofing it up that they were shaking like leaves. We were hard at work checking tables, the chaffing dishes and Sterno burners when the first guests came drifting in. Lucie and Adrian, the most social of us, broke off to see to coffee and water service for those folks. Marlo and I continued the serving line preparations. Marla was bustling around the kitchen putting the finishing touches on her dishes with her regular assistant.

I suppose there is one in every family, but I was still disgusted when an older guy pinched Lucie's backside. It was bad enough having some of the slightly sloshed single gals checking out us guys and a whole other ball game having drunken men scope out our Lucie. In my defense it wasn't just me who took offense.

We had divided the room into roughly four quadrants to see to the guests needs, and to keep their water glasses and coffee cups full. We were total absorbed in our sections when I felt something shift within the room. Something was *wrong*. The change was subtle but swift. I snapped my head around to where the strongest pull was. I was fast but Adrian was quicker. He was already moving across the room. I set my pitcher of water on the nearest table as I rushed past, ignoring a request for coffee.

Marla was checking the main line to be sure that the food still out, was the right temperature. She caught my quick movement out of my section and was at my side in moments. We were in time to watch the angry guest lurch to his feet and roar, "Clumsy girl! I'll see that you're fired!"

Fired up is more like it, I thought in my head. I could see Lucie's furious gaze sizzling back at the man. Adrian slid the last couple of feet to her side and scowled at him. Lucie was not backing down.

He seemed surprised to find himself faced with two servers and then four.

"What's the trouble here?" Marla asked in her calmest, most professional tone.

"This... this... girl spilled water on my best trousers! I want her fired! This instant!" he blustered back at her.

"She is one of my best workers. I have never known her to be careless." Marla answered with confidence. Lucie looked ready to growl or maybe even bite. She held her tongue instead. I resisted the urge to put a hand on her arm. This was her fight.

"I said I want her FIRED!"

"How about if I move her to another section and replace her with this young man?" Marla asked him while flipping her hand in my direction to indicate me.

"Don't you have another girl?" His tone disgusted me. It was almost wheedling. It held the edge of a greasy salesman. This was the kind of guy who thought all women loved him and couldn't understand when they didn't respond like he expected to his advances. He was the kind of guy who gave all of us a bad name.

Marla's response was crisp and sure, "No sir. I will move her and you will have the young man here to see to your needs."

"Well... IF she'll pay to have my slacks dry cleaned and she promises to be nice... then I suppose she can stay."

"Luce, go to Owen's section and take over. Aid, help her." Marla mumbled to us and gave Adrian a look that said, "Keep watching her back."

I surveyed the rest of the table while Marla spoke. They all looked like they wanted to crawl into a hole. None wanted to stand up to him but clearly none supported him either. Most were whispering to their neighbor and looking painfully embarrassed.

"Uncle Fred! What are you doing?" the bride demanded as she stomped in our direction.

"This," he seemed to realize that Lucie and Adrian were walking away. Adrian had his arm around Lucie. Her back was stiff, her head held high. "I mean, that clumsy girl spilled on me."

The bride wore a ferocious scowl. "Let me guess... You grabbed her ass and she didn't like it. Get out! You are NOT ruining MY reception! I won't have it! I warned you. Now you apologize right this minute and then leave."

I was shocked that Uncle Fred was so easily cowed. He apologized to Marla and slunk from the room. I turned to the bride with raised eyebrows.

"I'm so sorry. I hope your server is okay. He doesn't mean any harm but... He doesn't understand boundaries and he loves young girls. I mean he... Oh never mind. Please stay. You're doing a wonderful job."

"Of course," Marla answered calmly, "We'll just get back to work."

"Thank you," the bride said sweetly and flounced off.

"I had no idea catering was such a tough business," I said softly to Marlo's mom as I tried to hold in a chuckle.

"You have NO idea," she sighed. She patted my shoulder and headed back to the buffet table checking guests as she went.

"Um, young man?"

"Yes, ma'am?" I said, turning to the lady nearest me.

"He really did pinch her and then he wiggled his eyebrows at her. She dumped the ice water right in his lap but he deserved it; there is no doubt in my mind. Tell the nice caterer not to be too hard on her. Please. She was doing a really good job."

"That's very kind of you. I'll be sure to pass it along."

The rest of the reception passed smoothly. When the dancing began Marla used Marlo and Lucie to help pack up the leftovers while Adrian and I covered the room. The cake cutting and other wedding silliness passed by with no sign of Uncle Fred or any other weirdness. Now that I was paying attention, I almost felt like I was being watched, but I decided I was just being paranoid.

It was a relief when the bride and groom left. Everyone else soon followed and we could proceed with the final clean-up. We worked like a well-oiled machine. Marla hardly had to say anything to us. I figured it was all the hours at the pawnshop together. Sure, we were doing something new to most of us, but we had become quiet intuitive about each other. I'd helped Marla before and Marlo had been helping her since he could walk, or knowing Marlo, maybe even before then.

As we were loading Marla's van Lucie finally told her side of the Uncle Fred story. We were all proud of her for standing up for herself. Marla would hate to lose a catering job but she would not have her staff treated like that. She gave Lucie a big hug so that she would know there were no hard feelings. Lucie threw her arm around Adrian and kissed his cheek. "Thanks again for coming over and staring him down, Buddy!" Adrian blushed to the roots of his hair. It made me smile.

We were all beat. We piled in the van and buckled up. We dropped off Adrian first. Marla got out and hugged him and thanked him again and made sure he was safely inside before we left for Lucie's. I caught her scowling at her phone. I could see the stiffness in her posture.

"What is it?"

"Unbelievable. They... they left. They left again. They met a recruiter from Washington who is interested in my brother and took off to see the campus. REALLY? Now, imagine if I was the kind of kid who threw parties or did drugs or... or... ahrrgggh." Lucie threw up her hands in total disgust. "They'll be back late on... wait for it... Monday! Happy Birthday to me."

"So..." Marlo said, eyeballing his mom, "We could maybe take you home or..?"

"No, Mar, I'll keep her, thanks anyway."

"Now wait just a minute. I can stay by myself, thanks, Mother," Lucie said with a glare in my direction.

"Luce..." I began but Marla gave her a hard look in the mirror.

"I don't think you should stay in that big house alone. Stay with us or with Owen. We'll stop by and get your things. Just in case Lucie, be safe. Be smart, stay with one of us," Marla pleaded.

And just think... Marla didn't even know about Kraeghton. I knew Lucie was caving when I saw her shoulders slump. At least getting down to Fallon, Nevada for Emiline Claremont's birthday shouldn't be a problem. Her folks didn't care what she did. As long as she caused no obvious trouble and kept her 4.0 they left her – completely and frighteningly – alone.

It was after midnight when we got to Lucie's. Her house was completely dark. Worse yet... it felt... wrong. I snatched Lucie's keys from her hand. She started to say something but took one look at my face and clamped her lips shut. I gave Marlo a look and told him that Lucie and I would be right back and that he could wait with his mom. Marlo gave me the classic single nod that he'd adopted to let me know that he got the real message. I saw his phone flash on and he began texting with the phone held down between his hip and the door as he continued to hold a normal conversation with his mom. A-ma-zing!

Lucie and I hopped out of the van and walked up to the front door. "You have the overprotective thing going again... what *is* it?" Lucie asked in a hushed voice.

"Someone was here."

"I hate this. I feel like your personal damsel in distress. It isn't right. It's not normal. Normal people don't have to walk around with a bodyguard. I don't want you to be my bodyguard." Clearly Lucie was nervous. She wasn't usually one to babble.

We approached the door and I touched it before I inserted the key to open it. Whoever it was, it wasn't Kraeghton. Another *watcher stalker*? Someone dark, with bad intentions had touched this door – but who it was and why they were here was unclear. Why did Lucie seem to draw these guys in like no other? Was she unlucky or did they find her as appealing as I did? Lucie stopped talking and was watching me closely. She was trying to be brave. She wasn't running, screaming, whimpering or clinging to me.

I silently opened the door and *felt* the house. It was clear now but it hadn't been. "Whoever it was, is gone, Luce. At least I can't *feel* anyone else here. Stick close just in case and never come in this house alone," I whispered, in case her house had been wired or bugged for sound.

"But we have an alarm," she whispered back as she moved to the panel and deactivated it.

"Come on Luce, you know Marlo can disable an alarm," I whispered back with a glare.

"I love Marlo but he is so NOT normal," she whispered back with a glare of her own. "Who would... never mind."

I tilted my head toward the stairs with two quick jerks to encourage her to move faster.

"You're so bossy," she said with an eye roll.

She gave *me* an eye roll? Really? "Let's do this."

"Fine." But she didn't move. She just looked at the stairs like she was searching for her courage. I watched her throat as she swallowed. I started to reach for her hand but she took a deep breath and started up. She walked with purpose, her back perfectly straight. She was both graceful and stiff. I admired the slight sway of her hips in her black slacks, as she walked in front of me, and the way the gold glinted in her hair where it curled gently around her shoulders. Six steps up, she turned to look at me. I quickly whipped my eyes up to her face and shook my head. I walked up beside her and we moved on up the stairs.

"You were watching my butt," she giggled. "It's got to be almost one, we worked all day, I had a break-in and you... You're such a... guy."

I shrugged. What could I say? She was right. I was a guy and she was worth watching – even at almost one in the morning.

At the top of the stairs I rested a gentle hand on the back of Lucie's neck to stop her from walking down the hall until I had a chance to check it first. I closed my eyes to focus, counting on her actual vision and my connection to her, to see what else was going on. Lucie froze as she felt my gift wash over her like a gentle electric tingle. I pushed my senses out and *felt* the house again. We had tried something like this at the shop but I'd never actually done this with her before. I kept all my abilities dialed way back when we practiced. I could hear her soft intake of breath as she saw the hall with her own eyes and *felt* it for the first time. I moved outward to the rooms upstairs and finally the whole house with my ability to sense darkness and danger.

"Wow," she breathed bringing a smile to my lips and causing my concentration to slip a bit. I let go of her and started to head down the hall. She reached out a hand and grasped my arm to stop me. "You continue to amaze me. You make my gift seem so small and unimportant. You... I can't imagine what it must be like to be you."

"Luce, it's just me. I'm the same guy you've know since sixth grade. I'm nothing special."

"Oh my God, Owen, you are so wrong. You are..."

I interrupted her. I couldn't have her thinking that I was any more important than anyone else on the team. "I can't let the stuff I do go to my head. I have to keep it real. I can't be better than the people I help. I have to relate to them and understand them. This job isn't easy. We have gifts but we make sacrifices too. Take you, for example. You can't tell your family who you really are or what you do.

If they even believed you – it wouldn't be safe for them or for you. I wondered why it was so hard to hide what I did from my mom. Now I know it's because she has a gift too. Hers is just so weak that *watcher stalkers* never paid any attention to her. Now that she has been 'exercising' it, her gift is stronger, but she is mainly useful to protect my brothers and boost my abilities. Well, that and all the 'mom' stuff she does. I don't want to undervalue her in any way. I would never have made it this far without her. You, on the other hand, have us. It's fortunate in some ways that your folks ignore you. It's easier to take you away. We need you Luce, you are important."

I turned from her and moved on down the hall. Lucie's hand dropped to her side and she continued to watch me for a moment and then followed me down the hall. I stopped at Lucie's room. I would've known the way even if I hadn't been here before because it had the most residual darkness.

"Luce, you are being *stalked*. We need to..."

"I know, Owen, I feel it too. I need to stay around people and in contact with you but I feel like they're just watching and trying to intimidate me right now. I sense that..." Lucie closed her eyes to concentrate. I watched her for a moment and they snapped back open showing me the light in her eyes – the knowledge. "Owen I can *hear* them. They don't want me. They want to use me to get to... YOU."

I stared at her. Kraeghton wanted her - to get even with me for ruining his plans in Florida. But he wasn't the one who was here. So now, the question was... who was after us? I started to ask why, but that was a dumb question. We were a power boost for *dark watchers* and we prevented the spread of darkness and chaos. Of course they wanted us. We promoted goodness and order.

"Come on, let's get you packed and out of here." While she gathered her things, I texted Marlo to tell him we were fine, the house was clear but that we needed a team meeting as soon as he could get one together.

We relocked her house when we were done and got back in the Saggio family van. Marla dropped us at my house and hugged us both. She whispered that she would see me soon for the 'you know what.' I thanked her. Lucie deserved to have a nice birthday.

Mom met us at the front door. She had gotten Marlo's text. She already had bedding on the couch for me. She wrapped Lucie in a big comforting hug. "I'm so sorry, honey. You're always welcome here. We want you safe."

"Thanks Lila, but I think you should be worried about Owen. They only want me to get to him. None of us are safe."

"None of us have been, ever since Owen discovered his gift, but what you both do is much more important than any one person. We just have to watch out for each other. Owen is powerful, that makes him valuable. Any of us, they would happily drain for a power boost but Owen... I think they'd rather turn him to their side. As a *dark watcher* he would be nearly unstoppable. They're wrong about him though, they could take anything and everything away from him and he would never turn. He has never been hungry for power. His desire to help people is too strong." Mom turned and looked at me fondly. "He keeps us all in his heart and even if we're gone, we'll always be there."

"Mom, that sounds... morbid. I don't want anything to happen to any of you. I would sacrifice myself for you, all of you. I'm not that important." Mom and Lucie both looked at me. "What?"

They shook their heads; it was almost comical to watch. They seemed to notice and both turned to smile at each other. Too much estrogen in the entryway for me. I turned and headed upstairs to change my clothes and brush my teeth. I paused in my room and looked at my bed. At least I had made it but I really should change the sheets for Lucie. I dropped my pjs and t-shirt on the floor and opened my closet to look for my extra set of sheets.

"What are you doing?" Lucie asked softly.

I leaned back to look at her past the closet door. "I was getting you fresh sheets. I... um... well, I haven't changed them since you were here last. I just thought... you know, it'd be nice if you had clean sheets."

Lucie snorted softly. "It's fine, Owen, really. How about if I help you change them tomorrow? Right now, let's just go to bed. It's late and I'm beat."

"That's not fair to you. I'm not being a good host."

Lucie shook her head. "My house has been invaded again. People want to use me as a human battery and they want to hurt my friend. It's well after one in the morning and we worked all day. Clearly sheets are a big priority."

She was being sarcastic but I was serious. "Luce, I just..."

"Look, you big dope, they smell like you. It will be like you're here with me and I will feel safe and I'll actually be able to sleep. You try to change those sheets and I'll tackle you and throw you out of here! Now go get ready for bed. Yeesh."

First I looked at her, stunned by her words and then I laughed a little but softly so I wouldn't wake my dad or my brothers. "Okay Lucie, you win. I'll hurry."

I picked up my stuff and rushed through the bathroom. I went back to tell her it was her turn. Only my bedside lamp was on. She'd opened up my bed so that she could crawl right in. She sat near the foot with one shoe in her hand and the other still on. She looked half asleep already.

"You okay?"

"Yeah, tired. Feet hurt and my butt hurts where that jerk pinched me. I'm not cut out to be a waitress. I almost punched him. I thought first, like you taught me. I went for the lesser of the evils and dumped the water on him. I'd been ignoring his comments but that was too much. He'd already put his phone number in my apron pocket and tried to grab a feel of more than one part of my body. Sicko."

"What? You didn't say anything. I would have..."

"Owen, no. You're not my personal bodyguard. I handled it. It's over. I'm tired and I'm venting. Let it go."

I hung up my tie and apron – Marla had them specially cleaned to maintain the logo and keep them looking crisp and new. I tossed my shirt, slacks and socks in my hamper. I shoved my shoes into the closet and still Lucie sat. I moved over and sat on the floor in front of her. I took off the shoe that was still on her foot and then took the other out of her hand. I set them both under the edge of the bed. Then I picked up her foot and began to rub the ache out of it. Lucie sighed. Her head dropped and her shoulders slumped. She thought I was being nice. I am a devious son of a... well, you know. I was trying to get the rest of the story from her clothes.

"Feels nice," Lucie mumbled sleepily. I worked my way up her leg to her calf and then I switched sides.

"Let's get you to bed. Tomorrow is another day."

"Mmmmm"

I helped her to her feet and untied her apron. I made sure to touch her sleeve too.

"Hey, Owen?"

"Yeah?"

"You can have all the money I made today if you will lay down on the bed and warm it up for me."

"Sure Luce, no problem." I watched her stagger to the bathroom.

The *visions* from her clothes told the story. It was worse than even she had let on. No one had stood up to the man. They seemed to be almost afraid of him or maybe just afraid of a scene. Either way they'd let the bullying go which made them all at fault. I found the man's number in Lucie's apron when I hung it by mine. I got a hit off of it too. This man was definitely on my 'to do' list. I flipped on my IPod, selected a playlist and sat on my bed.

Mom came in as I was laying down on it. "What do you think you are doing?"

"Just warming it up. I swear. She asked me to."

"Hmmm. So how did it go?"

"Working for Marla is great. We did have to deal with a not so nice man and Marlo told you about Lucie's misfortune. Mom, she has got to stay here whenever her parents are gone. I don't want her alone in that house. In fact..."

"You want to set a trap."

"Yeah, I think I might. Hey, did Marlo ask you about a team meeting?"

"He's trying for tomorrow. I'll see if I can get your dad to take your brothers to a matinee. We'll meet here."

"Good."

Mom pushed off from the doorframe. She held her fingers in a V and then pointed from her eyes to me and back. *I'm watching you.* Yeah, Mom, I get it. I smiled at her and nodded. She blew a kiss to me, called a soft good night and melted into the darkened hallway.

Lucie was back right after Mom left. She looked even more tired. She had taken off her makeup and brushed out her hair. "Thanks."

I got up, let her lay down and covered her up. "I'm glad you warmed it up but I shouldn't have kept you up. It wasn't fair."

I sat on the edge of the bed. "It's okay to let people take care of you sometimes, Luce."

I thought she was going to cry. She closed her eyes and took a breath. I became aware of the song playing... Nickelback's *Trying Not To Love You*. Yep, the story of my recent life. I hung my head, sighed and started to get up. Lucie lunged at me and hugged me tight.

"Don't feel unappreciated. I want you to keep saving me. I just wish you didn't have to. Maybe someday, I'll save you."

I inhaled the scent of her hair. What I would give to just stay here. She wasn't as good at pushing me away when she was tired or upset. Someday. "Luce, you do save me. You just don't see it. I've gotta go. I'll see you in the morning." I kissed the top of her head, pulled her arms from me and... yep... walked away. I headed slowly downstairs and sat on the couch. After a moment I flopped onto my side and fell asleep without even putting the blanket over me.

I dreamed of Lucie. It was all the little things. I dreamt of holding her hand, her smile and her laugh. I thought about the times when she held her body close to mine. She was warm. I could smell her shampoo. She reached out and ran her fingers through my hair. It was so real. Something changed. I realized that I was... awake. I opened my eyes. I was covered by a blanket and Lucie was just about out of sight up the stairs. She had been watching me sleep again but this time I slept right through it. Bummer. I rolled over and tried to go back to sleep. The house was still quiet and the sun wasn't all the way up yet.

NINETEEN

I don't know what finally woke me up. It was either the smell of breakfast cooking or the hushed conversation going on. I lay there and eavesdropped. Not my best quality. Dad didn't think that Lucie should be staying with us. Mom felt the opposite. Under my protection was the best place for her. Mom wished she was here all the time. No one at her house could protect her like I could.

"It's wrong I tell you. I know he likes her. She seems to like him too. She shouldn't be here."

"Brad, seriously!" Mom whispered angrily. "You know what kind of people they are. What they did to you. What they did to Owen. We can't let them get their hands on Lucie."

"I suppose not. It just feels like a recipe for disaster. I was a fifteen-year-old boy once."

"You have to trust him," Mom answered firmly.

"I know. I'm just having a hard time not blaming him for all this. I try but... Don't look at me like that. If he didn't have that weird ability none of this would have happened."

"Please accept that your father was part of the problem. Then work on accepting that what Owen has is a GIFT. He helps people. If we have to pay for that then *I will* gladly. How can you not see the big picture?"

"I'm trying, Lila. I'm taking the little boys to see Dad and then I'll take them to a movie. I'm doing that for *you* so you can have your meeting. I'm helping. Nowhere does it say I have to like it."

Yikes. I felt bad for my dad but I found him so frustrating too. I quietly got up and headed upstairs with the blanket and pillow tucked under my arm. I found Alex at the top of the stairs. He scooched over to let me pass.

"You know you're the main topic of conversation between them?" Alex asked. For once I hadn't a clue what he was thinking.

"Sadly, yes," I replied hoping for neutral ground.

"I'm sorry that it's like that for you. I get to hide in the middle." Good old Alex. He made me snort softly. Yep, he liked to fly under the radar too. I tossed the pillow and blanket off to the side and sat next to him. "Am I going to be like you?"

"I don't know. Do you really want to?"

"Yeah, I think I do."

"Do you want to know?"

"Yeah, I do. I think if I wait to find out the feeling is only going to get stronger."

"What feeling Alex?"

"I don't know. Being around all this stuff makes me... want it. I'm starting to think that I have something too. You probably think that's stupid."

"Alex, no! Why would you say that?"

"Well, can you tell if I'm like you?"

"I don't know. I haven't ever tried. I'm not like White Eagle. He told me he had a feeling about me but he didn't know for sure until I was fourteen. Maybe we won't know until then about you. I could try. Don't get your hopes up though. I think we need White Eagle." Alex seemed to brace himself. I reached out with my gift and looked at him. I tried to think about what White Eagle saw. I couldn't make that work. I don't see colors like White Eagle, for me it's light or dark. "I'm sorry, Alex. All I can tell about you is that you're good person. That certainly is a good start, right?"

"I guess."

"I'm sorry. Don't take it as bad news. Take it as a maybe. No matter what, you are valued, needed and appreciated for who you are. Don't ever forget that."

"Kay."

I threw an arm around him and gave him a half hug. "It smells like breakfast is about ready. How about if you wake up Lucas while I jump in the shower?"

"Kay. Hey, Owen?"

"Yeah, Buddy?"

"Whether or not I'm like you... I still want to help."

"You are one awesome brother, Alex."

"I know," he replied with a laugh.

I snuck into my room and found some clean clothes to put on after my shower. Lucie was curled up in a ball on her side, hugging a pillow to her chest. Her hair streamed out behind her. In sleep she looked peaceful and young. The bedside lamp was still on so I silently turned it off. My playlist was still quietly running on the IPod. She made me smile. She had on my shirt again. Maybe I could peel her out of it today and replace it with another one. Maybe I could find one that would go better with her wardrobe. It was nice just to listen to her breath. For now, she was safe.

Lucie was waiting when I opened the door to the bathroom. She rushed in, hugged me and pushed me out all without a word and without looking at me. I suppressed a chuckle. I tossed my pjs in my room and decided to strip my bed. I tossed the comforter onto my desk chair and pulled off the sheets. I pulled my hamper over and tossed the sheets on top. I guessed I'd have to do laundry today with everything else. I pulled the clean sheets out of my closet. I snapped open the bottom sheet and was letting it float onto the bed when a streak of orange zoomed onto my bed. Our cat... great. How did he do that? He could hear clean sheets from a mile away I swear. Now the game began. Could I get the sheets on without getting scratched or attacked? He wasn't mean. He was playful and he LOVED sheets. He would run under and around them as you tried to work, getting completely in your way.

I sighed and turned up my music. I managed the bottom sheet okay. I only had to pull him out three times. I picked up the top sheet and his eyes dilated to complete roundness. He laid his ears back and wiggled his behind, ready to attack. What a goober. I snapped the sheet out over his head and he leapt joyfully into it as it floated down around him. I tried to smooth it out over the lump of his body in the middle of the bed. I tucked in the bottom and tried to tuck in the bottom side edges. An orange paw reached out to swipe at me. I was mostly able to evade him. I wasn't so lucky on the other side. "Ouch!" I snarled when he nailed me. "Son of a..." I jerked my head up when I heard giggling from the doorway. Lucie.

"I told you I would help. I didn't appreciate how badly I was needed." Her grin was huge and her eyes sparkled. "Ron, kitty, kitty, kitty, come here boy."

"Merrow?"

"Ron, kitty, kitty. Who's a good boy?" And that was all it took. The little traitor slid out from under the sheets and pranced over to Lucie his tail waving in a big question mark, his posture happy. Lucie scooped him up and nuzzled him. "We'll meet you downstairs. Wash your hands and I'll fix up your scratch."

Sometimes life just wasn't fair. Lucky, rotten cat. I swear he looked at me over Lucie's shoulder with a look like he'd won. I looked at my hand. It was starting to drip so I left the bed and grabbed my hamper and headed downstairs.

Lucie fixed my hand true to her word. Washing it would have been fine but I wasn't going to pass up on the extra attention. Dad left with my brothers right after breakfast and everyone else started arriving shortly after. Mom, Lucie and I cleaned the kitchen. I brought in chairs from the other room and we all squeezed around the kitchen table. Adrian, Marlo, Sarah, White Eagle, Mom and Lucie all looked at me expectantly.

I looked at White Eagle. "Um, thanks for coming."

"Owen, this is your meeting. You're in charge here," White Eagle said calmly.

I stared at White Eagle. A silent communication passed between us. My *watcher*, my meeting. I gave him a nod and took over. It was weird to be in this role. It was weird to be the leader of a group of such talented people. I did not feel worthy.

We firmed up our early June visit to Fallon, Nevada to celebrate Emiline Claremont's 90th birthday and to reconnect with Mitchell, her *watcher*. Marlo showed us the phony choir retreat permission slip we would use for Lucie. Adrian and Marlo's parents thought we were going camping again. Sarah would be the person who would answer the phone if Lucie's parents happened to call. Next we talked about Lucie's situation. Marlo and Adrian could relate. Their parents didn't know what we did together either but they were not being stalked by *dark watchers* and we could always claim guy time if we needed to get together. I wondered if we could make it three more years without having to let more people in on our secret. Lucie hated having to be with one of us at all times either in person or by having her phone GPS on and giving us updates but she understood it.

Marlo would do what research he could to see who our new player might be. Sarah and White Eagle would keep up on the local police information. All of us would be alert for anything suspicious. The four of us would train every single day until we left for Fallon. White Eagle, Sarah and Mom would join us at our practice sessions whenever they could. We needed to be ready. I also warned that this could just be a feint on Lucie and they were looking for weakness. They could come after any of us.

I turned the floor over to Sarah who gave us an update on Trevor and Willie. More and more evidence was mounting. He would likely get the death penalty – whether or not it would be enforced was another matter. It was out of our hands and up to the courts. We were scheduled to go to Astoria on Friday to notify Trevor's mother and sister. It was a furlough day for our school district so we would all go. We would take the van.

Marlo cleared his throat. "I have some news myself." All heads turned in his direction. "Lucie, since we had narrowed our search down to two girls from the '50s, having eliminated the one who died from breast cancer in 1995, I believe I've found your sobbing girl from… 1956. I have meshed what I found from school records and newspaper articles. Her name is Bettylou. She was suspended from school toward the end of her senior year because back then you couldn't be pregnant and attend. The baby was put up for adoption. The likely father of the baby, her boyfriend, died in a motorcycle accident before the birth. I found a picture of them in the yearbook when they were juniors. I believe that if we can get into those records and reunite the mother and… her child, we can put your ghost or whatever she is, to rest."

"Wow," Lucie breathed. She leaned over and put her arm around Marlo. "Thanks, Buddy. You really are the best. You're my favorite. Don't tell the others," she said with a twinkle in her eye and then she turned and winked at my mom, causing all of us to laugh.

"But you told me I was the best," Adrian said with a laugh.

"That was yesterday. What have you done for me lately?"

Lucie stayed with us Sunday night too. Mom drove us and Marlo to school on Monday. The three of us passed Lucie around all day to keep a close eye on her. Marlo confided loud enough for me to hear when it was his turn, that he thought Lucie was tougher than he was but that it was always good to have a buddy. Lucie gave him a huge grin and threw her arm over his shoulder.

While he was still in her good graces, Marlo sprung her birthday dinner on her. She gave me the evil eye but was nice to him. Go figure! Marlo and his family, Adrian and his family, White Eagle, Sarah and all of my family gathered at my house for a planned potluck that Marla put together. Lucie cried when Marla brought out a mini three layer blue and white cake. My brothers and Adrian's sister had made posters and had decorated the dining room. After we ate cake and ice cream, Lucie opened presents. Adrian got her a t-shirt with her favorite rock band on it. Marlo had put together a digital photo frame with a bunch of pictures of all of us. Mom and Marla had gone in together on a gift card to the book store at the mall. White Eagle and Sarah got her a gift card for music. I was nervous about her opening my gift in front of everyone but sucked it up and handed it to her after seriously considering shoving it in my pocket. Lucie looked at the small box and then at me. Her eyes glittered. I knew I would always remember how she looked. Most of her hair was in a pony tail but several strands around her face had escaped to curl against her skin. She took a deep breath and slowly untied the bow. She lifted the lid with the same care. She finally peeked inside, reclosed the lid, opened it again and bit her lip. I thought she would cry.

"What is it with you and birds?" she asked in a husky voice.

Every eye in the room turned to me and it was silent as a tomb. I cleared my throat. "Well... it's a combination of things. It's what I wish for you and what I see in you. I want you to be free to live your life. I see the beauty and grace of birds in flight and I think of you. The ceramic bird I gave you last year was a delicate and resilient bird. It looks small but it's tough in its own way. You're the bird, Lucie."

Lucie stood up from her seat on the couch and hugged me. The room broke into applause. She laughed and begged me to put the necklace on her. She gently traced the bird in flight as I hooked the clasp for her. She spun around in enthusiasm. "How does it look?" I had no idea – all I could see was her.

Mom looked at me and moved between us. "It's beautiful and perfect for you. Come let Sarah see it and Marla."

"Me too," piped up Adrian's sister.

The days passed and we continued to pass Lucie around, never leaving her alone. She took it all well. She kept her GPS on and Marlo tracked her tirelessly. We practiced every day as planned. I never let her go to her house alone. Most nights we stayed at the pawnshop or went to my house until nine or ten at night. She wore her necklace every day. Perhaps she never took it off. Friday finally came. I once again put on the suit. It had only needed minor adjustments by Sarah's tailor friend. I packed some jeans and a sweatshirt for the beach. Mom hugged me goodbye. Dad grunted at me. I walked down to Sarah's house where White Eagle was waiting and we loaded up. We picked up Marlo, Lucie and Adrian and hit the road.

The trip this time was happy and lighthearted. What we had to do was serious but I knew in my heart that Trevor's mom already knew he was gone. The final news would bring her peace. I can't explain it but it felt really... good to be together like this. We were bringing something to a close and we were together. I was learning to appreciate the small moments. I looked at each face in the van and thought about how much I loved each of them in their own way – my other family. They meant everything to me.

I didn't want this time to end but soon enough we were pulling up in front of the familiar house. "Adrian, Marlo, you stay with White Eagle. Lucie, you come with us," Sarah said.

"What?"

Sarah looked at me. "I have the feeling she needs to meet Lucie. Am I wrong?"

I took a moment. Sarah was right. I could feel it too. I felt that pull in my belly. Sarah might not have a gift even as strong as Mom's, but to be an agent she had to rely on her gut. She hadn't lasted with the bureau as long as she had and ended up in the special unit as she was in without having a good sense of things.

"Come on Luce, let's go. Sarah is not wrong. She knows people. She is almost as good at it as Mom is." Lucie looked at me nervously but took my offered hand.

Sarah smiled at me. "You make me blush. I don't have a gift like you do."

"Not like I do, no, but you do have a gift. It brought us together. You knew who I was even before White Eagle did. You see it in Alex too, don't you."

Sarah looked at me and her eyes widened a bit. "Maybe I do." She almost sounded surprised.

"He asked me the other day and I *looked* at him. I couldn't see it then, but I do now. I see it because you do. I trust your judgment," I said with a smile. I kept ahold of Lucie's hand and hugged Sarah with the other arm. "Lucie is the girl who found Trevor. His mother will believe that she is a psychic."

Lucie looked ready to run. "I'm not."

"We know that. She doesn't. It's okay to be nervous and scared but she's a nice lady and this will help her to understand and accept. She has a bit of a gift herself. Come on ladies." Sarah took my arm on one side and I kept ahold of Lucie's hand on the other. The front door opened before we even hit the driveway. Trevor's mom stepped out, looked at us and began to cry.

"He's really gone, isn't he?" she asked in a broken voice.

"I'm so sorry for your loss," I said softly. Sarah put an arm around her shoulders and turned her back toward the house. Lucie and I followed behind.

"I knew it. I felt it. About two weeks ago I knew for sure. I've been waiting."

"We had to be possitive," Sarah told her gently. "I'll make you some tea. This is Lucie. She's the one who..."

"My boy... he talked to you didn't he."

Lucie's mouth fell open at her words. "He... yes," she stammered.

"Thank you for giving us peace," Mrs. Vance said softly and she hugged Lucie.

Sarah and Trevor's sister came in from the kitchen with tea. We talked a bit more and Sarah provided her with the appropriate documentation. She also gave her Mica's contact information. Sarah explained that Trevor was not the only victim. Lucie told her how brave Trevor had been and that he had almost gotten away. She also told her that if not for him we wouldn't have found the others. It seemed to be just what she needed to hear.

As we left, Lucie leaned over and put an arm around me. "So this is what it feels like when you close a big case. This is why you know it's worth it. It *is* worth it. All of it, even the *dark watchers*. No one can take away what we did for Mrs. Vance."

"Yeah, Luce, it keeps me coming back too," I said smiling at her.

"Did I tell you how good you look in that suit, Agent Ryer?" Lucie asked playfully as she punched me lightly in the belly with her free arm.

I stopped walking and faced her. "No, tell me." The mood shifted immediately. Lucie had kept it playful and light. I saw in her face all the things she wished for and thought she couldn't or shouldn't have. She took a step toward me, her arms out; then a frown marred her perfect brows and she turned and got in the van.

Well, what did I expect? Just friends and the rest of our group was waiting. I sighed and crawled into the way back to change my clothes as we headed to the Columbia River Maritime Museum for some fun. White Eagle didn't even wait for me. He pulled out, nearly knocking me over. I figured it was his way of giving me an agility test. I hung my suit up once I was again looking like a normal teenager.

We had some fun around town, saw the museum, the Astor Column and the Flavel House, had some lunch and drove south to walk on the beach before heading home. Lucie kept her distance from me, preferring the company of either Marlo or Adrian. I tried to relax and just be myself but she was making me sad. What had I done now? Marlo snapped a ton of pictures to upload to Lucie's photo frame. We posed several shots of all of us and then some smaller groupings on the beach. Marlo captured several amazing shots. He got a great one of Sarah and White Eagle and one of Lucie. The Lucie shot was almost haunting. She was looking away from the camera, tucking some loose hair behind her ear, the look on her face both sad and joyful, and her eyes had picked up the grey of the Oregon surf.

The week passed much as the last one had. If Lucie's parents were gone, she was at my house or at least with one of us. We traded her off at school like a prized possession. The rumor mill had started up. It was the first time all year that Adrian did not have a girlfriend so there was much speculation about which of us Lucie was actually dating. On the rare occasion I saw her brother he just scowled at me. He never once pulled me aside or tried to talk to me. What he was thinking was anyone's guess. His body language said be nice to my sister or else. I wanted to laugh – I was the last person who would hurt Lucie.

We had all of our gear packed and loaded in the van Friday morning. White Eagle and Sarah met us in the school parking lot as the final bell rang. I drove first while White Eagle slept in the back. When I got tired, Sarah would take over and then she would wake up White Eagle to drive the final stretch. We were driving straight through to Emeline's in Fallon. It was a ten and a half hour trip with no stops though we would be stopping for dinner and gas part way down.

The trip began with happy chatter. Marlo whipped out his laptop, figured out all of our homework assignments and made a schedule for us. The rest of them started on what they could with Sarah kibitzing in. White Eagle was smart. He had brought earplugs and was making good use of them. I was to focus on driving and not talk. They didn't say I couldn't listen in. I even made a few comments. Marlo submitted the assignments that he could electronically. He even sent in one of my papers that he finished for me by asking my opinion as I drove. Have I mentioned lately how awesome Marlo is? I must take him to college with me.

We hit Eugene after five o'clock and traffic was picking up. We found an Applebee's just off I-5 in Springfield and pulled in for dinner. We hoped that most of the traffic would have found its way home by the time we were on the road again.

Lucie sat next to me for the next leg of our journey. I was secretly thrilled but a little surprised by her choice. She had been more or less avoiding me since we'd been at the beach. We picked away at more of our homework. The goal was to get all of it done on the drive. She had brought acupressure wrist bands to ward off her tendency to get motion sick. She was doing well riding in the center of the first row of van seats behind the driver. Marlo had sat next to her on the first leg.

Adrian for some unknown reason liked the back. He and White Eagle were softly snoring within minutes of us pulling out of the restaurant parking lot. Adrian was less interested in homework than the rest of us. He did what he had to do but he could care less if he got a few C's on his report card. For him high school was a social activity and women were a priority. The rest of us pulled out our Biology stuff. The more I thought about Adrian the more stumped I became. When I couldn't stand it anymore I blurted out, "How come Adrian doesn't have a girlfriend?"

"What that has to do with animal diversity, I don't know!" Lucie laughed. "Oh wait – I get it! Are you saying Adrian is an animal?"

"I'm sorry, I'm off topic and no, I don't consider him an animal," I said, giving her shoulder a gentle shove as I smiled at her. "I got to thinking about it and pretty soon it was all I could think about. It's weird and so unlike him. "

"I know, right? But if you have the back story it makes sense."

I waited. Lucie looked at me and her eyes sparkled. She loved it that she knew something that I didn't. Marlo turned in his seat to look at us. Apparently he didn't know either.

"So... Adrian confided in you? And not us?"

Lucie's smile was so big I bet her cheeks hurt. She shook her head, but then she couldn't stand it anymore. "He likes my friend, Brenda, but I warned her about him and his long list of broken hearts so she's leery of him. He has been chasing her for almost two months. It's a new record for him as far as I know. She's starting to cave. I have never known him to try for so long. He usually just moves on. Brenda likes it that I can vouch for his activities lately. This would be a whole new kind of relationship for him. He has never had to work so hard. Would you believe that he only asked me once to help? He is truly trying and I say, 'good for him.'"

"Wow," Marlo said softly. "I can't believe it. He must really like her."

"Well, I think she's adorable, funny and smart but then she is my friend."

"Nice," I said.

By the time it was White Eagle's turn to drive it was getting too dark to see. Lucie chose to sit by me again and in no time had snuggled into my side to sleep. Sometimes I don't get her but I would take what I could for now. I wrapped my arms around her and was soon asleep myself. A flash woke me up. I opened one eye, realized it was Marlo taking a picture and went right back to sleep. I don't know when I've slept better. I may have been in a strange position, and would likely wake up with a kink in my neck, but with Lucie wrapped in my arms what could be better. I wouldn't trade it.

I felt the van pause. I figured we must be coming into town. I'd be sad to get out of the van because it would mean giving up holding Lucie and I hated that idea. I felt the van pause a few more times as we hit lights going through Fallon. I held Lucie tight and tried to cushion the movement of the van so that she would sleep on. I knew when we pulled off the main road and onto the long drive to Emiline's house.

When we reached the end of the drive, White Eagle parked and he and Sarah held a whispered conversation. I only caught snatches of it but it sounded like they were leaving us in the van to sleep. Yes! Sarah scribbled a quick note which she folded so it would stand up by the windshield within easy view. Then they exited the van and went up to the front porch.

I tried not to move as I watched them through the windshield past the driver's seat. I didn't want to wake Lucie. I was afraid if I did she would leave. I saw Mitchell open the front door and let them in. He looked happy to see White Eagle and I watched Sarah hug him. Classic Sarah. I sighed, tightened my arms around Lucie and went back to sleep.

Lucie's movement woke me. Dawn was just breaking, tinting the inside of the van with a pink glow. I looked at her and smiled. She looked rumpled and confused. I could hear heavy breathing from both Marlo and Adrian.

"Ugh, I wish I could've brushed my teeth," she whispered.

"You can go into the house and do that if you want. No one is up yet but why don't you stay?"

She looked at me with a mix of regret and determination. "I don't think I... trust myself to stay. I need to go to the bathroom anyway."

"Lucie, why do you... fight this thing between us?"

"We have to work together. We're a team. You're my mentor. Everything will get all mixed up if we... it's a bad idea. It's probably just because you save me all the time anyway..."

I started to speak but she moved toward me so I stopped. I thought she was going to kiss me. I wanted her to. She stopped, shook her head and leaned away from me.

"No. Show me to the bathroom, please," she whispered.

"Okay, Luce. Okay."

I walked her in, showed her the bathroom and found Emiline already in the kitchen. Sarah and White Eagle were each crashed on a couch. I figured Mitchell was asleep in his room. I knew that his dad had been deployed and his mom had gone overseas with him on a new contract. Mitchell was finishing his senior year with Emiline.

"How are 'ya, boy?"

"Good and you, Miss Claremont?"

"You call me Emiline. You've earned it."

"Yes, ma'am."

"I'm right as rain and still feisty."

"I'm glad."

"Thank y'all for coming down to see us and help me celebrate. I really pushed that stubborn mentor of yours. We needed to have a meetin' and plan for Mitchell's future. He's good, but he's not safe alone the way things are gettin'," she rasped in her elderly voice.

"Why? What's up?"

"My gut's been churnin', a sure sign somethin' bad's comin'. Mitchell wants to start community college here, but if something happens to me I want him with y'all."

"I see. What does White Eagle say?"

"He wants him with me as long as possible. He thinks I still have a lot to offer and he's stretched pretty thin. He thinks I have years. I'd say months. I can feel it."

"It's true he's stretched a little thin. I have a *watcher* of my own now, so he's taking care of all four of us, in a way."

"Do you now? I thought you were an extraordinary one. The best I've ever seen."

"Thank you, Emiline, I'll try to live up to your high expectations."

She barked a laugh as Lucie came around the corner. I smiled at her and waved her into the kitchen.

"Emiline, this is Lucie Ness, my *watcher*. She's a locational. She hears *dark* things."

"I'm pleased to meet you, my dear. Aren't you a beauty! Mitchell will be drooling. His ability is to know something *dark* will happen right before it does. He's pretty handy to have around. It's hard to compete with your mentor here, though. I have never known someone to not only have more than one ability, but to be both a *watcher* and a mentor. He's a force to be reckoned with." I blushed and ducked my head. "And still shy and humble I see."

Lucie laughed a soft laugh. "Yes ma'am. He is the humble one of our group. He doesn't see his own value. He thinks he's just another ordinary guy."

I shook my head and decided to change the subject. "So what's up besides coffee? How can I help? We brought a bunch of food. Do you want me to bring in the supplies?"

"Are you changin' the subject?" Emiline asked, twinkling at me.

"Yep," I answered with a half smile. She was kidding, right? I hated being the center of attention.

"Fine, let's get the grub goin'," Emiline laughed.

As we cooked I told Lucie the story of our first meeting and how Emiline had tried to shoot me. Soon our laughter had Sarah and White Eagle up. Mitchell showed up in the kitchen soon after and Emiline was right... Lucie did make him drool. Great. He couldn't take his eyes off her.

White Eagle sent me to wake up my buddies in the van. Marlo woke up in a great mood but Adrian was grouchy. No surprises there. When I got back to the kitchen Mitchell and Lucie were talking and laughing. I tried not to snarl or growl. I did grind my teeth a little though.

After breakfast, Mitchell took Lucie and the guys out to do chores, spar and shoot. I got to watch from the window as I helped clean the kitchen and we began our mentor powwow. Emiline pretty much restated everything she had said to me. White Eagle was still oddly resistant to her plans for shipping off Mitchell.

He completely interrupted my green-eyed monster when he asked what I thought. All I could think was - about what? I pulled myself together and took a minute to answer. I decided on a question instead.

"Do you doubt what Emiline feels?" I asked, truly curious.

"Nope," he answered right away.

"Then I'm as confused as she is. What is the problem? I like Mitchell. Everyone else seems to also. He would be a great addition to the team." Except for the Lucie part I thought.

"I believe that he should stay with Emiline as long as possible. He should stay with her until there is absolutely no other choice. He was found *here* for a reason. This is his... territory or his area to cover. If he's in Oregon then this part of Nevada goes unprotected by a *watcher*. It makes me nervous. As much as I believe in Emiline's gut, I worry," White Eagle responded slowly and with great thought.

"Maybe you worry too much, Earl. You and I have been out of the game for many years until recently. I understand what you're saying about this being his area but what good is he if he isn't fully trained? I don't know if he is ready to take on a *dark watcher* alone. I feel next to useless at this point," Emiline retorted.

"I disagree. Mitchell would not have come to you if you weren't meant to have him," White Eagle argued back. Then he turned to me. "What do you think, Owen?"

"I can see both sides. Emiline, you must have something extra special about you that brought Mitchell here. When the time comes we will welcome him with open arms for more training. I wonder if part of the reason he is here is to protect *you*?"

"To what end? I'm old, I'm frail and I'm cranky. I disagree but I accept your decision. You are the new generation. I'm on my way out."

"Ms. Claremont, I would never assume that I know more than you do about being a ment…"

Emiline interrupted, her sharp words cutting right over mine as she held me in her steely gaze. "Young man, you are like nothing I have ever seen before. You are the most powerful force of good in the area if not the nation. Now don't go getting bigheaded but do realize who you are!?!" Now… Any luck on finding others?" Emiline asked. Sarah remained silent and listened attentively.

I was too stunned to speak but White Eagle had my back, "We're working on it. Sarah has been incredibly helpful. She is more of a consultant now, but for years she worked with a unit that she thought…" He turned and looked at her as if wishing that she would tell her own story.

Sarah took over, "I seem to have a limited ability myself. I can sense young people who will become *watchers*. I recognize people like you, Mitchell, White Eagle… You get the idea. At first I thought that my unit was being helped by psychics. Over the years I became suspicious and felt that there was more to it. Then I met Owen. He saved my life and he could not hide who he was from me anymore, no matter how hard he tried."

Sarah took a deep breath and looked at White Eagle. He nodded at her and she continued. "When Owen went on the Washington D.C. trip, Earl and I were very worried about him going as a new *watcher* but we didn't want to ruin the experience for him and we knew that he was going with Adrian and Marlo. So I pulled in some of my oldest, most trusted contacts. I was able to get in touch with a mentor there. Owen took out a *watcher stalker* and left him unconscious in the Smithsonian Natural History Museum. He and Lucie got away and the *dark stalker* who seemed to be after Lucie is now in special custody. My contact in D.C. also works for the FBI; quite a neat trick in my opinion. He doesn't have any *watchers* himself now, but he watches for *watchers* and teams them up. Even to Earl this was something new. He is far away and busy so we don't talk much."

Sarah cleared her throat and continued, "When we knew something bad was going down in Florida with Owen's family, I was able to find someone like myself to help, before his family even left. Owen seems to be a magnet for the big and ugly out there. I think his strong power draws the darkness to him. Owen's grandfather has money. At first Kraeghton, a powerful *dark watcher*, posed as a businessman and went after the grandfather for money. He soon took over his life and pulled in Owen's dad, who is a talented chemical engineer. Then Kraeghton soon discovered that he was really on to something when he overheard Owen's dad complaining about his strange son. Kraeghton understood what Owen really was and he tried to set three traps that we know of. He's still out there, wounded and dangerous. My contact there was Mica. When we found her, she was already working the case from another angle. Her sister was a watcher so she gets it. Now you have a recap of who we have found and what we've been up too."

"Do you work with this Mica's sister?" Emiline asked.

"She is… no longer alive, but Mica has been a blessing."

"So you know there are watchers in the D.C. area but you don't work with them and you now have no contacts in Florida," Emiline concluded.

"That's about right," White Eagle spoke up.

"So where do we go from here?" Emiline queried.

"We celebrate your birthday and train the kids the rest of today. When you have nothing left to offer Mitchell, then he will come to us until he is ready to be on his own. In the meantime we will not give up looking for others," White Eagle finished, sounding firm.

White Eagle and Emiline continued to work with me on my mentoring skills while Sarah watched. How she stood it, I don't know because much of it was mental. We also practiced looking for talent. I showed them how I had learned to press out my ability. They were both surprised. Then we worked on White Eagle's trick of blending skills and people together. Next we pulled first Lucie and then Mitchell in so I could practice on them. I was exhausted by lunchtime.

After lunch I got to work with the 'kids' on physical skills. We did a lot of sparring and we practiced teaming up on each other. We had brought our fighting gear. Mitchell was the biggest of all of us but both Adrian and I could still take him. We had been at this much longer than he had because it was not Emiline's gift. Mitchell did have scary quick reflexes but I suspected that he had learned to expand his gift like I had. Mitchell was the clear winner when it came to shooting however. I was beginning to suspect he could take a *dark watcher* but I didn't like the way he looked at Lucie. Maybe I was oversensitive. He was a good guy and she wasn't mine to claim but I didn't have to like it! I tried to pretend it didn't bother me. Lucie, my strength and my weakness.

As we cleaned up the gear, I watched Mitchell pull Lucie aside to talk. I could feel myself bristling.

"Stop it," Marlo said elbowing me firmly in the ribs. "You won't help the situation by getting all jealous and making an ass of yourself."

I glowered at him but he did have a point. Marlo tilted his head to the side and gave me a 'really?' look. "I know you hate it but I can tell you like Mitchell. He's a good guy. If it's meant to be, Lucie will find her way back to you. She always does. Be patient. How far can she go? She's stuck with you as a mentor."

I hung my head. "Thanks, Mar. I don't always want to hear it but you do give good advice."

We headed in to see if Adrian was done with his turn in the shower. Marlo went next while I started putting leaves in the table. Coming in without Lucie was the hardest thing I'd had to do in awhile. When Lucie and Mitchell came in a bit later, laughing and smiling, I found myself grinding my teeth – again.

A few friends of Emiline's and Mitchell's showed up with potluck dishes for dinner. Sarah had made a magnificent birthday cake.

Marla Saggio's, it was not, but still one of the best I've seen. People were happy and friendly. The party spilled out of the house and into the yard. Emiline seemed to love the attention but I could see her getting tired as the evening wore on. By eight she was bidding the guests goodnight. By eleven, we were done cleaning; the last dish washed and put away. We all camped out on the living room floor. Sarah got Mitchell's room. I was so tired I think I was asleep before my head hit my pillow. I wanted to keep my eye on Lucie, but exhaustion won.

Emiline was up again at dawn. Old habit, she told me. I figured she couldn't sleep but didn't want to say so. I helped her get breakfast ready. She looked like she had a lot she wanted to say to me but for some reason she held back. I tried to encourage her but it wasn't in my nature to pry. Maybe I should have.

Emiline hugged me tightly when we were ready to load the van after breakfast. "Go be amazing," she whispered in a harsh voice.

"I will do my very best," I said hugging her back.

I felt I owed Mitchell something. I struggled to find the right words. "When the time comes… we'll be expecting you. You'll have a home with us."

"Thanks, Owen, but my home will always be here. Emiline is leaving this place to me. I may come to finish college, but… well, this will always be my home. I agree with White Eagle, I'm meant to be here in Nevada. It's something I feel."

I nodded. That, even I could understand. I loaded up behind White Eagle. Marlo and Adrian had already claimed the way back. Marlo had out his laptop and was typing away. He looked completely absorbed as he scowled and grunted at it. Adrian met my eye and shrugged, with a 'who knows?' kind of look.

I was gnashing my teeth once again as Lucie hugged Mitchell goodbye. She might be hugging him now but she would be sitting with me for the next several hours. As she climbed in, Lucie looked at me and shook her head. She buckled up saying nothing. The van was silent as we pulled into town to gas up for the road.

"Hey Luce," Marlo called from the back of the van. She turned to look at him. He looked like he was trying to figure out how to cushion a blow. "Umm… Your girl from the hall at school is... Bettylou McMurtry for sure. I have found her full records and her current address. It looks like she never married and never had any other children. She ended up dedicating her life to helping other young girls in similar situations. Over the years she's been quite the advocate. She gave up a baby for adoption in May of her senior year. She ended up getting a GED later. She must have been too angry to go back and graduate. They had suspended her from school, but after all, it was the fifties. The records about the baby are so old that they are only in hard copy and they're sealed. I mentioned before that we might need to get to them at the agency holding them. Now I know that is the only way we will get them. I think I have all the information on the agency we will need to break in. I don't see any other way than to sneak into the agency to look at those records if you want to reunite the mother and child but it's up to you. If you want to get in – I can help make that happen." Marlo cleared his throat and looked at me nervously.

Lucie looked at me. "Can we?"

"If that's what you feel needs to be done, then we will find a way."

Sarah and Adrian both looked at me with surprise on their faces but kept their mouths shut. White Eagle stared straight ahead and drove on without uttering a word.